W9-AVF-463

Praise for the novels of Mindy Klasky

Girl's Guide to Witchcraft

"What fun! *Girl's Guide to Witchcraft* is a charmer of a story from
start to finish…. With her great characters and delightful prose voice,
Klasky really brought this book alive for me. Recommended highly."
—Catherine Asaro, award-winning author of *The Misted Cliffs*

"Mindy Klasky's newest work, *Girl's Guide to Witchcraft,* joins a love story
with urban fantasy and just a bit of humor…. Throw in family troubles,
a good friend who bakes Triple-Chocolate Madness, a familiar
who prefers an alternative lifestyle plus a disturbingly
good-looking mentor and you have one very interesting read."
—*SF Revu*

Sorcery and the Single Girl

"Klasky emphasizes the importance of being true to yourself
and having faith in friends and family in her bewitching
second romance featuring fledgling witch Jane Madison
(after *Girl's Guide to Witchcraft*)…. Readers who identify with Jane's
remembered high school social angst will cheer her all the way."
—*Publishers Weekly*

"The entire cast of this book comes to life, making it almost painful to
witness Jane's misplaced trust and inherent naivete. Klasky,
who first wrote about witch Jane in *Girl's Guide to Witchcraft,*
keeps you entranced from start to finish."
—*Romantic Times BOOKreviews*

Magic and the Modern Girl

"Filled with magic—both of the witch world and the romance world—
complicated family relationships and a heavy dose of chick-lit humor,
this story is the perfect ending to the series."
—*Romantic Times BOOKreviews*

"Librarian (and practicing witch) Jane Madison learns a lesson in love
and spell casting in Klasky's lively latest
(after *Sorcery and the Single Girl*)…. Klasky's whimsical flair
makes this a fun entry in a series still building momentum."
—*Publishers Weekly*

Also by MINDY KLASKY

Jane Madison series

GIRL'S GUIDE TO WITCHCRAFT
SORCERY AND THE SINGLE GIRL
MAGIC AND THE MODERN GIRL

MINDY KLASKY

How Not to make a Wish

MIRA®

MIRA

ISBN-13: 978-0-7783-2737-0

HOW NOT TO MAKE A WISH

In loving memory of my grandfather, Maurice Getz

CHAPTER 1

I LOVE THE THEATER. THE THEATER IS MY LIFE.

At least that's what I told myself as I suffered my third sneezing fit in an hour.

Standing in the costume shop at the Fox Hill Dinner Theater, I extracted a linty tissue from my pocket and blew my nose, trying not to pay attention to the clouds of dust swirling in the overhead fluorescent lights. If I let myself think about how much debris filled the air around me, my lungs would seize up and I'd collapse in front of a dozen feather-covered costumes from *Gypsy*.

"Gotta have a gimmick, Kira Franklin," I muttered to myself.

A gimmick—that was the name of the game in the cutthroat world of Midwestern dinner theater. And without one, Fox Hill would be out of business in less than a month. Anna Harper, the dinner theater's artistic director and my boss for the past seven years, was fully aware of our company's dire straits. She'd been hinting for months that I should get my résumé out, that I should try to nail down my dream job at Landmark Stage, the Twin Cities' newest theatrical darling. In fact, she'd pretty much told me that my next paycheck would be my last—the theater loved me, couldn't work without me, but just couldn't afford to keep me, blah, blah, blah.

Alas, my Fox Hill credentials weren't likely to spark interest from the Landmark. Like it or not, I'd limited my marketability by staying with Anna for as long as I had. Every time I applied for a position with the prestigious Landmark Stage—even just working in the ticket office—I received a polite, anonymous, form-letter rejection.

Nevertheless, barring a miracle, Anna was going to have to cut me loose. But we wouldn't go down without a fight. Prior to hiring some starry-eyed kid right out of high school, Anna had decided on one last money-making scheme: selling our old costumes to the public. We were trying to be as festive as possible as we launched our last-ditch bid for survival—we had taken out full-page ads in both the Minneapolis *StarTribune* and the *St. Paul Pioneer Press* announcing our grand sale: Evening gowns! Dance wear! Halloween costumes for young and old alike!

We played up the glamour, providing a long list of our hit shows from the past decade. We kinda, sorta, maybe hoped that no one would focus on the fact that most of the costumes were designed for a handful of quick outings on stage. We absolutely refused to make any guarantee that seams would hold, that sequins would stay attached, that feathers and ribbons and bows would last through a single wearing at a glamorous society ball.

That's why *we* kept a costumer on hand during all performances.

A costumer, someone to run lights, someone to run the sound board, people to change sets and hand out props—it could take more than a dozen backstage folks to mount one of our productions. And I was the person in charge of all of them, at least until I was laid off. Kira Franklin, stage manager extraordinaire.

Okay. That wasn't really the way that I thought of myself. I always stopped after the "manager" part.

But my father added the "extraordinaire" when he dutifully attended each of our productions. And so did my high school debate coach. And the handful of friends that I managed to rope into seeing individual shows, most often by handing out coupons for free dessert at our luscious gourmet buffet table (two entrées nightly!).

Come to think of it, most of my friends had dropped the "extraordinaire" a few years back, too. Maybe it was our Christmas production of *Miracle on 34th Street,* with a well-developed seventeen-year-old playing the little girl role, because we just couldn't find a kid who could stick to our rehearsal schedule.

Truth was, the Fox Hill Dinner Theater was not a leading light in the Twin Cities' theater community.

Let me explain a little more about who and what and where we were. You've probably heard of the Mall of America, right? The largest shopping mall in North America, with more than four hundred stores? Employs 12,000 people? Built around an amusement park, with a flight simulator, aquarium, and real live (okay, dead) dinosaur walk? Visited by forty million people each and every year?

Fox Hill was about a mile south of there.

We were located in an old strip mall, space we took over from a Woolworth's that was driven out of business by the big box stores even farther down the road. We had a decent-size "house" with seating for five hundred. There were two steam tables to serve dinner, and a thrust stage that reached into the audience, bringing musicals so close that patrons could practically touch them. But in a metropolitan area with a thriving artistic community and more than one hundred theaters, large and small, Fox Hill had its work cut out for it.

And things weren't exactly helped by the fact that our next-door neighbor was a porno-movie theater—the Fox Hill Cinema. You might have thought that dirty movies were a losing business proposition in the wake of the Internet and perfect-for-home-viewing DVDs. The fading grande dame, though, had cleverly diversified to stay in business with its three-screen emporium. Two showed the latest skin flicks, and one showed art films.

It could be really interesting to watch the line at their ticket window. It was pretty easy to tell who was in line for the Truffaut retrospective, and who was waiting for *Goldilust and the Three Bares*. At the dinner theater, we tried to promote ourselves to the first group, and we hoped that the second crowd didn't wander through our doors by mistake. You had to take your customers where you found them, though. Isn't that one of the primary rules of business? Well, it should have been.

"Kira? Are you in here?"

As if to answer, I sneezed again. "Yeah. In the back room."

Maddy Rubens pushed aside a sliding rack of thirty-six identical dresses—the irresistible Paris Originals from last year's overly optimistic production of *How to Succeed in Business Without Really Trying*. Maddy was a lighting designer who had worked at Fox Hill on occasional gigs between the handful of dream jobs that she'd landed in New York, the more usual local productions, and the rare-but-lusted-after West Coast projects. More important, Maddy was my housemate and best friend.

"Jules and I finished going through the jewelry," she announced. "There's enough crap out there for a dozen high school proms. Tiaras up the wazoo, and enough pearls to strangle a decent-size horse."

"Gives all new meaning to the phrase 'costume' jewelry," I said.

"We're calling it a day and going to get burritos. Are you coming with?"

My stomach rumbled. Even though I'd had an Egg McMuffin with double hash browns for breakfast, I'd worked through our supposed lunch break. In fact, I'd had nothing but coffee since coming in that morning—four of my jumbo java mugs' worth. I'd brewed it first thing, taking elaborate care to put out the sign that read "Kira's Stash." I liked my coffee twice as strong as anyone else did, and I'd finally conceded the necessity of labeling my own carafe after poor Anna had been kept awake for thirty-six straight hours following one particularly long dress rehearsal with nothing but my java for sustenance.

"Burritos sound great," I said, "but I want to finish up *Kismet*."

"The costumes will still be here tomorrow," Maddy said, reasonably enough. "You work too hard."

I sighed. "I don't work hard enough. I told Anna I would have all of this stuff ready by last Friday."

"The same Anna who's signing your walking papers next week?" Trust Maddy to tell it like it was.

"Come on," I said. "Could *you* just walk out? Leave all this behind?" Maddy snorted, but I knew that she was every bit as tied to the theatrical world as I was. We weren't in it for the money—both of us, along with Jules, could barely afford to pay my father rent on the second-floor apartment he provided us at well below market rate. We were in the theater because we loved it. It made our hearts sing, as corny as that sounded. We loved the creativity, the feeling that we were making something from nothing.

Either that, or we were bug-eyed crazy.

"Yeah, you're right," Maddy agreed reluctantly, as I'd known she would. "But you still have to eat. Let's go! Jules is treating. We're going to get chips. With extra salsa. And guac-a-mo-le…" She turned the last word into a seductive song.

I shook my head reluctantly. "Nope. I wouldn't enjoy it,

with this stuff hanging over my head. But tell Jules that buying tonight doesn't get her off the hook for the Scrabble victory dinner she owes me."

Jules—Julia Kathleen McElroy—was the third occupant of our apartment. She was an actress. After spending years trying to top the charts in the Twin Cities theater scene, Jules had settled into a comfortable career doing industrials, training films for companies. Her most successful role had been "Stubborn Defendant" in *You're Being Deposed? Expect the Worst*.

"Fine," Maddy said with a resigned sigh. But then she took a step closer to me, resting her blunt-fingered hand on my arm. "Just tell me with a straight face that this doesn't have anything to do with today's date."

"Today's date?" I asked, and I almost managed to sound puzzled. What could I say? Acting wasn't *my* strong suit. I knew it would be overkill to say, "I don't have a date today. Do you?" Besides, I could never be quite *that* blasé about the greatest disaster in my entire life.

"Kira," Maddy remonstrated.

I shook my head. "It doesn't have anything to do with today's date." I said the words with the rote certainty of a small child reciting multiplication tables.

"I don't believe you."

I raised my chin and looked straight into her piercing blue eyes, forcing myself not to blink my muddy-brown ones. (Read: I braced myself to lie through my teeth.) "Madeline Rubens, I swear on my next and last paycheck and all else that is holy that my skipping burritos tonight has nothing to do with today's date. Cross my heart and hope to die." She just stared at me. "What? Do you want me to spit in my hand, so we can shake on it like five-year-olds? Make a blood oath?" I looked around with a cartoonish manic grin. "There's got to be a dagger or two in here somewhere. Where's the stuff from *Camelot?*"

Maddy rolled her eyes. "Okay, then. We'll see you at home. Cheerio!"

"Wait," I called before she could walk away. "I thought you and Colin broke up last week."

"We did." She shrugged. "I just haven't broken the habit of saying 'Cheerio' yet."

I couldn't help but laugh as she left the costume shop. Maddy changed boyfriends more often than the porno house next door changed its movies. Colin had lasted two full weeks, which was typical. In the five years that Maddy and I had been house-mates, only one guy had made it to a month, and that was because Maddy had spent three weeks on a road trip.

No fuss, no muss—when Maddy was bored she moved on, pleased to have learned a few words in a new language, or a couple of idiomatic expressions. Colin had actually taught Maddy the rules for cricket. Come to think of it, Gordon had taught her those rules a couple of years ago, and Nigel, a few years before that. Cricket comprehension didn't last much longer than love, in Maddy's book.

My life would have been so much simpler if I could just treat men, treat relationships, the way that Maddy treated hers.

I'd lied to her. Of course, my decision to skip burritos had everything to do with the date. January 7. One year ago today, I had been left at the altar by TEWSBU, The Ex Who Shall Be Unnamed.

Okay. Not quite literally at the altar. We'd planned a civil ceremony.

But I'd worn a white dress, with a veil and a train and everything. Maddy and Jules had stood beside me in personalized bridesmaid gowns. Their dresses had been made out of an emerald-green silk that actually worked well for both of them. Predictably, Jules had selected a stunning strapless sheath that showed off her willowy form, while Maddy enjoyed something substantially less revealing. My father had worn his tux. Judge Saylor, one of my father's former law firm partners, had stood at the front of the room, smiling and friendly as the minutes ticked by.

But TEWSBU never showed.

I wasted a couple of hours imagining every possible disaster that could have befallen him. People who worked in the theater were superstitious by nature, our imaginations heightened by the dramatic fare we consumed every day. I pictured my beloved mutilated in a car crash. I imagined him cut down by robbers when he stopped at the drug store for a silly, unnecessary disposable camera. I panicked that the stress of the day, the excitement of fulfilling his lifelong dream of perfect, permanent married love, had all proved too much for him, had brought on a heart attack.

Drawing on my experience as a stage manager, I'd started phoning hospitals. I had created so many contact sheets for so many shows—complete with blocks of emergency contacts in boldface type—that I knew most of the numbers by heart. My cell phone grew hot beside my ear as sympathetic nurse after sympathetic nurse reported that they had no patients matching my professionally accurate description of my fiancé.

Sometime during phone call fourteen, he left a voice mail. My so-called beloved was a director. His message used our common language, the patois of the theater that we both lived and breathed. He was sure I'd understand eventually, he said. He'd only just realized it himself. The blocking of our entire relationship was just not right.

Blocking. Where the actors stood when they said their lines.

I had spent the night of my would-be wedding, precisely one year ago, kneeling on the bathroom floor of the Hyatt Regency. Maddy and Jules had taken turns holding my torn-down updo off my face, offering me damp paper towels and glasses of cold water to rinse my mouth.

The guests—cast and crew from dozens of local shows, long-lost relatives, scores of my father's law firm partners—had pasted on fake smiles and eaten their filet mignon with merlot reduction, their potatoes Anna, their haricots verts. And I had eaten nothing as I tried to imagine how I could possibly face everyone the morning after.

I had eaten nothing that night. But I'd made up for it during the intervening year.

For twelve months, I had solaced myself with alternating treats of sweets and savories. In my frequent bouts of self-loathing when I thought about what I was doing to myself, I was disgusted by the amount I had consumed. Sure, I was tall—five foot ten—but there was a limit to the pounds that even my height could camouflage. A monolith of empty ice cream pints towered in my mind, mortared together with crumpled bags of Doritos, shredded boxes of Cheez-Its. My candy wrappers alone, laid end to end, could have spanned the Grand Canyon, and I couldn't bear to picture the veritable ocean I had consumed of the perfect comfort food: homemade Tater Tots hot dish.

I also couldn't stand to think of the four different wardrobes crowding my closet—four different sizes of clothes, laid out in a neat sequence, like my stage manager scripts. After rebuying jeans for the third time, I'd gotten smart and given in to elastic waistbands—bulky sweatshirts, fleece pants, all in black because I desperately believed the color was slimming.

What did it matter? I spent most of my time backstage in a

dark theater. Why did I need a real wardrobe, anyway? It wasn't like the dating gods were showering gifts upon me. There might be dozens of theaters in the Twin Cities, but TEWSBU had friends in all of them. Stupidly, I was still caught off guard when theater people nodded as I introduced myself, a distant glint of recognition in their eyes. I was *that* one, they all seemed to say. And then they all darted not-surreptitious-enough glances at my ever-expanding waistline, silently saying, "Well, no wonder he left her."

A lot of theater people could be superficial. That came from judging actors on their body types, day in and day out, defining whether they could fill a role based on how they looked. But the most frustrating thing about all of my weight gain? My chest was still flat as a board. At twenty-eight years of age, I could still get by wearing an undershirt, instead of the engineering feats of lace and wires that other women proudly sported.

I was jilted, fat, flat, and miserable.

And the absolute worst part was, I couldn't even drown my sorrows in alcohol. Sharing a few six-packs with girlfriends had carried me through the loss, years back, when my boyfriend broke up with me freshman spring at the U. And when I kicked out my sophomore beau, I already had a bottle of chardonnay waiting on ice. Tequila shots dulled the pain when my junior year beloved turned out to have a side thing going with my then-best-friend. And each and every time I broke up with one of those meaningless senior-year guys, a legally purchased martini had marked the occasion.

But at some point in the past six years, since I'd been cut loose from the serious business of college partying, I had become allergic to alcohol. It was really strange—if I took a sip of wine, a swallow of beer, touched my lips to anything stronger, I could feel my cheeks turn bright red. The handful of times I'd tried to go beyond that warning sign, I'd been rewarded with blotchy hives that itched like the devil.

My doctor had shrugged and told me that allergies sometimes develop later in life. She'd shaken her head at my dismay and reminded me that I was actually pretty lucky. After all, no one really *needed* alcohol to make it through the day. I could avoid it easily enough, she'd chided. It wasn't as if I had a severe allergy to eggs or wheat, to something that would put me constantly in danger of a reaction worth a hospital visit.

Yeah, that was me. Lucky. Lucky like a Minnesota Vikings fan, watching my team forever slip out of contention.

I brushed my hands against my black fleece pants and turned toward the rolling racks of *Kismet* costumes. There were a dozen outfits for dancing girls—long, flowing harem pants in pastel colors, each matched with a scandalous golden bra. The boys' outfits featured similar pants, but in saturated hues.

I started to hum "Stranger in Paradise" as I attached price tags to each of the frothy creations. I couldn't imagine anyone actually wearing one in public, but then again, there were a whole lot of men and women who thought nothing of donning slut-wear for Halloween. We just had to find a lot of people willing to buy almost a year in advance.

Somewhere nearby, we must have stored the accessories from the show. If I remembered correctly, the dancing girls had worn elaborate veils in one scene and necklaces of gold coins in another. The men had sported ruby-studded sashes, and we had to have at least a dozen scimitars. The *Kismet* cast would never have made it through airport security. If, you know, they were actually going anywhere. It wasn't like Fox Hill productions traveled to New York, or Hollywood, or anywhere else smacking of theatrical power or prestige.

Absentmindedly, I tugged at the third rolling rack, ready to find the small pieces and finish my work for the day. A loud, metallic clatter made me jump back, and I bit off a curse. If the necklaces had fallen, they'd send coins flying all over the shop floor. It would take me forever to collect the debris.

I quickly realized, though, that no jewelry had fallen. The clatter I'd heard had been loud, echoing, not the tinkle of scattered metal. I squatted beside the rolling rack and reached beneath to retrieve whatever had fallen.

That motion had been a lot easier thirty pounds before. My hand came down sharply on something metal. I dragged it back and sat down hard, eager to relieve the pressure on my knees.

A lamp.

A brass oil lamp, with a high delicate handle and a long, gently curved spout.

It must have been one of our props—we had dressed the set with all sorts of pseudo-Arabic bric-a-brac. I could still remember the props master coming in from Goodwill, thrilled to have found a string of glass beads that looked like they'd just surfaced in the local bazaar. We'd joked about who'd had such tacky decor in their own home before donating it for our greater good.

The oil lamp in my hands was absolutely filthy, so caked with dust and tarnish that I wouldn't have thought it metal if I hadn't heard it fall.

Huffing and puffing more than I was willing to admit, I clambered to my feet and stepped back to the center of the costume shop. I raised the lamp toward the bare lightbulb overhead, hoping to make out some stamp on the bottom, something that would let me jack up its price for our current desperation sale.

Shaking my head, I pulled the sleeve of my sweatshirt over my wrist and rubbed at the brass, trying to polish off its coat of grime. Pressing harder, my fingertips brushed against the curved brass spout.

An electric shock jolted through my arm. The force was strong enough to make me yelp, and I dropped the lamp with another ungodly clatter. My fingers jangled violently, and I shook my hand as if I could make the pain fall away, drip off like splatters of boiling water. My heart pounded so hard I couldn't speak, couldn't even swallow, and for just a second, I thought that I had somehow, impossibly, managed to electrocute myself.

I kept on breathing, though. Kept on breathing, and kept on watching, even as my jaw dropped in disbelief.

Fog poured out of the brass lamp's spout.

Okay. I was a stage manager. I knew how to generate fog onstage. I knew how to make great billowing clouds with dry ice. I knew how to generate clammy banks that hugged the floor, twining around actors' ankles, making audiences shiver in anticipation of London accents and wolves howling on moors. I knew how to create a soft, fuzzy mist with fine droplets of heated oil, a shimmer that could diffuse spotlights and make a crowd believe that they were lost in a dream, that they were in the company of Broadway stars who belted out ballads as if their fictional lives depended on it.

I could order up atmospheric effects in my sleep, recognize them—any of them—from twenty paces.

This was no atmospheric effect. This was real. This fog swirled as it emerged from the lamp, shimmering with its own inner light. It expanded and twisted on itself, writhing like a living thing, glinting beneath the fluorescents. I could make out flashes of cobalt and emerald, ruby and topaz.

I blinked, and the fog disappeared.

In its place was a man. A man wearing a white polyester suit with wide lapels, and a black synthetic shirt with an ungodly, buttoned-up white vest. He was tall, a good head taller than me, and so skinny that I wondered if he might be ill. As I gaped, he shot his right hand up in the air, striking out his left leg in a perfect 1970s Disco Fever dance pose.

A tattoo wrapped around his right wrist. The ink was compelling; it drew my eyes, even as I gaped at the bizarre sight in front of me. I could make out a delicate tracery in red and gold, individual tongues of flame outlined in jagged black. The design made me shiver, as if it spoke to some dark, secret memory deep inside my brain.

As I stared, absolutely speechless, the guy smiled and tossed his blow-dried hair in a way that I was apparently supposed to find seductive. "Hey, foxy lady! Ready to boogie on down with a wish?"

CHAPTER 2

FOXY LADY? HAD I SUDDENLY BEEN TRANSPORTED back to 1977? Was this John Travolta wannabe really talking to me like we were on the set for *Saturday Night Fever?*

I tried to answer.

I tried to say something, anything, form any sort of verbal response.

But my mouth just wouldn't work. My mouth wouldn't work, my brain wouldn't work, my entire body was about to collapse on the costume-room floor.

This guy was real. He was flesh and blood. I could reach out and touch him—him and his white disco suit. And all of it—suit and man—had appeared from nowhere. Not from nowhere, my brain screamed. From the lamp. I had conjured him out of the brass lamp by rubbing the damned thing.

"You— You're a genie," I croaked.

He tossed his blow-dried hair and lowered his dance-ready right arm. "Psych! Who else would grant you a wish?" He stared at the *Kismet* costumes with a distinct look of disgust. "Well, bummer. Are these the threads everyone is wearing these days?"

I started to laugh.

I couldn't help it. First, it was the way the guy sounded like a reject from *That '70s Show*, like an extra who had been cut because he was just too...obvious. Almost immediately, though, I pictured everyone walking around on the Minneapolis streets, dressed like some Hollywood dream of a harem, come hell or high snowbanks.

Once I started to laugh, I couldn't stop. Nervous tension, the stage manager part of my brain diagnosed—I was still recovering from the jangling electric shock that continued to make my fingers tingle, that made me want to shake my arm and restore the proper blood flow to my fingertips. Partial electrocution, then near asphyxiation by jewel-toned fog... And now this bizarre...genie (could he really be a genie? What sort of crackpot dream was I having?) who sounded like a cross between a valley girl and Casanova.

With a supreme effort of will, I managed to smother my totally inappropriate laughter and gasp, "Who *are* you?"

"I'm Teel."

"Teel?"

He sighed in obvious exasperation. "Teel," he repeated, like it was Jason, or Michael, or any other name I should have known. He pulled himself up to his full height—and a rather impressive height it was—and he cocked his head at an angle that made him look more like a curious parrot than a killer disco dancer. My treacherous laughter bubbled up again. He was not at all amused. "And what is so funny about that?"

"It's just..." I had to concentrate. I had to pay attention to what was happening here. If nothing else, I could pretend that this was a play. A musical, like everything we performed at Fox Hill. There. That was calming. Why *hadn't* we ever done a musical of *Saturday Night Fever*? Was there one, in stage form?

Concentrate *now!* I said, "I thought…"

But what did I think? What was I going to say? Why couldn't I make two brain cells rub together to form a single coherent sentence? Oh. There was one. Why hadn't I left with Maddy when she tried to take me out for burritos? I could have been eating a burrito and chatting with my housemates about silly Twin Cities theater gossip, and not worrying that my past year of sorrow and self-indulgence had finally driven me mad, finally made me see apparitions.

That apparition wasn't going away. In fact, it was only looking more annoyed with every second I delayed. I tried again. "I expected…" One last time. "Teel! I was expecting something a little more majestic. Aladdin, maybe. Ali Baba. Something more exotic."

"And I suppose they call you Scheherazade." He sniffed.

I realized that I probably wasn't the first lamp-rubbing human to comment on his name. I took a deep breath and exhaled slowly. There. I finally had my nervous giggles under control. "I'm Kira Franklin."

I started to extend my hand to shake his, but one glance at his flame tattoo made me stop. I'd seen a lot of tattoos in my theater days, but there was something about Teel's wristband that kept me from completing my simple civil gesture.

There was power in those flames. They were brighter than any tattoo I'd ever seen. Stronger. Purely different. Other.

To cover my prickling awareness, I glanced at the brass lamp, glinting now in the center of the room. "Hey!" I said. "How did that thing get so clean?" Even to my own ears, I sounded afraid.

Teel's eyes flashed in the predatory way of all terminally cool dudes cruising dark discos for foxy chicks. "Chill, baby," he crooned. "It's cool."

Despite everything, despite my confusion, despite the utter bizarreness of a man springing to life in the middle of the costume shop, I gritted my teeth at his patronizing tone. His eyes narrowed, and he asked, "Too much?"

"Nobody calls me baby," I said.

He rolled his eyes. "Another feminist. Let me guess. Susan put you up to this."

"Susan? Who's Susan?"

His laugh was tight, a little nasty. He took a step away from the brass lantern, his shoes—black ankle boots with substantial, clunky heels—thudding on the linoleum floor. "She must be having a great time watching us. Where is she hiding? Susan?" He thrust his hands through the feathers and fluff of our *Gypsy* costumes. "Susan! Enough joking! Where are you?" His voice turned fawning as he called out, "Come out, come out, wherever you are!"

"Um, I don't know any Susan," I said, before he could begin attacking another rack of costumes. Well, I did know a Susan. Two, in fact. But not one who was going to be lurking in the Fox Hill costume shop on a Sunday afternoon in January. Not one who knew a genie named Teel. I was willing to bet money on that.

"Of course not." He glared at me, clearly not believing a word I'd said. "What is this place supposed to be? Backstage at a theater? Well, you'd better brush up on your acting skills if you expect anyone to believe that line."

Despite myself, I blushed. "I'm not an actor!"

"Obviously not." He sighed and looked around the rest of the costume shop. "Susan! Come on! Tell me you forgive me, and we can get back to planning our little getaway to the Poconos." I shook my head, but he held up one commanding hand. "Susan? Susan! This isn't funny anymore!"

"Teel!" I said, sharply enough that I finally commanded his

attention. "There really isn't any Susan. I don't know who you're talking about."

"Yeah, yeah, you don't know Susan, and I've been abandoned to the first idiot who rubbed my lamp." He completed a head-to-toe survey of my admittedly grimy self and shook his head in disbelief. "I dig it. Susan is still upset about catching me with Connie. She's going to make me pay. But where *did* she find you?" Before I could retort, Teel made his voice as sweet as the corn syrup we used to make stage blood. "Susan, that girl meant nothing to me!" Silence. Silence, which Teel broke by howling toward the ceiling, "What! Are you trying to get an extra wish? You *know* I have to follow the rules! I can't hand out extras to anyone. I've already told you. That never works."

"Wishes?" I gasped. He'd mentioned them the second he appeared out of the lamp, but I was only now realizing that I was part of a real-life fairy tale. Me. The woman who was so unlucky, she just made donations to charity, instead of buying scratch-off lottery cards.

Was I really going to get three honest-to-goodness chances at happiness? He couldn't be serious. Wishes were impossible.

But not less possible than a man materializing out of a brass lamp

Teel suddenly blinked, as if he were seeing me for the very first time. Me, and absolutely no hope of Susan. He stared for a long minute, and then he exhaled, breathing out with a force that seemed to deflate him like a collapsing balloon.

"Susan isn't here, is she?"

"That's what I was trying to tell you." He looked so crestfallen that I had to add, "Maybe we can find her, though."

"What year is it?"

For a moment, the question stunned me. Here I'd thought that my genie was a fashion lunatic. In an instant, though, I understood. He must have been forced back inside his lamp in the seventies, at the height of disco, bad hair, and slang that made my teeth ache. He didn't intend to dress like Disco Stu; he just didn't know any better.

"The year?" he prompted again, and his tone was sharper.

I told him, and he started to swear under his breath, linking phrases with a fluidity that would have impressed any playwright. Curse words hadn't changed much in the past few decades. "Dammit!" he finally wound down. "Dammit all to brass shards!" Okay. Maybe he had a few odd oaths up his white polyester sleeve.

Sighing explosively, he raised his fingers to his right earlobe and tugged twice, hard.

Another electric shock jolted me from head to foot. This one wasn't as strong, though, as the spark that had set everything in motion. Instead, I felt like I'd been shuffling across a carpet in wool socks, then touched my finger to a doorknob. Nevertheless, I blinked and jumped back.

And when I opened my eyes again, Teel had changed. His white polyester suit had metamorphosed into midnight-black sweatpants, in-seam pockets slightly turned out. His dress shirt and vest had melted away into a stretched-out black sweatshirt. His blow-dried hair was gone; he now sported unruly curls, messy, as if he'd spent an afternoon working in the costume shop.

In fact, staring at him, I realized that Teel had just patterned himself as a mirror of me. He must have believed that I was the height of current fashion, that I was a perfect model for him to fit into the world around us.

Poor guy. He was really in a fix if he was relying on me for fashion guidance.

"There," he said, dusting off his hands in a universal gesture of completing a job well done. I could still see the flame tattoo on his wrist, poking out from beneath his sweatshirt's sagging cuff. If anything, the individual tongues of fire were more compelling against the black than they had been against the white disco disaster. My eyes kept drifting toward the inked image, unaccountably drawn to its sharp, clear lines. Teel nodded. "*That's* more like it."

"My thoughts exactly," I said weakly, knowing that I needed to say something else, anything; I needed to fill the silence. "Um… So I guess you don't have any idea how your lantern ended up on our set? From *Kismet?*"

Teel stared at me, a distinct frown creasing the space between his eyebrows as he evaluated me. Now that I knew I was a model, of sorts, I was increasingly uncomfortable. How could I possibly match up against the fashion goddesses of the seventies? Was he comparing me to Farrah Fawcett? Angie Dickinson? Wasn't she from the seventies? Both women—truth be told, almost any women—were certainly more endowed than I. And definitely slimmer.

Or maybe Teel simply disapproved of the almost-invisible coffee stain on the front of my sweatshirt. "Kismet?" he snapped. "There isn't any kismet in *my* being here. So, where exactly are we?" His voice seemed flatter than it had. Less flamboyant. I realized that he'd left behind his 1970s slang, apparently absorbing my contemporary language as he took on my clothes. Still, he clicked his tongue in frustration, a timeless sound meant to speed my answer along.

"At the Fox Hill Dinner Theater." Teel's exasperated expression indicated that he was looking for additional information. I hastily added, "In Bloomington. Just south of Minneapolis. Minnesota."

"Well, rub my lamp and tell me another one," Teel muttered.

"Where did you come from?" I asked. "I mean, before the lamp."

"The Upper West Side." He blinked, and then enunciated very clearly, as if I might be an idiot. "In Man-hat-tan. New. York."

I grimaced. "I know New York. I'm a stage manager here at the dinner theater. I've taken plenty of trips to New York."

"So, this *isn't* the end of the earth. It just looks like it." Teel glanced around.

"We're not half bad!" I had to rise to Fox Hill's defense. No wonder Susan had ditched Teel's lamp. She'd probably dropped it off at her own Goodwill shop, starting its decades-long cross-country trip. Given Teel's snotty attitude of New York superiority, it wouldn't surprise me if Susan had had a very good reason to be angry with the guy.

"But you're certainly not half good." Teel looked at my dusty clothes, and he scarcely bothered to gesture at the racks of costumes around us. "Let me guess. *A Chorus Line* passes for cutting edge around here?"

Despite myself, I sighed. "We haven't done it." I remembered the fights that Anna had gotten into with the board of directors. They'd disliked the "tits and ass" song; they thought it was too suggestive. Somehow, the board managed to ignore the theater marquee next door, boasting the so-called film *Jack and the Giant Stalk*. I didn't think we needed to worry about "suggestiveness" on stage if our clientele was brave enough to get through our front door. But no one had listened to me.

Teel sighed in disgust. "All right, then. Let's get this over with. What's your first wish?"

"My first wish?"

"Oh, come on. You've got to know about the genie gig, even here in the middle of nowhere. You rub the lamp, out comes the genie? You make all sorts of unreasonable demands? I'm your slave until I've granted all your wishes? Peace, love, and granola…"

"You're serious."

"Serious as the New York City blackout. The sooner I grant your wishes, the sooner I can figure out where Susan went." His voice softened as he mused to himself, "Stupid girl. She must have thought I really *was* interested in Connie. She should know by now that I only do those things to freak her out."

Three wishes. A genie was sitting in my costume shop, waiting to grant me three wishes before he left to track down his now-middle-aged main squeeze.

I closed my eyes, imagining everything that could be mine. Unimaginable wealth—I could create my own theater company! And find a better landlord than my father, in the meantime.

But filthy lucre would be a pretty selfish use of a miracle, wouldn't it? I should go for something *real,* something meaningful—forging world peace, ending hunger everywhere, eliminating illness from the face of the earth.

Of course, if I eliminated illness, then people would live longer. They'd eat more, put a strain on all their local food resources. That stress would inevitably lead to battles over territory. And the battles would result in poor nutrition, compromised medical care, and…illness. We'd be right back where we started.

Just to make sure I wasn't being too negative, I opened my eyes and squinted at my benefactor. "I suppose eliminating disease from the entire world is out, right?"

Teel sighed in exasperation. "What is it with you people? Nine out of ten people want eliminating disease as their first wish." He shook his head. "Look, I can get you the disease thing, if you really, really want it. But it'll take some time. I mean, I've only got so much power, and something that affects so many people…"

"How much time?" I asked, curious despite myself.

"A couple of centuries, give or take a decade or two."

"I'd be long dead by then!"

"Yep." He nodded. "You, and everyone you know. And I'd only be able to cure the things we know about now, as we get started with your wish. Diseases that come up while I'm in progress would still exist."

Even so… Could I truly pass up the opportunity to try? But then Teel continued, "I have to warn you, though. I tend to get a bit distracted. I might forget what I'm working on, partway through. Especially after you're gone and can't remind me."

"That would be cheating!"

"It's only cheating if I drop your wish intentionally. Sometimes, my attention wanders. And something that takes centuries to complete? You've got to be realistic. Ten out of ten people are. Every single one forgot about the disease thing after I explained."

I had to be realistic. With a genie standing in the middle of a dinner theater. Okay, eliminating disease was right out. "World peace?" I asked.

"Arg!" His exasperated shout made me jump. "Eight out of ten go for peace once disease is off the table! It's the same deal. North America isn't bad on the international peace front, and Europe would probably come in line in a decade or two. But North Vietnam? The Soviet Union? I hope you have a lot of very prolific children—it'll take generations before they would see any positive result, even if I start work today."

His general language might have been updated when he adopted my contemporary clothing, but someone would have to get him caught him up on world politics. I wasn't inclined to be a history teacher, though. I was still stinging from his statistics, lumping me together with every other person who'd ever cast a wish. There'd be plenty of time to let him know the Cold War was over. First, I had to try one more wish for the betterment of mankind. "Hunger?"

"What is it with you people? Six out of ten—let's feed the world." He'd shrunk his voice to a mocking little pout. "At least with disease and war, there are *some* people who aren't suffering right now, right at the beginning. But *everyone* gets hungry, given a day or two. It'd take at least five hundred years for a genie like me to wipe out hunger—and that's assuming no population growth, a stupid assumption in light of how fat and happy everyone would become."

Well, then. No wonder only sixty percent of us lucky wishers were stupid enough to suggest saving children from starvation. I sighed. At least I could say that I'd tried, if anyone ever asked. The big things were impossible; they were never going to work. That left more manageable projects. More realistic ones.

Zoom in on me.

I glanced around the costume shop, taking in the pitiful price tags I'd placed on our racks of clothing. Fox Hill was staggering along. It might manage to last another season, maybe even two or three, once they got rid of my pitiful salary and cut back in other desperate ways. But dinner theater was never going to be my future. It wasn't going to support my professional career as a stage manager—it had already closed some of the more important doors in the region.

And truth be told, I didn't want to do musical theater forever. I needed something else. Something bigger. Something *more*.

The problem was, I had to have *some* sort of job in the theater, and I needed it now. Other people could float for a month or two between jobs, rely on their savings to carry them through a temporary gap.

If *I* didn't have something lined up by the time Anna gave

me my last paycheck, my father would finally have the opportunity he'd craved for years. He'd be able to insist that I apply to law school. That, or I could very well find myself looking for a new place to live, along with a new job.

Dad wasn't a terrible person; he wasn't even terribly unreasonable. He just wanted to know that his only child was financially safe and sound. So long as I was getting paid to "play" in the theater (Read: Work my fingers to the bone making productions happen), he'd stay off my back.

But if I waited until Anna gave me my last check… If I didn't have something else lined up, something big and recognizable… Something that even my father would view as worthwhile…

I needed a gig with the Landmark Stage. I needed to work on a production at the brightest star in the Twin Cities' theater firmament. One show, no matter what it was, no matter who the director was, and my local reputation would be set. My local reputation and—if I played my cards right—my career.

I tested the notion, tugging it in one direction, pulling it in another. It wasn't too much to ask of a genie; it wouldn't take years to fulfill. It would have a minimal impact on other people. The actors and crew for the show would end up better off for my involvement—I was a damned good stage manager, if I did say so myself!—and the only possible person to lose out would be the stage manager I ousted from the job. At least that person probably already had great credentials or fantastic connections; otherwise, they wouldn't be working at the Landmark in the first place.

The more I thought about it, the more I liked the idea.

"Anytime today, sister!" Teel said, breaking into my reverie.

I glared at him. Weren't genies supposed to be submissive? Wasn't he supposed to yield to my wish and my command? Oh, well, there was no reason to get him riled up, just before

I asked him to do something for me. I took a deep breath and said, "Make me the stage manager for Landmark Stage's next production."

He rolled his eyes. "That's your first wish?"

"Yes!" I heard the defensive knife beneath my words. I almost asked him how many wishers out of ten asked for the Landmark.

"You have to phrase your request in the form of a wish."

What was this? *Jeopardy?*

Still, he was the genie, and I was just the lucky girl who'd found the lamp. I took a deep breath and enunciated: "I wish I were the stage manager for Landmark Stage's next production." Before Teel could respond, I started to think about all the things that could go wrong with what I'd said, so I hurriedly added, "Here. In Minneapolis. The new Landmark Stage. The one that just opened last season. The—"

"I've got it," Teel said dryly. He raised his fingers to his earlobe, staring at me, as if he were daring me to change my mind. I bit my lip and nodded. "As you wish," he said, and he tugged at his ear twice.

Another electric jangle shot through my body, freezing my breath inside my lungs and making me painfully aware of my heart's stuttering beat. The tiny hairs on my arms rippled to attention and then settled down, but not before I felt the entire room surge *closer* with Teel's energy.

Even as the electric shock faded away, my cell phone started to ring. I had the volume set on high, so that I could hear it above the hustle and bustle of cleaning out the costume shop. The raucous repetition of "There's No Business Like Show Business" sounded cheap. Vulgar.

Grimacing, I dug the phone out of my pocket, flipping it open with fingers that trembled in the aftermath of Teel's electric discharge. A local number was displayed across the screen, a strange one I'd never seen before. Teel stared at me in fascination, as if he'd never seen a cell phone. Which, I realized, he never had.

I'd explain later.

I pressed the tiny button to activate the call and put on my most professional voice. "Kira Franklin speaking," I said.

"Kira!" A voice boomed down the line. Over the airwaves. Whatever. "Bill Pomeroy here, from Landmark Stage."

I gaped at Teel, who had figured out enough about the device in my hand to smile smugly. "Bill," I said, suddenly aware that I needed to respond, needed to say something, needed to keep this conversation moving forward.

"I know this is incredibly short notice," said the Twin Cities' darling-of-the-moment director. "I've just cast my production of *Romeo and Juliet*, but our stage manager has a family emergency. I need someone to fill in and your name is at the top of my list for possible substitutes. First rehearsal is tomorrow, and we open in three months. Any chance that I can convince you to drop whatever you're doing and become my stage manager?"

CHAPTER 3

AFTER ACCEPTING BILL POMEROY'S INVITATION AND agreeing to attend the next day's rehearsal, I collapsed to the floor of the Fox Hill costume room, staring at Teel in amazement. The genie merely nodded in smug satisfaction; apparently, he was accustomed to the adoration of wishers like myself.

"Can I see that?" he said, gesturing toward my cell phone, which I passed to him numbly.

He started punching buttons at random. I vaguely wondered if my package included calls abroad, because Teel was certainly going to connect with *someone* if he kept up his nonscientific exploration of the phone. I could hardly tell him to stop, though. Not when he had just granted my first wish. Not when I owed him my greatest professional success to date. Not when I—I!—was going to stage-manage Landmark Stage's next production. What were a few bucks spent on a call to Ulan Bator, in exchange for guaranteed career advancement?

I hadn't read *Romeo and Juliet* since high school, but that was okay. I could skim through it that night—there had to be a copy somewhere in the apartment that I shared with two other theaterphiles. Besides, I'd get to know the play by heart in the days and weeks to come.

Three months till opening night. That made it an April opening. April—a time when a lot of theaters do "hard" plays, thought pieces, demanding productions to make up for the froth of *A Christmas Carol* and other holiday fare.

I swallowed hard. We could do it. Three months was a century, in theater time. Or so I tried to convince myself.

Teel looked up from the phone. I could hear the double ring that meant he actually had managed to punch in an overseas number. "Ready for your second wish?"

Second wish? Now? I could barely process that my first had been granted.

"Sain by noo?" came a voice from my phone. After a pause, it repeated, *"Sain by noo?"*

"Give me that!" I said to Teel, snatching back the electronic device. I snapped the phone closed, cutting off my dear correspondent from Outer Mongolia, or wherever Teel had actually managed to reach. I gave the genie a dirty look, but he only shrugged, as if people grabbed cell phones from him every day.

"Your second wish?" he repeated, glancing at his flaming wristband the way a normal person would glance at a watch.

"Do I have to make the decision now?" Two wishes left. That suddenly seemed like such a small number. Such a forlorn possibility. Especially when I saw how easy "one" had been.

Teel sighed. "No. You can wait."

I glanced at the brass lamp. "So do you go back in there, while I'm trying to decide?"

He shook his head vigorously. "Absolutely not. I get to roam free while you make up your mind."

That didn't sound like such a good idea. I tried to remember my elementary school afternoons spent eating junk food in front of the TV, watching syndicated reruns. On *I Dream of Jeannie*, things always went wrong when Jeannie was allowed out of her bottle. Of course, she referred to the guy who released her as "Master." I didn't see Teel becoming that submissive anytime in the near future. (Read: I couldn't imagine Teel *ever* bending to my will.)

But could I be certain that he was telling me the truth? What if he disappeared without granting me the rest of my wishes?

Then again, was I really any worse off, with only one wish awarded, than I had been when I woke up this morning? I tried to erase the suspicious tone from my voice. "So how do I get you back, when I'm ready to make my next wish?"

He nodded toward my right hand. "Just press the flames together, speak my name, and I'm bound to come to you."

The flames?

I looked at my fingertips for the first time since Teel had poured out of the lamp, the same fingertips that had jangled with sparky energy when he'd worked his magic in front of me. If I angled them just so, I could discern vague outlines across the whorls of my fingerprints—flames that seemed to be tattooed in transparent ink. My right thumb and each finger on that hand were marked.

I pressed my thumb and index fingers together and squeezed. "Teel," I said loudly.

"Ow!" He gave me an annoyed glare. "I'm right here!" He raised his own fingers to massage his temples and said crossly, "Do you want to make another wish now, or not?"

"Not yet," I said meekly, staring at my hand in amazement. I couldn't keep from asking the first question that popped into my head. "Why do you care, anyway? I mean, isn't it better to be out of the lamp than locked up inside there?"

He scowled at me and drew himself up straighter. "Of course

it's better to be outside. But we genies have certain standards. The Registry keeps statistics on every wisher we assist."

"The Registry?"

He rolled his eyes. "The administrators who keep track of all us genies. The ones who decide who gets to be advanced." I must have looked as confused as I felt, because he sighed and started over. "Each genie is obligated to grant wishes. If we take too long to grant them, we get shoved into one of the backwaters."

"Backwaters? Like what? Like Minneapolis?"

"Like Regrekistan."

"Regrekistan? I've never heard of it."

"Exactly."

Well, how I was I supposed to argue with that? Instead, I tried to trace his scattered logic through to its most likely end point. "And if you grant your wishes quickly, where do you get assigned?"

"It's not so much the assignment—most of us stay in the States, or Europe. Or China—there's a long tradition of wish-granting there. What we're hoping for, what we're *all* hoping for, is time in the Garden."

His voice changed as he said the last word. The disco playboy disappeared completely. The impatient taskmaster fled. The exasperated worker who struggled to keep both of us on task utterly vanished. Instead, Teel sounded wistful, longing. His face relaxed, as if he were sleeping.

I almost hesitated to repeat, "The Garden?"

"It's beautiful there." He sounded like a man talking about his first kiss. "The Garden nurtures our spirits, our…souls. We genies become one with the natural world, the world we are otherwise forced to manipulate, to change. The Garden is the only place where we're truly at peace. The oldest genies, the ones who have granted hundreds of thousands of wishes, are allowed to stay forever. Not just visit. Not just linger for a day, a week, a month. A year…"

Hearing his voice trail off in wistful memory, I wasn't quite sure what to say. Part of me felt like I should hurry up and make my last two wishes—who was I to deny bliss to a genie? But part of me wanted to hold on to my treasures, wanted to take time to think things through.

The momentary spell passed as quickly as it had descended. Teel appraised me shrewdly as he urged, "I don't suppose you're ready yet?"

I shook my head.

"Then I'm going to spend my time learning what wonders there are in—" he pursed his lips into a scornful pout "—Minneapolis. As soon as you decide—"

"I'll…" I touched my fingers together but refrained from adding pressure. Before I could say anything else, my genie turned on his Converse-clad heels and glided out of the Fox Hill Dinner Theater.

I wanted to call out to him. I wanted to tell him to be careful, to remember that things had changed in the intervening decades since he'd last been out in the world. I wanted to tell him to put on a coat; the January evening would be cold. I wanted to tell him to walk past the Fox Hill Cinema without even glancing at the movie posters for *Joe White and the Seven Whores*.

But he was gone before I could say a word.

The next morning, I stopped at Club Joe for a cup of coffee to fortify myself before heading in to my first rehearsal at the Landmark. The guy behind the counter looked at me strangely when I asked him to add four shots of espresso to my latte, but he finally shrugged, chewed on his lip ring, and complied. The first sip of the drink hit my bloodstream like gasoline sprayed on a fire.

I tried to convince myself that my pounding heart was just a product of overpriced coffee. I knew, though, that it was really about working at the Landmark, working with some of the Twin Cities theater community's leading lights.

Teel and his wishes and my sudden professional elevation still seemed completely unreal. I hadn't even had a chance to share my news with Maddy and Jules yet; they had both spent the night with their respective beaux. Ordinarily, I was thrilled to have the apartment to myself, but I had spent most of last night fighting the urge to phone them both, to demand that they come home to keep me company (and to verify that I hadn't lost my mind).

Now, hovering outside the rehearsal room at the Landmark, I was as nervous as a kindergartener on the first day of school.

The Landmark had launched after a massive capital campaign, and they'd used their millions to build a state-of-the-art rehearsal facility on the ground floor of their theater space. The idea was to make theatergoing transparent to the audience, to let people buying tickets at the box office peer through glass walls at actors creating the very plays they would later see on stage. Patrons would be so impressed by the hardworking actors, the theory went, that they would gladly shell out more for tickets. And invite their friends. And their relatives. And every other person they knew in the Twin Cities.

I couldn't say whether the notion had resulted in additional ticket sales, but I knew that the open rehearsal room impressed me. The walls were clear, shimmering planes of glass, which made me wonder who had to clean them. They were fitted with venetian blinds, to hide the actors when they worked on sensitive scenes. Now, though, everything was open, inviting. The huge space was filled with the best and the brightest actors around.

I'd come a long way from Fox Hill. Or maybe my sense of

awe was just inspired by the fact that I hadn't needed to hurry past a bunch of porno patrons to get in the building's front door.

Two dozen chairs had been placed in a neat circle. Looking at them, I felt a pang of guilt—setup was my responsibility. Would *be* my responsibility, I nodded to myself, as soon as I had a key to the theater and an understanding of the director's expectations.

As suddenly shy as a wallflower at homecoming, I tried to convince my legs to carry me out of the shadows and into the brightly lit rehearsal room. I clutched my cup of coffee in a suddenly sweaty palm, as if it were a lifesaver thrown to me from the deck of some passing ship.

I stared at the actors and wondered if my first wish had been sheer, unadulterated stupidity.

There was Jennifer Galland, winner of three Ivey Awards (our local equivalent of the Oscars). The last time I'd seen her on stage, she had been dressed in a stunningly beautiful Edwardian gown, performing—alas—in a deeply flawed production of *The Importance of Being Earnest*. (She'd had an ideal sense of comic timing, but everyone else in the show had worked under the mistaken belief that Wilde had written a tragedy. Of epic proportions. And even more epic length—the show had run nearly four hours.)

Now Jennifer was wearing a pair of the rattiest blue jeans I'd ever seen outside of my own apartment. Her plain white T-shirt looked like a refugee from a bargain bin. Her honey-colored mane was pulled back in a bouncing ponytail, and she seemed to have forsworn all makeup. Nevertheless, she was stunning, gorgeous in a way that poets describe as dewy, and teenage boys record as "totally hawt." She was solid Juliet material, or I was no judge of casting.

I sighed and glanced around the room, daring myself to

count the number of men whose tongues were lolling about their ankles. That was one thing about working on a Shakespeare play—the casts were hugely weighted toward males. I'd worked on one production of *Julius Caesar* in college where the men's dressing room became so overcrowded that they'd taken over the women's, forcing poor Calphurnia and Portia into a broom closet.

Counting up Jennifer's admirers, I received my first shock of the day.

There were at least a dozen women in the room. Many more women than men. For a Shakespeare play. For *Romeo and Juliet*.

I skipped through the roles in my mind. Juliet. Her nurse. Lady Montague. Lady Capulet. That made for one nubile romantic lead and three dried-up husks.

Even if every designer on the show was female, there were still too many women in the room. And the designers weren't all female. I recognized David Barstow, a lighting designer who had beaten Maddy out of at least three dearly desired jobs in as many years. He was talking to Alex Munoz, a successful local sound designer. Bill Pomeroy—the director who had made my wish come true—crouched beside him, nodding as Alex pointed out something on a sheet of scratch paper.

No, the designers were certainly not all women.

What was going on here? Was this some elaborate joke? Had Teel somehow corrupted my wish, brought Bill Pomeroy into the loop, only to embarrass me and tell me that my dream job was not actually going to happen? Was I doomed to return to Fox Hill, with everyone laughing at my idiotic self-deception, everyone in on the joke except for me?

But how could Teel have managed that? How could he have known what I would ask for before I did? How could he have worked things out with Bill in such a short time and made my cell phone ring—especially when he'd quite obviously never seen a cell phone before I'd freed him from his lantern?

Who was I fooling? If I was willing to accept a genie who could grant wishes, I had to be willing to accept a genie with a wicked sense of humor. Didn't I?

Call me an idiot, but I took a deep breath and walked into the rehearsal room.

Bill looked up as I crossed the threshold, and a huge smile broke across his face—the smile of a grateful man, a relieved man. Not a man who had just pulled off the cruelest joke in the history of Twin Cities theater.

"Kira!" he said, and his exclamation sifted silence over the rest of the room. "Our savior! I'm thrilled that you could join us on such short notice!"

He walked across the room and offered his hand, along with a smile that was as bright as the light reflecting off his shaved skull. He wore a tight black turtleneck tucked into black denim jeans; his outfit looked like a crisper, cleaner, much more tailored version of mine. Fine lines spidered beside his eyes, a crinkling maze that reminded me just how long he'd been a theatrical god in Minneapolis, well before he'd landed this plum job at the Landmark.

Still holding my hand, Bill said earnestly, "Maria was so relieved to hear that you accepted our offer. Her mother was discharged from intensive care this morning and she should make a one-hundred-percent recovery. Maria asked me to tell you, explicitly, that she feels so much better knowing that you've stepped in to take care of things here."

Maria. That must be the stage manager I'd displaced. I'd never met her before—didn't even know her last name. I suspected that Teel's magic had eased Maria's concern by giving her a false memory of my work. What crisis, though, had sent

Maria's mother to the ICU? I fervently hoped it was something wholly unrelated to my wish, something completely independent from Teel's magic.

That had to be the case, right? Maria's mother had to be in the hospital *before* I made my wish, before Bill called to offer me the job. Teel might have harnessed another person's misfortune, but I couldn't be responsible for actually making a woman ill. Could I?

I glanced uneasily at my faintly tattooed fingertips. Before I could say anything, though, Bill gestured toward the circle of chairs. He shot his sleeve and tapped his wrist at the spot where most people wore a watch. He had none, but he conveyed a sense of time-driven urgency with the gesture. "Come on, everyone. Let's get started." He nodded toward the seat beside him, and I took it, figuring that I could best assist him if I were by his side, even if I had no idea of his agenda for the day's meeting. I gulped another swallow of coffee and braced myself for whatever was to come.

Everyone grabbed a chair, scooting the careful circle into a more comfortable, random shape. Water bottles joined coffee cups on the floor, and a couple of people shrugged out of sweaters. Bill added to the aura of casual ease, starting by having everyone go around the circle and give their names. I was grateful that he didn't have us say anything else—our favorite movie, our favorite drink, our preferred sexual position.

Yeah. I'd had directors foist some really strange icebreakers on a group, all in the name of smothering first-day jitters.

I wished, though, that Bill *had* asked people to state their role in the production. I wanted to know why there were so many women present, so many more than I had ever expected for a classical show. With a chill, I thought of a production of *Twelfth Night* that I'd seen in college, where "the melancholy

Jacques" had been played by seven actors. They had chanted in unison, like a traditional Greek chorus, creating a perfect hash out of the Bard's famous Seven Ages of Man speech. Oh, you know it. It's the one that starts, "All the world's a stage…" It doesn't gain anything by being recited by seven people at once. Trust me.

I swallowed hard and ordered myself to pay attention as Bill started to speak.

"Thank you, all, for joining us today. You are some of the bravest actors and designers I know. Some of the most courageous stars of the Twin Cities, who will be remembered for this production for years to come."

Courageous.

What required courage? I had to admit, I wasn't very brave. I was a stage manager, and a damned good one, but I would never be described as…

Bold, Bill Pomeroy went on. Intrepid. Daring. Gutsy. Venturesome.

Venturesome? The guy was a regular thesaurus, his words tumbling over one another as he exhorted his cast.

I glanced at the glass walls of the practice room, at the venetian blinds. Was Bill planning a *Romeo and Juliet* in the nude? Was I about to discover that my days next to the Fox Hill skin flicks were actually the best possible training for my new gig?

I swallowed hard. Why hadn't I asked more questions? Why hadn't I hesitated before accepting my first wish on a platter?

I could not keep my eyes from Jennifer Galland. She was staring at Bill eagerly—some might say *ardently*. I could see her breathing, and I was suddenly uncomfortably aware that the adjective "perky" would probably be featured in any accurate description of her anatomy. I stared down at my own sorry, sweatshirt-clad body and hoped that the rest of us would not be expected to join in the courageous display of bared flesh.

Just as I started to worry about wasting my second Teel-wish getting out of this production, I forced myself to tune back in to Bill's speech. "*Romeo and Juliet* has become one of the touchstones of our popular culture. Ask any educated person, and they know the phrase 'star-crossed lover.' They know that 'a rose by another name would smell as sweet.' They know 'what light through yonder window breaks.' Our goal—our *mission*—is to get people to think about this play in ways they never have before. We will get people to hear the words, to see the action with totally new ears, completely opened eyes."

The actors were eating this stuff up. They leaned forward on their chairs. Their eyes glinted. They licked their lips, ravenous cats ready to pounce on a prize.

Bill sat back, smiling benevolently as he held out his hands to the room. "But you don't have to trust me. You don't have to take my word for it. Let's read through a quick scene, just so that you can hear the difference our production will make."

The actors all reached into their bags, digging around to extract their copies of the script. As if reading my mind, Bill passed a copy of the play to me. There were thousands of editions of *Romeo and Juliet*, of course, with different footnotes and annotations. We would all work from the same version, so that we could more readily find our lines, more easily follow every action on and off the stage.

I took my copy gratefully. Once I got home, I would create my stage manager's notebook, cutting apart the binding and taping individual pages to blank sheets of paper. With the added margins, I could add copious notes, record the blocking, write in light cues and sound cues, keep track of all the details a stage manager needed to control behind the scenes.

For now, though, I followed Bill's excited instruction to turn to Act II, Scene II. "You all know this passage. You've known it for years. Listen, though, as we challenge society's most basic expectations. Jennifer? Drew?"

Jennifer cleared her throat and tossed her ponytail, as if she were impersonating a bobby-soxer at a Frank Sinatra concert. She held her script with her left hand, using the fingers of her right to trace beneath words. When she spoke, her voice was high and light, like Marilyn Monroe giving her most airheaded line reading ever. "But soft! What light through yonder window breaks? It is the east, and Juliet is the sun."

I knew the line. As Bill said, we *all* knew the line. I could picture Juliet standing on her balcony, staring out at the night-time stars, thinking about the guy she'd just met, the love of her life, the boy—man—she was willing to risk everything for, abandoning her family, her nurse, everything she had ever known and loved and respected.

Except, Jennifer was reading Romeo's lines.

She completed the monologue, delivering every familiar phrase with the same whispery, ultrafeminine pout. And then, a male voice chimed in from right beside me: "O Romeo, Romeo! wherefore art thou Romeo?"

I started to laugh.

Obviously, this was a game that the company had worked out before I arrived. This was a joke, a hazing for the new kid. They were getting back at me for having missed casting calls, for having joined the production just in the nick of time.

Except I was the only one laughing.

I felt the weight of two dozen stares like a physical thing. Jennifer's perfect features arrayed themselves in a frown. The man who had responded to her delivery, Drew Myers, who had read Juliet's lines, looked like I had tripped him while he was carrying a ten-course meal into a dining room. He was startled, and angry, and a little bit embarrassed.

Bill's paternal voice was gentle. "Exactly," he said, as if someone had finished arguing some point with the eloquence of a Harvard debater. "Let's step back and take a look at what happened here. Jennifer, how did it feel to deliver Romeo's lines?"

Jennifer glanced at me, then looked at the script in front of her. She stared up at the ceiling, as if she could read a response there. "It felt…" Her voice was her own again, husky, seductive in a way that her little-girl whisper could never be. She licked her lips, tossed that ponytail. I was really starting to hate that ponytail. "It felt liberating," she said at last. "It felt like I was shrugging off centuries of expectation. Of belief. I was able to break out of what everyone *thought* I should do, *thought* I should be. I felt free."

"Excellent!" Bill beamed. "And Drew? How did it feel to deliver *your* lines?"

As Drew swallowed and shook his head, I had a chance to sneak my first good look at the actor. I knew him by reputation. We'd never worked on a show together, but according to the well-greased wheels of Twin Cities gossip, half the actresses in Minneapolis had fallen for his California-surfer-boy good looks. His broad shoulders filled his often-washed cotton shirt; he wore khakis with a casual ease that let me know he was comfortable with himself, with his place in the world. While formulating a response to Bill's question, he set his script down across his knee, freeing his hands to flex, as if he were trying to rein in all the mysteries of the world.

If Drew had responded to the proverbial "call to central casting," he'd report for duty as Leading Man. His hair was tousled, as if he hadn't taken the time to comb it when he'd tumbled out of bed that morning. (I sternly pulled my thoughts away from an image of him in bed.) Streaks of gold glinted through rich dark blond; if he'd been a woman, I'd have known that he paid handsomely for the highlights. (Since he was an actor, he might have paid, as well, but chances were he was just damn lucky. Besides, I didn't detect the brassy perfection of even an expert hairdresser's touch.)

Drew's eyes were a deep brown, so dark that they were almost black. As he blinked, though, I could just make out sparkles of green, adding depth, complexity. His bone struc-ture was amazing—hey, theater people are taught to analyze things like that, with complete and utter dispassion! His cheek-bones were strong, and he had just a hint of a cleft in his chin.

I was half in love—and totally in lust—before I heard him reply to Bill's question. The strangled crush of my heart against my ribs was only heightened by the adorable shrug he made as he laughed in rueful embarrassment.

"It was a total mind-trip, dude. It was like Juliet was totally hawt for Romeo. You know, first love."

Okay. So Drew wasn't going to win any elocution contest. But I was more than willing to help him remember the heat of first love.

Bill jumped to his feet, almost turning over his chair. "Exactly!" Drew's answer apparently gave our director so much energy that he had to pace behind us. I half turned in my seat, so that I could follow him as he gesticulated. "Reversing our gender roles makes us think about the meaning of everything we say, everything we do. It makes us listen to our old assump-tions with new ears. It makes us ask ourselves whether we really mean all those things that we've always said, whether we truly believe all those thoughts that have been pounded into us since we were children."

He waved a frenetic hand toward Drew. "Does it have to be

the woman who stands on the balcony, waiting for her love to arrive?" He pounced toward Jennifer. "Does it have to be the man who finds the first courage to speak?" And then, he rounded on me. "What social strictures bind us? Why do we react the way we do?"

I quaked a smile, which felt like the tight-jawed grin of a skull.

Bill waited. And waited some more. "Seriously, Kira," he said at last. "Why do we react the way we do?"

Well, I supposed I should be grateful that I was being included in the discussion. I should appreciate being brought into the fold right away, from the very beginning. If only the fold weren't quite such a freakishly bizarre place.

Bill spread his hands in appeal. "Why did you laugh, Kira?"

"I—" I cleared my throat. "I laughed because they took me by surprise. I laughed because I wasn't expecting to hear those words said by those people. I associate the lines with a certain type of behavior, a certain attitude."

Bill nodded gravely, and the entire cast mimicked him, like the audience on Oprah's show. Any minute now, he was going to invite me to share my story, to bring in Dr. Phil for a consult. "Go on," he said, and I realized I still wasn't off the hook.

"I laughed because I was uncomfortable," I said. Even if I hadn't been uncomfortable then, I was now. That should count for something.

"Yes!" Bill said, and suddenly he'd gone from Oprah to preacher. The cast caught their collective breath, clearly enchanted by Bill's power, taken in by his aura. I wouldn't have been surprised if they'd broken out in song, perfect pitch, one and all. Or maybe that was just my background, coming to the Landmark from so many years in musical dinner theater.

At least I knew what I was supposed to say now. I knew

exactly how I was supposed to react. "Society has led me to respond to romance in certain ways, to react to love stories with certain expectations."

"Precisely!" Bill exclaimed, and the cast nodded its frantic approval. "Kira, here, is saying exactly what we expect our audience will say. She is the voice of the people. Vox populi."

Really? Me? I was all that? I suddenly found the cover of my script fascinating. (Read: I became excruciatingly aware of everyone studying me like I was some exhibit in a zoo.)

Bill went on expansively. "In the next three months, we're going to study Kira's reaction. We're going to focus on what we know, what we believe, and where there are gaps between those two. We're going to examine why our society does the things that it does, what we can change, how we can make things different. And along the way, we're going to change the way that the Landmark, the way that the Twin Cities, the way that the United States of America thinks about art!"

The cast applauded.

They actually applauded, as if they were at a play themselves. For just a moment, I thought that Bill might even garner a standing ovation.

What had I gotten myself into? Were these folks stark raving mad?

Or was this what the real theater world was all about? Was this what artists were really doing, instead of rehashing old musicals while their audience tried to sneak second helpings of dessert from the buffet?

I'd asked for change, and I'd certainly gotten it.

Bill made a few more points. He talked about production design, and how he wanted the play to appear, visually. He explained that in the same way that we were exploring the reversal of genders, we were going to explore the reversal of classes. Our

Romeo and Juliet were not going to live in palaces. They were going to live in sewers beneath the Verona streets. They weren't going to dress in silk and velvet; instead, they'd cover themselves with whatever rags they could salvage from the rotting landfills around them. They weren't going to duel honorably, with swords flashing in a public square. No, they would fight their battles with nunchucks, tossing in a kick or two to the groin.

We were going to stage a *Romeo and Juliet* like no other. Of that I could be sure.

Bill wrapped up by announcing a full read-through the following morning. The actors eagerly gathered their belongings, chatting animatedly as they headed out the door in groups of two and three. I glanced around the now-ragged circle of chairs, grimly amused to see that even gender-bending revolutionaries neglected to throw away their own empty water bottles and coffee cups. I shrugged and stacked the chairs into four piles, easing their metal legs together, one on top of the other. Then I started to collect the debris. Some stage manager tasks were always the same, no matter how adventuresome the company.

As I was scooping up the last cup, I heard Bill's voice from behind me. "Kira, I want you to meet our set designer, John McRae."

I straightened up to find the Marlboro Man staring at me. He was tall, but a bit slouch-shouldered. His hair was a little too long, as if he hadn't made time to visit a barber for several weeks. It was wavy and black, with a sprinkling of gray around his temples. This guy had spent more time in the sun than dermatologists currently recommended; he had gentle crow's feet by his eyes. His mouth was set in an easy smile, but it was half obscured by a mustache—a look that had gone out about twenty years before but somehow seemed to suit him.

Maybe it was the plaid shirt he wore, and the well-worn

jeans. Or the toes of his boots, scuffed and comfortable. But I could totally picture him swinging up into a saddle, clicking his tongue in a near-silent message to his horse, riding off into the sunset.

I automatically extended my hand to complete Bill's introduction, only to realize that I was still holding the lipstick-printed dregs of some actor's latte. I would have shifted the cup to my other hand, but those fingers were already splayed around a trio of Red Bull cans. At least one of our cast members was prepared to match me, milligram for milligram, in caffeine consumption.

John reached out and took the paper cup in his left hand, offering me his right to shake. "Pleased to meet you," he said, and I was pretty sure that he was smothering a laugh at my expense. What the hell. I'd been ready to laugh at our entire production.

Bill glanced toward the door and saw that his lighting designer was about to leave. "Dave!" he called out. "Wait up! I want to talk to you about just how dark we can make the fight scenes."

As he hurried away, I turned back to John. "Sounds pretty grim," I said.

"Sounds pretty something," he said. I caught the hint of a drawl, hiding beneath his wavy hair and warm brown eyes.

"You aren't from around here, are you?" I asked, almost kicking myself when the question came out sounding like something from *Gunsmoke*. Or *Bonanza*. Or any of the other ancient Westerns that haunted late-night TV.

He shook his head. "I moved up from Dallas about six months ago."

"At least you got to enjoy our summer."

He grinned. "I can barely remember it now."

"It'll get colder before spring. And we'll have a lot more

snow." I watched Bill walk Dave Barstow out to the front door of the theater. I figured I could venture a question or two. "So, did you know about this whole gender-switch thing when you signed on?"

"Pomeroy and his 'concepts.'" John shrugged. "I've worked with him on a half-dozen shows over the years. He starts out with big ideas, and grows them bigger."

"I'm not quite sure where else this one can go."

"Just you wait," he said with an easy smile. "If Bill says he wants sewers, you can be sure they'll be the nastiest, slimiest ones you've ever seen."

"Great," I said, trying to chase a note of doubt out of my voice. "I've always heard that he's thorough. At least we don't have a smell designer on staff."

"Don't put it past him to add something like that before we're done."

"Scratch and sniff in the programs?"

"Maybe more like those fancy perfume ads in magazines." He shrugged. "The audience can rip open Eau de Sewer when they read about the cast. Catch 'em by surprise."

Surprise. I'd said I wanted a change. I'd said I wanted to do more than I had at Fox Hill. I'd said I was up for the challenge. "I can't wait." Success—I'd hit the right note. At least John laughed with me.

He glanced at the oversize clock on the wall. "I've got to swing by the lumberyard this afternoon, but a bunch of us are grabbing dinner at Mephisto's tonight. You up for it? Around six?"

Mephisto's.

The restaurant was a couple of blocks away, conveniently located near half a dozen of the small theaters in downtown Minneapolis. It was actually called Mike's Bar and Grill, but all the theater crowd called it Mephisto's, because Mike looked like the devil, and his burgers were enough to lead anyone down the path to Hell.

I loved Mike, and I adored his food, but I hadn't set foot in Mephisto's for over a year. The place was one of TEWSBU's favorite hangouts. By unspoken arrangement, he'd gotten it in our…divorce. After our non-wedding, I'd had no desire to hang out in the familiar restaurant, to chance running into him. My belly flipped at the idea of going there even now.

Besides, I should head home to prepare my script. I should do some research on past productions of *Romeo and Juliet*, on other directors' attempts to turn the story on its head. I should do some laundry and wash my hair and iron my sheets into flawless perfection.

But John was offering me a way to meet my new theatrical family. He was opening the door for me to join the cast, to move forward with the camaraderie that they'd clearly already begun building through auditions.

Besides, Mike's burgers were really, really good.

I stooped to pick up one last wayward water bottle and was a little unnerved to find John looking at me when I straightened. His expression was relaxed, patient. His weight was distributed evenly on his feet, as if he could wait all day for me to make up my mind. Without saying a word, the man projected calm steadiness, the exact opposite of the tempestuous TEWSBU. "I'd love to join you," I said before I was even sure that I'd made up my mind.

"Great," John said, with another easy grin. "I'll see you there at six. Have a great afternoon."

I waited until he'd left before I dug my phone out of my backpack. Glancing around the room and shaking my head about the strange rehearsal I'd just witnessed, I auto-dialed my father. I nearly dropped the phone in surprise when he answered the line directly; I always got his secretary.

"Hey, Dad," I said, recovering quickly. "I'm finishing up here at the theater. Can I swing by in half an hour?"

I was already turning off the lights in the rehearsal room when he said yes.

CHAPTER 4

MY FATHER'S SECRETARY, ANGIE, WAS BUSILY TYPING away when I got to his office. "He's on the phone," she said, scarcely glancing at the Space Shuttle hardware that substituted for a telephone on her desk. She tracked three phone lines for my father, and she supported two other attorneys full time. It wouldn't have surprised me if she could launch nuclear weapons from that thing.

"Should I come back?"

"He'd probably welcome the interruption now. It's been a long day."

"I know what you mean," I said, sighing dramatically.

"Aren't you ready to leave the theater, and come take a normal job here at the firm?" Angie knew that my father had been encouraging me to do the same for at least the past ten years, since I'd been a sophomore in high school.

I grinned and gestured at my black sweatpants. "What? Give up my life of glamour?"

She snorted. "I just want to report to your father that I've done my part. You'd better go on in, before someone else comes around."

I thanked her and dipped my hand into the M&M's jar on the corner of her desk. She filled the thing every morning—when I was a kid, I believed her when she said that fairies replenished it at night. Now, knowing that Teel and his ilk were roaming the streets, I wondered what it would take to find a real magical candy stock boy.

I picked out all of the green M&M's and started crunching away as I knocked on Dad's door frame. As Angie had predicted, he waved me in. I shrugged out of my coat and dropped into one of the chairs across from his desk. He glanced at my black sweats, briefly registering disapproval, but then looked away. We'd decided a long time ago which battles were worth fighting.

He was speaking in his Logical Lawyer voice. "I've got to have the rider by noon tomorrow, Chuck. My clients wanted this deal closed in December. They're already set to walk away." I listened to the squawk of disagreement on the other side of the phone and smiled. Knowing my father, his clients didn't need to close the deal until Independence Day.

As Dad gave a patient, professional reply, I glanced at my fingers. The flame markings were barely visible, here in the office light. If I twisted my hand just...so, I could make out a slight flicker, but there was nothing that anyone else would see. Nothing that my father could pick up from the other side of his desk.

I realized that I wasn't going to tell him about Teel.

After all, how many lawyers could listen to their daughter say that a genie had granted her three wishes? How many caring parents could let *that* one go by, without calling for immediate medical intervention?

I didn't have any way to prove that Teel existed; I couldn't show that I was speaking the truth. My housemates—they just might understand. They'd heard enough crazy things from me over the years; we'd had serious discussions over whether certain theaters were haunted, whether Shakespeare's Scottish Play could actually bring bad luck when its name was said aloud.

But Dad? Not so much.

I looked around as he made conversation-finishing noises. His office hadn't changed in years. He had two corner windows, looking out from the twenty-seventh floor of the IDS Tower, the tallest building in Minnesota. Life as a partner at Franklin, Cromwell and Hopkins had its perks.

Although my father would never admit it, his practice had been infinitely more successful than even he had originally predicted. The firm now boasted three hundred attorneys who devoted their time to every conceivable field of civil and criminal law. Profits per partner were the highest in the Twin Cities.

As Dad insisted on reminding me, every single time I stopped by. I started a mental stopwatch as he hung up the phone. "Good afternoon, sweetheart," he said, paternal warmth replacing the legal chill that had been in his voice.

"Hey, Dad. Aren't you supposed to be at home watching TV and eating bonbons while your associates fight the good fight?"

"Someone has to mind the ship," Dad said. "Those profits per partner don't generate themselves."

Wow. Under a minute. The old man still had it.

I glanced at the shelves that lined the side wall. Scattered between mammoth books were dozens of Lucite cubes, records of transactions completed to the tune of millions of dollars. Each block contained a miniature version of a stock offering, my father's brilliant legalese shrunk and preserved forever. I didn't know who had started the tradition, but some trophy company must be making a killing.

In the center of the legal memorabilia was a picture frame— a plain silver rectangle holding a professional black-and-white portrait. My mother.

She had the same unruly curls that I'd inherited, and I knew that her eyes were the identical brown as my own. I could just make out the upturned tip of my nose when I looked at hers. Now that I'd put on my post-TEWSBU weight, our chins were different, but when I was at my slimmest, we looked like sisters.

She'd died of leukemia when I was three years old.

I had a few memories, images that I held on to with the ferocity of a child clutching her favorite teddy bear. I could feel Mother coming in to kiss me good-night after an office holiday party, her hair still cold from the winter air outside. I could remember her laughing as I blew out the candles on my third-year birthday cake. I could hear her reading *Goodnight Moon* to me, and I remembered shouting out "Good night, nobody!" even though I was supposed to be quieting down and getting ready for bed.

But mostly, I knew about her from stories that people had told me. She'd wanted to go to law school, had always planned on starting classes after I was in elementary school. She'd planned on practicing environmental law, suing the corporate bastards and cleaning up every last one of Minnesota's famed ten thousand lakes.

She hadn't lived long enough to achieve her dream.

In twenty-five years, Dad had never remarried. I'd never really thought of my father as a lonely man, as a grieving widower. No one did. The only concession he'd made to grief was that he'd moved out of the house that he and Mother had bought when the firm first turned a profit. He'd said that he couldn't imagine living there without her.

But I did.

The house was a giant old thing, just off Lake of the Isles, in one of Minneapolis's oldest districts. It had two rambling stories, a full attic, and a basement. After Mother died, Dad just locked the door and rented us a town house in the suburbs. He couldn't bear to live there, but couldn't bear to sell it.

After a couple of years, he got around to trying to rent out the place, but no one wanted a home that large. Ever the practical lawyer, he'd consulted a tax and real estate colleague, who'd suggested renovating the house, turning it into two large apartments. Dad had agreed, and the work had been completed almost twenty years ago.

Lucky for me.

Maddy, Jules, and I now lived in the second-floor apartment. In deference to Dad, I had the front room, a spacious bedroom that was built into the turret on the corner of the building. Maddy's and Jules's bedrooms looked out over the backyard; they might not be able to glimpse the lake from their windows, but they had the same hardwood floors, the same solid plaster walls, the same long-polished oak door frames. We enjoyed a gigantic living room, and a kitchen that more than met the needs of three women who were always on the run.

And we paid about one third the market rate for our rent.

That discount more than made up for the handful of things that weren't ideal about the house. Our downstairs neighbors, the Swensons, were in their seventies. They occasionally phoned upstairs, asking us to walk more quietly across our hardwood floors. Maddy, Jules, and I sometimes resented the fact that the Swensons got to park in the single garage *and* in the driveway, while we had to forage for street parking. And there was always a debate if we had Chinese food delivered after nine o'clock at night; the drivers from Hunan Delight absolutely could not grasp the idea that they should ring the buzzer for upstairs, rather than downstairs.

Nevertheless, the arrangement worked pretty well. (Read: We could forgive a multitude of neighbor sins for dirt-cheap lodging.)

I unzipped my backpack and took out the January rent check. My roommates and I might have a sweetheart deal, but payment was still due promptly. I handed it across Dad's desk and said, "Here you are. Signed, sealed, and delivered."

"Thank you." He slipped it under a paperweight shaped like a gavel; I knew that it would be deposited by noon the next day. "How are you, Kira? How are things at Fox Hill?" Dad hated the fact that I worked in the theater; he worried—justifiably—that it was economically unstable.

I shrugged. "I'm fine. But you should know, I've left Fox Hill."

He raised his eyebrows. "I thought we had an agreement, Kira. When you finish up at the dinner theater, you'll take the LSAT."

The Law School Admission Test. The standardized test necessary for me to apply to any law school in the country. Dad had pushed me to take it since the day I graduated with highest honors from the University of Minnesota. I'd majored in English (a compromise—he had argued hard for Poli Sci, and I'd wanted a degree in Art, Design, and the Performing Arts). Despite my mother's aspirations, I had absolutely no desire to be a lawyer. I knew too much about how the profession worked; I'd been raised with stories of associates slaving away, trying desperately, frantically, to prove that they were worthy of elevation to the partnership.

I kept my voice light through years of hard practice. "That wasn't precisely our agreement, Counselor. I said that I'd take the LSAT if I lost my job. I started my new job today. Before Fox Hill formally let me go."

Dad frowned. "And this new position? Where is it?"

"The Landmark Stage."

"The Landmark? There was an article about them in the paper last Sunday!"

"Yes, there was," I said, deciding not to take offense at the surprise in his voice. "You are looking at the Landmark's newest stage manager…extraordinaire."

He smiled fleetingly, but then pursed his lips. "And let me guess. This new show is something outrageous and edgy. Something that will alienate three-quarters of your potential audience before you even open the door."

"We're doing Shakespeare, Dad. *Romeo and Juliet*." There was no need for him to know about our little gender shift—not right now, in any case.

He nodded slowly, but I could see him marshaling his legal arguments. "When does the play open?"

"The first week in April."

"And how long does it run?"

What was it with the cross-examination? I wasn't sure how long the play would run—I hadn't even thought to ask. It was important, though, to make my new employment sound solid. Stable. I took a gamble that my father would not be intimately acquainted with the performance schedules of local theaters and gave the answer for a typical play. "Eight weeks."

"And then what?"

"Excuse me?"

"What happens after that? After *Romeo and Juliet* closes?"

I sighed. I'd been so excited by Teel's little magic trick that I hadn't even begun to think about the *next* step in my career. "This show is going to get me noticed, Dad! Everyone pays attention to what the Landmark does. The director is a genius! People are going to see the show, other directors, other producers. I could go from the Landmark to the Guthrie, Dad!"

"You could," my father agreed. He got up and walked around his desk, sitting in the client chair next to me so that our knees almost touched.

Despite the fact that the firm had gone to "office casual"

several years back, Dad still wore a suit and tie every day. He thought such an image was most appropriate for a lawyer of his stature; it was expected of a name partner. Nevertheless, he'd shed his jacket while he was working, and he'd loosened his tie with a couple of impatient tugs. Now he glanced at the photo of my mother, as if he were consulting with her on the next thing he was going to say.

"Kira, I know there's a chance that you could go to the Guthrie. There's also a chance that when your show closes, you'll be done. Finished. Not for any bad reason, not because of anything you can control. But you've chosen such a difficult field. Theater is so unreliable."

"Dad, I'm a grown woman now. If I want to take chances, I'm allowed to do that!"

"You're right. You are. But I'm not doing you any favors if I let you take those chances without your completely understanding—and assuming—all of the risks."

My stomach turned over. "What do you mean?"

"As you just said, you're not a child anymore. I shouldn't treat you like one. I shouldn't subsidize your rent, pay your way at the Lake of the Isles house."

I glanced at the check I'd just given him. "You're kicking us out? Me and Maddy and Jules?"

He shook his head. "I wouldn't do that to you. We have an agreement. We always have."

I remembered to breathe again.

He went on, though, before I could enjoy too much relief. "Part of that agreement, though, is that you'll support yourself. If things fall apart in the theater, you need to have somewhere to go, something to do. You need a safety net."

"I do have one!"

"What, serving burgers at Mike's Bar and Grill?"

I flushed. I was going to say working as a *hostess* at Mephisto's. Dad was right, though, as usual. The servers got better tips.

I forced myself to take a deep breath before launching round 3,427 in our endless dissection of What Kira Should Be When She Grows Up. "You know what theater means to me, Dad. I've told you about that feeling I get when I walk into the building, when I start a new show, when I realize the potential that's there."

He nodded. Well, that was better than having him interrupt to interrogate me.

"You also know that I have a great deal of respect for what you do. I'd be an idiot not to." I gestured out the window, at the dusky Minneapolis skyline spread before us, already growing dim with the winter's early sunset. "Maddy and Jules and I know just how lucky we are to live where we do, and I know that your practice has brought us a lot of that."

His eyes narrowed as he tried to identify the parameters of my rhetorical technique. I could see the wheels turning inside his head, calculating how to dissect my points, how to craft his own argument in response. I hurried on before the questioning deposition could resume.

"But the simple fact is that I don't feel the same way about the law as I do about the theater. I don't get that same rush when I walk into a courtroom. I don't get all trembly inside when I look at the closing binders on your bookshelves. That's not a statement about you, or about your firm. It's just a statement, a fact, about me. About how I feel. About who I am."

"There are ways of compromising, Kira."

I immediately pictured myself stage managing *Inherit the Wind*. *Witness for the Prosecution*. *A Few Good Men*. Plays about the legal process. That probably wasn't the sort of compromise he meant.

Dad pressed on. "In the past, I've argued for your following a traditional path—taking the LSAT, going to the best law school you can get into, accepting a job at the best firm that will have you. But you don't have to work at a large firm. You could specialize in lawyering for the arts—museums, theaters, other cultural institutions. You can combine your loves." He interrupted himself, raising a hand in anticipation of my protest. "You can combine your *love,* singular, for the theater, and your practicality, your common sense, your ability to organize and communicate. All the characteristics that make you a wonderful stage manager."

Man, he was really good at this. But I wasn't about to cave that easily. "I don't get it, Dad," I said. "We've talked about my being a big-firm lawyer for years. Why are you only bringing up alternatives now?"

He sat back in his chair and caught his lower lip with his teeth, shaking his head. The action made him look twenty years older. Much less certain. Much less sure. "I'm worried about you, Kira."

"Worried? I'm—"

"An entire year has gone by."

What was the deal with the calendar? Did every single person I knew have the date of my failed wedding etched on their reminder list? Sure, *I* had been counting the days, but it had never occurred to me that anyone else was so concerned.

He held up a hand to keep me from retorting. "It's been a year, and I don't see anything changing. We've never really discussed what happened, and that's all right. I'm your father, not your best friend. But it's obvious to me that you aren't happy. It's obvious that you're dissatisfied with the direction your life has taken."

A protest died in my throat. I looked down, suddenly blinking away tears. My elastic-waist sweatpants filled my vision, silent confirmation of everything my father said.

He dropped his voice. "Kira, I'll be honest with you. Before you got here tonight, I had decided to make you move out of the Lake of the Isles house, to make you face reality, instead of coddling you in your made-up little theater world."

My eyes shot up, but he shook his head, holding up a hand to keep me from protesting.

"I *was* going to tell you that. But your news about the Landmark made me change my mind. You've gotten out of that dinner theater. You've taken the first step in a year toward moving on with your life. But I'm still worried. I still need to see more."

"What's 'more'?" I sounded like a sullen teenager, but I couldn't help myself.

"More is knowing what comes after. More is knowing where you'll go after this show closes." He took a deep breath and reached for a sheaf of papers on his desk. "More is taking the LSAT in June. The application is due on May 13. I've prepared all the pages for you. You just have to sign."

"You what?" I was so astonished that I almost dropped the papers that he handed me.

He shook his head. "Just expand your options, Kira. I can't stand to see you like this any longer. I can't stand to know that you're so unhappy, while nothing ever changes."

I wanted to fight back. I wanted to tell him that he was punishing me because he'd spent too much money on the wedding, money that I'd never asked him to spend, serving the perfect dinner to two hundred of his closest friends and business associates. I wanted to tell him that he was pushing me into law because he wanted to boast to his partners, wanted to tell them that I'd gotten into Harvard or Yale or whatever. I wanted to scream that he didn't always get what he wanted, he couldn't always shape the world into some perfect, flawless entity that functioned precisely as he mandated.

But he already knew the world wasn't perfect.

The portrait of my mother at my back reminded him of that every single day.

He only wanted what was best for me. And how could I argue that having options wasn't the best course? I didn't have to *go* to law school. I just had to take the stupid test.

But I wasn't going to give in quite that easily. "Okay," I said, but I rushed on before he could even register my acquiescence. "I'll take the LSAT, *if* I don't have another theater job lined up by the May application deadline."

"A theater job as good or better than the one you've got at the Landmark," he bargained.

"I won't go back to Fox Hill," I assured him. There probably wouldn't even be a Fox Hill to go back to.

I could see that he wanted to say more. He wanted to place more restrictions on me, make more demands. But he settled for extending his hand.

Ever since I was a little girl, we'd sealed our deals with a handshake. I'd agreed to try Brussels sprouts, agreed to make my bed every morning, agreed to be home by my too-early, completely unfair, totally overprotective curfew. I folded my fingers around his and shook firmly.

He leaned forward and kissed my forehead, making me feel like I was five years old again. "Thank you, Kira. I knew that you'd see reason."

I smiled and sat back in my chair. Who was I kidding? I was never going to be a lawyer. I had a new job at the Landmark. And, if worse came to worst, I had two unused wishes up my sleeve.

CHAPTER 5

IN THE END, I CHICKENED OUT ON GOING TO Mephisto's. I felt bad—John's invitation had seemed genuine enough, and I could practically taste one of Mike's burgers. But I'd spent too many months avoiding the place, too much time worrying about whether TEWSBU was there, what he was doing with his post-me life.

Besides, I hadn't seen Jules and Maddy since getting the Landmark job. My entire life had been turned upside down in the best of all possible ways, and I hadn't had a chance to gush about it with my housemates.

Alas, I'd apparently spent my entire allocation of luck finding the brass lamp and summoning Teel. Traffic was terrible on Hennepin as I left Dad's office, and it was well after seven by the time I got home. I needed to park three blocks away and walk back to the house. When I finally got to our walkway, I saw that the lights were on downstairs. I consciously resisted the temptation to slam the entry door. It wasn't the Swensons' fault that parking spaces were scarce around the lake.

By the time I got upstairs, I was in a foul mood—and ravenous besides. Maddy took one look at me and said, "Hunan Delight?"

"I thought you'd never ask."

Jules chimed in from the sofa, where she had her ballet-perfect legs thrown over the couch's arm. "We've just been waiting for you to get home, so we could order. Who knows when we'll all be home at the same time again?"

Home. The apartment that Dad might raise the rent on, if I didn't square away another theater gig. If I didn't take the LSAT.

No reason to bring down my housemates with that little wrinkle. Yet. Instead, I mustered enthusiasm to say, "That's right! Maddy, you start tech rehearsals next week, don't you?"

As a lighting designer, my housemate's life would be crazy for the next seven days, while the cast learned to perform their play with all her lighting cues in place. Maddy would be in a foul mood, too. She hated making changes to her design when actors couldn't remember to stand in specific spots to deliver specific lines.

Her current show was called *Jack and Jill;* it was a kiddie production that retold Mother Goose rhymes. Maddy had been grumbling over her lighting design for months, complaining that the director had the imagination of a rock, regularly insisting that Maddy's design be "brighter!" and "happier!"

"Yeah," she said, putting on a brilliant fake grimace. "And Jules is heading out of town with Justin."

"Not till Sunday!" Jules said. Justin was her long-time boyfriend, a lawyer who would have made my father proud. Justin's firm was based in Los Angeles, and they had a retreat every winter, bringing in all their lawyers from across the country to enjoy fine wine, gourmet food, and endless seminars on how to sue corporate America. Jules had decided to accompany

Justin for the three-day retreat, and then they were going to indulge in a well-deserved vacation.

I pouted just a little. Maybe my father's life plans for me weren't really so far off. Law firm life—wining, dining, and enjoyable recreation with a perfect boyfriend? Oh. That's right. I didn't drink. I certainly didn't need to eat any more. And I didn't have any boyfriend, perfect or otherwise.

Maddy must have sensed my change of mood from parking-frustrated to love-life-morose. She waved the Chinese menu in front of me enticingly. "What'll it be?" She already had the phone in hand.

"Hot and sour soup, with an extra packet of crunchy noodles," I said. "And crispy sesame chicken."

What could I say? Even if Chinese food *could* be healthy, I didn't need to obsess about making it so. And despite the conversation with my father, I was feeling celebratory.

I had a genie on my side.

Maddy nodded and started punching in numbers as I shuffled back to my bedroom. Slipping out of my Converse All Stars, I tossed my backpack onto my desk. There was a soft *clunk*, and I remembered that I'd shoved Teel's lantern deep into the recesses of the bag that morning. I'd been strangely reluctant to leave it behind in the apartment; it was almost as if I feared my position at the Landmark would evaporate if I didn't keep the thing with me.

Glancing over my shoulder toward my open bedroom door, I considered taking out the lantern, bringing it into the living room to show Maddy and Jules. They'd never believe my story about Teel if I didn't bring absolute proof. I pulled out the lamp, staring at it in the light from the overhead fixture.

It gleamed as if it were lit from within. There was something…satisfied about its appearance, something peaceful. Serene. Just looking at it made me feel peaceful and calm.

I brushed my fingers against the metal. Tiny vibrations shuddered up my hand, as if the nearly invisible tattoo across my fingertips was shimmering in harmony with the lamp. Two more wishes, I thought. Two more chances to change my life in any way I wanted.

"Kira!" Maddy called. "Come on! Are you going to play Scrabble?"

My housemate's voice jerked me back to the present. I wondered how long I'd been standing there, how long I'd been caressing the brass lamp, dreaming of the treasures Teel could give me. I blinked hard, as if I were waking up after a long, restless night. "Um, yeah," I called back. "But just a sec. I want to show you something."

I started to carry the lantern out the door, but it didn't want to go.

Okay. I knew it was an inanimate object. I knew it didn't really have *wants,* couldn't possibly have desires. But it grew heavy as I carried it, suddenly so massive that my arm sagged, my muscles trembled.

I turned back to my desk, and everything was normal.

Scowling, I shifted my grip on the lamp. My fingers must have slipped on its graceful, swooping handle. It must have been weighted, originally for ease of pouring oil, I guessed. There. I had it firmly in hand this time. Two steps toward the door, though, my fingertips started buzzing, itching with a ferocity that was on the edge of stinging.

I wasn't an idiot. The lamp obviously didn't want to leave my room.

Shrugging, I set it on my desk. As I moved away, though, it fell over on its side, with a *clunk* that was mostly muffled by my backpack. I was getting exasperated now—I wasn't a clumsy person by nature, and there was nothing I had done that should have made the lamp fall.

I righted it and turned to go, only to find that it had fallen again.

So. The lamp didn't want to come with me, *and* it didn't want to stay on my desk. At least it didn't want to stay *upright* on my desk.

This was utterly bizarre. The lantern hadn't had any problems in my father's office; I hadn't sensed it jumping around inside my backpack then. It hadn't moved around while I was driving home; there had been no strange lamp behavior in the car. It hadn't clunked against my spine through the canvas of my backpack as I walked the three blocks from my car.

And then the answer dawned on me. The lamp didn't want to be seen by anyone other than me. It hadn't rebelled at Dad's, in the car, during my walk, because it had been hidden.

After everything else that had happened in the past two days, thinking of a brass tchotchke as a sentient object didn't actually sound that strange. I took the lamp from my desk and opened my closet door. By now, I wasn't surprised that it was *happy* with that choice; I could feel its satisfaction tingle through the tiny flames on my fingertips.

It was even happier when I shoved it into my hamper. It almost sang when I covered it with my coffee-stained sweat-shirt from the day before.

I was still looking at my fingers when I went back into the living room. I forced my voice to be normal, nonchalant even, as I asked, "So what did you guys order?" Before they could answer, I said to Maddy, "Don't even bother. I know you got the hot and sour soup. And Eight Treasures Chicken."

Maddy stuck out her tongue. "Am I that predictable?"

I grinned. "If it makes you feel better, you can claim

'reliable.' 'Dependable.'" The truth was that Maddy had chosen hot and sour soup and Eight Treasures Chicken every single time that we'd ordered Chinese in all the years I'd known her. If she had selected anything else, the world would have slipped off its axis. The moon would have crashed into the sea; the earth would have spun into the sun.

That, or I would have been so astonished that I couldn't have eaten my own meal.

Jules looked up from her perch at the table in the corner of our living room. She had the Scrabble board set up, all of the tiles turned upside down in the top of the game's box, ready to be selected and played. She flashed me her killer smile. All of us were Scrabble fiends, but Jules had a dictionary embedded in her brain.

I still didn't understand why Julia Kathleen McElroy had given up on her stage career. She said it was because she was only ever cast as a romantic lead, and she knew that she couldn't continue that once she lost her looks. That sounded so grounded, so centered, that I knew it had to be a lie. I think that she'd had a bad experience, losing out on one coveted role a few years back. When she succeeded at her next audition, for an industrial training film, she never looked back at the crueler, more objectifying life of live theater.

Jules still looked the part of the girl who got the guy. Her shoulder-length black hair was thick and straight, possessing a magical texture that let it take a curl and hold it, no matter how hard rain or snow fell outside. Her eyes were so green that she was regularly asked if she was wearing contact lenses, which might have annoyed her if her natural vision had not been twenty-ten. Her skin was tawny, and her cheeks were permanently flushed; she looked like she had just come from a tennis game on a sun-drenched court in the Riviera.

If her looks weren't enough cause for hating her, her love life just might be. Jules had been dating the same guy since high school. She and Justin had been Homecoming Queen and King; they had been voted Most Likely to Marry. The only reason they hadn't tied the knot yet was that Justin was playing the law firm game, cruising through the ranks at a firm even larger than my father's. Justin promised Jules that they would get married the year he made partner, when he would be able to spend enough time with her, all the time in the world.

Me? I would have taken the perfect guy, whether he had to work late or not. But what could I say? The delay worked for Jules and Justin. And Maddy and I had never needed to look for a new roommate.

"What did you order, Jules?"

She smiled. "Corn and asparagus soup," she said. "And Ants Climbing Trees."

"What's that?" We'd been ordering from Hunan Delight for years, but Jules still managed to find exotic dishes that I'd never noticed on the menu before.

"Spicy pork over cellophane noodles," she said, as if ants and trees were as common as peanut butter and grape jelly on Wonder bread. "Want to try some, when it gets here?"

"No, thanks," I said, a little too quickly.

It wasn't the fact that it was spicy—I liked my food hot. It wasn't the pork; I was an avowed fan of The Other White Meat. It wasn't even the cellophane noodles; in the past year, I had developed a love for all carbohydrates, without discriminating against any grains of origin.

I just didn't like to share my food.

I'm not sure where the aversion came from. Some kids throw fits if one type of food touches another on their plate. Other kids hate to eat green vegetables. Still others refuse to consider trying anything other than chicken fingers or mac and cheese, preferably the neon-orange kind purchased in a bright blue box.

Not me. I was a good eater, even before my TEWSBU-inspired binges took control of my life.

I just didn't like to share, didn't like people digging around on my plate with chopsticks or forks, snagging the perfect bite that I'd saved for last. Of course, I knew that I was acting like a baby. I knew that the vast majority of mature adults enjoyed tasting one another's food. I knew that Chinese food, especially, gave people a chance to try new flavors, to experiment with textures.

So, I felt a little guilty. And that guilt kept me from trying other people's dishes, even when they freely offered their own food.

Jules laughed. She found my aversion to sharing hysterical. She wasn't above testing me when we went out, asking me for a French fry, or begging for a forkful of salad. I had learned to look her in the eye and call her bluff, volunteering to place an order for a whole new plate of whatever I was enjoying.

What could I say? I was a freak.

As if to confirm my self-diagnosis, the buzzer rang, indicating that the delivery guy was at the front door downstairs. Jules said, "I'll get it." She brandished her wallet. "And that will close out last week's Scrabble debt in full." We played for a dollar a point, and Jules had hit a really bad stretch, getting stuck with a U-less Q in three consecutive games.

Maddy and I made noises of agreement as Jules scurried downstairs. I heard the Swensons open their door, and I winced. The delivery guy had obviously rung their doorbell before—or after—he'd rung ours. The financial transaction at the front door was muffled, but I heard Jules say, "Sorry, Mrs. Swenson. Would you like some dumplings?" There was a mumbled reply, and then Jules said, "No, I don't think any of us has ever gotten indigestion from eating this late. I'm sorry they got the bell wrong. Again."

She sprinted up the stairs and closed our apartment door, leaning against it in pantomime of being chased by wolves.

"Brave, brave woman," Maddy said sardonically.

"What were you going to do if she took you up on the dumplings?" I asked.

"Act astonished that Hunan Delight forgot them," Jules replied, shrugging as she carried her bounty to the kitchen counter. She made short work of parceling out the bright red containers, and we were soon crowded around the Scrabble board, slurping soup before we got to our main dishes.

Knowing how to build tension in a dramatic scene, I waited until they had both selected their seven tiles, hiding them on their trays. Jules flipped over a *W.* Maddy flipped over an *N.* I flipped over an *E.* I got to go first. I pretended to study my tray as I fished out a piece of tofu from my hot and sour soup. I touched one tile, then another, and then I put my spoon back in my bowl. "So," I said, drawing out the word. "I got a bit of good news yesterday."

"Your father's dropping our rent by a hundred dollars," Maddy said, taking a moment to crumble more fried noodles into her soup. Jules followed suit. I glanced down at my black sweatshirt, momentarily regretting my double order of noodles as I recited my ten thousandth resolution to return to my pre-wedding-abandonment weight.

What the hell. I was celebrating. If I was going to eat crispy sesame chicken—fried chicken in a sweet, hot sauce—a few extra noodles in my soup couldn't hurt. I added a thorough handful, taking time to break them into pieces as I enjoyed the anticipation growing on my housemates' faces.

"Um, not exactly." I refused to let my LSAT obligation get in the way of my good news. There'd be plenty of time for my housemates to tease me about my study books for the exam, the endless logic questions that I'd leave strewn about the apartment.

"You found the crown jewels from Camelot!" Jules offered.

"No." I frowned. I'd forgotten they were missing. Oh well, that garage sale bonanza was going to be up to Anna to continue. The Fox Hill fund-raiser already seemed very far away. Fearing the next crazy guess my housemates might lob my way, I took pity on their curious faces. "You, dear friends, are looking at the Landmark Stage's latest stage manager."

"What?" Jules said, her perfect brow creasing into a frown as she parsed my words, comparing them with her encyclopedic knowledge of local theater productions.

"Really!" Maddy said at the same time. "For what? One of their summer shows?"

"Nope." I shook my head. *Romeo and Juliet.*

Jules said, "That's impossible! That's opening in three months! They must have set the stage manager ages ago."

My conscience prickled just a little at her words, and I resisted the urge to stare at my fingertips, at their ghostly film of a flame tattoo. Maria's mother was going to be fine, Bill had said. I didn't need to worry.

Instead, I raised my chin and announced, "I got the call from Bill Pomeroy yesterday, just as I finished tagging the costumes. His stage manager had some family emergency." I looked down at my lap, feigning modesty. "I was the first person he called. We had our first rehearsal today."

My housemates cooed with a gratifying level of support. Maddy said, "Wait a second. That's the show with Drew Myers, right?"

I surprised myself by blushing as I thought of our leading man's, er, leading lady's square jaw. "That's the one," I said.

"That'll fill a few seats in the house."

I shrugged and tried to sound as if I hadn't noticed how gorgeous Drew was. "The whole cast is good."

Maddy waggled her eyebrows. "I'm not talking about acting ability. He played Happy in that *Death of a Salesman* I worked on last year. And just about every woman in the audience had a smile on her face every time he walked onstage."

We all laughed. It felt good to share the joke with my housemates. We all knew the Twin Cities theater scene. We all knew just how important this Landmark job could be. I let their kind words break over me, thinking how long it had been since I'd had great news to share.

That could have been because I'd been sacrificing my career for TEWSBU's, when he and I were still together. It could have been because I'd turned down three great stage management prospects in the year that we were engaged, jobs that would have meant traveling out of town, away from my so-called sweetheart. It could have been because I'd let myself loll in the Fox Hill hammock for too long, lulled into complacency by a steady paycheck, even if that paycheck was lean, and I was bored to tears with second-class renditions of musicals designed to do nothing more than please the masses.

But all of that was behind me now. All of that was history. And I hadn't even told my housemates the most amazing thing. I glanced at my fingertips again. The flames were too faint to make out in the living room's shadows. They were never going to believe me when I told them about Teel.

"There's something else, too," I said, immediately silencing Maddy's and Jules's chattering congratulations. "I didn't totally get the job on my own," I said. "I had help."

"Help?" Maddy asked, spooning up the last of her soup.

I nodded. "I was cleaning up the *Kismet* costumes, and I found a brass lantern. It must have been part of the set decoration. I started to polish it, when all of a sudden—"

I couldn't speak.

Just like that, I couldn't form words. I moved my mouth, but nothing came out; I was as silent as if someone had punched the mute button on my personal remote control device.

I coughed, and that sound was audible. I took a sip of water and started again. "I started to polish it," I got out without any trouble, but when I tried to say, "and a genie came out," I was knocked utterly silent again.

"Are you okay?" Maddy asked, putting down her own spoon. "Are you choking?"

I shook my head. "I'm fine," I said, my voice totally, completely normal.

My housemates stared at me as if I were nuts. Which, all of a sudden, I was beginning to think I might be. I took my last mouthful of soup, swallowed it. There was nothing wrong with my throat. Nothing wrong with me at all. I gritted my teeth, suddenly more determined than ever to complete my story. "I was tagging the last of the *Kismet* costumes, when I knocked a brass lantern onto the floor. When I picked it up, it was filthy."

There. That had been easy. I gripped my spoon and clenched my jaw. I took a deep breath, exhaled slowly, and then measured out each word, concentrating on the sounds like a student learning a new language. "I…polished…it…and…then…a—"

Crash.

Without warning, my hand swept across the Scrabble board. I tried to stop my fingers, tried to interrupt the sweeping motion, but it felt like my grip no longer belonged to me. I had no control. I knocked over the game board and all of our tile holders, sending little wooden letters flying across the room. As if for good measure, I turned over Jules's soup bowl, sending her half-finished corn and asparagus flying across the table, toward my unsuspecting chest.

"Kira!" Jules exclaimed.

Maddy sprang into action, whipping her napkin off her lap and trying to mop up the disaster. Fortunately, Jules's soup was no longer steaming hot. My tough-as-armor sweatshirt blocked most of it from my skin.

"I am so sorry!" I said. "I—" How could I explain what had happened? I didn't even have any *idea* what had happened.

"That's okay," Jules said wryly. "I'd had enough, anyway."

Maddy's napkin was quickly soaked, though, and mine had been sacrificed to the initial deluge that seeped down to my lap. I shrugged in disgust and said, "I'll be back in a sec."

I pushed away from the table as Maddy and Jules started collecting the Scrabble tiles. They made concerned noises, but I assured them that I'd just had a really strange cramp in my hand. I saw them exchange a look, but they let me go.

I closed my bedroom door behind me and peeled off my sweatshirt. Something had happened there. Something strange. A distinct power had taken over my hands, a definite force that had emanated from the tattooed flames on my fingertips.

I opened my closet door and reached toward the hangers where another half-dozen sweatshirts waited. Before I could seize clean clothes, though, the world around me disappeared.

Yes, I know how bizarre that sounds. Believe me, it was more bizarre when it happened to me. One moment, I was peering into my closet, shaking my head at the strangeness that had overtaken my life. The next, I was standing nowhere, surrounded by nothing, peering at nobody.

Automatically, my arms folded across my chest, as if I could shield my less-than-stunning décolletage from the complete absence of anything familiar around me. I looked around frantically, wondering if I'd accepted Teel's magical presence too easily. Maybe my first instinct had been correct. Maybe I truly was going nuts.

I glanced down at my feet—they were firmly anchored on top of an invisible surface. I tried shuffling my toes to the side. I kept my balance, which implied that the absent floor extended beneath me in an even plane, but I still couldn't feel anything of substance. Cautiously, I crouched down, trailing my fingers beside my sock-clad toes.

Nothing.

The space around me wasn't warm, wasn't cold. It wasn't hard, wasn't soft. It wasn't dark, wasn't light. It was like a memory of something from before I'd ever lived, like my personal recollection of what my life had been like a year before I was born.

"Hello?" I said, half expecting the sound to disappear as it left my lips. I surprised myself, though. My questioning greeting was audible—flat, tentative, but clearly heard.

"Hello" came a reply out of the absence. I whirled around, catching a little scream against the back of my teeth.

A woman stood in front of me. She was tall, her looming height made even greater by the four-inch stiletto heels on her leather boots. She stared at me like she had every right to be there, like she *belonged* in this bizarre world of nothingness. She looked me up and down with an amused glance, her gaze lingering on the roll of fat that hung over the band of my sweatpants. I flushed with embarrassment. The exposure of those so-called love handles was momentarily worse than the surprise of believing myself stark raving mad, of finding a perfect stranger in my nightmare.

Even as my brain chittered inside my skull—*there was a stranger, here, in the literal middle of nowhere!*—I realized that the other woman had never known the embarrassment of an extra roll of flesh. She was bone thin, heroin-chic thin, cover-model thin. Her hair was dyed jet black, and it was piled on top of her head in a complicated swirl that reminded me of Amy Wine-house. She wore a laced-up bustier that revealed far more than it covered, and black low-rider leather pants that were tucked into those unbelievable boots. Her face was a palette for more makeup than I wore in a year—her eyes were outlined in heavy kohl, and her lips were painted a heavy burgundy. She'd added a beauty mark just to the right of her natural lip line.

She reached one ornately tattooed arm behind her and tugged a sweatshirt out of the nothingness. When she handed it to me, I saw the flames tattooed around her wrist.

"Are you a genie?" I asked before I could stop myself. I was embarrassed as soon as the question left my lips, but I was also strangely relieved. I could ask the question. I could say the word *genie,* the word that I'd been unable to get out back at the table, back in the real world.

"Teel," the woman said, in a deep, throaty voice. "I do believe we've met." She smirked and extended her hand to shake mine.

I backed away.

"Don't be like that," she said. "I should have said something before, when we were in the theater, but I forgot, with the time change and all."

Back at the theater. This woman knew I'd been at the theater. My fingers tingled, as if they were responding to the tattoo on her wrist, as if they were electrically charged by their proximity to that ink. I tugged the new sweatshirt over my head, moving as quickly as possible so that the apparition in front of me couldn't disappear.

"F-forgot?" I finally stammered, when I realized that I had to say something. What else had Teel *forgotten?* I'd think a little thing like the ability to change gender would be at the top of her—his—her list.

Teel shrugged. "What do you think of my new outfit? Things are a lot more…diverse out there these days. It's a lot more interesting than when I went into the lamp."

I nodded weakly, wondering where she'd spent the past twenty-four hours. It sure seemed like she'd given up on tracking down the mysterious Susan. Probably just as well, with all the time that had passed. "So," I said, still trying to make sense out of things. "A couple of tugs, and you just become whatever you want? Gender doesn't matter?"

"Gender, race, nationality…" Teel yawned, spreading crimson-painted talons in front of her mouth. "If I can work wishes like yours, it's easy enough to change my appearance, don't you think? Speaking of which, have you decided on your second wish?"

"Have I…? No!"

She puffed out her cheeks and sighed. The action was strangely comforting—perfectly *human* disappointment in the midst of so much strangeness that my head was buzzing. "Not even an idea of what you're thinking about?" I shook my head, and she gestured at the space around us before she wheedled, "I just thought that if you could see this, if I could show you the Garden, then you'd understand why it's so important to me."

"Th-the Garden?" I couldn't see anything at all.

Teel took a deep breath, as if she were savoring the most delicate fragrance imaginable. "Well, the front gate, at least."

I peered into the absence of space. "Um, I don't see any gate."

"Right there?" She frowned at me. "Wrought iron. Covered by morning glories?"

I stared where she was gesturing, but I couldn't make out anything at all. "I'm sorry," I said. "I really don't see it."

"Next thing, you'll tell me you can't smell the lilacs."

I shook my head, feeling strangely like a failure. "I'm sorry," I said again.

"Then I shouldn't have bothered," she said, sulking. "I thought you might have been different. You might have been one of the ones who can see." She sighed. "I could have come to your bedroom, just as easily as bringing you here. We could have talked there."

"Um, what did you want to talk about?"

Teel frowned at me, taking a minute to adjust the cascade of her black bouffant and to tuck herself into her bustier a little more securely. "There's something else I should have mentioned when you summoned me." She caught my gaze. "I'm a secret. No one can know about me. About genies. About the wishes."

"Why not? I mean, I've got to explain the changes in my life somehow!"

"That's part of the magic. No one will ask. No one will care."

"But Maddy and Jules will! They just watched me try to talk about you, about what happened! They just saw me make a complete idiot out of myself because of you!"

"They won't remember it when I send you back. I've taken care of that. Just don't mention me to anyone else in the future, and we won't have to go through these diversions."

"But you don't have to be afraid of Maddy and Jules! They're not going to hurt you."

Teel gave me a dark look. "When wishes are on the line, people do crazy things." I started to protest, but she shook her head and held up a hand in the universal sign for "stop." "It's the one rule. You can't negotiate it. You can't tell anyone about me. Promise."

"But—"

"If you want your other wishes, promise."

Well, when she put it that way… "I promise," I said, sounding as reluctant as a kid agreeing to clean her room on a gorgeous weekend day.

"Fine." Teel nodded, as if we'd just signed some formal written contract. She looked to her left, toward the supposed Garden gate. "You really can't see it? Or smell it?" She sounded wistful. I shook my head. "Then I'm guessing that you can't hear the brook, either, or the birds?"

She sounded so sad that I wanted to lie. I wanted to tell her that I could sense her entire Garden, that I could understand how wonderful the place was, why she wanted to get inside so desperately.

I thought about making two quick wishes, just so I could help her.

But then I thought about how wonderfully my first wish had turned out. Sure, I wanted to help Teel. I owed her. But I couldn't just throw away the possibility promised by those two remaining chances. I hardened my heart, even as she said, "No wonder the other genies said not to bother."

"The other genies?"

"We were talking yesterday, after our weekly productivity meeting."

"Productivity meeting?" Somehow, my genie had absorbed the worst of twenty-first century business-speak. I almost preferred Teel's outdated disco slang.

She rolled her eyes. "All the genies who are out of their lamps get together to discuss marketplace trends in wishing. We update our statistical databases and talk about ways to increase wish-flow." She made it sound so bureaucratic and boring, I half expected her to yawn. "I told them I was going to try bringing you to the Garden, to see if that changed your wish-making process."

"I see," I said, even though I couldn't see anything at all. My mind boggled at the idea of a bunch of genies sitting around a table in a conference room. The corporate image actually made it easier for me to hold on to my decision to wait on my other wishes. It was one thing to help *Teel,* the genie who had already made my life so much better. It was another to be a pawn in some sort of bizarre corporate genie game that I didn't begin to understand.

Teel sighed, glancing wistfully at the invisible gate. "I might as well take you back. But you'll think about your other wishes? Make them soon?"

"As soon as possible," I said.

Teel raised her crimson talons to her earlobe and tugged twice. Electricity jangled through me, head to foot, and then I was standing, alone, in my bedroom. As if on cue, there was a knock on my door. Jules's voice was carefree as she called out, "Kira, are you ready? We've got the food dished up, and we're ready for you to make the first move on the board."

She didn't sound like a woman who had been cheated out of half her asparagus soup. She didn't sound like someone who had just scrambled after game pieces scattered across the dining room floor. Teel had been as good as her word. My housemate recalled nothing of the scene I had made. "Yeah," I called. "I'll be there in just a sec."

When I got back to the living room, Maddy looked up from the table. A bowl sat in front of her, filled with rice, chicken, and eight delectable vegetables in a brown sauce. By her right hand, there were several cellophane wrappers, and the golden shards of fortune cookies. She was smoothing three slips of paper beneath her blunt fingers.

"Maddy!" I exclaimed.

"I couldn't wait," she said. "You know I like to eat my fortune cookie first."

"Great," Jules grumbled, manipulating her chopsticks

expertly to raise a huge bite of cellophane noodles to her lips. "You could have let us open our own."

"Yeah," I said, grateful for the distraction, for any conversation that led away from why I'd been hanging out in my bedroom while our Chinese food grew cold.

Maddy shrugged. "The Buddha helps those who help themselves."

I rolled my eyes and asked, "Which one was mine? What does it say?"

Maddy shoved a curling slip of paper across the table. "Romance enters through a hidden door."

They both laughed, a little too forcefully. I knew that they were thinking about TEWSBU, about the disaster at the Hyatt Regency. I forced myself to smile with them, and we were soon eating copious amounts of the best Chinese food in the Twin Cities. But every time I looked at that curling slip of paper, the barely visible flames on my fingertips tingled, reminding me of my remaining wishes.

CHAPTER 6

THE NEXT MORNING, I WOKE UP RAVENOUS, DESPITE having polished off all of my crispy sesame chicken the night before (*and* having enjoyed a celebratory handful of Oreos after winning our Scrabble game, due to placing "quiz" on a triple-word score with double points for the Q). I mowed my way through the kitchen, supplementing a bowl of Cap'n Crunch with a couple of Little Debbie Nutty Bars that were sitting, abandoned, in the back of the pantry. My housemates had cleared the premises well before I awakened; I was usually the last one up.

I didn't bother making coffee; I'd have time to grab a caffeine-fortified cup at Club Joe before the *Romeo and Juliet* read-through. Before stepping out the front door, I dragged my knit muffler across the lower half of my face. The temperature had settled into its heart-of-winter basement; I doubted that the thermometer would climb to zero during the day. I felt all the more cheated because the sky was a shocking blue, not a cloud in sight. A true Minneapolis winter—when it got too cold to snow.

I couldn't continue complaining, though. The barista at Club Joe added my four shots of espresso without treating me like a crazy woman, sending me on my way so efficiently that I got to the theater with a full half hour before the cast was supposed to arrive.

Someone had already opened the front door, though. Lights were on in the rehearsal room, and chairs were distributed in a neat circle. I called out a tentative hello, but no one answered.

Slinging my backpack onto the floor, I dug out my notebook and a handful of pens. (I always kept extras ready; cast members inevitably forgot their own, and I wasn't about to stop a perfect scene to rummage around if mine ran out of ink.)

As ready for rehearsal as I could be, I closed my hand around my coffee cup, gripping the paper sleeve as I administered a healthy dose of caffeine. When I lowered the cup, the eerie tattoos on my fingertips caught the light. I shifted the coffee to my left hand and gazed at my marked hand as if it were some fascinating museum display.

I wondered if anyone else could see the mark of the flames. I mean, Teel had kept me from telling Maddy and Jules about my wishes the night before, about the impact the genie was making on my life. It wouldn't make a lot of sense to offer that sort of protection and then let anyone who cared see the magic writ large, literally, on my hands.

"Morning, Franklin" came a deep voice from behind me, and I started as if I'd been doing something dishonest.

I curled my fingers into a fist and turned around, fighting to quell a guilty crouch. John McRae stood in the doorway. His nose was red from the cold, and he stamped his feet as if he despaired of ever restoring circulation to his toes.

"Good morning," I said. Meeting his easy grin, I felt guilty about ducking out of the cast get-together the night before. "I—I'm sorry that I didn't get over to Mephisto's last night. My housemates and I ended up having dinner at home—one of them is about to start tech rehearsals and the other is going on a cross-country trip. I won't be seeing them for weeks."

Stop, I told myself. This guy doesn't need your entire life story. Just. Stop.

"No problem," he said, shrugging. "Most of us left around eight, anyway. Had to be ready for today's rehearsal."

And that was that. No federal case. No need for endless apologies. No need for further, contorted explanations, about TEWSBU or Teel or anything else.

"Did you set things up?" I nodded toward the circle of chairs.

"Yeah," he drawled. "I got here early and figured I might as well be useful. Mandatory morning calisthenics."

I grinned, more at the image of this laid-back cowboy doing some official military workout, than out of any actual amusement about the rehearsal room. "Thanks. I feel like I'm not carrying my weight around here." I almost winced at my own words. Leave it to me, to call attention to my weight. Desperate to change the topic of conversation quickly, I nodded toward a heavy cardboard tube in his hands. "What's that?"

"Drawings for the set. Left 'em in the truck by mistake and had to go back out there." He peeled off his coat and shook his head ruefully. Even though I was a big fan of Minnesota, I understood his reaction to the bitter winter cold. It must be particularly difficult for him, Texas transplant that he was. He brandished the tube. "They're sketches, really. Bill wanted to photograph them this morning, to use as a background for some pages in the program."

I tried to hide my surprise. At Fox Hill, the program was always a last-minute scramble, proofread by me—or anyone else awake enough to see straight—a week before the show opened, then sent off to Kinko's for quick printing, folding, and stapling.

I tried to sound a little bored, like I was used to the Landmark's professional way of producing programs. "May I see?"

He smiled self-deprecatingly. "I thought you'd never ask."

We crossed to the worktable against the wall. I was impressed by the way his strong fingers pried the cap from the end of the sturdy tube—I always needed to resort to screwdrivers to lever those stupid things out. John's hands were large, tanned, even in the middle of winter.

I remembered my own tattooed fingers. Suddenly, I was overcome with the urge to test him, to test the visibility of Teel's magic. As John unrolled the sheaf of papers, I made a point of anchoring two corners, spreading my right hand across the white surface of the paper. I tilted my wrist to make the iridescent fire shimmer as much as possible.

From my perspective, the flames glowed; I could make out specific licks of crimson and vermilion and topaz, as if the design was stamped there in Technicolor. I waited for John to leap back in astonishment, to swear in surprise, to stare at my hands in slack-jawed amazement. Or, at the very least, to dip his head and say, "Cool tats."

Instead, he tugged at his belt, deftly detaching a tape measure to weigh down my side of the drawing. "Thanks," he said, anchoring the curling far side himself. He gestured at the top drawing. "For the opening scene, I picture the guys on this platform, looking down on the rest of the town square. Bill and I talked about moving each scene lower, deeper into the streets, into the sewers." John's twang softened his words, made them less of a lecture and more of a conversation.

I wasn't ready to give up on the tattoo thing quite yet, though. I pointed vigorously toward another area of the drawing, as if I were showing off the world's most expensive manicure. "What's that?"

"A trapdoor," he said, oblivious to the magic sparking before his very eyes. "We'll use it to take out Friar Laurence, at the end of his first scene."

Nothing. He obviously couldn't see the marks on my fingertips. Teel would remain a secret, even if *I* saw evidence of magic every time I waved my hand.

I blinked and actually paid attention to the drawing for the first time. Now that I was no longer trying to measure my Visible Genie Quotient, I could see that John had done a great job of capturing his design ideas. His drawings were obviously only sketches, ideas that would be modified as they were turned into models, then actually constructed by the Landmark's renowned carpentry shop. But the lines were firm, the overall design confident, quietly competent in a straightforward way that many theater designers lacked.

"How will you handle the balcony scene?" I asked. Even as I voiced the question, I remembered Jennifer and Drew reading the day before. I resisted the urge to wrinkle my nose—as much as I respected Bill Pomeroy's daring ideas, I didn't like the notion that the gimmick of reverse-gender casting might ruin the audience's appreciation for the stagecraft evident in John's drawings.

"We'll use this platform here." He gestured toward stage right. "Juliet's bed will fold down from the back wall. I want it out there, really obvious, so that her—his—whatever…" he said, stumbling over his pronouns, and I wanted to tell him that I sympathized. Teel had made me question my own use of the English language, just the evening before. I could only imagine how confusing the next few months would be here in the theater, with genders switching minute by minute. "Her sexuality," he finally continued, with enough irritated emphasis that the second word unexpectedly made me blush, "is clear from the start, but I also have to get it out of the way for the entire ballroom scene. That's when this level doubles as the entrance hall." He shrugged. "I might go down in history as the first set designer to give Juliet a Murphy bed."

I laughed—it just struck me as funny. There we were, talking about one of the greatest lovers in all literature, and the only thing I could picture was every bad slapstick routine I'd ever seen, with mattresses slamming into walls at the most inopportune times. "That Juliet—she's quite a decorator."

John still seemed annoyed by the pronoun confusion. A quick frown creased his forehead, and he rubbed a hand down his mustache. "Damn fool casting," he muttered.

"Don't let Bill hear you say that," I warned teasingly, glad that I wasn't the only person who found our courageous production a little…silly. At least at this stage. Maybe rehearsals would change my mind.

"Don't let Bill hear you say what?" The question, predictably, came from Bill himself. "Ah!" our director exclaimed, coming to look at the drawings. "Wonderful! I want the entire cast to see these, so that they can start to live the physical realization of this show."

Live the physical realization. (Read: "Get familiar with the set." But "living the realization" sounded so much more grand.) John rolled his eyes just the tiniest bit, and I bit my lower lip to keep from smiling with him.

Most of the actors had drifted into the room while we'd been talking, and Bill quickly called everyone to order. "All right, everybody! Take your seats! We've got a lot to do today!"

The group settled down immediately, with a tangible air of expectation. This was a company of professional actors, intent on making theatrical magic come alive for themselves, for their director, for the audiences that would be stunned by our creation, come April.

Surreptitiously, I dug out a listing of the cast that Bill had given me the day before. Working my way around the circle, I made sure that everyone was present, on time for this important first read-through. I was pleased to see that I could match every name on my printout to a face.

Bill called on John to explain his basic design, to annotate verbally the perfectly clear sketches, for everyone's benefit. I used the time to go back around the circle, to test my ability to name every cast member without the aid of my written list.

Just as I got to Drew Myers, he looked up. It was almost like he'd heard me call his name. His dark brown eyes met mine, hints of green sparkling as if we were in the middle of an animated conversation. His smile was immediate, dazzling. Surprised by the unexpected attention, I looked away, pretending that I'd been distracted by something in the general area of the rehearsal room door. When I gathered my courage to glance back, Drew was leaning over to whisper something to the actress sitting next to him.

I fought off a scowl. Why hadn't I just smiled back at Drew like a normal person? Why hadn't I accepted his silent offer of friendship? What the hell was wrong with me?

I knew what was wrong with me.

Drew Myers was the most gorgeous guy I'd seen in ages. He was the first man to make me catch my breath in…I couldn't even say how long.

I was afraid of my reaction to him. The last time I'd felt like that, I'd ended up engaged to the guy. Engaged to TEWSBU. I wasn't going to make that kind of mistake ever again—not if I needed to avoid every smile from every actor in every play I ever worked on, for the rest of my life.

I folded my flame-tattooed fingers into a fist and bent over my notebook, forcing myself to take meticulous notes as Bill instructed everyone to turn to the first page of their scripts so that we could begin our read-through.

At the end of the read-through, a group decided to go to Mephisto's. It was two o'clock when we finished the rehearsal; enthusiasm was wearing thin as everyone grumbled about being hungry. The cast filed out quickly, but John stayed behind to help me with the chairs. Again. After accepting his assistance, I could hardly refuse his invitation to grab a burger with everyone else.

Even if I was leery of Mephisto's. Even if my pulse started to quicken as we hurried through the bitter cold to the nearby block of low-rise, family-owned businesses.

The storefront wasn't anything to look at from the street. Careful lettering on the plate glass window announced Mike's Bar and Grill. That same window was half covered with theater posters from productions dating back to the 1970s.

Hmm… Teel would have been perfectly at home there, if he'd first manifested in the back room of the dive. At least his disco suit would have been deemed "retro" instead of simply weird.

Inside, the lighting was dim, the tables were close together, and the bar took up the better part of the left-hand wall. There were private rooms in the back, each large enough to host the cast and crew from a medium-size show on opening night. The food at Mike's was simple and good—burgers, fries, and onion rings, with a killer green salad for leading ladies constantly on diets. Not that I'd ever actually ever tasted the salad in all my years of coming to the place, but I'd been told that it was good. At least, the blue cheese dressing was to die for. (Read: Leading ladies lie to themselves about what they eat just as much as everyone else does.)

Mike Reilly, our very own Mephisto, was the father of four daughters, each of whom had struggled to make her way in the local theater scene. Kelly, the oldest, had actually succeeded enough that she'd left us all behind, for Broadway (or off-Broadway, or off-off-Broadway, or for a few bit parts in a community theater in Queens—we never asked for too many details).

Two-thirty in the afternoon was an odd time for anyone to arrive at Mephisto's; Mike was more likely to see customers stroll in at two-thirty in the morning, after a particularly grueling rehearsal. In fact, when John and I ducked through the door, Mike was behind the long zinc bar himself, a clear sign that his evening staff had not yet arrived.

"Kira Franklin!" he exclaimed as I stepped into the dark restaurant. I blinked to hasten my vision's adjustment. He set down the rag that he was using to wipe clean the spotless bar and settled his hammy fists on his hips. "How long has it been, stranger?"

"Just about a year," I said, surprised to find myself grinning, despite the reason that I'd kept my distance. Mike had been one of the invited guests that night at the Hyatt. I was certain that TEWSBU still ate here on a regular basis; he'd always claimed that Mike spiked the French fries with crack.

Well, it was funnier when he said it. Back when I'd thought everything he said was funny.

I wiped my suddenly slick palms on my shapeless sweatpants, trying to cover my awkwardness with an attempt at being polite. "Have you met John McRae?"

"Met him?" Mike boomed. "I've fed him half his meals since he came to town. How you doing, John?"

"Just fine." My set designer (*my* set designer! I was still incredibly thrilled to think of the Landmark's staff as my own) smiled easily and crossed the room to the bar. Mike had already pulled a dark and foamy mug for him—it looked like John had an unfathomable appreciation for Guinness. Smiling laconically, John looked over his shoulder and said, "What'll you have, Franklin?"

But Mike was a better bartender than that. He'd already scooped up the largest of his glasses, filled it with ice and shoved three limes onto the rim. As he shot the glass full of tonic water from his six-button dispenser, I tried to calculate how many times I'd bellied up to his bar.

I retrieved the glass from Mike with a grateful smile, sneaking the quickest of glances at John to see how he registered the non-alcoholic beverage. About half the guys I met thought I was the strangest specimen of humanity they'd ever met outside a zoo. The other half gave me a sad little smile and a half shake of the head; most of those immediately launched into a conversation about loved ones who were twelve-stepping through some program.

John didn't seem to notice what I was drinking. Instead, he said to Mike, "You taking orders out here? I'll have a black-and-blue burger, with fries."

I thought I saw Mike's smile tighten as he turned to me. We both remembered that TEWSBU loved Mike's Cajun-spiced hamburgers, built around a pocket of blue cheese that melted into a redolent sauce more compelling than any gourmet kitchen's snooty offering. "Cheddar and bacon," I said, determined not to let John's unfortunate order get me down. And then I decided to toss all care to the wind. What the hell, twelve months was too long to stay away from Mephisto's. "And grilled onions and—"

"Mushrooms," Mike finished. "Welcome back, Kira. It's been a long time."

I tried to think of something to say, but all of my responses sounded awkward. It occurred to me that I owed John some sort of explanation; the guy had no idea of my sordid past. But

I wasn't quite sure what to tell him, how much anyone would want to know about the greatest embarrassment of my life.

Typically, Mike saved the day. "I half expected to see you in here asking for an apron, Kira." As I'd alluded to my father, Mike was famous in the theater community for handing out jobs to those in need. When roles were really scarce, Mike had one waiter per table. When shows were doing well, though, you could wait half an hour for the place's one harried server to take your order. We theater folks were always grateful when it took a long time to get refills on drinks.

"The rumors of my demise were greatly exaggerated," I said with a grin that was only slightly forced. I had Teel to thank for that, of course. I rubbed my tattooed fingers together, shivering a little at the electric tingle that hummed down my spine.

"Glad to hear it," Mike said. "Go ahead, you two. Everyone's in the Mamet Room. I'll bring your food when it's ready."

The Mamet Room. Every time I ducked through the velvet curtain of the private space, I felt like I should swear like a sailor. Swear, and talk as fast as possible and tell everyone about my sex life, in the raunchiest terms imaginable. Yeah. As if I had a sex life at all. Mamet just brought that out in a girl. Or at least his plays did. I'd cut my teeth on his early piece, *Sexual Perversity in Chicago*. It wasn't as bad as it sounded. Really.

Still, I was more comfortable in the neighboring Shakespeare Room, all things being equal.

John held the curtain for me as I ducked into the Mamet, careful to keep from spilling my tonic water. I pasted a smile onto my face, the better to greet my new acting family. Mechanically, my eyes swept over the bevy of actors, the women who were going to play Mercutio and Benvolio and Paris. And Friar Laurence. After our morning read-through, I was more convinced than ever that the show was going to be strange. Wonderful, groundbreaking, breathtaking. But strange.

I shrugged mentally. "Strange" was how a theater made its reputation. "Strange" was how a company made its mark. Besides, who was I to talk about strange? Me, the woman with a genie at her beck and call?

I tried to brace myself against the silly swoop I knew my belly would make when I caught sight of Drew Myers. Sure enough, he was sitting with his back to John and me, right by the entrance. There were a couple of chairs open beside him, and I knew that it would be the most natural thing in the world to take a few steps forward, to put my glass on the table, to sit beside him.

I ordered my feet to move, but they refused to listen. I told my smile to stretch a little more widely, but my teeth seemed to get in the way. I instructed my voice to form a greeting, but I had apparently forgotten every word I knew in the English language.

It had been a long time since I'd tried to socialize with anyone, much less with a drop-dead gorgeous guy like Drew. I'd grown accustomed to living in the convent of my apartment. It was harder than I'd expected to make the transition back into the real world.

In fact, I felt as stifled as I'd been when Teel kept me from mentioning the genie stuff to my housemates. Worse, even, because I knew there wasn't anything magic about this. Nothing more magic, that was, than the fact that Drew was unbelievably, unfairly handsome.

But he was an actor, I remonstrated with myself. The type of guy who had a dozen women hanging on him, even on a slow day.

"Hey, y'all," John said, putting an end to my internal debate by pulling out a chair for me—the chair closest to Drew!—and taking another for himself.

There was a chorus of greeting, and I was freed to sit down, my momentary awkwardness released. I took a sip of tonic water, hoping that the bitter tang would cool the furious blush that I could tell was painting my cheeks.

Drew spared me a small smile as I put my glass back on the table, but even that blast of casual half-normal wattage sent my stomach tumbling over itself. "Hi, Kira," he said. I could not think of a reply; I was unable to muster a single complete sentence in English.

I glanced at John, hoping to find that he was miraculously prepared with some topic of conversation. Instead, he was already talking to a woman across the table, a pretty brunette whose name I suddenly couldn't remember, despite the fact that I'd seen her here, in Mephisto's, for years, before TEWSBU led to my self-banishment. The woman was playing Tybalt, Juliet's cousin, the brute who thinks with his sword instead of his brain. John was nodding at something she was saying, something about how a winter storm was expected to blow through by Monday.

I gulped my drink and turned back to Drew, simultaneously pleased and chagrined to be on my own. I forced myself to say, "So, this production is going to be like nothing I've ever seen before. Did you know about the reverse casting when you auditioned?"

Drew smiled again and shrugged with the sort of frat-boy abandon that made me want to run my fingers through his already-tousled hair. (Read: I was ready to invite him home then and there, regardless of what Maddy and Jules might think when they saw a guy—a guy I'd only mentioned once before— swaggering through our front door.)

I'd forgotten what it was like to be this interested in someone. I'd forgotten what it was like to plot out conversations three ex- changes down the line, to have a constant monitor running in my head, reminding me that if I asked about *this*, I was likely to open up a line of discussion good for another five minutes; if I asked about *that*, I could glean a minimum of seven minutes....

I used to be really good at this game.

But that was before TEWSBU. Before the past year of self-enforced celibacy, and the year before that of engagement, and the year before that of exclusive dating with the guy I'd believed was the man of my dreams.

Wow. I'd been out of circulation for a long time. Could it really have been three years since I'd experienced this breathless, pounding, flushing feeling? (Yeah, there was that time I had the flu, last January. But that didn't count.)

In fact, I was so far out of the swing of things, I'd forgotten to listen to Drew's answer to my question. He'd said something about the auditions, about Bill's plans for *Romeo and Juliet*, something that would have given me some idea—any idea— what to say next. And I'd missed it, because I was anxious, feeling sorry for myself, sorry for the me whose life had been ruined by an insensitive, cold-blooded, bastard ex-fiancé. I drained my glass, searching for my next line.

Luckily, John had overheard whatever Drew had said, and he dropped easily back into our conversation. "I wish I'd been there for those callbacks," he drawled. "Just to see the expression on y'all's faces, when Bill told you to switch roles."

Again, Drew dazzled us with that smile. Dazzled me, anyway. I was pretty sure that John wasn't affected. "I thought it was an acting exercise, you know? 'Think about what Romeo's sword feels, as it plunges into Juliet's breast. Feel that emotion. Act out the role of the sword.'"

I laughed, and John joined in. We'd all worked with our share of touchy-feely directors. Method acting in its simplest form—it was a technique where actors tried to re-create the emotions of their characters by drawing on their past experiences. It was one thing, though, for someone to build Ophelia's insane love of Hamlet by thinking about an actual failed high school romance. It was another when directors pushed Ophelia-actresses to build their madness on the loss of some other relationship, say a childhood friend who'd moved away. Or, in one disastrous production I had stage managed in college, on the loss of a favorite angora scarf.

That production gave all new meaning to Hamlet's line, "There's the rub."

Yeah, we theater people were strange.

Drew's good-natured mocking of the audition process was what I needed to finally put me at ease. At last, I could remember how to breathe, how to act like a calm, cool, and collected stage manager, instead of like a seventh-grader at my first school dance. Thinking of another method-acting disaster, already famous in Twin Cities theater lore, I asked, "Did you see the *Richard III* they did last year at Epiphany?"

Drew smirked. "Dude! It's one thing to make Shakespeare come alive, but it was totally broken to give Richard a sword fetish. Especially with those leather costumes."

John said dubiously, "I wish I'd seen that."

"No you don't!" Drew and I both said at the same time.

As we laughed together, Mike pushed his way through the velvet curtain. He swooped my plate down in front of me, bowing from the waist as if he were a courtier and I was some type of queen. John didn't get quite the same level of attention, although Mike made sure that a bottle of ketchup rested evenly between us. Like a mind reader, he replaced my empty glass with a full one, saying, "And another tonic water, extra lime. Anything else I can get for you guys right now?"

I shook my head, breathing deeply of the magical smell of

fresh-from-the-fry-basket potatoes. Why had I stayed away from Mephisto's for so long?

As if he'd read my mind, Mike favored me with a broad smile. "Enjoy. Kira, it's great to have you back."

"It's great to *be* back, Mike," I said as he returned to the bar. Before I could devote an appropriate level of attention to adding salt and pepper to my fries, Drew leaned close, settling one hand on my sleeve. He nodded toward my fresh beverage and said, "I went to Alateen for years. That really helped me learn how to deal with my father."

"Yeah," I said, slipping into my well-rehearsed explanation, even as my adrenaline glands pumped into overtime at the thought of his hand touching me. *Down, girl,* I thought. "Actually, I'm allergic to alcohol. I'm not an alcoholic. Um, not that there's anything wrong with that. I mean, not that it's different from any other illness. Like tuberculosis."

Damn. I was usually a bit more smooth than *that*. I fought the sudden, ridiculous compulsion to tell him about my allergy symptoms, to explain that my cheeks would turn bright red (as if he could tell the difference, given how furiously I was blushing), or that my palms would start to itch, or that my mouth would begin to tingle.

Yeah, that would make me really popular.

Before I could commit any more social crimes, I took the time to cut my burger in half, grateful that my black sweatshirt would camouflage the worst of my gustatory sins.

My first bite of burger was even better than I remembered. Swallowing hard, I sat back in my chair with a sigh. Drew laughed, which made me sit up a bit straighter. "Dude, I don't think I've ever seen anyone enjoy one of Mike's burgers that much, even when I was on the late shift."

"You used to work here?"

He ducked his head, as if admitting to a secret past. When he smiled up at me through his eyelashes, my heart did another round on the flying trapeze. "Guilty as charged. I've had my share of auditions that didn't go as planned. Mike's a totally great guy."

"He is," I agreed.

"So how long have *you* been coming here?"

I laughed. "Is that like, 'What's your sign?'"

Drew aped the worst sort of pickup artist, smoothing a non-existent mustache and leering as he said, "What's a nice girl like you doing in a place like this?"

I giggled. *I. Giggled.* Me, the girl who hadn't talked to a new guy in a year. The girl who had sworn off men for the rest of my life.

I couldn't help it. He was funny. He was knockdown gorgeous, breezily friendly, and he was funny.

I played along, remembering the almost-forgotten steps in the dance of flirtation. Barely wasting a moment to wipe my hands on my napkin, I settled my fingers on his forearm, daring to measure the taut muscle beneath his soft cotton shirt. My belly—or something lower—dove when I let myself imagine the dusting of dark blond hair that was sprinkled across that forearm. I immediately forbade myself from even looking at his hands, because I knew that I would completely throw myself off track if I even *thought* about what those fingers could do.

Instead, I answered in my best mock-little-girl voice, a parody that would have put Jennifer Galland's rehearsal voice to shame. "Me? A nice girl like me?"

I summoned my finest smile to let him know that I was totally joking, that I was completely aware that we were playing, acting out stereotypes more absurd than the worst plays either of us had ever worked on. He grinned back, and I realized for the first time that one of his front teeth was just slightly out of alignment. For some reason, that tiny flaw, in the midst of his otherwise unblemished Leading Man perfection, made me swoon.

Almost literally. I was back to the silly, heart-pounding, throat-closing, belly-tightening impossibility of talking to him.

Apparently unaware of the crisis building in my traitorous body, Drew nodded toward my plate. "Are you going to eat all of those fries?"

"Please!" I said, and I hoped he wouldn't realize how abnormally high-pitched my voice had become. I was so excited that he'd continued our silly conversation that I barely heard what he'd said.

"Kira Franklin deigns to share her French fries! Will wonders never cease?"

For one insane moment, I couldn't place the voice. I'd heard it so many times in my dreams—in my nightmares. I must be imagining it here, in Mephisto's, surrounded by my new cast, sitting next to my new crush.

I'd had endless discussions with that voice. I'd ranted to it. Raved. Told it exactly what I thought.

But now, hearing it for real, I was struck utterly dumb. Knocked as silent as some poor heroine in a Jane Austen novel. Thrown absolutely and completely for a loop.

TEWSBU. The Ex Who Shall Be Unnamed. Here, and in the flesh, in the middle of the Mamet Room.

How had I not noticed that he was sitting here with my cast? *My* cast. From *my* show. From *my* new life.

I thought a long string of expletives, but I managed to reduce them all to a choked, "Wh-what are you doing here?" as I spotted him halfway down the table.

A strange silence fell over the room. In one breath, all of the chatter drained away, all of the mindless discussion about the morning's rehearsal, about Bill Pomeroy, about the production that we were devoting the next three months of our lives to create.

Gone.

After all, we were all experienced in the theater. We all knew good drama when it came and slapped us in the face. We all recognized an exciting little play being performed in our very midst.

I forced myself to meet the eyes of the man I'd pledged to marry. They were as blue as I remembered, an amazing blue, a blue that he always—always!—emphasized with an offhand touch of color, a perfect broadcloth shirt, a subtle silk tie. Today, he wore a casual tee; I'd give my next wish from Teel if it wasn't Hollister's newest color.

His smile was the one I remembered as well—his perfect white teeth, never capped, in a world where half our acquaintances had their paychecks deposited directly into their dentists' accounts. His white smile was all the more striking because of the strong lines of his cheekbones, the worn hollows of his cheeks that always made him look like a tortured artist.

He sounded totally normal and utterly untortured when he answered my stammered question. "I'd never pass up one of Mike's burgers, you know that, Kira. Besides," he said with an indulgent shrug, "I wanted to meet the people that Steph is going to spend the next three months with."

Steph. Stephanie Michaelson.

As if a cameraman were laying out my heartbreak on film, my focus changed from the face of the man I once had loved to the puzzled pout on the lips of the woman sitting next to him. As we'd gone around the circle yesterday, she'd introduced herself without a hint of who she truly was, what she truly meant to me. She was playing Mercutio, Romeo's best friend. A reckless free spirit who managed to make a pun, even as he died at the end of Tybalt's sword.

I wished I had a sword, right then.

I glanced at Drew, who had frozen with my French fries halfway to his lips. I could see that he was confused, embarrassed, wondering why it was such a big deal that I'd agreed to let him take some of my food. After all, I had a generous plateful. I felt obligated to say something, to smooth over the situation, to make everything better.

"Please!" I said, and my voice was twice as loud as it should have been. "Have my fries! Eat them all!"

I pushed the plate toward him and looked down, suddenly all too aware of my shapeless sweatshirt, covering up my shapeless body, hiding the shapeless blob that I'd become in the past year. Tears burned behind my eyes, and I blinked furiously to keep from shedding them. I tried to swallow away the searing mixture of embarrassment and shame, of outright rage that coated the back of my throat.

I was furious. Mike should have told me that it wasn't just us cast members here. It wasn't just the *Romeo and Juliet* crowd hanging out in the back room. He knew me. He knew what this encounter would mean to me.

I stared at my burger and tried to remember how I had ever enjoyed fried onions and mushrooms—right now, they looked like noxious slime, oozing from beneath the bun. Somehow, I pasted a smile on my lips and said to Drew, "Really! I mean it! Have all the fries you'd like! I couldn't eat another one! Please!" I shoved the plate in front of him, eager to get as far from it as possible.

I wasn't lying. The plate of food was ruined. I wasn't going to touch them. I might never eat at Mike's again.

And TEWSBU laughed. He laughed in that easy, confident way that I had admired so many times. He laughed like a carefully calculated director, like a master craftsman who was used to having the attention of everyone in the room. He laughed like a man who pitied the less fortunate. "I didn't *think* you'd actually share your food. Give it away, maybe, but never share. It's nice to know that some things never change."

I pushed back from the table and scrambled to my feet, suddenly wondering if I could keep down the few bites of late lunch that I'd managed to swallow before everything had collapsed around me. Out of the corner of my eye, I saw John jump up, as well. Smart man. He recognized a madwoman when she was flailing next to him. Like the laid-back cowboy he resembled, John was clearly ready to protect his herd, to keep the cast safe from my insanity.

Now that everyone was staring at me, I became completely self-conscious. These people—the cast that I was going to live with, eat with, drink with for the next three months—they were staring at me like I was some kind of selfish, hoarding freak.

They'd all made the connection now, even the ones who hadn't realized exactly who I was, who hadn't remembered year-old gossip when we went around the circle the day before, reciting our names. But now they all knew. Now they could all phone up their friends, text messages to actors they'd met three, four, five shows back. They had a story to tell. I could *see* them storing away this little circus scene for the next time they needed to pity a fellow actor—a character—on stage.

And beneath that pity, on a few of the faces, the final emotion on the hit parade—a tiny curl of disgust. Disgust at a person who didn't fit into their mold of Body Beautiful, into the self-conscious, size-zero vision of perfection that so many cast members strived for.

I couldn't look at Drew, couldn't force myself to see how his face had changed. I couldn't make myself recognize the jagged shards of the flirtation that had seemed so natural only a few moments before, the easy, silly chatter that had just seemed *right*.

I had to get out of there. I had to get away from Drew, away from the cast, away from TEWSBU, away from my past.

I jumped back from the table so fast that I knocked over my chair. I fumbled for it at the same time that John did. We nearly bumped heads, and he reached out a hand to steady me, saying, "Easy, Franklin."

I leaped away as if I'd been stung, my eyes starting to burn from my concentrated effort not to blink. I scrambled for the straps of my backpack and turned on my heel, ducking under the velvet curtain before my flight unlocked everyone else, set them free to move, to speak, to laugh.

"Kira!" Mike called as I burst into the front room.

"Gotta go, Mike," I said, with too much energy. I fumbled in my pocket, found a crumpled bill, looked down just long enough to realize it was a twenty. "Thanks. Keep the change. It's been way too long."

And then I was bursting through the front door, bulling down the sidewalk, gulping in great breaths of freezing air, and trying to remember what it had been like before TEWSBU had ruined every last thing in my life.

CHAPTER 7

SIX HOURS LATER, I WAS ENSCONCED ON THE LIVING room couch, doing my best to drown—er, feast—my sorrows. I had changed out of my stage manager sweats into my home layabout clothes, a disreputable flannel robe that any normal person would have burned half a lifetime ago and a pair of enormous fluffy slippers that had once been red. I had my hair pulled back in a ponytail that was messier than anything Jennifer Galland had ever considered wearing, and it certainly wasn't flopping around in a cute counterpoint to whatever I was thinking.

I was studiously scraping the bottom of a pint of ice cream. Foolish me—I had thought that I would never eat another bite when I'd fled Mephisto's in shame. Like clockwork, though, my belly had started to rumble at seven o'clock, refusing to take a microwaved cup of frozen broccoli as an answer.

I had been forced to reach for the hard stuff: Ben & Jerry's New York Super Fudge Chunk. This was an emergency, after all.

I knew from personal experience that some people (Read: My perfect housemate, Jules) could make a pint of ice cream last for an entire month. Every night, after she finished her well-balanced dinner (consisting mostly of leafy greens, with small portions of lean protein and the occasional ounce or two of whole grains), she would permit herself a single spoonful. If one of the delectable "super fudge chunks" lodged on the edge of her spoon, she counted that in her night's allotment, skimping on smooth chocolate ice cream to make up for the candy treat.

Sometimes, I hated Jules.

For me, a pint of Ben & Jerry's was a single serving.

Feeling a little sick to my stomach, and a lot sick at heart, I huddled deeper into my robe. I was fumbling wanly for the TV remote between the sofa cushions when Jules waltzed out of her bedroom, wearing a tiny black dress that barely covered half of her erogenous zones. She'd pulled her hair into a smooth updo. I knew that she was wearing makeup, but I couldn't see where her naturally flawless features ended and M·A·C began. I vaguely recalled that she and Justin were going to some gallery opening, the last event on their social calendar before they headed out to California.

She paused in front of me. "Are you going to be okay?"

"I'm fine," I said, burrowing deeper into my flannel cave.

"You don't look fine."

I bit off a sharp reply. I wanted sympathy, not badgering. "I *will* be fine," I amended.

Jules perched on the arm of the couch. "You do know that getting out of that relationship was the best thing you ever could have done, don't you?"

"Obviously," I said, sighing and staring down at my pitiful self. I had let a dollop of ice cream slip off my spoon sometime during my administration of frozen pain medication. The chocolate stain added character to my robe.

"Seriously," Jules said, shaking her head with a vehemence that would have led to a French twist disaster for an ordinary human woman. "We've been through this about a million times. You are way too good for that smarmy, superior jerk. You would have been miserable if you'd gone through with the wedding. You would have hated yourself every single morning that he skated off to *his* production, taking the lead over every single one of yours."

"I would have learned to deal with the misery," I grumbled, knowing that I was acting like a two-year-old.

"Yeah," Jules said. "You deal with misery really well." She bent down and scooped up my empty ice cream carton. "If you were still with him, you'd never have been able to take the job at the Landmark."

"I would have!" I argued. Teel would have found a way for me to take the Landmark job. But I couldn't tell Jules about Teel.

Jules grimaced. "That man's career was too 'important' for the bastard to make time for your *wedding*. Do you honestly think he would change travel plans or casting calls or anything else, just because you landed your dream job? Come on, Kira. It's time to pick yourself up. Get back on the horse."

Unexpectedly, I pictured John McRae, with his cowboy slouch and his drawl designed to calm a frantic bronco. "I hate horses," I said sulkily, pulling my hands up into the sleeves of my dilapidated robe. "The only time my father took me to a petting zoo, the pony ate my sweater."

Jules sighed in exasperation, then stalked into the kitchen, perfectly stable on heels that made my arches ache just to look at them. By the time she came back from disposing of my comfort food remains, I had pulled the lapels of my robe up to my chin. She shook her head as she stared at me. "Seriously, Kira. Do you want me to stay home with you?"

What good would that do? We'd both sit on the couch and watch the latest episodes of some grating reality show. I would ignore the stupid television as I drowned in guilt, knowing that I'd kept my best friend and housemate from yet-another-perfect-soiree with Justin-the-perfect-man at wherever-the-perfect-locale, where Jules would have eaten three bites of whatever-the-perfect-food that whoever-the-perfect-hostess was serving.

Me? Bitter much?

I forced myself to sit up straighter on the couch. "No, Jules. I'll be fine. Really." She looked at me with the shrewd disbelief of a longtime friend. "I mean it," I said, seasoning my words with a resigned sigh. "I'm going to get all of my sulking done tonight. I'll be as good as new tomorrow. I promise."

Jules clicked her tongue. She knew me too well.

"Okay," I amended. "I might sulk for tomorrow, too. But I'll be fine once I get it out of my system. Once and for all. Really."

Jules glanced at the clock. "You'll call me if you need anything?"

Yeah. Like I'd ever be able to reach Jules on her cell phone. Half the time she forgot to charge it, and the other half, it was buried deep in her purse, set to vibrate so that it wouldn't interrupt rehearsal or filming or whatever.

"I'll call Maddy."

Jules laughed. We both knew that Maddy's phone was surgically attached to her ear. "Where is she, anyway? Are they still rehearsing?"

I shrugged. "I think she was planning to blow off some steam with Bachelor Number One. Some guy she started seeing last week. Mauricio, I think she said his name was."

"Italian?"

"Probably." I shrugged. "You know Maddy. A few weeks

from now she'll tell us it had been true love, but he had to sail for Rome." I threw a mock hand of desperation against my forehead, as if I were watching Maddy's one true love disappear into the sunset. While Jules and I were well accustomed to Maddy's frequent breakups, it remained a mystery to me how she managed to get over her guys so quickly, how she was ready to look for new blood a single day after sating herself with farewell sex.

I was never going to sleep with a guy again.

"When will she be home?" Jules asked, and I wasn't certain if she was still concerned about me, or if our resident house mother had moved on to worrying about our sex-crazed housemate.

"Tomorrow? Day after? Her note didn't say, but you know how she gets during tech rehearsal weeks." I nodded toward the white board calendar in the kitchen, where we supposedly kept one another up-to-date on our comings and goings. Maddy's hastily scrawled note said, "Ciao, bellas! Piu tarde!"

Jules snorted. "Let's call her tomorrow, to make sure she isn't lying injured in a ditch."

"Yeah," I agreed. "She wouldn't appreciate our interrupting her tonight." When I saw Jules's frown start to crease her carefully glossed lips, I scowled. I knew that she was questioning whether I'd have the nerve to interrupt Maddy if I needed anything. "Go, Jules! I'll be fine! I promise!"

And, finally, she did.

I turned on the television and started flipping through channels, but the offerings were even worse than I'd expected. Each show that I paused on featured a team of brilliant young professionals, all pitted against one another for money, fame, and fortune. Everyone was friends now—it was only a few minutes after nine. They had another forty minutes and three commercial breaks before they'd be at one another's throats.

I wished that I had another pint of Ben & Jerry's in the house.

In the days immediately following my broken-off wedding, I'd bought ice cream by the carload. I always had some in the freezer, no matter how much I'd already consumed that day, that week, that month. I'd hoarded Ben & Jerry's the way my father kept Zantac in every room of his house. You can never have too much protection, he'd explained to me once, when I'd laughed about spotting the little round tablets on his three-season porch in the middle of winter.

I just needed a little more protection. About a pint more.

During an interminable commercial break (Who would get voted off? Geneen, who had stabbed her teammates in the back? Or Denysia, who was the most likely to enjoy long-term success and thus threaten all the other contestants?), I replayed my little drama of the afternoon.

I'd been a fool to let myself think that Drew Myers might be the guy for me. Sure, he'd given me the time of day. He'd been willing to flirt over a burger and fries. But in the long run, he had to know that I was damaged goods. Everyone in the theater knew that I was broken, and nothing was going to change that. Nothing was going to heal me.

I'd made the wrong wish with Teel.

I shouldn't have wished for the Landmark. Sure, that had gotten me out of the dinner theater racket. It had moved me away from the unfortunate neighboring porno movie house; it had let me escape from temperamental tenors and high-strung sopranos.

But it was nowhere near enough of a change. My wish hadn't whisked away the broken world around me, the aching disappointment that I knew far too well, that I'd lived with for far too long. Disappointment with TEWSBU, yes, but even more importantly, disappointment with myself. Disappointment that I had let myself become That Woman, the bitter ex-fiancée, the one who falls apart completely and manages to spend the rest of her life living the romance that never was.

I should have wished for a perfect score on the LSAT and entrance to Harvard Law. At least that would have made my father happy. Dad deserved a little wish fulfillment after all the money he'd wasted on my non-wedding. So what if the thought of spending the rest of my days as a lawyer made my blood run cold? I'd learn to like it. My mother had wanted it badly enough. And I certainly wasn't getting anywhere in the theater. Not with TEWSBU dogging every step, even months after he'd left me in the dirt.

I sighed, and my robe slipped loose around my waist. When I gathered it up to launch Stage Two (or was it Three? Or Four? Or was I up to a billion?) of my patented pity party, I couldn't help but stare at the ice cream stain on the flannel.

What had I been thinking, drowning my sorrows in Ben & Jerry's? Again.

Consuming a pint of meaningless fat? Again.

Riding the roller coaster from sweet to savory to sweet? Again.

I shook my head in self-disgust.

In the past year, I'd truly developed terrible habits. I'd trained myself to fall into oblivion with the help of food. My temperament, my body, and my self-respect were all taking major beatings. Repeatedly.

I needed to lose the extra weight that I'd gained. I needed to kick my fat-slob self to the curb. If getting rid of TEWSBU was supposed to be such a blessing, such a growth opportunity, such a grand chance to become a better person, then why not make other dramatic overnight changes?

I hauled myself off the sofa and shuffled across the living room. My bedroom door was half open, and I blinked as I stared at the mess inside. What was going on with me? How could I—a stage manager by profession, a professional organizer and tucker-in of loose ends—stand to live in such utter confusion and disarray?

When had my nice, neat life slipped so far out of balance? And why had I let it stay slipped for so long?

I waded through the mess and pulled open my closet door. Aside from my sweats, I had fewer than a half-dozen outfits now. A half-dozen things that I could wear out of the house without fear of being arrested for indecent exposure.

It hadn't always been that way.

I shoved hangers to the side, pushing my way back three months, six months, a year into my past. There. I hadn't lived in black before TEWSBU left me. I had that green silk blouse, the one that never went out of style, that always managed to bring out the golden glints in my hair. I had that Fair Isle sweater, a classic burgundy and gray that made me feel chic in a timeless, Audrey Hepburn way, every single winter that I'd slipped it on since my senior year in college. I had the charcoal slacks that zipped up the side, the ones that made me look positively lanky.

I had a great wardrobe, clothes that made me feel good, clothes that made me like myself, even on the gloomy days, even on the days that seemed too dark and depressing to haul myself out of bed.

At least I had, a few zillion calories ago.

I could try Weight Watchers. Or Jenny Craig. Or Atkins, or South Beach, or Zone or whatever we were calling low-carb eating this week. I could watch what I ate for a year or two, monitoring every single bite as I regained control over my life, as I took back the balance and the happiness that had been mine before the non-wedding.

Or, I could call on Teel.

Was it really superficial for me to use a genie to lose weight? He'd already said I couldn't use my wishes to solve the big problems. If I was never going to succeed with major humanitarian efforts, was it really that bad to ask for a little nip and tuck? For a little—all right, a *lot* of—liposuction?

It wasn't like I was just asking for help in losing weight, I argued with myself. *That* would be superficial. No, I was asking for a return of my personal confidence. Personal strength. A jump start, so that I could best take advantage of my new job, my new life as a rising star in the theater scene. (Read: My new show with Drew Myers, a certain treacherous voice whispered at the back of my brain, but I hushed it to immediate silence.)

After all, I'd read a lot of articles about how fat people suffer discrimination. If I kept looking like this, I'd never be considered for the best jobs. Directors would always see my size first, my competence later. I would never line up another theater position. I might as well give in to my father's demands right now and complete my LSAT application that very night.

On the other hand, if I managed to lose all the weight at once, I'd be inspired to keep it off. I'd eat like Jules for the rest of my life. I'd swear off Tater Tots hot dish forever. I'd be a new person overnight, forget about waiting till the first of the month, or the winter solstice, or the New Year, or whatever arbitrary "new beginning" I set myself to initiate the transformation that just never seemed to happen.

I'd do it now, and then I'd keep it done, once and for all. Forever and ever. Amen.

Before I could lose faith in my justification, I reached into the back of my closet, digging to the bottom of my clothes hamper to find the magic lamp. Grubby laundry might not be the recommended swaddling for an artifact of such value, but

I'd been hard-pressed to find another safe place to store my treasure. I'd lived with my housemates for too long—they wouldn't hesitate to rummage through my desk for a postage stamp or a pencil with a sharpened tip. Even my dresser wasn't totally sacrosanct; Jules routinely borrowed my T-shirts to work out in, when she hadn't had a chance to do her own laundry. I'd considered stashing the brass treasure beneath my mattress, but the lamp was large enough and lumpy enough that I'd suspected I wouldn't get a wink of sleep.

So, dirty laundry had been my choice.

Anyway, it wasn't like Teel was ever going to know.

I collapsed onto my bed and closed my eyes. I only had three wishes; I couldn't afford to squander one. But the more I thought about asking for this change, the more I imagined myself back where I'd been a year before, wearing my old clothes, moving with my old confidence, climbing three flights of stairs without a nagging catch of breathlessness. This was *right*. I could feel it in my bones. My aching, nutrition-deprived bones.

I scooted up to my headboard and sat cross-legged where my pillows would have been, if I'd bothered to make my bed that morning. Or the morning before. Or the morning before that.

I'd have plenty of time to straighten my room after making this wish, I told myself. Plenty of time to live my new life. To get things back under control.

I stared at my hand, barely able to make out the flame tattoos on my fingertips. I rubbed my thumb across my fingers, and it might have been my imagination, but the pattern started to glint a little more, to shine, as if I'd trailed my hand through glitter.

I picked up the brass lamp and checked the flame markings again. They were definitely clearer where they touched the brass. The metal was warm under my fingertips, much warmer than the lantern should have been when it had just been plucked from a pile of dirty laundry. The temperature felt good, made my fingers *want* to rub some more. The metal seemed to hum with its own energy, like static electricity made audible.

I pressed my fingers together, hard, and said out loud, "Teel!"

Immediately, fog poured out of the lamp—glinting, gleaming mist that shimmered with ruby and emerald and cobalt. The shape within coalesced more quickly than it had in the costume shop; I blinked, and a body stood at the foot of my bed.

"Ready for your second wish?"

I almost dropped the lamp. The guy who stood in front of me was a chef.

He was dressed all in white, in the traditional double-breasted jacket and a huge toque. His sleeves had been hastily folded above his elbows; I could envision him in the middle of preparing some hectic feast for a hundred honored guests. He clearly had enjoyed a fair amount of the food he generated in this persona; his belly sloped beneath the starched coat as if he were pregnant with triplets. "Teel?" I asked, although I knew that it had to be my genie.

"At your service," Teel replied. I wondered if he'd actually found his way into one of the Twin Cities' finer restaurant kitchens, or if he'd merely taken no prisoners at Williams-Sonoma after spending a day watching the Food Channel. Either way, I found it more than a bit ironic that he was dressed like a chef when I was about to ask to lose a year's ill-acquired weight.

Teel took a long look around us, his bushy eyebrows coming together in a frown as he acknowledged my stained and faded bathrobe, my matted fluffy slippers. He stared at the chaos of my bedroom, shaking his head in amazement. "I think I could send over a sous-chef or two, to help you straighten things up around here."

"I don't need a sous-chef," I snapped. "I just need some time. Time to get things done, when I'm not working on a play."

"At least let me get you a vacuum cleaner," Teel said. After a sharp double-tug on the lobe of his fleshy ear, a machine appeared, already plugged into my wall socket. The tattooed flames around Teel's wrist gleamed against the high-end Dyson Absolute. As a stage manager, I recognized the model immediately. I had to appreciate my genie's willingness—and ability—to conjure up the very best.

Nevertheless, I said, "Later." I was a bit annoyed that he thought my homemaking skills were more important than any other reason I might have summoned him. He looked disapproving, as if my slovenliness put one of his Michelin stars at stake, but I staved off any further judgment by saying, "I've chosen my second wish."

"Magnificent!" he boomed, as if he had just unveiled a particularly succulent standing rib roast.

Yum. Roast beef. Maybe I could put off my wish-making for a meal or two…. At least until I was feeling a little better. A little less raw about TEWSBU.

No. That was the sort of thinking that had gotten me into this mess. "I've decided that I want to lose weight," I said quickly, before I could change my mind, and I immediately grimaced. I sounded just as stupid and superficial as I'd been afraid I would. I hurried on. "I want to get back to the weight I was before my wedding. The wedding that didn't happen. You know what I mean. I want to be the person I was then, physically at least. I mean, I wouldn't mind being that person mentally, or emotionally, or, well, whatever."

What was it about defining my wishes that made me so confused? The same thing had happened when I'd tried to confirm my wish for a better job; I'd found myself spewing modifications to my own words, new thoughts, details, explanations.

When Teel stayed silent, I said, "So, how about it? Can you make me lose the weight I gained during the past year?"

He blinked. "Oh! Are you through explaining everything?" I narrowed my eyes, and he held up his meaty hands, as if to assure me he was only joking. "So it took you two full days to get around to *that?*"

"What do you mean?"

"Changing your physical form. Seven out of ten women ask for modifications to their physical appearance as their second wish."

Something about his matter-of-fact tone set me on edge. His matter-of-fact tone, or the way that I was just another statistic to him, just another random woman who had found his lantern and made my demanding wishes? Stung, I said, "And the guys? Don't they ask for physical changes?"

He shook his head. "Not exactly. They might ask for specific physical traits, the ability to do specific things, but they don't go for the full body overhaul."

"Seven out of ten?" I couldn't decide if the ratio made me feel cheap, or if it gave me comfort.

"But most women ask for something really striking. You know—full body, full face, complete upgrade." He stared at me, once again taking a survey from the crown of my head to the arch of my feet. I couldn't help but feel like I came up a few points short in his overall estimation. "You sure you don't want to consider something a little more radical than just losing a year of bad choices? I really can do a lot, if I do say so myself." He gazed appraisingly at me, as if I were an entire salmon waiting for his chefly expertise.

I should have been offended. I mean, here was my genie,

practically telling me that my body was below average, my face was a disappointment. Or would be, once he'd magic-blasted away those pounds.

But I sighed. "I'm really not trying to get a *perfect* body out of the deal," I said. I tugged at my straggling ponytail, removing my elasticized band so that I could run my fingers through my curls. The motion helped me to think. "I just want what I had. I want what was mine. What I lost when TEWSBU left me."

TEWSBU. I pronounced it the way it always sounded in my head, so that it rhymed with "who's blue."

"You lost me." He settled his hammy fists on his hips. "Who is this two's boo?"

"The Ex Who Shall Be Unnamed. The guy I was going to marry."

"So, you want to lose the weight to get back at him?" Teel frowned, his entire face pulled into the expression beneath his towering toque. "I can do that for you, but I have to tell you, it's a really lousy idea."

"It's my wish, isn't it?"

"Of course it's your wish. And you know I'm eager for you to make it. But spending a wish just to get revenge at someone… Nine out of ten women regret spending a wish to get back at a lover."

"Nine out of ten!" I wanted to ask him how many women *had* lovers to get back at, at least as much as I did, but I thought the answer would probably make me so depressed that I'd give up on the whole genie thing altogether, and just seek out another round of Ben & Jerry's expert treatment.

"Nineteen out of twenty," Teel offered, "if you count the lesbians who want revenge against their partners."

Where did he get this stuff? Was there some Genie Statistical Abstract that he kept at his flame-touched fingertips? It didn't really matter, though. I swallowed hard and tried to clarify my wish. "I'm not trying to get back at anyone. I'd be totally happy to never see TEWSBU again. It's *me* that I want to change. *Me* that I want to get into line."

Teel nodded, his bluff features turning the motion into an avuncular commentary. "And twenty pounds will do that?"

I curled my lips into a snarl of self-disgust. "Thirty."

"In one year!" I thought his eyebrows might never descend from beneath his pleated hat.

"It's been a bad one," I said.

Teel looked around at my room, at the black sweatpants piled haphazardly on my desk, at the crumpled socks beside my bed. My trash can glittered with candy bar wrappers, and towels from my morning shower were clumped at the foot of my bed. "I can see that."

And I could see it, too. I could see how I'd let my weight get out of hand, the same way I'd let everything else fray and scatter. The same way I'd let my confidence spin away, go whirling off into the darkest recesses of my mind. It was time to take charge. Time to get back on track. I looked Teel in the eye and said, "I wish that I weighed what I did before my wedding was called off."

Holding my gaze, Teel raised his fingers to his earlobe. He paused long enough for me to take a breath. Another. Another.

Speak now, or forever hold your peace.

I nodded affirmatively, a tiny, determined gesture. "As you wish," Teel said, and then he tugged his ear twice.

The electric jolt was stronger than I expected, more violent than I'd remembered from our exchange back in the costume shop. The jangling energy made me catch my breath; it froze every cell of my body. My mind decided to cry out; my throat tensed up and my lungs began to expand, but I couldn't move, couldn't give voice to the sparking pain.

But then, the agony was over. The electricity was gone.

I stared down at my body. The belt of my flannel robe was suddenly slack, letting the fabric gap open. I gasped in surprise, and the movement of my lungs felt different, easier, cleaner. I ran my fingers down my sides, closing them around my waist—the waist that I had not felt for months.

Everything had changed. I took a step, and I realized that I was feeling my thighs moving through the air, no flesh chafing against flesh. I raised my fingertips to my throat, felt the sleeker line of my chin, the sharper hint of my cheekbones.

I laughed, then breathed deeply to fill my lungs again. Looking down, I realized that something was different, something was…wrong. Something was not me, neither my pre- nor post-TEWSBU self.

"Um, Teel, you improvised a little." I stared down at a pair of firm, shapely D-cups that I'd never had in my life.

"Those?" he said with an elaborate shrug. "I thought you'd appreciate a little Chef's Surprise. Think of it as dessert."

I knew that I was supposed to be annoyed with him, frustrated that he'd gone beyond the strict four corners of my wish. But just that once, I decided to forgive him.

CHAPTER 8

THIRTY POUNDS.

The next morning, I was still trying to get my mind around the meaning of thirty pounds. If I pictured thirty blocks of butter molded around my waist, okay, that was a lot. But it wasn't like I'd been one of those morbidly obese people they wrote newspaper articles about, the ones who are physically incapable of getting out of bed. Even at my heaviest, I wasn't a poster girl for the annual scare stories about the dangerous food at the state fair, about how Pronto Pups and deep-fried Snickers will kill you.

But I had to admit, dropping thirty pounds overnight made me incredibly aware of myself, made me realize just how much I'd changed in the past year.

It wasn't only the weight. I'd harmed myself by doing more than eating nonstop. I'd built up some really bad habits, truly destructive ways of thinking about myself, about my life.

The morning after making my second wish, I lay in bed after I woke up. My first thoughts were the same that they'd been every morning since TEWSBU left: I was alone. I was alone, and the pillow beside me was untouched; the sheets were still tucked in on the far side of the queen mattress, pristine after I'd made up the bed the night before.

That morning, though, the empty bed wasn't an accusation. It wasn't a defeat. Rather, it was a special present that I'd left for myself. I'd slept in the center without any fight about who was stealing the covers, about who had whipped the blanket and the sheet into such a tangled froth that it was necessary to remake the bed just to doze back to sleep.

Something about losing those thirty pounds had helped me to sleep more soundly than I had in months. I hadn't awakened once, didn't remember a single bad dream.

When I stumbled into the kitchen to grab some breakfast, the white board stared at me. Maddy had been home some time during the night; she had scrubbed away her Italian greeting and posted in its place: "Guten morgen allerseits!" Beneath the message, Jules had printed in her bubbly script, "Do we get a scorecard?" She'd turned the bottom of the question mark into a heart.

Wow. Mauricio had lasted a mere six *days*. Was that a comment on where Italy and Germany stood in world history? Current events? The relative skills of those particular lovers?

Poor Mauricio. I hoped that Maddy had let him down gently. As for Herr Wunderbar, whatever his actual name might be, I doubly hoped that he had a strong constitution. He was going to need it in the nights to come. Whatever had brought about Maddy's linguistic change, I'd slept through the transition, like a sleek, svelte Rip Van Winkle.

I was sure that I'd hear more about this romantic development the next time Maddy and I managed to be in the house at the same time, but I was going to be crazy busy, with *Romeo and Juliet* getting into full swing, and I wasn't quite sure of

Maddy's schedule, only that her play was opening in a few days. She would spend most of her free time making last-minute changes to her lighting design. Herr Wunderbar would be put on hold before getting the full range of her attention, and we, Maddy's intrigued housemates, would have to wait to hear all the details about this new so-called love.

I shrugged and glanced at the kitchen clock. Jules and Justin must have headed out to the airport already, jetting their way to Santa Barbara and the ill-gotten fruits of Justin's legal career. Like a patient taking my temperature, I asked myself whether I was jealous, whether I wanted to be at a law firm retreat. The answer was still no. I continued to recoil instinctively at the thought of following in my father's footsteps, of fulfilling my mother's dream.

I had to admit, it made my life a little easier, having no housemates around. There was no one to notice that my robe was sashed tighter around my waist. No one to say that I'd regained my bridal figure. No need to explain away the change, since I was fairly certain Teel hadn't relaxed his rules about my mentioning his very existence.

I opened the cabinet above the stovetop, automatically reaching for my box of Cap'n Crunch. Except this morning, I didn't really want that nostalgic brown sugar boost—even if it did come with Crunch Berries. If I was going to be perfectly honest, I'd have to admit that the cereal was so sweet it made my teeth ache.

In the past, I'd treasured that ache; it reminded me of early mornings in elementary school, when Dad had poured me a bowl of golden barrels to go with a tall glass of milk, before sending me out in the winter snow to walk the four blocks to school. Surely, it was coincidence that I'd ended up with a half-dozen cavities by the time I was ten.

I shoved the cereal back into the cupboard and opened up

the fridge instead. We housemates generally did our own grocery shopping, but we'd been together for long enough that we could supplement a meal from one another's stock without launching World War III. I pushed aside Maddy's packaged ravioli and sniffed at a carton of orange juice, only to discover that it was well on its way to becoming citrus wine.

But there, toward the back of the top shelf, was the perfect breakfast—a container of lemon yogurt. It had to belong to Jules; I'd never bought the stuff, and Maddy was more of a frozen-waffle kind of girl, on the rare occasions when she found herself home for breakfast in the first place. I shrugged. I could replace a container of lemon yogurt easily enough, before Jules got back from California.

I actually ended up liking the flavor. It was cold and creamy, and the lemon taste was just the right amount of tart—my lips weren't frozen into a permanent pucker.

I ducked into the bathroom as soon as I finished breakfast. My morning shower was…interesting. While I might have soaped and shaved a slim body thousands of times in the past, I'd never had the opportunity to clean one that was quite as well…endowed as Teel had left me. I frowned as I wrapped my towel around my chest, not trusting my casual terry tuck to stay in place. I surprised myself, though, by making it back to my bedroom without unscheduled interruption.

It wasn't until I opened my chest of drawers that I realized the problem that Teel had created. Sure, I could slip right into my old trousers, the earliest ones in the archeological site that was my closet. But I was going to need some new bras before I could show off the current state of my upper body. For that matter, I'd need some new blouses, as well; anything tailored that I currently owned would either be baggy at the waist, or it would gap open across the bust.

Shrugging, I pulled on my familiar black sweats. It was better to lounge inside the now-oversize jersey knit, than to tumble out of one of my older blouses. Besides, there was something comfortable about the clothing, something that let me hide from myself, from the new me that my genie had charged into existence just the night before. I'd scope out a new wardrobe soon enough.

I found a parking space just one block from the theater and still had time to drop into Club Joe for a large skim latte, with my requisite four shots of espresso. The smell of the coffee almost knocked me over—it was so rich, so perfect. In fact, all of my senses seemed on fire after Teel had worked his little magic trick the night before. The lemon yogurt had tasted *more;* my shower had proved more refreshing than any five minutes of hot water had a right to be. Even the cloudless sky seemed brighter—as if I'd never seen that shade of blue before. The temperature wasn't any warmer than it had been the day before, but now I smiled as my breath fogged the air in front of me.

I dug in my pocket for a set of keys that Bill Pomeroy had given me. The key ring was enormous—I felt like I was some sort of medieval keeper of a castle as I spun through the bits of brass. The front door key had a green plastic sleeve wrapped around its top. Green for go. Green for new growth.

I laughed at myself and pulled the door closed behind me.

I hadn't even ventured into the actual theater yet; all of my time had been spent in the glass-walled rehearsal room. Well, no time like the present. I fumbled for a few minutes but managed to find the key to the door between the lobby and the theater itself. Sipping my coffee, I walked down the house right aisle.

A bare lightbulb shone from the center of the stage, glaring atop a plain iron floor lamp. Ghost lights were a tradition in most theaters. Some people said that they were mandated by the actors' union, Equity. (They weren't.) Some said that they were required by management once Equity came into existence, so that rehearsals could be completed without needing to call in a union stagehand to turn on the lights. (They weren't.) Some said that they were demanded by theater owners, after an unlucky burglar fell in a darkened theater and broke his leg and sued successfully for damages. (They weren't.) Some said that they were left to placate ghosts, so that the production would not be haunted. (Maybe, just possibly, they were used for that.)

Whatever the explanation, setting out the ghost light was one of the stage manager's last responsibilities at the end of every workday. My counterpart for the Landmark's current production had dutifully done so, and I used the glare to find my way into the wing at stage left.

The current show was a hypermodern version of *The Crucible.* The set was made out of plain gray blocks, structures that could be fashioned into a church, a cottage, the bare, desperate life of earliest America. The show was already up and running—they'd have the theater space for another month. Then we'd strike their set and create our own, replacing their dry, austere construction with our underground Verona.

Every theater was different, but every one was the same. I could smell dust in the legs, the utilitarian black velvet curtains that cut off the audience's views of backstage. I wondered what John would do to mask the angles for our production; the amazing sketch I'd seen didn't show anything. The plain black that worked so well for the stark *Crucible* would likely be replaced by something reminiscent of Verona, fabric patterned after stone or something similarly evocative.

Squinting into the shadows, I just managed to make out a

panel of multiple light switches on the wall. Palming the entire set flooded the backstage area with harsh white overheads. The back wall of the theater was made of cinder block. It was painted a flat black, a color that swallowed up light, hiding a myriad of minor flaws. I looked above the stage and saw a dozen pipes, heavy metal rods that held mammoth lighting instruments and several backdrops.

The stage manager for the current production could not exactly be called a neat freak. The floor was gritty with dirt, and a number of dust bunnies looked large enough to consume unsuspecting small children. Two wooden tables were pushed up against the walls, holding a jumble of props and bits of costumes, all interspersed with trash—a broken-toothed comb, a sprung hair scrunchie, a dozen sheets of paper covered with doodles and telephone numbers.

A large garbage can stood beneath the light switches, almost overflowing. I sniffed sharply, but I couldn't smell rotting food—at least *some* professionalism was evident there. A dozen chairs were scattered in the space, a few of them stacked, but most lying on their sides, as if someone had kicked them over in an acting exercise, then forgotten to clean up. A push broom lay on the floor, just waiting for people to trip over it, or to step on the bristles and brain themselves when the handle came flying up.

If this was the caliber of stage management expected at the Landmark, my first wish might not have been as unfair as I once had feared. The *Crucible* stage manager wasn't doing a great job—at least not from the look of things back here. Maybe the Landmark really needed a stage manager who could *manage,* someone like me who could keep a professional theater neat and clean even in the midst of a chaotic production.

Maybe I *could* land another job before my father's May LSAT deadline.

I took a few steps further into the wings, reaching for a glinting silver doorknob. It turned easily enough, but the door groaned as it opened. I'd have to scare up some WD-40. A creaky door like that could make itself heard in the last row of a theater, especially during a quiet scene onstage.

At least the light switches were where I expected them to be on the wall. I flipped both to reveal a dressing room as disorganized and messy as the rest of the backstage space. Mirrors lined the far wall, with frames of bare lightbulbs carving out space for individual actors to sit and apply their makeup. A dozen bulbs were missing, though, a clear indication that someone had not paid attention to the most basic of facilities (not to mention the risk of leaving a bare light socket accessible in a busy workspace). A makeup-stained T-shirt was crumpled on the counter, and a disgusting fluff of hair teased from a now-missing brush skittered across the floor in the breeze of my own footsteps.

A double door occupied almost all of the wall to my left, its intriguing access cut off by a hefty padlock. I jostled my massive key ring again, determined to see what was back there. Of course, it was too much to hope that the appropriate key would be clearly labeled. Aside from the green plastic cap for the front door key, there was nothing to distinguish one bit of brass from another.

Sighing, I set my backpack on the floor and decided to try each one. Once I found it, I'd put it beside the green one. That would have to do until I could create some labels, until I could turn the key ring into a useful tool instead of a frustrating guessing exercise. Steadily, I started testing each option, one by one.

I was halfway through the ring when I heard the voice behind me. "What's a nice girl like you doing in a deserted place like this?"

"Ah!"

I'd never thought of myself as the sort of girl who screamed. I'd never believed that I was the type of stage manager who would jump three feet into the air when she was taken by surprise. I'd never imagined that I was the sort of woman who would whirl to face an intruder, shoving her hand deep inside her backpack to pretend that she had a super-secret weapon ready to dispatch an invader.

"Oh," I said weakly. "Hi, John." As soon as I realized it was him, I felt a little embarrassed, ashamed about running out of Mephisto's without even saying goodbye. I breathed a silent prayer that he hadn't noticed (Read: That he'd somehow been struck blind and deaf as I staggered out of the Mamet Room like a drunk madwoman).

"I didn't mean to startle you, Franklin." John McRae took a lazy step back, holding his hands out by his sides, as if to prove that he was harmless.

I began to say that he hadn't surprised me, but that was stupid; he obviously had. I settled for shrugging and saying, "I should have expected other folks would show up early for rehearsal."

"I wanted to check out the fly space. I don't think there's enough room up there to do everything Bill wants, flying in the sewers and all. Not if he really wants the tunnels deep enough to hold slime."

"Slime?" I hadn't heard that part of our staging plans. I was intrigued, even as I started to think of everything that could go wrong with slippery wet sets.

"We are going to turn the theatrical world on its *ear*," he said with a shrug, managing to capture Bill's trademark excitement even as his own twang stretched the last word into two syllables. "Do you have the key to the catwalks on that ring?"

I held up the useless tangle of metal. "I'm sure it's here somewhere. Nothing's labeled, though."

"What good is that?" he asked, with a good-natured snort.

"My thoughts exactly. Here. You're welcome to find it. I've got to get out to the rehearsal room, get things set up for today." I passed him the heavy ring.

"I'll bring them back when I'm done."

"If you're going to walk around back there, be careful. It's a real mess."

He glanced at the careless disarray around us, obviously as critical as I was of the state of the other stage manager's handiwork. He said, "The Landmark was lucky to get you on this show, Franklin."

Even though I was starting to agree with him, I could feel myself blush. The Landmark hadn't been lucky. They'd been manipulated by a genie. They'd been forced by my wish. I muttered something about how this was a lucky chance for me, too.

John took my keys and started to walk away, but when he got to the door, he turned back. "I was sorry you left Mephisto's so quickly. I hoped we could talk some, figure out a calendar. Start meeting with the other designers."

Damn. Of *course* he'd noticed I'd run away. He'd seen and heard everything—my flirting with Drew, my embarrassment at the hands of TEWSBU. He had even tried to pick up the chair I'd knocked over—how had I even imagined that he wouldn't notice my crazed departure?

Without thinking, I folded my arms around my belly, trying to wrap in the surge of nausea that came whenever I thought of the man I'd almost married. As my fingers closed around the fabric of my sweatshirt, though, I became even more self-conscious. The cloth pulled beneath my grip, emphasizing my waist, making my newfound bust stand out. I wiped my hands against my thighs with all the subtle aplomb of a zebra at the lions' family reunion.

"Yeah," I said, when the silence had stretched out for way too long. "Sorry about that. I remembered that I had to get home to, um, take care of some stuff. This show came up out of nowhere, you know, and I didn't really have a chance to clear my schedule."

John nodded slowly. "Uh-huh," he said. "Mike said it must be something like that."

Mike. Mephisto himself, who knew everything about me. What the hell else had he said?

"I—I've got to get out to the rehearsal room," I stammered. I clutched my backpack to my side as I ran away.

A couple of actors were already waiting outside when I crashed into the lobby. As I opened the door for them, I said hello. Jennifer Galland and Stephanie Michaelson. Perfect. Just the two women I most wanted to see. Not.

Suddenly, I wondered how long TEWSBU and Stephanie had been going out. Had he left me for her? Had they been together for a full year? *Had he started dating her before he broke up with me?* Surely I would have heard *that* piece of gossip, if it were true.

I pasted a smile on my face, refusing to think about how idiotic I must have looked the night before. For her part, Stephanie smiled and pretended that we were perfectly good friends.

I led the way to the rehearsal room, hoping that they'd both interpret my flushed cheeks as some type of stage manager's eager beaver will to do good. As soon as Stephanie entered the room, she sat on the floor, splaying her legs in front of her as she engaged in a serious stretching regimen. I wondered if she thought we were doing a walk-through, something that would require actual physical exertion, but then I realized that she was probably just used to showing off her spectacular actor's body. Her incredibly well-endowed actor's body. Her so-well-endowed-that-she-absolutely-could-not-have-come-by-that-chest-naturally actor's body.

As if I had.

I wondered if TEWSBU had been attracted to her because she didn't look like a stunted teenage boy. I couldn't help but wonder what he'd think of the twin gifts that Teel had given me. What had my genie called them? Chef's Surprise?

It didn't matter. It absolutely didn't matter. TEWSBU was history.

And if I repeated that to myself often enough, I might actually come to believe it some day.

As the rest of the cast drifted in, I covered my confused jealousy by handing out phone lists that I'd printed that morning. When I got to Stephanie, I looked away, giving both of us a chance to build up the pretense that we liked each other. Within fifteen minutes, it didn't matter, anyway; the whole cast had gathered, and the room was humming with activity. Bill worked the crowd, saying hello to everyone, smiling and nodding and touching each person to say hello—a fleeting brush of his fingers on a hand, a sleeve. Each of the actors seemed to tune in to Bill's frequency, to vibrate with a tightly controlled enthusiasm as he moved to the far edge of the circle of chairs. Within seconds of his sitting, everyone was poised, ready to start.

Bill panned his gaze around the group, his smile growing. "Perfect," he said. "As you know, most shows would start to rehearse scene by scene. Well, we're not most shows. We're going to do things a little differently. We've got a lot of work ahead of us, figuring out the social bonds of sex and of gender, deciding where to shred our audience's expectations. We'll all work together for a couple of weeks, exploring issues that will be important for every actor, for every scene. Before we start, though, I want each of you to engage in a little thought experiment. Drew? On your feet."

Of course, Drew had come in with all the other actors. I'd purposely not looked him in the eye, not paid any special attention to him, not acknowledged that he was the man I'd been willing to share my fries with. It seemed safer that way. More normal. More sane.

Who was I kidding?

I *had* noticed that he was wearing jeans. Comfortable, well-worn jeans, that looked like they'd known every line of his body for a lifetime. He had on a khaki T-shirt, as well, topped by a soft flannel shirt that must have been washed a million times. And his smile was every bit as dazzling as it had been the day before, perfect because of that one tooth that was just a hair-breadth shy of straight. Unconsciously, I found myself repeating the ten digits of his phone number, like a magical incantation.

As Drew took to his feet, I was immediately struck by the same swooping sensation that had led me to act like such an idiot at Mephisto's. And that belly flip only became worse when Bill said, "Kira, could you stand up, as well?"

Obediently, I got to my feet, suddenly aware of being the target of two dozen eyes. I resisted the urge to clutch at my sweatshirt, to tug the fabric into some invisible magical shield. Wildly, I wondered how my flame tattoos would look against the fabric now. Could any of the cast make out evidence of Teel, when John had not seen it the day before?

I resisted the urge to shake my head as I forced my attention back to the rehearsal. Bill nodded as he stalked around Drew and me. The fluorescent light glinted off his freshly shaven scalp. He spoke to the cast, harnessing every drop of his legendary charisma. "Ordinarily, I'd leave Kira out of this. Let her work her stage manager magic." He smiled at me, and my lips automatically curved in response, even as I wondered what he had in store for me, for us. "But for this exercise, I need to call on someone who isn't in the cast. On a *woman* who isn't in the cast."

A woman.... That certainly didn't make me feel any more comfortable. Drew flashed me a parody of a wolfish grin, leering with an actor's comic exaggeration. The cast laughed good-naturedly, but I couldn't even begin to reciprocate. Somehow, I feared that whatever Bill had up his dramatic sleeve was going to be a lot more embarrassing than my offering to share my food. And it just might be a hell of a lot more intimate.

Our fearless director went on. "People, as we work through these scenes, I want each of you to become aware of the conflict inherent in our casting. We've waged a battle by switching genders. You need to understand the struggles that the opposite sex goes through every day, the fights that they engage in every waking moment. These roles will be new to you. Your knowledge of your own flesh and blood will be shocking, astonishing, new. You must learn what your bodies have to say to you, what your bodies *would* say to you, if they possessed different chromosomes, different genes, different genders."

Bill paused deliberately, taking the time to meet the eyes of each and every one of his cast members. He lingered for the longest time on Drew, as if he were trying to think some secret message to his star, trying to speak some hidden truth, mind to mind. Still holding Drew's gaze, Bill said, "Kira, what do your breasts say to you?"

"Excuse me?" My voice sounded like a crow's, cawing against the honeyed sweetness of the director's hypnotism.

Bill shook his head, never breaking Drew's gaze. "Kira, I need you to help us. All the other women in the room must start to think of their bodies as male. All of the other women must learn to question their senses, their sensations. But I need a woman to teach us. Teach us men. Teach Drew. Kira, what are your breasts saying to you right now?"

I wanted to melt into the floor. I wanted to run out of the room. I wanted to flee the scene faster than I'd run out of Mephisto's the day before.

But I was a professional stage manager. My job was to support my director. I closed my eyes and took a deep breath. And then I said, "They're embarrassed."

"Yes," Bill crooned. "Go on."

I started to cross my arms over my chest, but realized that my breasts wouldn't like that very much. I forced my hands to dangle awkwardly by my sides. "They don't like to be the focus of this much attention." I thought of Teel's wicked smile when he'd done his work the night before. "They're not used to being noticed. Not used to being talked about. They'd like for you to focus on the men now. To ask about their…" I wasn't sure how crude my breasts would be, how inclined they'd be toward slang. I decided that my breasts were more the clinical type. "To ask about their testicles."

The cast laughed. Even Bill was amused. "Thank you, Kira. Now, Drew? How did Kira's breasts make you feel?"

That was going too far. It was one thing to ask me to give a voice to my recently enlarged, if carefully hidden, body parts. But asking Drew to respond, and in such a personal way? I thought he would refuse. *I* would have refused.

Instead, he said tentatively, "They, like, totally confuse me."

Well, that was deep. He sounded like some surfer dude. At first, I thought that he was mocking me, mocking Bill's exercise. But no. Drew's face bore the perplexed frown of a high school student caught unprepared during a trigonometry pop quiz.

Bill said, "That's the man-you speaking, Drew. That's the man-you who was listening to Kira. What would Juliet's breasts say?" Drew squirmed, but Bill said, "No. Don't tell us. Not with words. Bring it to your reading. Let us hear it when Juliet first speaks to her nurse."

Drew's jaw tightened, and he nodded. Around the circle, half the actors were nodding. I could see them talking to their own phantom organs, all of them building silent bonds to their characters' gonads.

I resisted the urge to roll my eyes.

This was theater, after all. This was a sort of magic. All I had to do was sit back and watch the cast at work. All I had to do was let Bill weave his dreams. All I had to do was believe.

It turned out, my talking breasts were the high point of the rehearsal. The rest of the time, the cast plodded their way through Shakespeare's immortal words, trying to become comfortable with the awkward-to-us "my lords" and "madams" as we turned our characters' genders upside down. We wrapped up just as it was getting dark outside, having taken only the briefest of breaks for lunch. People shuffled out in small groups, and I listened to the strands of conversation as I stacked the chairs, extremely conscious of my talkative female body.

When I was finished, Bill thanked me for my help. I tried to believe that he wasn't staring at my chest, but I wasn't at all sure that was the case. As he got to the door of the rehearsal room, though, he stopped and said, "What's this?" I turned around in time to see him pick up my key ring, along with a slip of paper. "Thanks, Franklin. Catch you later," he read, curving the last three words into a question.

"Oh," I said. "John borrowed my keys to do some work backstage. He must have left them there, instead of interrupting the rehearsal."

Bill tossed the ring to me. "See you tomorrow, Kira."

"Have a good night." I glanced down at the keys, readily

finding my old green standby. But now, I could make out a dozen plastic caps, each sporting a white paper label. The gleaming rectangles were filled with perfect, steady letters.

Costume shop. Catwalk. Prop closet.

John had labeled my keys.

Somehow, the gesture made the whole day a little bit better. The neat handwriting canceled out a little of my shame about Stephanie, about TEWSBU's girlfriend. The labels covered at least some of my embarrassment, speaking for my new breasts in a roomful of strangers. The keys locked away a fraction of the desperate sense of breathless imbalance I still felt every time I looked at Drew Myers, every time I met his green-flecked eyes.

I made a mental note to thank John the next time I saw him. It was good to have another professional technician working on the show. I wondered when he'd left the keys outside the door. I could only hope that it was late in the rehearsal—well after my vocal breasts and I had settled into our chair and disappeared inside our sheltering baggy sweatshirt.

I tried to imagine what my down-to-earth set designer would have said if he'd been in the room for my interpretive role. I was surprised to find myself blushing, all over again. No, I didn't really want to know what practical John would have said. Not at all. Not when his sardonic words would have been delivered in that already-familiar Texas drawl, stretching out my embarrassment even more.

We were producing art here at the Landmark. *Art*. I just had to remember that, as I locked up the theater and took my new breasts home.

CHAPTER 9

BY THE TIME I GOT HOME, THE STREET LAMPS WERE on, and it had started to snow—tiny flakes that would make for a relatively easy workout when I shoveled the driveway in the morning. Over the years, I'd become a better forecaster than the guys on television; it didn't take a lot of Minnesota winters to learn that the early and late storms of the year featured a lot of heavy, wet snow, while mid-January's bitter cold made the flakes smaller and grainier.

Years ago, my housemates and I had settled on a snow-clearing schedule. The Swensons were far too old to be tackling our driveway and sidewalk on their own, even if they did get preferential parking privileges. Maddy, Jules, and I took charge of the snow removal, and Mrs. Swenson kept the flower beds in perfect order during the too-short summer months. The arrangement might not be absolutely fair (some winters dropped so many feet of snow that the flower beds were almost-forgotten memories), but between the three of us in our upstairs apartment, the shoveling wasn't too much of a burden.

I'd take first shift, handling this initial snowfall. We rotated responsibility, liberally factoring in allowances for our diverse rehearsal schedules. Maddy and Jules also had the boyfriend cards to play; if they'd slept over at their beaux, they were hardly expected to come home for snow maintenance. Years ago, we'd decided that shoveling was just One of Those Things—not worth fighting over. Sort of like borrowing food from the fridge.

That reminded me—I still needed to replace Jules's lemon yogurt.

Shaking my head at my forgetfulness, I carried my stuff into my bedroom. I started to dump it all onto my bed, but then I took a minute to put things where they belonged. My backpack went on my desk, next to the LSAT application that Dad had completed for me. I draped my coat over the hook behind my door.

As long as I was on such a neatnik binge, I decided that I might as well do my laundry. I excavated the pile from the back of the closet, placing Teel's lamp in a place of pride on my desk. I was home alone, so there wasn't any chance of it being discovered by anyone else.

It took me about thirty seconds to separate the whites (my sheets) from the darks (every other garment I owned.) The washing machine and dryer were in the basement; I made short work of carrying down my first load and getting it going.

I had just stepped back into the apartment when I felt the electric charge that I'd come to associate with Teel. It started in my fingertips. I looked down just in time to see my flames flare brightly, and then the jangling energy flooded through my body. I squeezed my eyes closed against the charge.

When I opened them again, I was back in the place of nothingness. It didn't frighten me as much this time; I didn't waste my time trying to peer into the distance. I didn't try to touch the floor, or any walls, or whatever invisible ceiling arced above me. I didn't even attempt to move. Until Teel spoke from behind me. "There you are!"

I whirled to face...her. "Couldn't you at least show up in front of me when you bring me here?"

"Sorry," she muttered. She was dressed like a schoolgirl, her long blond hair held off her face by a black velvet headband. She wore a uniform, a durable polyester skirt in a hideous green-and-white plaid, a too-tight white oxford shirt, and a skimpy hunter-green cardigan. The outfit was ruined—or some might say, perfected—by knee-high black boots, sleek leather that left a few inches of vulnerable leg starkly visible. The vampy look telegraphed that the entire schoolgirl thing was intended as a joke.

That, and the bracelet tattoo of flames that sparked bright in the dull light of this nowhere place.

"Nice," I said wryly. I shook my own hand, still trying to drive away the remnant tingle of my magical transportation.

She twisted a few long strands of hair around her right index finger, taking time to chomp on her gum and blow a bubble before saying, "Totally awesome, huh?" She blew me a kiss.

"You're not quite my type," I said.

She shrugged. "Are you ready to make your third wish?"

"No," I said, shaking my head. "It's only been what? Twenty-four hours? Not even that!"

I expected her to be exasperated with me. Instead, she took a couple of steps away, raising her hands to curl her fingers in front of her. It didn't take a lot of imagination to realize that she was grasping the invisible-to-me iron gate. She closed her eyes and leaned back, breathing so deeply I thought she'd pop off one of her uniform buttons. "Can you smell that?"

"No." I only realized after I'd answered that she'd meant the question to be rhetorical.

"Really?"

"No. I really don't know what you're talking about."

"The hyacinths are, like, totally in bloom."

In college, I'd stage-managed a production of Strindberg's *The Ghost Sonata*. Part of the play took place in the other-worldly Hyacinth Room. I had spent three days tracking down a bottle of perfume scented like the flower so that the cast would understand the imagery of the words they were reciting. The aroma had been intense, floral, the very essence of spring.

I definitely wasn't able to smell hyacinth here. Curiosity got the better of me, and I asked, "How many more wishers do you have to serve before you'll be allowed in?"

Teel sighed, like every disgruntled schoolgirl who had ever faced a parent's absolute injustice. "Two. After you."

Wow. So close. I wondered how long her visit to the Garden would last—she'd made it clear that she wasn't senior enough to stay there forever. But the wistful expression on her young, perfect face almost made me come up with a random third wish, just so that she could enter—for any amount of time.

Almost. But not quite.

"I'm sorry," I said. "I'll think about it. I really will. But I'm just not ready yet. And your dragging me here won't make me decide any faster."

She looked up at me through heavily mascaraed lashes. "Yeah. I was just bored." She stretched the last word into three full syllables.

"Really?" This was the first time I'd really thought about Teel's life outside of my presence. I suddenly remembered Susan, the woman who had apparently locked Teel in his lamp decades before. Had my genie looked for her in the here and now? Had...*he* tried to track her down? Or had he realized that the intervening years had severed their relationship completely?

It felt too prying to ask about Susan, especially asking a girl who looked like the only person she'd want to date was on the cover of *Teen People*. Instead, I asked tentatively, "What do you do when you're not with me? You don't just stand here by the gate, looking into the Garden, do you?"

"No. That would just, like, make me feel sorry for myself." With a perfect pout like that, she could get *herself* on the cover of any magazine.

"So, what? Are you walking around Minneapolis?" That might explain the boots. Not the bare skin flashing between her skirt and the leather, but the boots at least.

"Yeah." She was slipping into typical teen communication, obviously peeved that I was asking too many questions.

"But how do you fill your time? What do you *do?*"

"A little of this. A little of that." She let herself look wistfully back at the invisible gate. "Shopping malls are safest. Or, you know, libraries. Movie theaters. Since you can call me, like, anytime, *to make your third wish,* I need to keep from talking to other humans. It would be totally bad form to disappear in the middle of a conversation, you know?"

Bad form. That was one way to put it. She could single-handedly have dozens of people committed to insane asylums if they ranted about talking to a disappearing minor. Or whatever form she chose to take.

Teel chomped on her gum, then wheedled, "I'd totally like to wrap things up here sooner rather than later, you know? Are you sure you're not ready for your third wish?"

I looked down at my chest. "Seriously, Teel. Do I have some sort of time limit? An expiration date?"

A sly thought flickered through her wide eyes, just a flash, followed by her biting her bottom lip. This incarnation would make a lousy poker player. Teel shook her head before rolling her eyes and sighing in teen exasperation. "Nope. I'm yours till you decide on your last wish."

"So how long do most people take?"

"The good ones?" She smiled winningly. "A day. Two at most."

Her attempted manipulation was so transparent that I snorted. "Too bad for you I'm not one of the good ones."

She sighed and tugged at her uniform skirt before whining, "Can I hang out with you, then? If I'm with you, I don't have to worry about being called away. I can talk to people and stuff."

Stuff. My genie's vocabulary was truly well-suited to her appearance.

Nevertheless, I felt a twinge of guilt. After all, if I could just settle on my last wish, then Teel would be on to her next wisher, that much closer to the Garden. I almost matched my genie sigh for sigh. If she wanted to hang out with me for a few days, could that really be such a big deal? "What do you mean, hang out with me? You'd stay here at the house?"

"Sure. While you're at home. And I'll go to work with you, when it's time for that."

I gritted my teeth. "It would be really hard to have you here. You won't let me tell Maddy and Jules what's going on, and I can't just have a houseguest appear out of nowhere."

Teel frowned, then reached up and tugged her earlobe decisively, twice. A ripple of nothingness stirred through the indeterminate air, as if a stream of not-quite-light was weaving into all the other not-quite-light around me. When I blinked, there was a man standing by my side.

He looked like the proverbial pencil-necked geek, with a generous overbite and ears too large for his head. He wore a white short-sleeved dress shirt, with an actual pocket protector. His brown Dockers were about two inches too short, and his white athletic socks almost blinded me where they flashed above his black lace-up shoes. Even the flame tattoo looked geeky on this guy, as if he'd gotten it years ago, the one time he'd gotten drunk on a debate team trip, pounding back froufrou drinks with umbrellas in them.

"I could be your boyfriend," he said, his voice cracking on the last word. "Someone you just met, that you've fallen head over heels for."

"Thanks a lot," I said, wondering what Teel saw in me that led him to become Nerd Guy, instead of some muscle-bound super-hero. I shook my head. "That's not going to work, either. I haven't been on a date in more than a year. They'd never believe that I'd fallen so hard for you—er, for anyone. Not without talking to them about it along the way. Not without sharing some details."

He scowled and pushed his taped Buddy Holly glasses back up the bridge of his nose. His annoyance combined with his overbite to make him look like a math-genius beaver who had just calculated the water-to-tree-trunk ratio of his latest dam and found the measurement wanting. "Fine. Be that way." Before I could reconsider, he said, "Can we compromise? I'll stay out of your hair while you're at home. But you'll let me go to work with you, at the theater?"

I heard the longing in his voice, almost as strong as when he spoke about the Garden. I heard the desire to be part of some-thing, to *do* something, to be rescued from the infinite boredom of avoiding human beings. I thought of Teel tagging along at rehearsal, though, lurking behind me every waking minute. Posing as my boyfriend, the King of Geeks. That was the last thing I wanted Stephanie Michaelson to see, to pass on to TEWSBU. The last thing I wanted Drew Myers to see, as well.

"You can come," I said grudgingly. "But not like this. Not as my boyfriend."

"As what, then?"

I racked my brain, trying to figure out something noncontroversial, something that wouldn't embarrass me, no matter how Teel played with the form. "A college student," I decided. "A theater major. I'll convince Bill that you need to shadow me for a couple of weeks for a class. An internship, I'll say. For TH 1322. That's a theater arts class called Creating the Performance."

I wasn't certain that I could sell the notion to Bill. Not if it meant having a stranger sit in on rehearsals, watching the delicate bonds that were building between the actors. If that stranger, though, could contribute to the production... If that stranger could help further Bill's crazy gender-bent conceit... "Show up as a woman!" I said. "Someone who can tell Drew Myers how a lovelorn thirteen-year-old girl thinks." Someone whose breasts were a little more conversational than my own, I thought, but did not say.

"You want me to be a teenager?"

I thought of the little vamp who had just been standing there in nothing space with me. Then I imagined the questions Bill was likely to ask, the directions he would push our star little witness. The last thing we needed was for someone to report the show to the police, citing corruption of a minor. "No," I said, making my voice firm. "You've definitely got to be legal. Just make it so that you remind them of Juliet. Can you do that? Do you know the play?"

The smile on Geek-boy's face was a little predatory. A lot creepy. "Yeah," he said. "I can do Juliet."

"Good." I tried to believe that this was an excellent idea. At least my breasts would never have to speak up at rehearsal, ever again.

As things turned out, Teel could have hung out around the house as my geek boyfriend, my lesbian lover, or my vacationing Aunt Minerva—Maddy and Jules would never have known. It was nearly two weeks before I saw either of them in person.

During that time, Maddy left a number of messages on the white board, all in pidgin German. From that, I concluded that her romance with Herr Wunderbar continued to flourish. If past experience proved an accurate predictor, the relationship had no more than a few days left before Maddy showed her dreamboat to the door. I hoped he was having as good a time as Maddy seemed to be.

Jules's trip to Santa Barbara was followed by a week of heavy work reprising her role as Stubborn Defendant for a new training video. This one was called *So You Lost at Trial, Here's Your Appeal!* I gathered that Jules was spending a lot of time stomping around in high heels, telling her "lawyers" all the mistakes they'd made when they didn't follow the instructions from earlier videos.

Rehearsals sucked up almost every waking hour for me. I left the house before nine every morning, and I was lucky if I got home before nine at night. Bill had a million problems for me to solve, a thousand new details were introduced every day. I was learning more than I ever thought I could, but I tumbled into bed, exhausted, every night.

As if the theater weren't enough to keep me busy, Teel pulled me into the nowhere space of the Garden every three days, like clockwork. My genie stared wistfully at the invisible iron gate, sighing about amazing floral scents that I could never detect. Teel adopted a different persona for each of those jaunts—one visit he looked like the classic genie-in-a-lamp with flowing Arabian pants and a turban; the next visit she became a spinster school-marm from the 1800s. Our trips to nowheresville got shorter and shorter—I still had absolutely no idea what I wanted to wish for, and I was disinclined to stand in nothingness while Teel wheedled.

After one particularly frustrating visit—Teel had adopted a beekeeper's suit, complete with a heavily veiled hat, so that I couldn't see his face as he berated me for my indecision—my housemates and I found a Thursday night to stay home together and order in from Hunan Delight. Outside, it was snowing lightly, and we'd made a big pot of oolong tea while we waited for our food. Jules had a set of porcelain teacups, white and handle-less, just like the ones in restaurants. The tea had nowhere near the caffeine content of the coffee that I regularly pumped into my veins, but it was hot, which was a substantial virtue.

I ran downstairs to pay off the driver. We'd placed the order early enough that the Swensons didn't get involved; even if their doorbell had been rung by mistake, they didn't get nasty until after nine o'clock.

Upstairs, I left my muffler looped around my neck, still too cold to take it off. Jules was flipping Scrabble tiles over in the top of the box while Maddy unpacked the order.

"Hot and sour soup," she said. "Eight Treasures Chicken. Here's your winter melon soup, Jules. And what *is* Dragon and Phoenix?"

"Shrimp and chicken, with vegetables, in a spicy sauce." Jules made it sound as common as pork fried rice.

"Did they leave my Hunan sauce on the side?" I asked.

"Yep," Maddy confirmed. "I can't believe you didn't order soup. And steamed vegetables? I don't think you've *ever* had steamed vegetables in all the time we've been ordering from Hunan Delight."

I laughed. "So you think that I should just get the same thing, every single visit?"

"Hey, I happen to enjoy Eight Treasures Chicken!"

"And I happen to enjoy steamed vegetables," I said.

Jules and Maddy exchanged A Look. Apparently, Jules was elected spokesperson. "Kira, Maddy and I have both noticed how you've lost weight. We hadn't even realized how hard you were trying. These past two weeks must have really made a difference—we can really see it in your face."

I felt a twinge of guilt. Dieters all across America would kill for a single wish from Teel. I brushed my flame-tattooed fingertips firmly enough that I felt the tingle up to my shoulder.

Sure, my new body had embarrassed me on its first public outing. But maybe it was time to grab the proverbial bull by the horns. Time to buy new clothes—at least a new bra, so that I could wear my old clothes without spilling out of them. No matter how crazy my schedule was, I had to be able to find a *few* hours for shopping. Right?

For now, though, I needed to create a distraction. "You know how it is. Sometimes a diet just clicks, and it's easy to follow. For a while, anyway. Until there's a pepperoni pizza on the table." We all laughed together, and then I edged the conversation away from me. "So," I said to Maddy. "How's the show? Did you finally make it bright enough and happy enough?"

"Oh, yeah. Just bright enough that the entire audience could see the curtain jam opening night. And they got a great view of the lid on the wishing well getting stuck. But it was all worthwhile when Bo-Peep totally lost it during curtain call. Her robotic sheep went right off the magnetic track and plunged into the audience. The kids got quite an education—they learned all sorts of new vocabulary words."

Jules made a face. We'd all seen our share of disastrous opening nights. She asked me, "Speaking of an education, how are Transgendered R & J getting along?"

"As well as can be expected," I said. "We've already gone through three boxes of Hefty bags, though."

"Hefty bags?" Maddy looked at me like I was nuts.

I nodded. "Bill's trying to turn everything upside down in

the show. Our fair Verona all takes place in the sewers. Bill wants the actors to think about slippery stuff, about slime beneath the city streets."

"Sounds really appetizing," Jules said, making a face. She pushed her spoon around in her soup.

I hurried on. "He wants everyone wearing a Hefty bag at each rehearsal. He says it'll help them keep in mind the 'oppressive nature of the streets.' I say it makes them all a bit, um, ripe by the end of a hard day's work."

"Eww," Jules said, bravely spooning up another dose of winter melon. I thought that the white broth looked disgusting, but I didn't say anything. I'd already done enough damage to everyone's appetite.

"Let's just say that some of them can carry it off better than others." I smiled wickedly, thinking of Stephanie Michaelson trying to preserve Mercutio's wit, her hair plastered to her head after an afternoon of swaggering around in a trash bag. If only TEWSBU could drop by rehearsal then…. Not that I actually wanted TEWSBU anywhere near our play. I forced my thoughts away from my ex. "Drew makes the whole thing seem almost normal."

"Dreeeeeew," Maddy said, drawing out his name. "Do tell!"

I blushed. I hadn't made my comment offhand enough. "There isn't anything to tell. He's just a really good actor."

Jules shared a sly glance with Maddy as she pounced on my words with all the bare-clawed determination of a starving panther. "I know that tone of voice! Really good actor. Right! Like you can tell that, with him reading all of Juliet's lines."

"He *can* read Juliet's lines," I protested. "That's the thing. When he says them, they actually make sense!" I heard the vehemence in my voice and I hurried to explain myself. "I know it sounds like I'm a little brainwashed, but I really think that

Bill was onto something when he did the casting. When a guy says, 'Deny thy father and refuse thy name,' it doesn't sound like a whiny little girl, daring her boyfriend to prove his love. A guy makes it sound brave. Defiant. Like a statement of belief."

Maddy sniffed. "That's just because we're preconditioned to think of girls as whiny and moonstruck, and to believe that boys are brave and serious."

"Exactly!" I said. "That's my point. That's Bill's point."

"And Drew?" Jules teased. "Is that his point, too?"

I decided that it was time to move on from soup to main dishes. Instead of replying to Jules's taunt, I scooped my dinner from the red take-out container onto my plate. Jules and Maddy both looked at my vegetables suspiciously, but I was truly pleased by the bright green of the pea pods, the soft yellow of the baby corn. I dipped the tines of my fork into my Hunan sauce and speared a bite of perfectly steamed carrot. "Mmm," I said while I chewed.

"You're not going to divert us with carrots," Jules said. "Come on. What's really going on with you and Drew?"

Oh, how I wanted to have an answer to that question.

I wanted to say that we'd had a dozen heartfelt conversations. I wanted to say that we huddled next to each other at every rehearsal, ducking out for a quick cup of coffee at breaks. I wanted to say that we shared private little jokes, secret glosses on the script, on the actors, on the way the show was evolving.

Unfortunately, our relationship—such as it was—hadn't progressed to that stage yet. He mostly hung out with the guys, talking about the Wild's losing hockey season. But every single time I talked to him, I got one of those ridiculous rushes, the sort of fits that made me giggle and gasp like I was in high school. When he looked up from discussing goaltenders and defensemen—even if he was just smiling absentmindedly as I called the cast to order—my heart started pounding like a wild creature trapped in a cage.

I was smitten.

I shrugged. "He asked me to run lines with him during lunch break yesterday."

Maddy rolled her eyes. "Isn't that romantic."

"Like you're one to judge!" I said. "Sometimes romance is more than just jumping into bed!"

I think I was more surprised by my vehemence than my housemates were. They both stared at me, and I put down my fork. I had to say something, so I muttered, "He brought me a muffin yesterday."

I didn't bother to say that he'd brought them for everyone who had the early rehearsal call. And Maddy and Jules didn't need to hear that I'd taken the last one out of the bag. And they definitely didn't need to know that the flavor had been orange coconut.

I hated coconut.

Teel had eaten my muffin, along with her own lemon pop-pyseed.

Nope. No need at all to bore my housemates with all the details of my busy theatrical life.

Jules speared a perfect butterflied shrimp and chewed carefully before asking in a breezy tone (Read: Changing the topic of our conversation entirely), "So, who's this Teel person?"

I almost choked on a bite of broccoli. "Teel?"

Jules nodded. "Stephanie Michaelson mentioned her at the *Little Women* audition on Saturday, at the Spirit."

Maddy interrupted. "I didn't know you were auditioning for *Little Women*! What made you try for that?"

"Who wouldn't want to play Jo?" Jules smiled.

Maddy snorted. "You? Jo? Maybe you could have pulled that off five years ago." She forked another one of the Eight Treasures into her mouth. "Don't look at me that way, Jules. You know how crazy this business is. Jo is supposed to be what, sixteen in the play?"

"Fifteen."

"And you're twenty-six. And you don't play young." Another bite of rice, to punctuate her evaluation. "Kira, come on, you have to agree with me! We all promised years ago that we wouldn't lie to each other. Besides, Jules, Laurel Martin is directing that show! She'll never cast an attractive woman if there's a dog she can put into the lead instead."

I shook my head. It wasn't that I disagreed with Maddy. Laurel was legendary for finding the ugliest women she could for her productions. She always managed to find the prettiest boys, too—she was partial to long lashes and delicate features, even when she was casting hardened, soul-dry villains. Local reviewers had commented on her decisions in both the *StarTribune* and the *Pioneer Press*, but Laurel wasn't about to change her ways. She craved the power that came with being the director.

Still, it wasn't kind of Maddy, telling Jules that she was too old for the role. Each of us was getting older, every single day. And the theater was a cruel world for a woman who couldn't play young.

When I remained uneasily silent, Maddy bulled on ahead. "Well?" she said to Jules. "How did the audition go?"

Jules drained her glass of ice water. She fiddled with her fork. She took a sip of tea. "She asked me to read for another role."

"Which one?" Any minute now, Maddy was going to produce a glaring white light, demand to know where Jules had been on the night of July the thirty-first.

Jules whispered, "Marmee." The mother.

"You're way too young for Marmee!" I said, glaring daggers at Maddy. And then, even though I wanted to avoid the topic of

Teel, I felt obligated to rescue Jules. Housemate loyalty made me slant the conversation back in a direction I would have preferred to avoid altogether. "So, Stephanie mentioned Teel?"

Jules flashed me a grateful smile. "Just to say that she'd been hanging out at rehearsals. Helping answer questions. I gather Teel's a bit, um, outspoken?"

That was one way of putting it.

"Bill has this weird Method thing he's doing," I explained. "He wants the men to understand how a woman thinks, how we feel. He wants to get a woman's view on the script, to share it with the guys, but he doesn't want the women in the cast to share their thoughts, their experiences. *They* have to get used to thinking like men."

Maddy and Jules looked skeptical. Let's face it. I'd been skeptical, too.

Maddy said, "So what's the deal? This Teel is like a translator?"

"Every time we start a new scene, Bill has Teel explain what she'd be thinking if she were Juliet. You know, when she first tells her nurse about seeing Romeo, about falling for this guy solely on the basis of looks. Teel takes an experience from her own past—from her real life—and shares it with the guys."

"Uh-huh," Maddy said.

Better Teel than me, I wanted to say. Instead, I tried to think of a good example. All I could remember, though, was the scene my genie had dredged up on her first day at rehearsal. Following our agreement, I had summoned her, pressing my fingers together and calling her name before driving down to the Landmark. Teel had chosen her appearance conservatively—she looked pretty much like every young college student on the University of Minnesota campus. Every one that weighed a hundred pounds soaking wet. And wore jeans slung low around her hips. And a scarlet thong clearly visible above her studded leather belt. And a short ribbed T-shirt that bared the silver ring in her navel. And four piercings in the cartilage of her right ear. And, of course, the flames tattooed around her wrist.

I'd made her wait in the lobby while I asked Bill whether she could join us. As I'd predicted, he'd been reluctant at first, worried about her taking his ideas, sharing them with journalists or reviewers or other cultural spies before he was ready to disclose our unique production. He'd run a hand over his bald head and squinted up at the ceiling, talking to me about the sanctity of the rehearsal room, the compact that the cast members made with one another.

But then he'd looked out into the lobby and seen the compact little package that Teel presented. I could almost literally see the wheels turn in his all-too-masculine mind.

Teel was no fool. She'd smiled across the lobby, biting her lip with just the right semblance of timidity. She settled her hand on her hip. I'm pretty sure that she nudged the tattoo just a bit, too, made it sparkle across the room.

Bill invited her to join us, as if she were some long-lost friend.

And in almost two weeks, he'd never looked back at his decision. At each and every rehearsal, I'd heard way more than I cared to about the imagined love life of my genie.

Okay, maybe it wasn't imagined. Maybe every single word of it was real. After all, Teel had lived through the sexual revolution. She had found her G-spot before my peers even knew that they were looking for theirs.

And she had a contemporary vocabulary to describe her experiences.

It wasn't as if I hadn't heard the words before. They were some perfectly good nouns. A few decent verbs. A shockingly apt compound adjective.

But there was something more than a little unseemly about

the way all the guys hung around her. Something inappropriate about the way they dredged up individual lines, asked about character motivation for each and every Elizabethan phrase in the script. There was something just plain icky about the way they worshipped Teel and her recollections, about the way they never seemed to realize that she went *way* beyond the text in her recollections.

"Give us an example," Jules urged, spearing another bite of spicy shrimp.

I fumbled for one that didn't make us all sound like perverts. "Well… We were talking about the scene where Juliet describes Romeo to her nurse, where she first learns his name. Juliet's line is 'Prodigious birth of love it is to me, that I must love a loathed enemy.' Drew asked Teel if she'd ever loved an 'enemy.'"

I leaned back in my chair, fiddling with my fork as I remembered how the conversation had played out.

"Teel told him about this time in high school, when she developed a crush on a guy who was completely wrong for her. She was a totally emo kid, a freshman on the literary arts magazine, in the photography club. But she fell for the guy who had the locker next to hers, literally the senior who was captain on the football team."

I closed my eyes for a second, remembering the energy in the rehearsal room as Teel had spun out her story. Once again, I had no idea whether my genie was telling the truth or not. She might have just been creating a script, entertaining herself because she didn't have anything better to do with her time. Then again, she really might have fallen for the wrong guy at some point in her past. She might have been taken in by a totally cut body, by a jawline too rugged to be true, by chocolate-brown eyes sparked by just a hint of green….

I dragged my mind away from Drew and told Jules and

Maddy, "She said, 'We did it in the locker room. After the team lost in the State quarterfinals. I'd come in to take pictures of what was left behind, the towels and the game programs and stuff. I hadn't realized that he'd still be there, sitting all alone.'"

Teel had started crying as she spoke. Her words became more graphic as she described the specific things they'd done, the details of how she'd lost her supposed virginity. Woven into her profanity was a true story of love and loss, the true heartbreak of a girl who'd thought she was making a connection but found out that she was only being used. The quarterback had hurt her, had pushed her fragile shoulder blades into the cement floor. But the real pain was the next day, when he'd pretended nothing had happened, that he didn't even know her. The real pain had lasted for the rest of the school year, when he never said another word to her, no matter how many times he saw her at her locker, first thing, every single morning.

I said, "A couple of the guys in the cast were blinking hard when she was through with her story. Bill whispered, 'Marvelous,' and he just kept staring at Teel, shaking his head. It was like she created something there. She made the story come alive. She gave Juliet's line, Juliet's enemy, real meaning."

Maddy and Jules nodded, beginning to understand. For some reason, I didn't tell them what had happened next. I didn't tell them about how the touching scene had broken up.

There'd been a sound in the doorway, a cross between a snort and a cough. I'd looked up to see John McRae standing there, rolling a sheaf of drawings between his palms. He'd nodded at me, and his voice was too loud, too rough for the shamed, chagrined men in the cast when he said, "You got a second, Franklin?"

I'd glanced at Bill for permission before following John out into the lobby. He was chortling as he spread out his designs.

"What's so funny?"

"The horseshit that friend of yours is selling," he'd said, taking a pencil from behind his ear and starting to point to a specific drawing.

I hadn't bothered explaining that she was, supposedly, my intern, not my friend. "How can you say that!"

"There isn't a word she said in there that's true." He'd planted his hands on the table, fingers spread wide to anchor the pages.

"How do you know?"

"How many high schools put freshmen's lockers next to seniors'?"

"I don't know! A lot of them, I'd guess!"

"And what high school on the face of God's green earth is going to let a freshman girl hang out in the boy's locker room after a game? Without a chaperone? A coach? Anyone at all? It didn't happen, Kira. I'm telling you. It absolutely didn't happen." He'd shaken his head, making me feel stupid for having been taken in.

I'd wanted to call him a liar. But I already *knew* that Teel wasn't what she seemed. I knew that Teel's very presence in the theater was an elaborate masquerade. She had told me that she was bored. Wasn't it possible—likely, even—that she was just spinning out her stories to spark her own interest?

I'd sighed in frustration and taken a look at John's drawings. "What is this?"

"The new design for Friar Laurence's cell."

"What's new about it?"

"Bill didn't say anything?" I'd shaken my head. "He decided he doesn't want to go with the trapdoor. Instead, he wants a culvert to fly in from the top."

"A *culvert?*"

John had shrugged, as if he were asked to create sewer systems for every play he worked on. "There isn't space to fly it in. We'll have to roll it on from stage left." He'd flipped back two pages to show me what he'd done. It was a good design, and it definitely added to the oppressiveness of underground Verona.

"What's the problem, then?"

"It's getting mighty crowded back there," John had said, pointing to the offstage space.

"We'll manage." I'd sounded a little skeptical, but I was sure that it would all work out.

"It's going to get expensive. Paying extra hands to move the damned thing."

"That's the Landmark's problem. And Bill's. We'll get by."

"I'm sure we will," he'd said, rolling up his plans and tapping them against the table. "I just wanted to make sure you knew what was going on." He'd looked at me steadily, inviting a return to our previous conversation, the one about Teel. I'd chickened out, though, and told him that I had to get back to the rehearsal. I was pretty sure that he'd watched me the entire time that I walked across the lobby, watched until I'd disappeared into the well-lit rehearsal room.

No, I wasn't going to share John's supposed insight with Maddy and Jules. No reason to make them think any more about Teel. Especially since my genie was sure to stifle most answers I could give about who she really was, what she was actually doing at our rehearsals.

In any case, I discovered an easy escape from the conversation. "Wait a second! Where are our fortune cookies?"

Maddy sprang up and grabbed them from the kitchen counter. "What?" Jules said. "You didn't get into them before the food?"

"You didn't give me a chance," she pouted. She worked her cookie free from its cellophane wrapper, crushing it into two pieces without further delay. "'You are about to go on a journey,'" she intoned. "Wunderbar!"

"Hey," I said. "How did we finish this entire meal without your telling us about the man of the month?"

Maddy waved away my exclamation, shrugging off her romantic interest as if he were already fading in her memory. "I figured I shouldn't waste your time. Gunther heads out to New York next week. He's a fight director. They're doing *Henry V* at Shakespeare in the Park next summer."

Jules laughed at Maddy's typical dismissal. She opened her own cookie and read, "'Today is a sunny day.' That's not a fortune!" she complained. "It's a weather forecast. And it's wrong!"

They both crunched on their cookies while I opened my own. The little slip of paper tore as I tried to take it out, but I could still read the words: "'A wise man wishes for good.'"

Maddy and Jules laughed at the simple sentiment, but the words sent a chill creeping down my spine. I dropped the cookie onto my unfinished plate of vegetables, taking the time to roll the fortune into a tiny scroll.

I wasn't a wise man. And I didn't know what was good. But I had a wish to make. A third wish—and it was starting to weigh heavily on me.

Jules was laughing and saying, "Really? But you don't even *speak* German! How can you communicate anything to each other?"

"Wait!" I said, consciously shaking off my dark mood. "German! Herr Wunderbar? Go back! What did I miss?"

Maddy regaled us with tales of Gunther the Fight Director for the rest of the evening, as we cleared the table and settled into a ferocious game of Scrabble. I lost by a hundred points, though, unable to concentrate on wooden tiles when I thought about what I might choose for my third wish. Maybe I'd be boring and ask for an entire new wardrobe. After all, if my *room-mates* had noticed the change in my appearance, then I might be just one killer outfit away from finally getting the attention of Drew Myers. If, that was, Drew could ever find my clothing more interesting than hockey. Or the stories that Teel was telling about her supposed deep, dark past.

And if I cast my third wish, then Teel would go away, wouldn't she? I wouldn't have to listen to her stories ever again. I wouldn't have to debate whether she was telling the truth or weaving elaborate lies. I wouldn't have to face John McRae's patient skepticism.

I wasn't ready to make Teel disappear. Yet. But I had to admit that the temptation was getting a little stronger every single day.

CHAPTER 10

THE NEXT MORNING, I STOPPED IN AT CLUB JOE before rehearsal, knowing that extreme caffeine was necessary—even by my inflated definition. We were starting on the balcony scene, the absolute essence of *Romeo and Juliet,* and I wasn't sure that I was ready to handle the theatrical revelations, Bill Pomeroy–style, that were certain to appear, by way of Teel.

I got to the shop about an hour before rehearsal was scheduled to start, so I decided to settle in at a table. I thought about buying a slice of pound cake to extend my "rental" of the space, but I figured there were already a dozen other customers snarfing up the computer connection for no more than the cost of a small coffee. I'd bought a large latte, with a shot of hazelnut syrup and four extra shots of espresso; that was more than adequate dues. With eight weeks to go till opening night, I was seriously considering having my paycheck direct-deposited at the coffee shop.

I dug out my script notebook so that I could review my ever-growing list of notes for the various designers. While John had been around a lot, focusing on the set, I hadn't seen Alex

Munoz, our sound designer, for days. Bill had decided that he wanted all of the actors miked, even—especially—the ones with strong voices. He wanted the option of running their lines through a reverb chamber, making it sound like their words were echoing in the tunnels beneath Verona.

The day before, Bill had also asked me to talk to David Barstow, the lighting designer. Bill wanted all of the colors taken down a notch from the ones they'd discussed months before—darker blues, deeper browns. David wasn't going to be pleased; he'd already told me that he thought we were going from a "mood" to a "statement." (Read: He was losing artistic control to an overbearing director.) I didn't care so much about Barstow's artistic integrity; I was just starting to worry about how many rolls of glow tape I'd need to buy to mark off every possible corner, doorway, and sharp edge on the twilit set.

There was something else that I was supposed to tell the designers…. Something that had come up at rehearsal the night before. I'd been about to write it down last night, when Drew had come over to get a couple of Advils. I'd lost my train of thought as I'd dug into my backpack, muttering words of comfort to ease his headache, resisting the urge to offer him a neck rub. A back rub. More.

I shrugged. The note would come back to me. Most likely in the middle of today's rehearsal, when I was frantically scribbling down something else entirely. Like "buy more trash bags." We'd gone through another two boxes. The women kept catching them on chairs and door frames, and they refused to wear the same bag after we'd taken a break, saying that they got slimy.

Slimy! That wasn't the thing I'd forgotten, but I remembered another note, one for the costume designer. I dashed out the word *sibilant*—a reminder that Bill wanted the costumes to slither audibly when the actors moved, not just to look reptilian. As I dotted the second *i* I heard a familiar voice say, "Is this seat taken?"

Drew.

Drew Myers, inviting himself to join me. With or without my future tense new wardrobe.

I was so astonished, I almost spat coffee all over the table. Realizing just in time, though, that such an action wasn't likely to endear the man to me forever after, I remembered to smile like an ordinary human being and gesture toward the extra chair. "Please," I said, trying to sound casual, like I'd known he was going to stop by, that he was going to talk to me.

"You are just the woman I wanted to see!" he said, rattling his cup in his saucer as he leaned closer across the table.

I couldn't help it. I smiled as if he'd just proposed.

Oh, I wasn't an idiot. I was pretty sure that he didn't want to see me, as *me*. He wanted to see me as stage manager. He wanted to ask me for a favor. He wanted me to do something related to the production. But even as I reminded myself about all that, a giddy little voice inside my head said, "I'm the woman he wants to see! I'm the woman he wants!"

I snarled at the voice to shut up, or I was going to make a fool out of myself.

"What's up?" I asked.

Right then and there, I should have been nominated for an Ivey—I was the undisputed lead actress in a major Twin Cities production that winter. Hell, they should have handed me an Oscar, too, thrown in an Emmy and a Tony for good measure. I'd made my voice sound perfectly light, easy. I was interested, but not overly eager. I was—in a word—normal.

"Did you happen to find my cell phone when you closed up last night?"

Crash! That clattering sound was the complete toppling of my expectations, the shattering of my dreams. Yeah, I'd told myself not to care, not to imagine anything special, not to generate a wisp of hope. I never was very good at listening to myself.

Unbidden, I pictured TEWSBU. I saw him shaking his head in disgust when I'd let my dreams get ahead of our reality. I saw him sigh in exasperation when I'd suggested that we take some time for ourselves, that we do something as a couple, that we pretend to be two people in love instead of two professionals working in the theater.

Drew wasn't TEWSBU, I chided silently.

No, Drew was the star of my current show. He was my current crush. And he was waiting patiently, as if I weren't a madwoman carrying on a conversation in the privacy of my own brain.

"You lost it?" I asked. This time, I didn't manage quite as perfect a tone of nonchalance. I let myself be distracted by the worried glint in his eyes. I barely kept from reaching out to pat his hand. *In sympathy,* I remonstrated with myself. I was going to pat his hand in sympathy!

He shrugged, looking like a grown-up Dennis the Menace. He hadn't shaved that morning, and his beard was coming in with glints of gold, tiny prickles that caught the light and darted it back toward my heart. "I know I had it yesterday morning, but when I got home last night, it wasn't in my pocket."

"Did you try calling it?"

He stared at me, thunderstruck, as if my suggestion involved the finer points of nuclear fusion and astrophysics combined. "Dude! I am such an idiot."

He was cute when he was self-condemning. Okay. He was gorgeous anytime. "You would have thought of it," I assured him. "After you got some caffeine into your bloodstream."

That seemed to remind him that he had a perfectly good five dollar cup of coffee sitting in front of him. He took a swig, raising his head with just a hint of a whipped cream mustache. A rather dashing whipped cream mustache it was, but I handed him one of my extra napkins. Stage managers always have extra napkins. We use them to help us resist the urge to lick off whipped cream mustaches from the lips of stunningly handsome leading men.

I fished my phone out of my backpack and punched in his number. Before the missing phone could start ringing, Drew said, "You know my number?"

I wanted to melt away. I wanted to slip under the table, escape out into the snow. I wanted to be anywhere but sitting in this coffee shop, listening to four tinny rings, trying to think of a reason why I could just dial up his cell without a second's hesitation. As his voice mail picked up, though, the perfect answer came to me. Perfect because it contained a single grain of truth.

"I'm a stage manager," I said, flipping my phone closed without leaving a message. "It's my job to know everyone's number. If Bill needs to reach you quickly, he shouldn't have to wait for me to look up your number. Or," I added quickly, "anyone else's."

Drew grinned. "Dude! So you memorized everyone in the show's? How about Bill? What's his?"

I looked Drew straight in the eye and rattled off ten numbers, a local area code followed by seven totally random digits.

"That's amazing!"

If he only knew. I figured I'd better stop the game, though, before he asked me to recite one of the actor's numbers, one that he might actually recognize. I tossed my phone in the bottom of my bag. "Try calling your phone at different times of the day. If someone's picked it up, they should answer."

"What other magic do you do?" he asked.

I patted my backpack and tried to smile demurely, all the

time resisting the urge to shout out and dance in the center of the room. He thought I was magic! *Magic!* I resisted the urge to look at my tattooed fingertips, to speculate on the real, genie-backed magic I could work. Instead, I fought a losing battle to sound offhand. "I know all the downtown restaurants that have private rooms, and the places that are open after midnight. Especially the ones with decent beers on tap."

"You're too good to be true!" He drained the last of his drink, settling the cup on its saucer with a finality that almost made me faint.

"Aw, you say that to all the girls," I deflected. Before I could rack my brain for additional banter, I glanced at the large clock on the wall. My disappointment was real, not an act, as I said, "I'm also a perfect alarm clock. We've got to get over to the theater."

He waited while I gulped the last of my coffee. As we both stood up, I was afraid that he was going to hold my coat for me. I could never find the sleeves when a guy did that; I always managed to snag the collar and force the garment awkwardly toward the floor.

Fortunately, he wasn't quite that much a gentleman. He *did* hold the door as we left, though. I let myself lean into his arm, pretending for just a second that he was going to pull me close as the winter wind stole my breath away. I imagined the heat of his body radiating through the sleeve of his coat, through the sleeve of mine.

I was truly head over heels. Truly, disgustingly, head over heels.

Bill and John were already in the rehearsal room when we got there. "Hi, guys," I said, tossing my backpack on a chair. "I would have opened up earlier, if I'd known you were meeting." All the same, I was grateful that I hadn't needed to walk away from Drew, leave him behind at Club Joe, just to make yet another tech meeting.

Bill barely glanced up from the worktable, which was covered with drawings. "We were going over new plans for the balcony."

Drew shrugged off his coat and came to stare. "Dude! What is that?"

John pushed back from the table, a frown pulling down his mustache. The pencil tucked behind his ear made him look like a cross between an absentminded professor and a plumber. He tapped with one blunt finger and deepened his Texas twang, obviously putting us all on. "That there is a gen-u-ine manhole cover." He dropped back into normal speech. "We're buying it from the city, from the repaving project they completed on Lake a while back. Those are the chains to support it." He gestured toward the sketched lines. "It'll fly in from the top. There'll be an iron circle welded around it, so you can open it like a porthole. You'll be able to lean out."

"Cool," Drew said.

But Bill was shaking his head, running an agitated hand over his pate. I noticed that *he,* unlike Drew, had taken the time to shave that morning, as he did *every* morning. The bones of his skull made him look hungry. Even more demanding than usual. "It's not enough," he insisted, clearly continuing a discussion that had started before Drew and I arrived. "The design will turn this into a play about chains. They're all the audience is going to see."

"I already explained," John said patiently. "We can't use wire. That thing is too damned heavy."

"If you can't figure out how to do this, I can definitely ask around. Someone has to be able to figure out how to suspend that manhole cover." I was shocked by Bill's nasty tone. He was like a child berating a babysitter who had told him that he had to go to bed early.

John didn't take the bait. "You can ask anyone you want.

Anything less than a one-ton chain puts every single actor on that stage at risk."

Bill sighed, thoroughly aggrieved. "We're creating a reality here! We're building a complete world, down to every last detail. If we show the audience a manhole cover, if we put the chains in plain sight, it will jar everyone out of the illusion. This is the *balcony* scene. This is *Romeo and Juliet*." He threw up his hands in frustration. "Drew, I'm obviously not getting through to him. See if you can explain."

Drew gulped audibly before spreading a blinding smile across his face. He clapped a hand on John's shoulder as if they were the best of friends. "This is *Romeo and Juliet,* dude."

John shrugged off the touch, barely managing to make his action look like a reflex and not a planned personal affront. He took a deep breath and exhaled slowly. When he spoke, his drawl was deeper than ever. "Why don't we ditch the manhole cover, the real one. I'll make one out of foam. Paint it up, put it under lights—not even the first row will be able to tell it isn't real."

Bill slammed his hand down on the table, making all of us jump. "Have you heard one single thing I've said? It has to be real! It has to be solid! In our Verona, men carry iron pipes instead of swords. They beat the walls to prove their manhood."

John looked at Bill as if the director had sprouted two heads. "Iron pipes?"

Bill turned on me. "I thought you were going to tell him about that change? I thought that you were letting all the designers know about the iron pipe swords!"

I winced. *That* was the note I'd been trying to remember in the coffee shop, the one that had seemed so obvious the other day that I hadn't even bothered to write it down.

"This isn't about Franklin." John refused to raise his voice to match Bill's. Instead, he softened his words, lowered his pitch, and told a blatant lie. "She told me about the pipes, but I thought your gals could try beating on something else for one damn scene."

I tried not to look surprised, tried not to give away the fact that John was covering for me. I don't know that Bill would even have noticed; he was spluttering over the notion of his "gals" being restrained from expressing their perfect creativity in any way whatsoever.

John pretended not to notice. Instead, he said, "What if..." He trailed off, staring at some invisible point in the middle distance. He nodded, and then went on. "What if we put the manhole cover on a frame? Hell, put five or six of them there, a dozen, make it look like some underground junkyard. We can weld the damn things onto two frames, roll them in from the wings. They can lock into place, solid enough for whatever clanging you want."

Clutching a pencil with fingers that seemed just a little too tense, John sketched out his thoughts, materializing the metal frames with a few brisk lines. I was impressed by how quickly he adapted his drawings; if I hadn't seen his temper flare, I never would have believed that he was making this up as he went along, that he had never considered massive iron scaffolding until two minutes before.

Bill narrowed his eyes as he studied John's drawing. "I like it." His nodding picked up speed. "Yes, I definitely like it. I knew you could come up with something, if you'd just take a moment to think."

John ignored the insult that trailed after the compliment. Instead, he scratched a couple of quick calculations on the corner of the drawing. After pulling a firm line at the bottom of a column of numbers, he said, "There's only one problem."

"What's that?" Bill's voice had turned sharp again.

"We'll need eight stagehands to move the frames. We already added four last week, for the sheet metal on Friar Laurence's cell. But we'll need four more."

Bill shrugged. "It's only money."

John shot a quick look to me, but I just raised my eyebrows and offered a minute shrug. I had already told him—I was responsible for making the show run. I didn't keep an eye on the checkbook. That was Bill's job. Bill and the producers. What were another four union stagehands, when we were creating *art?*

John said, "Then let me talk to the guys down in the shop. I'll see what we can do."

Bill looked at his wrist theatrically. He still didn't wear a watch, but we all knew that he was chiding us for losing track of time. "We've only got eight weeks left."

"I've never been late delivering a set yet," John said. He squinted at his drawing. "I need to make some new measurements, make sure these frames'll fit backstage. Can I borrow your tape measure, Franklin?"

I extracted the tool from my backpack. I wasn't an idiot. I could see that John wanted to talk to me. I suspected that he wanted to get our stories straight on the lead pipe thing, to make sure that there wasn't anything else I was supposed to have told him. I wanted to say that I was sorry, that I hadn't meant to add to the challenge of dealing with our temperamental director.

Before I could move, though, Bill picked up his script, making a big show of turning to the proper page for the day's rehearsal. He was clearly ready to start. I handed the tape measure to John, trying to send brainwaves that I'd catch up with him later. He nodded, either reading my mind or just accepting the tool, and then he slouched off into the lobby.

I heard John mutter a greeting to someone, and I looked up,

expecting to see Jennifer. Our Romeo still hadn't arrived; it was unlike her to be late.

But no. It was Teel. Of course.

She always made a grand entrance, at least ten minutes past the time rehearsal was called for. I'd spoken to her the first few times it happened, but she wasn't about to change her behavior on my ineffective say-so. Somehow, I didn't think my genie *ever* changed her behavior, for anyone.

Bill tolerated her tardiness, accepting Teel's outrageousness in a way that he never would have tolerated with one of his actors. Bill never looked at his bare wrist when Teel was late. Bill liked Teel. Everyone liked Teel. All the men, at least.

My genie had outdone herself today. She was wearing a tiny black T-shirt, a scrap that looked better suited to a Barbie doll than to an actual adult female. Apparently, she hadn't been able to find a bra to match. I made a mental note to turn up the heat before the next rehearsal.

Teel's makeup overcompensated for her lack of undergarments. She must have discovered liquid eyeliner in her ramblings around town, along with a shade of lipstick that reminded me of a fire truck. Alas, a hairbrush seemed beyond her magical ability.

Before I could say anything, my entire body jangled with the energy that meant Teel was working her magic. My eyes closed without my permission. My skin crawled with the full force of my genie's dangerous electricity. When the shock faded to a dull tingle, I forced myself to look around.

Nothing.

I was back in the nowhere space. This time, I was smart enough to look behind me. No Teel, though. No intern-strumpet, no schoolgirl, not any of the guises I'd previously seen. I sighed in frustration and turned forward again (not that it made any difference to me, in the great nothingness outside the supposed Garden).

And Teel was waiting, an earnest grin on his face. He was dressed as an electrician, with a clipboard in his meaty hand and an embroidered name tag on his chest. A tool belt was slung low around his waist, bristling with insulated pliers, wire strippers, and a half dozen other tools. "Looking for me?" His voice was a bit higher than I expected, and he supplemented his words with a nervous laugh, running plump fingers through his ginger hair.

"What the hell are you doing? We're supposed to be at rehearsal!"

"They won't miss us." The burly guy cocked his head, as if he heard something in the distance. He scratched at his freckled nose. "The stream is running high in the Garden," he said. "You can hear it from here. There must have been a lot of rain lately. Look how much the vines have grown!"

I refused to stare at nothing, refused to pretend that I could see some monsoon-inspired overgrowth in my genie's invisible happy place. Instead, I grumbled, even though I knew the answer. "How could they not miss us? We just disappeared in front of them!"

"We've been through this before. Even though you refuse to acknowledge it, the Garden exists outside their time, outside their space. We could stay forever, and they wouldn't be any wiser. Not that we'd want to stay today, with thunder coming in like that."

"What thunder?" I had heard absolutely nothing. In fact, even Teel's voice was muffled, as if my ears were stuffed with cotton balls.

He blinked. "You don't hear that at all? You didn't just see that flash of lightning?"

My exasperation gave way to a gnawing twist of curiosity. Would a rainstorm drench Teel and leave me completely dry? Before I could speculate further, my electrician genie brandished his clipboard at me. He poised his pen as if he were ready to check off some very important box on his master cover sheet. "So? Ready to go with your third wish?"

"I told you! I'll ask when I'm good and ready!"

"I just thought that you might have forgotten—"

"Not likely," I growled, "with you throwing yourself around rehearsal every day."

He flinched, and I thought that my words might have sunk home. Before I could relish the victory, maybe even make him back off on the sexpot intern bit, a rapturous smile spread across his face. "Can you smell that? Rain on fresh-turned earth. Is there anything better?"

"You're nuts," I muttered. I knew the smell that he meant. In my world, though, it was the middle of winter.

I realized that I was jealous of him, jealous of his magical senses. Jealous of his ability to sense the Garden.

"Not nuts," he said, an appealing earnestness shining through his freckled features. "Just eager to get inside. To get into the Garden, where I belong. Me and all the other genies who've earned a visit."

Grudgingly, I folded my arms across my chest. "Well, I'm not ready to help yet. And dragging me here every other day isn't going to make me decide any faster." I knew that I sounded petulant, but I felt pressured, confined. The gray nothingness around me was oppressive.

"I just thought that if you could see it, if you could understand what it means to me…" There was honest wistfulness in his voice, true longing in his clear blue eyes.

"I can't, though," I said. "Teel, you have to promise that you'll leave me alone between wishes. Promise that you'll let me make up my mind. You can't keep bringing me here. I'm never going to see what you're talking about, to smell it, to hear it."

"If you could…" His tenor almost cracked with longing.

I was embarrassed to hear his desire so plainly. "I can't," I said, my voice harsher than I meant for it to be. "Promise, Teel. Don't bring me here again."

He stared into the distance, and I knew that he was looking at dazzling flowers, listening to a lyrical stream, tracking the progress of the invisible storm. He swallowed hard. "I'm sorry. I thought that I could share all of this with you, help you to understand who I am. Who all genies are."

I shook my head.

He sighed and said, "All right, then. I promise."

Sadly, as if he'd just learned of a traumatic death in his family, Teel raised his blunt-fingered hand to his ear. He tugged twice.

And we were back in the rehearsal room.

Back with Drew and Bill. Back with Teel dressed like an extra from Sluts on Parade. I started to exclaim, to shout out in amazement, but Teel merely spared me a sly grin and a wink. Smiling broadly, she greeted Bill with an air kiss, then gave Drew a quick hug. I glared daggers at her, all goodwill engendered in the invisible Garden completely dissipated.

Teel was utterly oblivious. I was trying to figure out what I could say, how I could put "my intern" to work—preferably in another building—when Bill barked, "Where the hell is Jennifer? She was supposed to be here fifteen minutes ago. Kira, will you give her a call?"

Give her a call. Well, that was a brutal return to my reality. Bill wanted me to punch Jennifer's phone number into my cell, quickly and efficiently. Without delay. From memory, as I had boasted to Drew that I could do, less than an hour before. I pasted on a sickly smile. "Sure," I said. "Let me just grab my phone."

I fumbled in my pants pocket, knowing it wasn't there. I reached into the side section of my backpack, pushing around the contents with an earnest determination, willing Jennifer to walk through the door before I could be proven a liar. "I think you put it in the main part," Drew said helpfully.

Great. At least he'd been paying attention to my every move. I plunged my hand in, shoved around the junk inside, and finally decided to find the phone. I took it out, flipped it open, flashed another smile at the men, this one more desperate. I wondered if I could point behind them, shout, "Look! Over there!" as I excavated my phone list and snuck a look.

Fat chance.

Just before I tried a one-in-a-trillion guess, Jennifer burst through the lobby door. "I am so sorry!" she was saying before she even made it into the rehearsal room. "My car battery died, and I had to wait for a friend to pick me up!"

Bill shook his head in disgust, but he settled for one more glance at his imaginary watch before starting to lead the actors in some physical warm-ups. Not surprisingly, Teel joined in with Drew and Jennifer.

Bill was always partial to yoga stretches—a few Cows here, a few Cats there, working out the kinks in everyone's backs as they crouched on all fours. In apparent deference to the morning's high tension, he coached them through some Warrior poses as well, then had them rest in Downward-Facing Dog. I was grateful that I wasn't part of the activity; even though Teel had carved thirty pounds off my ass, I didn't particularly want to be shoving it up in the air.

I caught Bill studying Jennifer's and Teel's forms, cocking his head to one side. I couldn't really criticize him, though. I'd made sure to take a prime viewing spot of Drew's exercises myself. It was my *responsibility,* I thought beatifically. If anyone overstretched and strained a muscle, I needed to be ready with the first aid supplies in my bag.

Next came the vocal exercises, tongue twisters designed to get lips and throat ready for the complexity of Elizabethan speech. Lovely lemon liniment. She stood on the balcony inexplicably mimicking him hiccuping. Which witch wished which wicked wish? Red leather yellow leather. I knew each of the precisely enunciated sentences so well that they formed the soundtrack to my dreams.

Only after we had retired a speed round of girl gargoyle, guy gargoyle did Bill declare us ready to work with the text. This was a crucial scene, he explained. This was the crux of the romance between Romeo and Juliet, the touchstone of romantic love for centuries of Western culture.

Jennifer took careful notes as Bill described the way a man would view the scene. She caught her tongue between her perfect teeth, nodding dutifully as Bill explained that when Romeo mentioned stars, he really meant sex. When Romeo talked about the moon, he was referring to sex again. When Romeo finally brought himself to mention Juliet's cheeks, he wasn't referring to her face, not at all. Not when he'd just spent ten lines talking about the fullness of the *moon.*

John returned at the tail end (no pun intended) of Bill's exposition. He'd apparently worked off his frustration; he was back to playing the laconic cowboy. He leaned against the wall beside the door, crossing his hands over his chest and making a show out of not interrupting Bill. He was chewing on a toothpick, moving the tiny stick up and down in the corner of his mouth. If he'd had a ten-gallon hat, he could have passed for a wranglin' man, just arrived from the Santa Fe Trail.

Bill concluded in a booming voice: "Sex, Jennifer! The entire speech is about sex! Romeo wants to get in Juliet's pants."

Jennifer nodded earnestly and said, "Let me see what I can do."

"Get a bag first." Bill nodded toward me, but I was already handing her a Hefty bag, with convenient holes already cut for her head and arms.

Drew took his, as well, nodding as enthusiastically as if I were handing him a cup of beer just pumped from a keg. I hadn't cut the hole for his head quite large enough, though, and he got stuck partway through. "Just a second!" I said, raising my fingers to rip the opening a little wider. My hands brushed across his hair, and I felt a thrill almost as electric as the ones that flashed through Teel's magic. Drew emerged with a rogue's smile on his face. "Hey, dude. There's something kinky about all this black plastic," he whispered, winking at me.

Knocked speechless, I resorted to smoothing the bag over his shoulders. His broad shoulders. His firm, virile, remarkably attractive shoulders.

I almost forgot that there were four other people in the room.

"Are you ready?" Bill asked dryly. I leaped back, picking up my script notebook as if it were a charm against the devil. As I scrambled for my pen, Bill nodded. "Okay, Jennifer. Go ahead." He sat back like a wiry potentate, rubbing a hand across his bald skull in eager anticipation of the fruits of his creation.

Jennifer took a few steps around the room. She lengthened her stride as she walked, drooping her right shoulder. She curved her hand toward her side, slouching along as if she was just waiting to give some dap to her homeboys. When she completed one full circuit, she shot out her left hip and looked up, squinting as if she could barely make out Juliet's manhole-cover window in the gloom of the underworld. "But, soft! What light through yonder window breaks?"

There was a soft snort by the door. I looked up to see that John was smothering his amused reaction with his hand, barely remembering to rescue his toothpick from the corner of his lips. "Sorry," he mouthed to me, and shrugged. The actors were so intent on the scene that they hadn't noticed.

"No, no, no," Bill was saying. "You *want* Juliet. There's nothing cerebral about this. Nothing noble or beautiful or touching. Lust, that's what I want to see."

Jennifer nodded, chewing on her lip. She took another lap around the room to get into character, and by the time she stood in front of the nonexistent manhole cover the entire room was silent, frozen with expectation—horrified expectation for some of us. "But, soft!" Jennifer brayed, sounding like a cross between John Travolta and Nicolas Cage.

"No!" Bill interrupted. "Lust, Romeo! You want to hump her! You're horny!"

This time, John actually laughed out loud; I couldn't have been the only one who heard his guffaws before they turned into a cough. Jennifer swallowed a furious look of despair and groped beneath her trash bag, clutching at her crotch and tugging her jeans with pit bull aggression. "But, soft!" she grunted. "What light through yonder window breaks? It is the east, and Juliet is the sun!"

"Yes!" Bill exploded. "Exactly! Pure animal attraction." He looked around wildly. "Teel! Teel! Ah, there you are. Now, what would Juliet think when she hears this sort of line? How would a woman feel?"

I wanted to roll my eyes. If Bill only knew Teel's true nature, he wouldn't be panting after her bare midriff quite so blatantly. He'd never let her be the voice of female reason, if he'd seen Electrician-Teel or Chef-Teel or Geek-Boy-Teel. Definitely not if he'd seen Disco-King-Teel.

But I had to admit, my genie played *this* role to a tee. "She's frightened," Teel said. "Overwhelmed." She lowered her voice to a whisper, and her lips quirked into a tiny smile as she looked at the flames locked around her wrist. "Excited."

Drew leaned closer to hear her last word. "Excited?" he repeated. "Dude!" He clearly had not expected that.

Teel nodded and stretched, as if she were trying to grasp the perfect words out of thin air. I thought she was going to sink her talons into Drew. "There's something about that power, about the demands that Romeo is making. They're a total… turn-on." She barely breathed the last two syllables.

Great. Perfect. My perceptive genie had just turned Shakespeare's most romantic female lead into Playboy's Miss February.

I spluttered, trying to figure out how to get this rehearsal out of the gutter. Couldn't Drew and Bill see that Teel was toying with them? Couldn't they recognize that she was a bored, manipulative woman, intent on dragging out every seductive stereotype ever imagined by an oversexed teenage boy?

I had to say something, do something, throw something across the room, if only to bring the rehearsal back to a basic level of human decency. A basic level of sanity.

John must have agreed, because he chose that moment to retrieve his drawings. He made an elaborate show of crossing the room quietly, stopping just short of tiptoeing around the perimeter in pantomime. His rangy frame, of course, drew everyone's attention. He stopped, halfway to the table, and shrugged elaborately. "Damn. I didn't mean to break things up."

Fortunately, that interruption was enough to bring everyone back to their senses. Jennifer asked for a five-minute break to think about her motivation for the rest of her lines. Bill lowered his head and rolled his shoulders, shaking out his arms as if he'd just wrestled the Minotaur into submission. Teel stood in the middle of the room, blinking her absurdly outlined eyes, the picture of tarted-up innocence.

And Drew looked around like a man awakening from a dream. He swallowed hard and stumbled toward a chair, jumping almost a foot into the air when a huge spark leaped from his fingers to the metal frame.

"Static electricity," John said as Drew yelped and shook his hand. "It's the worst damn thing about winter up here. Of course, those plastic bags don't make it any better. They come out of the box already charged."

I narrowed my eyes and glared at Teel. There must have been more to her sexual innuendo than even I had suspected. She must be purposely spicing things up with her magical powers. What had she told me when she'd begged for permission to come to rehearsal? She was bored, waiting for me to make a wish? Obviously, playing with Drew Myers had become an antidote to her boredom.

To her credit, she met my gaze and shrugged, the picture of innocence. I said to no one in particular, "I'll bring in a humidifier tomorrow. That should help."

John nodded. "Can't hurt, with all the extra metal on the set. We can set up a couple backstage."

Earlier, those words would have sounded like an invitation to battle with Bill. They would have heightened the tension in the room, upped the ante. Now, though, our brilliant director only nodded. His voice was firm, paternal, as he said, "I know you're still not sold on this yet, John. But I can see it in my mind. I'll work harder, I promise, so that you can share just what it is I'm seeing. I'll get you to believe me, to understand."

And right then? In that one second?

I *did* believe him. I understood. Even with—especially

with—the crazy gender shift, even with the darkness, the gloom, the slippery, sibilant sewers that Bill thrived on, I believed him.

After all, anyone could do an ordinary *Romeo and Juliet*. *Fox Hill* could have done an ordinary *Romeo and Juliet*. The Landmark was different. The Landmark was special. Our show would be talked about for ages.

I was so supercharged from my sudden rush of confidence, from my remembering that this production was what I'd always wanted, what I'd always hoped to achieve in the theater, that I almost missed Teel sauntering over to Drew. She made an elaborate show of reaching into her jeans and digging something out of her too-tight pocket.

"Oh, Drew," she said, in a voice that sounded like it was just for him. A quick tingle up my arm, though, let me know that she was broadcasting her words through magic. She meant for me to overhear. "I meant to tell you right when I got here. I must have picked up your cell phone by mistake yesterday. I don't know *how* that could have happened." She giggled, sounding like a more-sexual Paris Hilton. "My bad!"

She took her time dropping it into his outstretched hand, making sure that her fingers touched his. I didn't even know if he was aware of his movement when he stepped closer to her, when he brushed against her too-tight T-shirt. When he thanked her, she tossed her head back and laughed, raising her hand to stroke her throat. I watched her tattooed flames glitter, matched by a suggestive jangle along the edges of my own tattoo.

A different fire, a hotter one, kindled in my belly. By the time Drew suggested they grab a bite to eat, my vision was actually sparking with anger.

Teel looked over her shoulder as they left the room. She caught my eye and mouthed, "Don't wait up!"

I barely remembered not to launch myself across the room and strangle her then and there.

CHAPTER 11

I HAD TO WAIT HOURS FOR JULES AND MADDY TO GO to bed that night. They wanted to play a game of Scrabble. Then they wanted to watch *Law & Order*; an old friend was playing the corpse in the first scene. To commemorate the role, Maddy popped a batch of kettle corn in the microwave.

I have never liked kettle corn. It's dishonest. It *smells* like popcorn while it's popping, and it looks totally ordinary in the serving bowl. But when I taste it, it has a hint of sweet beneath the salt, a dessert flavor that just doesn't belong. Nevertheless, I took a handful, just to be sociable, and I ate the kernels one by one. I successfully drew out my serving, so that Maddy and Jules had emptied the bowl by the time I was done.

Ordinarily, I really enjoyed the evenings that all three of us were home. This time, though, I just couldn't wait for them to get tired, to go to their rooms, to close their doors and give me some privacy.

I had decided to call in my third wish.

Sure, I'd told Teel to leave me alone, just that afternoon. I'd told him that I'd make my wish on my own schedule. I'd told him to back off from dragging me into his invisible Garden.

But that had been before *he* had reverted to the trampy *she* I was sick and tired of seeing at rehearsal. That was before *she* had done everything she could to seduce Drew Myers. That was before *she* had purposely driven me insane, with her innuendos and her seductive looks.

As soon as I was certain Maddy and Jules were both asleep, I dug Teel's lantern out of my closet. As always, the metal was warm to my touch. Almost without thinking, I started to rub the side, my fingers aching for the familiar tingle, the promise of the magical energy.

I could feel my pulse beat strongly, echoing through the almost invisible flames tattooed across the ridges and whorls of my fingerprints. I pressed my fingers together, letting the energy spark against itself. "Teel," I actually said out loud.

This time, I was completely braced for the full electric shock. I was absolutely prepared for the jewel-toned fog that coalesced in the center of my room. I was one-hundred-percent ready for the light to shimmer through the fog, to settle into a human shape.

I'd somehow forgotten, though, that the shape wouldn't necessarily be familiar to me.

Teel was a black man. A *very large* black man. His belly spilled over his pants, testing the limits of his suspenders. He wore a white oxford shirt that had to have a twenty-four-inch neck; even then, a roll of flesh sagged over the back of the collar. A white canvas bucket hat sat comfortably atop his head. His hair was gray, where I could see it, and his skin was medium-toned—more seasoned oak than mahogany. He raised a hand as big as a dinner plate and rubbed at the back of his neck. The tattoo was clear around his wrist; the golden flames were highlighted, almost as if they'd been painted on.

"You rang?" he said. His voice was deep and melodious, the reincarnated tones of Paul Robeson. He could have given elocution lessons to James Earl Jones.

I didn't trust him, though.

This wasn't some avuncular guy, offering to help with whatever problem I was having. This was *Teel*. This was my meddlesome genie. He could raise one of those ponderous hands to his ear, tug twice, and look like the slutty little tramp who had haunted our rehearsals for the past too-many weeks.

Without preamble, I said, "I've decided on my third wish."

I'd tested the sentence in my head a dozen times during the evening. I wanted to sound calm. Confident. Not like a jealous witch.

"Indeed," he boomed.

I looked straight into his eyes, the caramel-colored irises that looked like they knew so much, could tell me so many stories. "I wish for Drew Myers to love me."

He laughed.

He stood there in the center of my bedroom, enormous hands folded over his belly like a beardless black Santa Claus, and he laughed. The sound started as a chuckle, a chortle, but it grew into a guffaw. He fumbled for his hat, used it to wipe at his eyes. Every time I thought that he was finished, he seemed to remember something else, some new private treat that was even more hysterical. Soon, he was wheezing for breath, staggering forward to rest one of his gigantic forearms against my desk. He fanned himself with the hat, gasping for breath.

When he could finally speak, he said, "Don't waste your wish on that."

"What?" I snapped. "You don't want me interfering with your own little seduction game?"

"My—"

I didn't let him finish his basso profundo expression of confusion. "I expected you to be happy that I've finally decided. I thought you'd be grateful to be one wish closer to your stupid Garden."

He shook his head slowly, still wheezing from his merriment at my expense. "You were right, Kira. I wasn't playing fair, taking you to the Garden. You need to make your wishes on your own schedule, not on mine. I've already promised not to force you back there. Why don't you wait until you've really made up your mind before you make your third wish?"

"I *have* made up my mind! I want Drew Myers to love me! You're just trying to talk me out of it because you like him, too. Not this you. The other you. The you who was at rehearsal."

He shook his head, all hint of amusement gone. "I've already told you—jealousy is bad for wishes. Nine out of ten women who make wishes based on jealousy end up regretting their decision."

"I am not jealous!" I protested. I'd had enough of his stupid statistics. What was he doing, pulling them out of thin air, the way he materialized himself? "Besides, you're the one who's been bugging *me* about finishing up. I'm just trying to help you out."

Well, that sounded like a good excuse. Altruistic, even. I wondered if genies could read minds. Would he actually *know* that I was lying? Or would he just assume so? I repeated, "I am not jealous."

Teel put his hands on his ample hips, using his current barrel chest to turn his Paris Hilton bubble voice into a monstrous parody. "Yes, Drew," he minced. "We women would feel… excited." The last three syllables were barely spoken, barely said aloud.

"That didn't make me jealous! That made me *nauseated*! You were manipulating him. Him, Bill…you reached out to Jennifer, too, didn't you?"

"I was just having a little fun. I *told* you I was bored."

"You can't screw with human lives just because you're bored!"

"But you can screw with Drew Myers's life?" Suddenly, the trickster was gone. Teel was staring at me intently, his butterscotch eyes like lasers.

"I love him," I said, fighting to keep my voice even.

"Spare me! Maybe you love the *idea* of him. Maybe you love the notion of a leading man who will sweep you off your feet, escort you to all the best parties. Maybe you love the thought of someone who lives at the top of your little social pyramid, someone who is instantly recognized as successful by every single person in the room. But you don't love *him*. Not as a person."

"That's a horrible thing to say!"

"It's the truth."

I couldn't believe the fury his words stoked in me, the rage that made my fingertips—tattooed or not—tingle. "For your information, not that it is any of your business, I have had all of that. There was a time when I *was* royalty around here. There was a time when people cared about me, paid attention to what parties I went to, who I talked to, what I thought!"

He shrugged, the motion rolling across his massive shoulders like an earthquake. "And what happened to change all that?"

TEWSBU had happened, of course. TEWSBU had left me. Abandoned me. Cut me down for life.

I shoved that image out of my mind, carved it from my consciousness as neatly as Teel had carved the poundage from my thighs. This wasn't about TEWSBU. This had never been about TEWSBU.

"I love him, Teel," I said. And then, because there might have been a misunderstanding, because my own thoughts were tangled and torn and confused, I said, "I love Drew Myers."

"You don't even know Drew Myers."

I fell into the whirlpool of thoughts I'd spun through for the past month, since that first day at the Landmark, when I'd walked into the rehearsal room and met Drew. "You're right," I conceded. "Sort of. I don't know him well. We only met a month ago." Teel was nodding, increasingly sure that he'd won this battle. "But," I said, holding up my hand in protest, "I know what he's not. I know that he's not pretentious. I know that he's not cruel. I know that he's not so conceited that he can't listen to other people, can't try new things, can't risk his dignity and his precious reputation for something new, something different."

He wasn't TEWSBU.

I didn't say that out loud. Teel really didn't know anything about TEWSBU; as a man or as a woman, he'd never understand.

And then there was the argument I didn't even try to make. Drew Myers was simply the most physically attractive man I'd ever met.

After all, wasn't that what my wishes were all about? Dream fulfillment. Shrugging off the miserable routine of a lackluster job for the glamour of the finest stage-managing position in the Twin Cities. Stepping out of a damaged body, into a stunning new one.

I was always the good girl. I was always the staid one. I was the stage manager, for God's sake, the person whose *job* was to pick up the pieces, to stay organized, to put each and every thing into its preordained place.

Just this once, I wanted to be the other girl. I wanted to play the romantic lead.

"I've made my decision," I finished. "That's my wish. For Drew Myers to love me." Then I started to think of all the things my trickster genie could purposefully misunderstand, all the ways that he could ruin this. "Drew Myers," I said again.

"The one who lives in Minneapolis. Who's playing Juliet at the Landmark. The one with blond hair—"

"I've met him," Teel said. The statement would have been saucy if it had been delivered by Intern-Teel. Coming from the gentle bear of a man in front of me, it just sounded sad. He sighed and said, "As you wish." He raised his fingers to his ear. The flame tattoo made his eyes seem to glow as he tugged once, clearly, with definite force, and then again.

I realized that I was holding my breath. Slowly, in control, I forced myself to exhale. I looked around the room, realizing that I'd somehow expected Drew to just materialize from some new stash of colored mist.

"That's it?" I asked.

"It's done," Teel said.

I looked at the phone on my nightstand. Bill Pomeroy had called to announce the fulfillment of my first wish. Was Drew picking up his own cell even now? Was he magically realizing that *he* had *my* phone number memorized, committed to some core knowledge that he'd never even suspected he had? Was he at least digging in his script notebook to find the cast list that I'd prepared for everyone, to look up my phone number on the sheet of paper that I had given him?

"What happens now?" I whispered.

"I don't know about you, but I'm beat." The black face creased into a smile. "That rehearsal took a lot out of me today."

I started to make some bitter retort, but he was already disappearing, already dissolving into a shimmer of ruby and emerald and cobalt.

He was gone.

I stared at the brass lantern on my bed. Four weeks ago, I hadn't believed that magic could exist. I hadn't imagined that a shape-shifting genie could weave in and out of my life, changing things forever. But Teel had given me my greatest opportunity ever in the theater. He'd given me back my sense of self, my sense of pride. He—if I believed him, and I had no reason not to—had just given me the love of my life. And I hadn't said goodbye. Or even thank you.

"Teel!" I called. "Wait!"

But it was all over. No more lying in bed at night, thinking about how I'd spend my next wish. No more nervous anticipation of where Teel would show up next, what the genie would do to embarrass me. No more brushing my hand against the lantern, just to feel the tingle, just to imagine the power I knew it possessed.

I was on my own. Totally and completely on my own.

Except for the tapping at my door. "Kira?" It was Jules. "Are you all right?"

She must have heard me cry out. Suddenly feeling a lot less nostalgic about my missing genie, I grabbed the lantern and tossed it underneath my bed. Just as I opened the door, I remembered that it was well after midnight. I was supposed to be sleepy, confused, barely awake.

"What?" I said, blinking hard at Jules's nightshirt.

"I heard you scream something," she said. "Were you on the phone?"

What could it hurt, if I told the truth now? Sure, Teel had made me keep his existence secret when he first came to me. He'd taken away my words when I tried to discuss him over Chinese food, muted me as thoroughly as a television set during a long commercial break.

But now? With my third wish spent? I should be able to tell Jules everything, to share all the strange things that had happened to me.

"No. I wasn't on the phone," I said. "I was—"

My throat stopped. One instant the words were there: normal, everyday words that I could utter as easily as I could speak my name. The next, I was opening and closing my mouth like a fish, my vocal cords apparently nonexistent.

"What?" Jules said, obviously confused.

"It was just—"

Nothing. There was no way I could say Teel's name. No way that I could move my body to the space beside my bed, that I could kneel down, that I could extract the lamp.

No way that I could tell her the truth.

"Sorry," I said. That word came easily enough. Whatever magic Teel had left behind knew that I'd given up. It knew the genie's secret was safe. Jules was peering past me, curiosity plain on her face. Glancing over my shoulder, I saw my bedroom as she must have—the bed covers still in place, obviously unslept in. I couldn't lie and say I'd had a nightmare.

I grimaced and twisted my neck from side to side. "I was just doing some crunches. Trying to get in shape. I don't know what happened. I got this weird cramp in my leg."

She looked down at my sweatpants dubiously. I shook my foot, as if I was shedding the last of a charley horse. "You should eat a banana," she said. "Get some potassium."

"Yeah," I said. "Sorry that I woke you."

"It's okay." She turned to go but stopped herself before moving down the hall. "Are you—"

"Kira!" The sound came from outside. My name, bellowed at the top of some man's lungs. "Kira!"

"What the—" I gasped, and hurried to my window. I tugged at the shade, snapping it up. It took me a second to process what I was seeing.

A car sat in our driveway, its engine running, its lights on. A man stood out on the sidewalk, arm wrapped around the lamppost to keep his balance as he leaned back, peering owlishly at my window. "*Kira!*" he shouted again, sounding for all the world like Stanley Kowalski in *A Streetcar Named Desire*.

It was Drew.

Drew Myers was standing in front of my house in the middle of the night, without a coat, without even a heavy sweater. He was rocking back and forth, getting more and more agitated by the second. He clutched a piece of paper in his hand, and he glanced from it to our front door, obviously checking the address, obviously making sure that he was at the right place.

"Oh, God," I said, and fled past the astonished Jules. Maddy was just stumbling out of her own bedroom as I jerked open the front door to our apartment. I hurtled down the stairs, hoping that the Swensons had suddenly become deaf enough that they hadn't been awakened.

No such luck.

"What in the name of—" Mr. Swenson huffed, opening his own door as I fumbled with the dead bolt to the entry hall.

"It's nothing, Mr. Swenson. I'm sorry, it's just a friend of mine, an actor in one of my plays."

"*Kira!*"

I swore and apologized again before I finally managed to get the door open. "Drew!" I hissed toward the street. "What the hell do you think you're doing?"

"*Kira!*" he said, with the joy of a small boy discovering a long-lost puppy. He staggered toward me, trampling across the snow on our front lawn.

"Damn fool," Mr. Swenson muttered, slamming his own door and turning three separate locks with a precision that told me I'd be doing more than shoveling snow to keep the household peace in the coming weeks.

"Drew, what is going on?"

He stumbled into the entry hall. "Kira! I'm so glad you're home! I had to see you!"

He was crying. He was honest-to-God crying; tears streaked his cheeks, and his nose was running. His hair stood on end, as if he'd just gotten out of bed, and he was wearing flannel pajama bottoms, with an ancient ratty T-shirt on top. He'd clearly crammed his feet into whatever shoes he'd been able to grab—one beat-up running shoe and a bedroom slipper that had seen better days.

"Drew, have you been drinking?"

"No!" He shook his head with the vehemence of Dennis the Menace. His teeth started chattering, but he was laughing, even as the tears continued to leak from his eyes. "Kira, I was sleeping. I was dreaming. I was dreaming, and it was raining. It was raining diamonds. And I heard this voice, and it told me that I loved you, and I woke up, and I knew that it was true! Kira, I love you!"

Teel had obviously outdone himself this time. Somewhere, locked away in his lantern waiting for his next victim, my genie must be chortling to himself, overjoyed with the scene he'd made here. Caused to be made. Whatever.

Well, that pleasure was going to have to last him a good long time. Who knew how many more decades it would take for Teel to be freed from his lantern again? Who knew how long it would take for some unsuspecting soul to rub the brass lamp? As Drew gave another shuddering sob, I personally vowed to toss Teel's lantern into Lake of the Isles, as soon as it was light out. Well, I would, as soon as the lake thawed. For now, I'd leave it stashed beneath my bed, where no innocent could stumble on it.

I gritted my teeth. "Come in, Drew. Wait! Let me go turn off your car. No, it's okay. I'll be right back. I'm not going anywhere. Drew, please, I have to turn off your car!"

He was like a hysterical little boy, laughing and crying all at the same time. I finally succeeded in slipping past him, darting out to the driveway. He'd left the driver's side open; the car was patiently chiming away to let everyone know that the door was still ajar. I reached in and turned the key, grateful for the sudden silence. I locked the vehicle and pocketed the keys.

Drew was staring at me, adoring, from the front porch.

"Let's go," I said, leading the way upstairs.

Maddy and Jules were waiting in the living room. I could tell that they'd been talking; who wouldn't have been, under the circumstances? I flipped on the overhead fixture to supplement the light that was bleeding out of each of our bedrooms.

"Maddy Rubens, Jules McElroy, this is Drew Myers." Jules offered her hand, which Drew took distractedly. He was busy watching me move across the room, into the kitchen.

It was times like this that I really wished I could have a drink. A stiff one.

Maddy said wryly, "We've met before."

"I—I don't remember," Drew said, barely managing the social nicety.

"Death of a Salesman," she said. "You were Happy." He blinked at her, clearly having trouble processing the conversation. "I designed the lights. At the Orpheum."

Drew suddenly nodded. "I remember! I remember the show! But we had a terrible stage manager."

Maddy sounded personally offended. "David Epstein is an excellent stage manager!"

"He's not Kira." Drew whirled toward me, a sappy smile painted across his face.

Maddy snorted. I could tell she thought Drew was drunk. I couldn't really blame her. Maddy said pointedly to Jules, "I have to get up early tomorrow."

"Oh!" Jules said. "I have an early day tomorrow also."

Well, no wonder my housemate was relegated to roles in industrial films. She sounded so stiff that no one could ever have believed her.

Maddy said to me, "You'll be okay?"

"Yeah. I'll be fine."

With one more exchange of meaningful glances, Maddy and Jules went back to their respective bedrooms. Drew looked at me expectantly. Okay. So I couldn't offer him a drink, courtesies of my stupid allergy. Even I wasn't enough of a caffeine fiend to mainline the stuff after midnight. Tea. We could have a nice, soothing cup of herbal tea.

Still trying to figure out the right thing to say, I dug around in the kitchen cupboards, coming up with a pair of chamomile tea bags. I felt Drew watch every move I made, as I filled the kettle, took out two mugs, two spoons, two paper napkins. I lit the burner and put the water on to boil.

"Honey?" I asked, and he nodded, as pathetically eager to please as a puppy. I quickly clarified, "I mean, do you want honey in your tea?" Disappointed, he shook his head. "Drew—" I started to say.

"Kira—" he began at the same time. "No. You go first."

I wasn't even sure what I wanted to tell him. It wasn't like I could say, "This is all a mistake."

I didn't know that it *was* a mistake. Sure, Teel had obviously had a bit of fun, granting this last wish. He'd indulged his sense of drama. He'd twisted my wish in a way I hadn't anticipated, turning my words upside down in ways that weren't quite fair.

But it was entirely possible that this story could still have a happy ending. After all, Shakespeare himself had written about just this situation. In *A Midsummer Night's Dream,* the fairies play tricks on the humans, making lovers fall for each other against all odds. At the end of that play, one of the men was still be-spelled, but everyone was happy.

I just had to treat Drew with dignity. With respect. Teel might have bulldozed my way into Drew's heart, but now that I was there, I could make things grow between us naturally. Once we'd had a chance to get to know each other in more… conventional ways, everything else would fall into place. It wasn't like we were total strangers. I'd become attracted to him because of the man I'd seen in rehearsals. Because I could ap-preciate him as an actor.

Because he was the most spectacular specimen of human male I'd ever laid eyes on.

And he was standing less than a foot away from me. His eyes were locked on my face. His lips quivered, just a little, as he breathed. I could smell his shampoo on his hair, something sharp, clean.

I chickened out, abandoning whatever confession I'd half planned on making.

"Hot water's ready!" I swept the teakettle from the stovetop, even though it hadn't yet begun to whistle. I poured into our mugs very carefully, pretending that the operation took the utmost concentration to complete. I unwrapped the tea bags, dipped them simultaneously, precisely, as if I were conducting some exotic type of brain surgery.

"Here you go!" I said brightly. I started to carry his mug to the table in the dining room, but then I realized that I wasn't sure I wanted him walking behind me, with both hands free—not in his current enchanted state. I shoved his cup into his right hand, then came close to pelting him with the plastic honey bear, just to keep him fully occupied. By the time we sat down at the table, I'd had a chance to form a plan.

"Drew," I said, pitching my voice to a tone of perfect

reason. "It's really common for people on a play to think they love each other. We spend a lot of time together, every single day. Bill has us working in really close quarters. This production is even worse than usual, because of the way the show's designed."

"I love the show," he said. "I love the show because you're stage managing it."

Okay. I knew it was a corny line. I knew that if Maddy were still standing here, she'd roll her eyes, pretend to shove a finger down her throat, probably even snort out loud.

But I had to admit that I was enjoying the attention. Even if this was all because of Teel's meddling, there was some perverse part of me that enjoyed having a man look at me—me! Kira Franklin!—with a look of perfect adoration.

Drew fiddled with the handle on his mug. "I know this must sound sudden to you. We've been working together for weeks, and it probably seems like I haven't even noticed that you're alive. I mean, with all the women in the cast, every single one of them there because she's got a great rack, you know, to make Bill's point about the sexes... And then, when your intern, when Teel started coming around and showing us what we were supposed to be thinking and feeling, and all that really hot stuff she said about the balcony scene..."

I cleared my throat, trying to get him to the end of his thought. He shook his head, looking utterly perplexed by the path he'd just walked down. "It's sudden," he said simply. "And I know I made a fool out of myself tonight." He nodded toward the window, toward the driveway where his car hulked, mute witness to his impulsivity. "It's totally like I'm watching myself on stage here. I can see myself doing these things, hear myself saying these lines. But at the same time, I know that they're real. I know that they're true. I know that they're totally how I really feel."

His eyelashes were still damp from the tears he had shed. He swallowed, and his Adam's apple bobbed.

"Drew," I said, hating myself. I had to explain. Even if I couldn't use the words "genie" or "magic" or "wish," I had to let him know what was going on. "It's not that simple. Things aren't what they seem."

"Nothing is ever what it seems. Dude, isn't that what our show is all about? Aren't we learning to ask ourselves questions, to see beneath the surface?"

I had to nod.

"Oh, Kira," he said, and the despair in his voice was so real, so tangible, that I thought my heart would break. "I'm not good at this. I'm not good at talking about my feelings." He closed his eyes, took a deep breath. He exhaled long, slow, as if he were trying to meditate himself onto a different plane. "I woke up from that dream tonight, and everything was different."

"I know," I said simply.

"This is going to sound like lines from some bad play, but it's like I was blind all those years. But now I understand. Now I know. I want to be with you, Kira. I want to be with you more than I've ever wanted anything in the world."

Damn, Teel was good. I plucked at my napkin. "Drew, I—"

"Please," he said, and his fingers closed over mine. "Please, Kira. Let's just see what happens."

His hand was hot from the mug. Carefully, tentatively, as if he were afraid I'd disappear, he leaned toward me. He touched his lips to mine, setting them there like a question, like a hope. I felt the shadow of his breath.

I kissed him back.

At first, it was a frightened kiss, a chaste kiss, the sort of kiss a lonely thirteen-year-old girl shares with the boy of her dreams. It changed, though. It grew. It deepened into another sort of kiss entirely until it was starvation, thirst, frantic, raving desperation.

His hands tangled in my hair, pulling me closer. I laughed, and he pushed back his chair, grating its legs across the dining room floor, somehow managing to tug me with him. I opened my eyes just in time to catch the wild look on his face; he'd already pulled his arm back, ready to sweep the kitchen table clear, to create a horizontal surface that I was almost certain— with my years of stage-manager expertise—would collapse like matchsticks beneath us.

"No!" I whispered urgently, knowing that Maddy and Jules would be out here in a heartbeat if they heard anything crash to the floor. I clutched his hand to reinforce my message, and then I pulled him down the hallway, through the door of my bedroom. Even as the latch snicked closed, his arms were tight around me, supporting me, consuming me. We staggered to the bed, toppled onto the comforter. He continued to kiss me, to tease me, to make me writhe.

After a lifetime, I caught enough breath to put my hands on his chest, to push him away for long enough that I could speak. "Just a minute," I said. "I just need to get—"

We were both panting as I wriggled out from underneath him. My backpack was sprawled across my desk where I'd left it. The first aid kit was snug in the front pocket. My fingers shook as I worked the plastic hasp; I'd never in my life been so grateful that I was a stage manager, that I was the queen of pre-paredness personified.

The foil packets were folded into the bottom of the plastic box. When I'd assembled the kit, I'd laughed at myself, wondering when I'd ever need them, when a cast member would require my foresight, would have the nerve to ask me for condoms. The absurdity of that imagined scene, though, hadn't kept me from adding them to my professional stash of emergency goods.

As I clutched my prize, Drew's hands closed around my waist, and he pulled me back to the bed.

By morning, I was glad I'd bought a three-pack.

CHAPTER 12

THERE WAS SOMETHING TO BE SAID FOR EARLY-morning rehearsals, at least when I got to wake up next to the leading man. Leading woman. Whatever.

Drew and I were jarred back to consciousness by my screeching alarm clock; I had purposely set it for 7:00 a.m., so that we'd have time to get ready before our nine o'clock cast call. We'd have to take a side trip to Drew's house, so that he could find some slightly more appropriate clothing than pajama bottoms and mismatched shoes.

I rolled out of bed and tugged on my bathrobe. Drew burrowed deeper into my sheets as I went out to start a pot of coffee. My sheets... The man I had lusted after for nearly six weeks was burrowing into my sheets.

Before closing the door to my bedroom, I glanced at the bed skirt. Teel's lantern was still shoved under there. What were people going to say, when my so-called theater intern didn't show up at rehearsal anymore? How could I account for the absent sexpot?

I wasn't complaining, I reminded myself. Teel had served her function. We were all better off without her, going forward.

And it wasn't like we needed any sexual interpretation for the day's work. Mercutio was going to die today, and I had to make sure that we had appropriate iron pipes ready. Not that anyone was actually going to beat Stephanie senseless. But I could dream about a little staged violence against TEWSBU's current girlfriend, couldn't I? Nobody would blame me for that.

Actually, I thought, as I breathed in the aroma of brewing double-strength coffee, Stephanie didn't bother me nearly as much as she had. I caught myself actually *wishing* that TEWSBU would drop by one of our rehearsals, wishing that he could see me now. See me in my dream theater job with my dream body, hanging out with my dream boyfriend.

My boyfriend.

That had been one hell of a third wish.

I poured a cup of coffee for me, then one for Drew, taking care to add a healthy splash of Jules's milk to his, along with a generous spoonful of sugar. I'd only seen him drinking lattes at Club Joe, and I had yet to encounter anyone who could match me, cup for cup, on the mud that I brewed.

Before I could sneak back into my bedroom, Maddy shuffled into the kitchen. She took one look at the two mugs in my hand and raised her eyebrows.

"What?" I said defensively.

"Company?" she asked, as if I regularly hosted overnight visitors.

I couldn't swallow my smile. "Yeah," I said. "Drew stayed over."

Maddy rustled in the freezer for a box of frozen waffles. "You go, girl. He *is* a damned good-looking guy. But what's the deal? You go for a year without dating anyone, and then Romeo himself comes beating down the door?"

"Juliet," I said, frowning. "Look, Maddy, just because it's taken me a while to get back on my feet—"

Maddy must have heard the defensiveness in my voice, because she shook her head. "I'm not saying there's anything wrong with it. It was just a surprise, that's all. I would have expected you to tell Jules and me more about him, you know, when you saw that things were heading…in that direction." She set her jaw and nailed me with a direct gaze. "I'm a little worried that you felt you couldn't share with us, couldn't tell us what was happening in your life."

I wasn't about to tell her that Drew's declaration of love had been a complete surprise to me, as well. Better that she think I'd been hiding the growth of a true, meaningful relationship, than she think that I'd tumbled into bed with the first guy in a year who'd swung from our street lamp and serenaded me by moonlight.

Which, come to think of it, I had. But this was different. This was safer. This was engineered by Teel. Even if Maddy didn't know that. She didn't know that everything was going to be all right. She was worried about me. In fact, from her perspective, she had every reason to be worried about me.

In a rush of sudden understanding, I set down the coffee mugs and gave her a quick hug. "I haven't seen much of you in the past few weeks," I said, letting some real remorse flavor the confession that I hoped would distract her, just a little bit. "Between my show and yours, and Jules being out in California, it's just been crazy around here."

"It's always crazy around here," Maddy said as her waffles popped up from the toaster. She nodded grudgingly, though, apparently accepting my explanation. She glanced at the whiteboard. "Jules is already gone this morning, and I'm heading out in half an hour."

I recognized the question she hadn't asked, the practical roommate concern. "Don't worry," I said. "Drew and I can wait to shower until after you leave." I blushed as I realized that sounded like we'd be showering together. Well, maybe we would be. Teel's little magic trick had certainly inspired other amorous excesses in the past few hours. "I'll see you tonight?"

"Nope," Maddy said as she finished dousing her waffles with syrup. "Gunther and I are going out to dinner. He wants to celebrate our three-week anniversary." It was my turn to raise surprised eyebrows. Maddy wasn't usually the sentimental type. Of course, she'd usually dumped her men before they had anything approaching an anniversary to celebrate. "What?" she asked. "It's a sweet gesture!"

"Yeah," I said. "Very sweet." An adjective I never thought I would apply to Maddy's love life—or to Maddy at all—in a million years. "We'll catch up soon."

"Yep," she said, catching a drip of maple syrup on one finger. "I want to hear *all* about what's new."

I blushed and snagged my cups of coffee before they could get even colder. Catching my breath, I ducked back into my bedroom.

Drew was lying facedown on my bed, his head buried in my pillow. I put the coffee on my nightstand and sat beside him, reaching out one tentative hand to his bare shoulders. Was this what I was supposed to do? How we were supposed to act? What if I had somehow miscommunicated my wish to Teel, managed to screw things up despite my most frantic attempts to provide clarifying details? What if Drew and I had shared some one-night special, and things were back to normal this morning? Back to horrible, awkward, no self-confidence normal this morning?

"Good morning, Gorgeous." Drew looked positively wicked, squinting through sleepy eyelids.

Well, I guess my wish was lasting for longer than one sheet-tangled night. "Hi," I said, and then because I didn't really know how I was supposed to respond to his apparent pet name for me, I said, "I brought some coffee."

He rolled over and sat up, letting the sheet bunch around his waist like the bed linens in some carefully scripted television show. I passed his coffee to him, and we clinked mugs together. Our eyes met over the rims of our cups. Once again, I marveled at the color of his, at the ordinary brown, made extraordinary by flecks of gold and emerald. He grinned as he took a sip.

He almost spit his coffee out; I watched him fight to swallow what he had in his mouth.

"You *drink* this stuff?" he yelped.

I swooped in to keep him from spilling across the sheets. "I added milk and sugar to yours! I like it strong," I said defensively.

"Dude, that's not strong. That's lethal. You could strip paint with that stuff."

"Sorry."

He reached across me to deposit his mug on my nightstand. "Besides," he said, and his crafty smile proved that it wasn't an accident when his fingers snaked into the loops of my bathrobe belt. "There are better ways to wake up than with coffee."

I thought of Maddy, taking her shower before she rushed out of the house. I had an obligation to my housemate, a duty to keep Drew engaged while she went about her busy morning routine. With a proud sense of honor, I succumbed to Drew's distraction. I never even heard Maddy close the front door when she left.

In the end, Drew and I were both pretty rushed, getting showered, pulling on clothes, slamming down some semblance of breakfast. He was thrilled by my Cap'n Crunch. (Read: He was thrilled by anything about me—except my coffee.) I borrowed another one of Jules's yogurts, savoring the peaches and cream as if it were a delectable dessert.

I could have eaten ashes and been happy.

We agreed to take Drew's car to rehearsal. We had to move it out of the driveway, anyway, so that the Swensons could get in and out, and it seemed wasteful for both of us to drive to the exact same place. As we maneuvered around Lake of the Isles, I was relieved to note that Drew's extreme goofiness from the night before had ebbed a little bit. I didn't feel like we were trapped in a bad play anymore; I wasn't quite as worried that Teel and I had manipulated him in some totally unfair way.

In fact, the sex that we had shared—repeatedly—seemed to have tempered him into something approximating the perfect boyfriend. He held the car door for me when we stopped at his apartment, and again when we parked near the theater. He shrugged good-naturedly when I suggested that we stop in at Club Joe for more coffee, and he rolled his eyes, smiling, when I had them dump half of Colombia's gross national caffeine product into mine. He held my backpack as I dug in the side pocket for my theater keys; I'd managed to disorganize everything with my frantic search for the first aid kit the night before. He greeted Stephanie and Jennifer with a distracted air, as if he barely saw his stunning coworkers, as if he only had eyes for me.

He even offered to go back to the car when I realized that I'd left my script on the floor. It was his fault, anyway. He was the one who'd distracted me after completing his parking maneuvers. If my head hadn't been spinning from his kiss, I never would have left the script behind.

Smiling as the door closed behind him, I turned to the routine task of setting out chairs. They were stacked neatly in the corner where I'd left them after rehearsal the day before. They weren't very heavy, but they were awkward to manipulate, and it was hard to take down more than one at a time.

"Oh!" Stephanie said, springing up from her warm-up

stretches and cutting off a chattering Jennifer midsentence. "You shouldn't be doing that. Let me get those."

I jumped back from the chairs as if they might carry some invisible contagion. "What?" I said stupidly.

Stephanie looked confused herself. "It's just—"

And then I saw her eyes go to my waist.

My baggy-sweatpants-clad waist. My nonpregnant, never-pregnant, Teel-skinny waist. My obscured-by-fabric-falling-straight-off-my-increased-bust waist. My still-hidden-by-sweats-because-I'd-never-made-time-to-go-shopping waist.

I could feel my blush steam crimson to the roots of my hair. I would have been every bit as mortified if I hadn't just spent the past several hours engaged in activities that could have made Stephanie's misinterpretation come true.

Jennifer stepped forward with an awkward smile. "Stephanie just meant that the chairs can be so noisy. We'll both help and then you can finish faster. She and I wanted to talk about the whole man-love thing, with Romeo and Mercutio. You know, does it become gay because two women are out there, instead of two guys."

"Yeah," Stephanie said, and I realized that she was a better actor than I'd ever suspected. She could certainly take a line when it was fed to her, and her reading was spot on. If I hadn't been drowning in embarrassment, I'd probably even have believed her. She raised her voice, the better to be heard over the imaginary clatter of shifting chairs. "The whole 'brothers in arms' thing has a strange tone with the switch."

Jennifer responded, her own voice pitched just loud enough that I could pretend to believe her lie. "That's probably what Bill is getting at, isn't it? One of the major things behind this whole interpretation?"

I had to let them help, had to let them pretend they had meant to help little old stage manager me all along. Together, the three of us wrangled the chairs into a rough circle, but the entire time I worked, I kept staring down. How could anyone think I was pregnant *now?* When Teel had erased thirty pounds *weeks* ago?

Sure, I'd had a couple of embarrassing moments in the past year, times when I'd ordered my typical alcohol-free drinks and seen the quick measuring flash of eyes to my waist. I'd even had one older woman gesture toward an escalator, smiling sweetly as she said, "Please, dear. It would hardly be polite for me to push *you* out of the way."

I'd told myself that those were exceptions. Minor oversights. The older woman had eyeglasses hanging from a chain around her neck; I'd pretended that she needed them for distance.

But now? Here? After my second wish was long granted, and I'd almost grown accustomed to the body of my dreams? It didn't make any sense. It wasn't fair.

I excused myself and hurried into the bathroom. Glaring at myself in the mirror, I turned to my right, then to my left.

As much as I wanted to, I couldn't actually blame Stephanie. I *did* look pregnant. There was something about the way the black jersey knit bunched around my waist. I pulled my sweatshirt waistband as low over my hips as I could manage and gritted my teeth. I had to go shopping that afternoon. It was time—long past time—to ditch my old clothes.

I was still tugging at the fabric when I stormed out of the bathroom.

"Whoa, Franklin!" I looked up in surprise as John McRae reached out to steady me. I'd been so intent on my appearance that I hadn't even noticed him crossing the lobby. "Is something on fire?"

I shouldn't have blushed. The words were innocent enough; they didn't have to be a reference to Drew and me, to the heat we had generated between my sheets the night before. I dug my fingernails into my palms, though, as my cheeks started to burn. Again. John—utterly unaware of the memories filling my mind—gave me a curious look. I muttered a greeting, and he followed me into the rehearsal room.

Drew was waiting for me, anxious as a lost toddler. "Kira!" he exclaimed. "Here's your script. Good thing we didn't leave it all the way back at your place."

I was only a little surprised that my capillaries let me blush a third time in less than fifteen minutes. I saw Stephanie and Jennifer register Drew's words, immediately parse them for the secret message of how we'd spent the night before. I couldn't bring myself to look at John; I didn't want to read the comprehension that would crease his face around his mustache.

"Thanks, Drew," I said, taking the binder and flipping through to the morning's scene. It was only as I stared at the typeset page that I realized Drew didn't even need to be at the morning's rehearsal. "I'm sorry!" I said. "I don't know what I was thinking! Juliet isn't even in today's scenes!" I lowered my voice and pretended that no one else was listening. "You could be home sleeping."

"I'd rather be here," he said simply. His statement made me feel warm inside. Supported. Loved.

That was stupid. It was absolutely too soon to talk about love. I couldn't plummet from crush through lust to love in less than twenty-four hours. At least not on my own. Not without Teel's help.

But I had to admit, I really liked the way it felt to have Drew slip into the chair next to me. And I loved, even more, the look of speculation that I caught in Stephanie's eyes as she joined us. I didn't even mind the more opaque expression on John's face, as he took in Drew's quick touch to my shoulder, as he acknowledged the nearly constant male attention I was receiving.

When Bill strode into the rehearsal room, he was positively thrilled that Drew was there. "Excellent! I was going to have Kira call you. We have some changes to make, changes that are essential to the play, and I want all the leads to know about them now."

I glanced at John, to see if he knew what Bill was talking about. He shook his head once, a short confirmation that he had no advance notice of what our director was about to announce. He started tapping a pencil against his leg, though, as he ran a hand over his mustache. Settling back into his chair like a man reminding himself to relax, he said, "What's it going to be now, Bill?"

Bill looked around at all of us, fairly bouncing on his feet as he gripped the back of his chair. "Supertitles."

Drew said, "Do you mean subtitles?"

"No. *Supertitle*s. Above the show. Up in the air." Bill's excitement was contagious; I glanced at my cup of coffee to see if he had somehow managed to gulp all of my caffeine. "They have them at the opera, translations so that audiences can know what's going on."

John kept his voice carefully neutral. "But *Romeo and Juliet* is already in English."

Bill's arms spread expansively. "Elizabethan English, yes! English that is four hundred years old. English that has been worn down, eaten away, changed so that it can barely be recognized by the average guy on the street. But we have the solution! We can translate! Picture it!"

Bill's fingers were splayed, jazz hands trying to bring down the very ceiling. Drew looked up obediently, almost as if he expected something to materialize from thin air. Stephanie, Jennifer, and the other women who had arrived to block out Mercutio's final battle exchanged glances among themselves.

Oblivious, Bill tossed his head back and howled his excitement. When he could speak again, he said, "And the best part is, all of you actors will be in on the secret! You'll come downstage and gesture toward the supertitles. You'll actively direct the audience's attention to the new words. Old, new, all of it will come together! We should be able to reblock the first three acts today."

Jennifer was actually the first to recover. She said, "So the supertitles will say something like "Romeo, oh Romeo, why do they call you Romeo?""

Of course, when she said it that way, it sounded absurd. Unnecessary. Just one further complication, for a production that was rapidly assuming the complexity of the D-day invasion. I waited for Bill to laugh, for him to say "Gotcha!" To bellow "April Fools'!"

But we were only halfway through February.

And the only fools were those of us sitting in the rehearsal room, trying to get our minds around the fact that we were going to have the first dumbed-down, supertitled *Romeo and Juliet* in the history of American theater. Or British theater. Or any other self-respecting theater, anywhere.

I swallowed hard and said, "Bill, you want to rework all of the blocking? So far into rehearsals?"

"This is *art*," my director reminded me, for at least the thousandth time. It might be art, but I questioned whether the actors could memorize new places to stand, especially when there were so many other technical tricks about this show.

John stepped forward to save the day. "Bill, it's too late to build a projection system. Too late to add a screen. Not with all the ironwork we have on the pipes."

Bill laughed. "I knew you'd say that. I knew you'd have some song and dance about why it can't be done. I already called a friend over at the Minnesota Opera. You have an appointment at noon, to be shown around their stage. They do it every show, so just forget about your 'can't be done.'"

For the first time in six weeks, I saw absolute rage on John's face. "Dammit, Bill, we don't have time to add supertitles! You're changing the set every goddamn day, and I can't go back now and add something totally new. Six weeks, Bill! We've got six weeks left!"

Silence.

Bill just stared at John in silence, his ebullience utterly deflated. The actors were shocked, too. They weren't trained to think about sets, about stage design, about tricks with lighting and sound and costumes. As a group, they were getting ready to switch from working in the rehearsal room to working on stage. They were eager to start moving in their sibilant slime-strewn costumes. They were excited about banging pipe swords against wrought-iron frames.

But they never really stopped to worry about how it all happened, how it all came to exist. They never worried about how stagehands built platforms and ironworkers welded manhole covers and stage managers tried to keep entire productions from falling apart at the increasingly weighty seams.

Drew spoke first, directing his best Leading Man smile at John. "Hey, dude. It'll all come together. You've got Kira to help you. Kira can do anything."

Any other time, I would have appreciated the vote of confidence. Just about now, though, I wanted to kick Drew's shins, smother his Pollyanna assessment before he made things even worse. John's silence felt heavier than the manhole-cover frames he'd designed.

And Bill just stared at his recalcitrant set designer. "Noon," he said, and then he glanced at his wrist, at his nonexistent watch.

John stormed out of the room.

I couldn't let him go. I was the stage manager—it was my job to keep the production moving forward, to keep everything on track. I jumped up from my chair, shrugging off Drew's hand as he reached out to keep me by his side.

I caught up with John on the sidewalk. "Wait, John! You can't just walk away!"

He shortened his stride, but he kept on moving. I crossed my arms over my chest to cut the winter chill.

"That is exactly what I'm doing." His voice was deeper than I'd ever heard it before. His words were more clipped; his Texas twang sounded almost like a British accent.

"John, you know that Bill's just excited about the show. He wants to make a splash. He's building the Landmark's name, building our reputation."

"He's flushing this show down the toilet."

"You don't honestly believe that," I said, although I was suddenly afraid that he did. I was suddenly afraid that *I* did. "He's daring, John. He's brave. He's the most charismatic director I've ever seen. You've watched—he's got the cast eating out of his hand, Jennifer and Drew, and all the rest of them."

John stopped. "Yeah, Drew is ready to do just about anything for this show, isn't he?"

I felt like I'd been slapped. "What is that supposed to mean?"

John stared at me for long enough that I wondered if he somehow knew about Teel. I wondered if he knew that I was a fraud, that Drew's sudden adoration was completely made up, that my body was a sad joke, that my very presence at the Landmark was all one cruel, manipulative excuse for professionalism.

But then he shook his head. "You're going to freeze to death." I realized that we were standing in front of a salt-stained silver pickup truck. John reached in front of me and unlocked

the door, tugging it open with an exasperated sigh. "Get in."
He shrugged out of his denim jacket, tossing the coat across
my lap. The plaid lining radiated heat from his body. I suddenly
realized that I *was* cold. I set my teeth to keep them from chattering, and I tucked my hands beneath the jacket's worn hem.
John closed my door as soon as I was settled.

As he walked around to his side, I glanced around the cab
of the truck. A copy of the *StarTribune* was fanned across the
bench seat. A wadded-up paper sack on top told me that John
had indulged in McDonald's for breakfast. The gear shift was
neatly wedged in Reverse, glaring like an exclamation point
from the steering wheel.

John slammed his door closed when he got in and then
leaned his head back against the padded headrest. His eyes
were closed. "I didn't mean anything by that crack about
Drew," he finally said.

My fingers were still freezing. "It's okay," I said.

"It's just that he was really pushing my buttons in there.
Callin' me 'dude.'"

"That's just something he says. He doesn't mean anything
by it."

"He's not in a fraternity anymore. He shouldn't talk like he is."

I wasn't comfortable with the conversation. Truth be told,
I thought that John was right. "Dude" was okay with actual
friends; but it did make Drew sound…immature. If we were
theater professionals, we should act like grown-ups. Sound like
them. That's what John was saying, and he was right.

But who was I to talk? I used my share of "totally" with Jules
and Maddy, sounding like I should still be chomping on Bubble
Yum and twirling my hair around my index finger.

And things had changed last night, things between Drew and
me. We were bound to support each other now, to stand beside

each other, if either one of us was questioned. I knew the drill. I'd perfected it with TEWSBU. I knew what it meant to be the affirming girlfriend, the one who always listened, who always agreed.

I expelled a deep breath I hadn't realized I'd been holding. That type of unquestioning support had been one of the things that had driven me most insane when it came to TEWSBU— to his career, to our engagement, to everything about my life with him. There had been times that I had known he was wrong, but he wouldn't tolerate my speaking out against him, even in the privacy of our own bedroom.

There was that time that he'd wanted to cast a beautiful woman as Antigone, just because she was beautiful—he'd said she'd fill seats in the theater, even though she was totally wrong for the strong-willed role. There was the time that he'd insisted on staging *Glengarry Glen Ross* in the round, even when everyone else could see that the play would be ruined by diffusing the audience's focus.

At least he'd never set *Romeo and Juliet* in the sewers. With slime. And supertitles.

I looked at John steadily. This wasn't really about Drew. There was no need for us to talk about Drew at all. This was about Bill and his artistic vision, about his plans for the entire production. "Come on, John," I begged. "Just go over to the Opera, okay? See how they do the supertitles. See whether we can get them up in time. If it's really not possible, then I'll back you up. We can go to Bill together and explain that it can't be done."

John shook his head, but he'd started to smile. "You realize that you're going to need *another* stagehand. Someone to change the slides."

I shrugged. "What's another person on the payroll, among friends?"

He laughed, the slow easy laugh that I realized I'd come to expect from him. "Want a ride back?"

"It's only a block. I can walk it. I don't want to make you late to the opera."

He shrugged. "Have it your way. I'd just as soon be late."

"Exactly," I said, and I was pleased when he chuckled again. Stage-manager mission accomplished.

I handed back his jacket reluctantly and let myself out of the truck, speed-walking back toward the Landmark. As it turned out, my cell phone rang when I was halfway to the theater's front door. I fished it out of my pocket, stopping Ethel Merman in midwail. "Hi, Dad."

"Kira."

Whoops. That didn't sound good. That didn't sound like a loving father, just calling to see how his one and only daughter was doing. I pasted on a smile, hoping it would carry over to my voice. "What's up?" And then, just to cut short whatever tirade I was owed, I said, "I've only got a minute before I have to head back into rehearsal."

Dad sounded like he'd been chewing on lemon peel; I could practically see his lips pucker. "I tried to call you at home earlier, but Maddy said you'd already left for the day."

Maddy. So he'd called while Drew and I... And I hadn't even heard the phone ring. "Yep," I said hurriedly. "I got an early start this morning." I tried to sound bright and cheerful. Like I wasn't hiding anything. Like I didn't have anything to hide. Like my housemate hadn't needed to lie to protect me from my father's inquiries.

"I'm a little surprised that you were able to wake up on time today."

Eww. What exactly did my father know? And how did he know it? I quickly settled on a perplexed "What do you mean?"

"I mean that Mrs. Swenson called me at the office this morning, first thing."

"Oh! That's all!" I was so relieved that I almost fell against the Landmark's heavy glass doors. I pushed through them, grateful that I was not going to have to discuss my sex life with my father. Sure, I'd been worried about Maddy and Jules overhearing Drew and me last night, but I was certain that our half-deaf downstairs neighbor didn't know what had happened in the bed above her. She or her husband. I could still hear Mr. Swenson muttering, though, as he locked his front door the night before.

"That's all? She was very upset, Kira."

Before I could come up with a good response, Drew slipped out of the shadows. He must have been waiting for me in the lobby, because he immediately sidled up behind me, slipping his hands around my waist. I leaned back into him as he touched his lips to my neck, nuzzling the sensitive spot just beneath my ear. I pulled away and turned to face Drew, holding a finger across my lips to keep him quiet as I said into the phone, "I'm sorry that we woke her up last night, Dad."

Drew pointed at himself, a goofy grin spreading across his face. I nodded as Dad said, "Having Chinese food delivered late at night is 'waking her up.' She made it sound like you all were having a party. She said that people were coming and going at all hours of the night, that car lights were shining in their bedroom window. People were screaming out on the sidewalk."

"It wasn't like that, Dad." My reply might have been more convincing if Drew hadn't taken the opportunity to wrap his fingers in my hair, to pull me close enough that I could feel his breath on my cheek. I hoped Dad couldn't hear him breathing.

"What was it like, then, Kira? What will the other neighbors say, when I call them?"

Wow. Mrs. Swenson must have really read him the Riot Act. Dad was always worried about his tenants, about our being good neighbors to the Swensons, but I hadn't been lectured like this since the first year that Maddy, Jules, and I moved in and decided to host a housewarming kegger.

Drew moved around me, his fingers cupping my Teel-created bust, teasing at the bra straps beneath my now-hated sweatshirt. It took all of my self-control not to giggle into my cell phone. I forced myself to put up a hand in the universal sign for stop. Drew looked like a berated puppy, but he took a single reluctant step backward.

"It was just one person who came by, Dad. His name is Drew. He's in the show at the Landmark. He's playing Juliet."

"Romeo," my father said.

I decided that this might not be the best time to clarify Bill Pomeroy's vision of gender relations. Besides, Drew was splaying his hand across his chest, silently asking if I was talking about him, *really* talking about him. "Dad," I said, putting enough emphasis on the name that my sex-starved boyfriend actually looked abashed. "I have to get back into rehearsal now. I promise we'll be quieter from now on."

"No more late-night parties?"

Since we hadn't had one in years, it was easy to agree. "No more late-night parties."

He sighed. "I know that you don't mean anything by it, Kira. It's just that things are very busy here at the office these days. Those profits per partners don't generate themselves, and if I lose half an hour listening to Susan Swenson tell me about how my daughter and her crazy friends were running around at all hours of the day and night…"

Profits per partner. We were back on solid father-daughter ground. "I'm sorry, Dad." I braced myself for the rest of the paternal speech, for the reminder about the LSAT, about the importance of my having options in life.

Instead, my father surprised me. "Kira…." He trailed off, though. I had never heard my father sound so uncertain. Unsure.

"What?" I said, honest concern leading me to push Drew off to arm's length, to half turn away and cover up my free ear, the better to concentrate.

"When I talked to Maddy this morning, she said that she's worried about you. She said that you've…changed."

Maddy. That little traitor! I forced my voice to be firm. "You know how Maddy is, Dad. She's always trying to control everyone. Always trying to make the world work exactly the way she thinks it should." I didn't wait for him to call me on the lie, to tell me that Maddy wasn't that way at all. "I have *got* to go, Dad. They're calling me from the rehearsal room. Goodbye." I snapped the phone off, almost before he could say his own, less angry goodbye.

Drew's arms were waiting before I had shoved the phone back into my pocket. It felt good to let him fold me into his embrace. I leaned my cheek against his chest, listened to his heart beating calmly, steadily. "Problems with the old man?" he asked.

I sighed and stepped back. "Nothing permanent." I glanced toward the door of the rehearsal room, already feeling a little guilty for having lied. "What *is* going on in there?"

Drew grinned and said, "Bill didn't even have a chance to tell us the best part about the subtitles before McRae took off."

"Supertitles," I corrected automatically, fighting a sinking feeling. "What's the best part?"

Drew grinned. "They're not just going to be, like, translations. They're going to be hip-hop. You know. Like rap! Dude!"

I shuddered, imagining John's reaction once he heard that. But John's reaction didn't matter. John's job was to make the technology possible, to get the slides projected onto the set. The only thing that mattered was that we were doing something new. Something different. Something that would make this production of *Romeo and Juliet* famous forever.

At least that's what I told myself, as Drew's distracting kiss took on a driving, rhythmic hip-hop beat of its own.

CHAPTER 13

AFTER REHEARSAL, DREW DROVE ME HOME. PERFORMING perfectly in the role of a solicitous gentleman, he insisted on dropping me off at the front door before trolling for a parking spot. I kissed him and hopped out of the car, ostensibly properly grateful to be spared the walk through the February cold.

As soon as the car was out of sight, though, I sprinted up the stairs to the apartment. A cautious "hello?" confirmed that neither Maddy nor Jules was around. I dashed into my bedroom and threw open my closet door. Digging out a handful of Hefty bags from my backpack, I immediately began collecting my old, oversize wardrobe.

In another life, I would have acted methodically, carefully stripping garments from hangers and folding them away for posterity. Now, though, I tore through the closet, desperate to complete my transformation before Drew came upstairs.

What had I been thinking? Why had I continued wearing my baggy clothes for so long? (Read: Why had I allowed base comfort and a crazy rehearsal schedule to triumph over even

the faintest hint of a fashionable wardrobe?) No wonder Stephanie had made her embarrassing mistake—I deserved it, for
being such a slob.

A frantic five minutes later, I'd accomplished my goal. I was
astonished to see how many bags I'd filled; I needed to shove
them into the back of my closet. Eating myself into emotional
oblivion had cost me an arm and a leg—in new clothes at least,
and that wasn't even factoring in the cost of all that food that
I'd consumed. I could only hope that someone at Goodwill
would enjoy the wardrobe I was leaving behind forever.

My final act of purification involved stripping off the sweats
I'd worn to rehearsal that day. I started to add them to one of
the Hefty bags, but then decided that I should keep this one
set. Treasure them. Always remember the way I'd let TEWSBU
ruin my life, the way that I'd eaten myself into misery and
despair (not to mention into a size 2X sweatshirt).

I shrugged into a body-skimming burgundy sweater that I
hadn't worn for more than a year, then pulled on a pair of
narrow-wale black slacks, as soft as velvet. Although I had
thought the sweater would be far too tight, it actually managed
to accommodate my new curves. I just looked very … healthy.
I was running a quick brush through my unruly curls when
there was a knock at the door.

"You poor thing!" I exclaimed as I let Drew in. I hoped that
the Swensons hadn't noticed that I'd left the foyer door ajar for
him to enter the building.

He collapsed on my bed, feigning exhaustion, like a man
who had just hiked miles through a blizzard. "I decided it
might be easier just to park in St. Paul."

"I am so sorry! It's not usually that bad around here." Secretly,
though, I was grateful that I'd had time to complete my closet
exorcism. I silently vowed to supplement my wardrobe the next

day, no matter what theatrical surprises Bill released upon us. "If I'd realized you were going to have to park so far away, I would have suggested going to dinner before we came back here."

"I'm not moving from that parking space until morning," Drew pouted. Before I could protest, he pulled me down beside him. "Even if it means that we starve to death. At least then we'll die together."

I did my best to reward him for his romantic words with a kiss. I even tried not to pout that he didn't admire my new clothes before he stripped them off me, garment by tantalizing garment. I sent a mental wave of thanks to Teel anyway, wherever he was now.

Drew seemed remarkably grateful for my genie's work as well. Not that he was inclined to be a particularly good judge of anything where I was concerned. Drew was completely, utterly smitten, entirely devoted to loving me, to pleasing me.

And that was such a wonderful change that I almost regretted that I would never see my genie again. Almost, but not quite. As Drew started to nuzzle the incredibly sensitive bundle of nerves below my right ear, an electric jangle built inside my body. This time, though, the tingling had nothing to do with magic. I gave myself over to the pleasure, forgetting all worldly concerns further than my bedroom door.

Of course, pleasure couldn't last forever. I eventually had to acknowledge that my stomach was growling with hunger. I eventually had to admit that I'd heard one of my housemates come in. I eventually had to sit up, to fumble in the dim light for the clothes Drew had strewn about with such reckless abandon.

"Yum," he said, reaching toward me after I slid up the side zip on my slacks.

I laughed and leaned down to kiss him on the nose. "As if you could do anything about it right now."

He looked down, as forlorn as a little boy who had lost his toy ray-gun. "I can try."

"I'll see what I can whip up in the kitchen, by way of a restorative." He started to push himself up from the bed, but I settled my palms against his chest. The heat from his body radiated into my hands. "Just relax," I said.

"But—"

"You've had a long day," I laughed. He collapsed onto my pillow with a dramatic sigh.

Jules was waiting for me in the living room, one leg flung casually over the arm of the sofa as she chewed the last bite of whatever healthful salad she'd thrown together for her dinner. "So," she said as I slunk in from the hallway. "You *were* in there. How was Loverboy last night?"

"Shh!" I glanced down the short hallway to make sure I'd closed my bedroom door behind me.

"What?" And then comprehension dawned. "He's here? Now?"

I nodded, unable to keep my happiness from spreading across my face in a silly schoolgirl smile. "I'm just getting us something to eat."

Jules leaped up and followed me into the kitchen. Trying to act as nonchalant as possible, I opened up the freezer. The possibilities weren't promising. There was a single Ziploc bag holding something that might have been a chicken breast, an Ice Age ago. I dug out the remnant of a loaf of bread, three or four slices with enough ice crystals to conduct a science experiment on cryogenics. Giving up my exploration of the Arctic, I tugged open the refrigerator door. I had a block of cheddar in the deli drawer. A couple of apples rolled around in the fruit bin. I shrugged. That would have to do.

When I stepped away with my pitiful harvest, I saw that Jules was staring at me. I expected a look of sly conspiracy, a "you go, girl" celebration of my newfound romance. I could have lived with an expression of shocked disapproval—after all, things *had* moved forward rather quickly with Drew. But I was utterly astonished to see the naked concern written across her features.

"What's wrong?" I asked.

She shook her head. "I guess I haven't seen you in a while." She gestured at my sweater and my velvet-soft trousers. "When did you get so skinny?"

I laughed. Jules's question was the perfect antidote to Stephanie's mistake that afternoon. Still, I knew that I couldn't tell her the truth, and I wasn't willing to ruin the evening by choking over genie-related words that would stick in my throat. I shrugged. "I've been working on it for a while," I said.

"And what are you wearing? A WonderBra?"

I blushed. "Jules!"

She glanced at the food I'd put on the counter. "That's not enough for dinner."

I was relieved that she'd moved off the topic of my Teel-enhanced figure so quickly. "We'll be fine," I said airily. "You know how life is during rehearsals. No time to get to the grocery store."

Jules turned to the pantry, digging around to excavate her own box of whole wheat crackers. "At least take some of these."

"I can't—"

"Kira, you have to eat!"

Wow. I couldn't remember the last time anyone had said that to me. "Okay," I said. I didn't want to turn this conversation into World War III. I should have planned better, should have gone shopping, even though the Landmark was consuming my every waking—and now, sleeping—moment. "I'll buy a replacement box the next time I'm at the store."

"Don't worry about it." I could see that she wanted to say something else. She kept looking at the cinched-in waist of my pants, at the swell of my sweater.

"Jules, I'm *fine*. I've just dropped a couple of pounds. You know that I had plenty to lose, after... Well..."

"Of course," she said. But I saw her eyes dart toward the whiteboard, as if she were seeking out Maddy's thoughts on the matter. *Bis Montag* was written there. I guessed that meant we'd see Maddy on Monday.

"Kira?" Drew's voice called down the hallway. I looked up to see him poking his head out of my room. He kept his body hidden behind the door frame; he obviously hadn't bothered to get dressed. His hair was tousled, and there was no possible way to pretend to Jules that we had not just been rolling around on my mattress. My heart clenched at the sight of him; he was adorable in an innocent, lighthearted way.

"Just a second!" I called, looking at Jules with just a hint of desperation.

"Go," she said. But she turned back to the pantry, seeking out a pair of chocolate pudding cups, the one sweet treat that she splurged on. "But take some dessert, too."

"Thanks," I said. And I tried to pretend that the living room was empty as Drew and I settled into our idyllic bedside picnic.

We quickly found a steady routine. Drew and I continued to hang out mostly at my place. He had a trio of frat-boy housemates who grated on my nerves with their constant high fives, beer-guzzling competitions, and comments that would have made a seasoned Hooters patron blush. Besides, their shared bathroom should have been condemned by the health department.

Drew and I barely made it to rehearsal on time every morning. Drew tagged along even when he didn't have to be there. I couldn't imagine voluntarily sitting through some of the scenes, listening to the same lines over and over and over again. Drew, though, insisted that he wanted nothing more than to sit by my side. I tried not to preen in public.

In the evenings, we took a break from Shakespeare. We caught up on watching all the movies that had been nominated for that year's Oscars, pretending to evaluate the performances until we let ourselves get distracted by reenacting the better romantic scenes. We introduced each other to our favorite restaurants. Once, we tried to walk all the way around Lake of the Isles, but we were defeated by incomplete snow removal and a bitter winter wind.

Every night, we collapsed into bed together. Simple cuddling wasn't part of Drew's exuberant expression of his boundless love; he was more an all or nothing sort of guy. And under Teel's spell, Drew wasn't about to settle for "nothing."

The play steadily progressed. A team of experts (Read: Musicians who were still trying to sign with a major studio) had been hired to complete the first-ever translation of *Romeo and Juliet* into hip-hop slang; we were supposed to get the words back by the first Monday in March, so that we'd have plenty of time to make the slides.

One of the metal frames for the manhole covers arrived, and it was huge—heavy and gritty-looking and capable of withstanding any assault with iron-pipe swords. The actors were gradually kitted out in their full costumes—sleek, rubberized things that were glued together instead of stitched. The costumes required copious amounts of baby powder to get on, and they had an unfortunate tendency to split along their seams. Any passing cops would be certain that we were holding huffing parties in the back room as we tried to seal the things up with aromatic glue day after day.

Teel's hot womanly commentary was originally missed, but the actors quickly recovered because they were almost completely submerged in their roles. Every single guy in the cast, though, made sure to tell me that he couldn't wait to attend Teel's senior thesis presentation in the spring. It wasn't until the fourth man (Lady Capulet) said something that I managed to wheedle details from Drew. Teel had told them that she was doing a performance art piece that examined gender roles and expectations. Basically, she performed a striptease set to a voice-over of great feminist texts from around the world. She started with a full Victorian costume and ended up in a bikini. Or less. Everyone was a bit fuzzy on that last bit.

Pity they'd never actually get to see the piece, now that Teel was gone.

In the meantime, Bill had demanded some sort of uber-Method acting for our cast. He'd instructed all the actors to stay in gender character even when they weren't at the theater. That direction had already caused some trouble: three of the women were threatened at a downtown bar after they insisted on using the men's room rather than the ladies'. Fortunately for me, Drew had decided not to follow *that* edict of Bill's, at least not when we got away from the Landmark.

On the home front, Maddy and Jules were fantastic about my newfound romance—even if Drew did present something of a challenge.

For one thing, he didn't play Scrabble. At all. One Monday night, the first one where all of us were home at the same time, Jules had already turned over the tiles when Drew and I traipsed in from rehearsal. She was waiting for a championship match.

Drew was eager enough at first. He sat down at the table, twirling his wooden letter rack between his fingers. But he had to wait for Jules to tell him how many letters to choose. And then, he had no idea how the double-letter squares worked. He got downright cranky when Jules built out a triple-word score that he'd left wide open, and it didn't help that she used the *Z* to score an instant thirty points.

That was the last time we all played Scrabble together—the game really isn't fun when your opponent only adds three-letter words to the board.

Ordering in from Hunan Delight wasn't much better. Drew was a sharer, and that upset the entire balance of our little tradition. He actually teased Jules for ordering Spicy Dry Fried Salted Squid. I didn't think that was tease-worthy; I was just astonished that she'd found it on the menu. In eight years, I was pretty certain that we'd never ordered squid before—dried, wet, fried or grilled. Even though Drew expressed dismay at the tentacles (what he actually said was, "Dude, are you really putting that in your *mouth?*"), he managed to dart in with his chopsticks enough that Jules finally passed the red carton to him with a barely suppressed roll of her eyes. I was just grateful that his attention was diverted from my own dinner. I ate quickly and managed to quell my shiver of distaste when Drew insisted on sampling the last few bites of my food.

Alas, Drew insisted on the idiotic childishness of adding "in bed" to our fortunes when we read them. Which might have been fine, if Jules had not opened a cookie that read "Use proven methods. Avoid shortcuts."

Even I found Drew's sophomoric braying a bit much to handle.

But every time I started to wonder if I'd made a mistake, if I'd acted too impetuously with my last wish, my new boyfriend did something to endear himself to me. Knowing my love of all things coffee, he tracked down a pound of kopi luwak, coffee beans that were, as the packaging discreetly read, "The World's Rarest Coffee Beverage." (Read: The only one to have passed through the digestive tract of a civet cat.) I couldn't bring myself to drink the stuff, but it was the thought that counted.

Drew was also ready with a back rub whenever we got home from rehearsals. He seemed able to read my mind about when I'd reached my breaking point with Bill's ever-more-bizarre staging ideas. He listened to me rant for three full hours the day that our inspired director instructed David Barstow, the lighting designer, to do away with every single light on the warm side of the spectrum. If it wasn't blue or gray, and cold, cold, cold, Bill didn't want it in our underground Verona. Never mind that every lighting designer in the world used warm colors to provide important *contrast* on stage.

The entire cast was wrapping up our first rehearsal in the actual theater space when Bill had another one of his brainstorms. "I just want to say one word to you," he announced to everyone after a particularly draining romp through the discovery scene, where Romeo believes his (her?) beloved Juliet is dead. "Plastic."

Of course, the actual line from the movie *The Graduate*, was, "Plastic*s*." With an *S*. Multiple plastics. But I wasn't about to say anything out loud. My mind was already reeling, as I tried to predict what new challenge Bill was about to introduce.

"Plastic," Bill repeated to his rapt cast. "That's the way to capture the danger. The oppressiveness. Kira, give John a call tonight. Tell him that we need to coat the floor with heavy-duty plastic."

The first thing I thought of was the fight scenes. The second was the Landmark's insurance premiums. I cleared my throat and put on my best Logical Stage Manager voice. "Bill? It will be really difficult for everyone to keep their footing if we cover the entire stage with plastic. Especially with all the slime we plan on using."

"Exactly!" he boomed, spreading his arms wide. "The floor will be a metaphor for the play's politics! Our staging will be a physical representation of the Prince of Verona's instructions to the Montagues and the Capulets. He tells them to be mindful. He says their lives are forfeit if they take one wrong step. We'll make that danger real."

I was pretty sure that John would see things differently. He hadn't made it to rehearsal in days; I knew that he was working long hours with the welders, trying to get the massive ironwork complete and delivered on time. He'd already made them redo Friar Laurence's culvert twice, because the sound echoed too loudly for the actors to be heard during those delicate scenes.

And then, to make everything worse, our fearless director exclaimed, "Picture it! The prince comes in for his first scene. He tells everyone that lives will be forfeited if the street fighting continues. He leaves, and a battalion of city workers, of stage-hands, comes in *right in front of the audience*, to lay down the plastic. The prince's word is made real, before our very eyes."

I was conscious of the very eyes of the cast, but I had to say something, had to make the protest that I knew John would make if he'd been there. "Bill, that's going to take a long time, to complete a transition like that in the middle of the scene."

He snorted. "Nonsense! If you have enough stagehands, you can do it in no time at all."

I pictured hordes of workers, waiting in the wings with plastic tarps. We could use the eight guys who would later ma-nipulate the manhole-cover screens. But to cover the entire stage? And to make sure the sheeting was secured at the edges, so that the actors didn't trip in the dark? It would take a dozen crew members at least. I took one look at the fanatic fire in Bill's eyes, though, and scribbled a note in the margins of my script. Four more stagehands. The union was going to love this show, even if the audience was mystified.

Bill nodded at my apparent acquiescence. "Let's start getting used to the new surface today. Unfortunately, Kira doesn't have the plastic ready, but I want everyone in their socks, right now. In your socks, and let's tape Hefty bags around your feet."

Unfortunately? What, did he think I could read his mind? That I could produce plastic sheeting out of thin air?

It wasn't like *I* was a genie.

Still, the cast had perfect faith in him. Not a single actor hesitated. Instead, they just looked at me like baby birds, expectant, confident that I would provide. I thought about making one more plea for common sense, but Bill was already looking at his nonexistent watch. I'd lose the battle. Why declare war in the first place?

One complete box of trash bags and two rolls of duct tape later, the cast looked like refugees from some horrific environmental disaster. Or a bizarre operating room with absurd sterilization protocols. Or something else that I was just too frightened to imagine.

We only had one fall that broke the skin. Stephanie was skating across the stage in her plastic getup, a guest at the fateful ball where Romeo and Juliet met. She took a tumble as she capered around, doing her best to manifest the trickster spirit so important to Mercutio. She broke her fall with an outflung wrist; it was just bad luck that Drew was standing in front of her, winking at me. The corner of his script notebook caught her palm, leaving a gash that bled copiously.

I apologized nonstop as I scrambled for my first aid kit. If Drew hadn't been clowning around for me, he would have noticed Stephanie's tumble. He would have snatched away the offending notebook.

At least I was equipped with gauze pads and a roll of white tape.

I shook my head as the cast ripped off their plastic booties at the end of the rehearsal. Drew helped to gather up the last of the garbage, shoving the torn bags into the trash can with an earnest smile. "Dude, that was so cool!" he said to me. "I could totally feel the uncertainty in Juliet's mind, when she was talking to her nurse."

"That was just fear that you'd break a leg. Literally," I added, thinking of the traditional theater curse for good luck.

Drew answered my tartness the way he always did. He folded me into his arms, kissing me until I began to relax. There was still stress in my life—there would be until the play opened— but this was a great way to deal with it. Nevertheless, I forced myself to push him away. "I've got to get going," I said.

"Where?" he whispered against my earlobe.

I shivered. "I told you this morning. I've got to drop off our rent check at my father's office. And *you* have to finish memorizing your lines. We're going to be totally off book, starting tomorrow."

"I want to run lines with you," he cajoled, backing up the suggestion with deft fingers that did surprising things along the line of my spine.

"Drew, we already talked about this!"

And we had. I'd told him that I needed one night at home. Alone. With Maddy and Jules, just us girls. Both of them had eyed me strangely when I followed Drew to bed the night before. More and more often, I could tell that they'd been talking about me when I walked into the room; there were too many conversations that stopped right when I came in.

Just that morning, Jules had caught me as I dashed out of the bathroom. I was tucking a brand-new white blouse into the waistband of my jeans. I'd found the pants at the back of my closet, stranded on the very last hanger, where I'd banished them after outgrowing them almost two years before. Now they zipped up easily, emphasizing the ample bosom that continued to surprise me.

"Wow," Jules had said tonelessly.

I'd grinned. "I don't even remember when I bought these."

"I can't believe how much you've changed, Kira." She'd frowned a little as she spoke, looking doubtfully at my chest, as if she were trying to remember if I'd always been so well endowed. An unreasoning spike of anger stirred in my belly. What did she have against my getting back in shape? How could she even begin to understand how excited I was to wear my skinny pants—Jules, who was always glamorous and gorgeous and fit? Before I could say something I'd regret, though, Drew came out of my bedroom, carrying my backpack for me.

"Ready?" he'd asked, settling a teasing hand against the small of my back as he guided us toward the front door.

As thrilled as I was with Drew's unending attention, I worried about the easy balance of my friendship with my housemates. It was time to clear the air—Maddy, Jules, and I would shift back to normal with a night of girls-only Scrabble and Chinese food.

Now, as rehearsal wrapped up, Drew's lips teased mine. "Call me if you change your mind." Exercising more willpower than I'd managed in decades, I pulled away from him. The February evening was particularly cold as I turned my key in my car's stubborn ignition.

At the law firm, Dad's secretary, Angie, looked up as I waltzed by her desk. "Hello," I said absently, already digging in my backpack for the check I was going to hand over.

"Hello, Kira."

That's when I noticed that something was wrong. By the end

of the workday, Angie was always frantically printing out documents for my father's review and signature. She always chomped on a wad of chewing gum that made her look like a big league pitcher for the Minnesota Twins. She always muttered a constant stream of threats to her printer, tearing open new reams of paper as if she were making sacrifices to a ravenous god.

But today Angie was sitting stock-still. Her desk was bare. Her hands twined in her lap. Her computer had gone to a screen saver, an endless chain of colored light spinning its way through an unknown maze.

I barely knew what to say. "Are you okay?"

"I'm fine."

I made out just a hint of emphasis on the first word. Angie was fine. If Angie was fine, but everything else was turned upside down… I turned on my heel and slammed open my father's door.

And was so surprised that I almost fell back into the hallway.

My father sat behind his desk, ramrod straight, his suit jacket rigid across his shoulders. His tie was perfectly knotted and close to his Adam's apple; he looked like he was ready to walk into contract negotiations with the archest of his enemies.

But that wasn't what surprised me. What surprised me was seeing Jules sitting on the couch, the one that had a full view of the Minneapolis skyline. And Maddy standing beside her.

"Come in, Kira," my father said.

I didn't want to. Summoning all of my courage, I met my father's eyes. "This can't be good for profits per partner," I said. I'd feared the joke would fall flat. I just hadn't realized how flat it could fall.

"Come in, Kira," my father repeated. "And close the door behind you."

I did. I had to clear my throat, though, before I could get

out any more words. "So, I'm guessing this isn't about the rent? This isn't about Maddy and Jules all of a sudden deciding that I can't be trusted to deliver our check?"

My father moved around his desk and gestured to the two Hitchcock chairs, which had been pulled into the stiffest conversation pit known to man. "Please. Have a seat."

I thought about saying no. I thought about saying that I didn't want to. I thought about saying that I was going to go out the door and come back in again, that I was going to rewind the last two minutes, so that the world would go back to normal.

Instead, I sat.

Dad joined me in the other chair, seeming not to notice that he had to step over the straps of my backpack to do so. Maddy seemed torn by both of us sitting; she looked around, so ill at ease that I almost didn't recognize her. Ultimately, she perched on the edge of the couch, twisting her blunt-fingered hands around each other.

I was a little surprised that Jules spoke first. "Kira, I asked everyone to get together tonight."

"What is going on?" I heard a note of fear in my voice and told myself that I was crazy. This was my *father*. These were my *housemates*, my best friends.

Jules glanced at Maddy, looked back at her hands. She wouldn't meet my eyes. "We're worried about you, Kira. We've been worried about you for a long time, and we finally decided that we had to do something."

My first—totally irrational—thought was that they had found Teel's lantern underneath my bed. Despite my being silenced by my genie, they had somehow discovered the magic that had permeated my life. They knew that I'd gotten my three wishes, and they wanted their own; they were willing to hold me hostage until they got them.

That was absurd, though. There was no way that my house-mates would have gone digging around under my bed. And even if they had, they would have brought the lantern with them—*if* they'd even bothered to tell my father. There was absolutely no reason to bring Dad into a discussion about Teel.

I crossed my arms over my chest. It seemed like a long time had passed since Jules had spoken, but I knew it could only have been a few seconds. "There isn't anything to worry about. I'm fine."

My voice cracked on the last word.

Maddy leaned forward. "You're not fine, Kira. You've changed."

"What do you mean?"

Maddy held my gaze with the ferocity that was her trademark. Madeline Rubens wasn't afraid of anyone. Or anything. "Kira, we know that you are anorexic. And we're here to help you."

Anorexic?

I shouldn't have laughed. But her accusation was so preposterous, so far from what I had feared she might say. Me? The woman who had eaten herself into a mountain over the past year? The woman who could match all three of them, bite for bite, on sweets or savories, on any snack in the world?

I glanced down at my arms folded across my Teel-induced cleavage, caught a glimpse of my newly retrieved skinny jeans.

Yeah. Me.

I stammered out, "Wh-what do you mean?"

Jules answered. "Sweetie, we only want to help you." Sweetie? She hadn't called me that since…since she'd been holding my hair back from my face in the Hyatt Regency bathroom, the night that TEWSBU left me. I started to protest, but she interrupted, using every ounce of her acting skill to override me. "We know that this has been a really tough year for you. We understand that you're just trying to control a little bit of the world around you. But you don't have to do it this way. You don't have to hurt yourself."

"I'm not hurting myself!" I snapped. "I'm not anorexic!"

Which didn't exactly prove my point. After all, what would I have said if I really did have an eating disorder?

My father took over, lending his gravest attorney-voice to the chorus. "Kira, as you know, Maddy and I spoke a couple of weeks ago. She just couldn't overlook your self-destructive behavior any longer."

I glared at Maddy, but I had enough sense to keep my mouth shut. Whatever she'd said then, she'd said because she was worried about me. I tried to sound as reasonable as possible as I said, "What happened a couple of weeks ago?"

But I already knew the answer. Maddy kept her voice even as she said, "Drew. Drew happened."

"Don't bring him into this!" I said. "He doesn't have anything to do with what I eat."

Dad shook his head, leaning forward in his chair as if he needed to distract me, needed to focus my attention away from the vulnerable Maddy. Yeah, right. As if Maddy had ever spent a day in her life being vulnerable. "You have to understand how all of this looks to us on the outside, Kira. One minute, you're working at Fox Hill, happy as a clam. The next thing we know, you've quit your job, taken up with some guy you'd barely even mentioned, and you've stopped eating."

"I haven't stopped eating!"

Jules sighed, then reached for a legal pad that rested on the end table. "We started talking, Kira. Maddy and me. We made a list of things." She glanced down, almost apologetic. "Strange exercise—crunches that make you cramp up, yoga in the middle of the night. New food habits: my yogurt for breakfast, instead of Cap'n Crunch. Steamed vegetables from Hunan Delight. One single handful of kettle corn, stretched out over an entire hour."

"I don't even like kettle corn! I've never liked it! I just ate it so that I didn't disappoint you guys! You know, my *best friends*."

Jules looked hurt, but Maddy was the one who replied in her bluff, no-nonsense way. "We *are* your best friends, Kira. But we've let this slide for too long. Jules and I were both shocked when we realized how much weight you've lost. We should have noticed sooner. We should have helped you solve your problem."

"I don't have a problem!"

I launched myself out of my chair, using my frustration to carry me across the office. When I got to the photograph of my mother, I stared at her for a long time. If she were here, she'd believe me. She'd explain to them that I wasn't sick. I wasn't anorexic. *She* would have noticed my weight loss as soon as it happened; *she* wouldn't have been fooled by some baggy sweats.

After all, she and I looked like sisters. Now that I'd lost my TEWSBU weight.

Unaware of my silent pity party, my father took up the attack. "Kira, you can't stand there and deny that you've lost a lot of weight. We all watched you after the…wedding." He hesitated before the word, as if he didn't know what to call it, didn't know how to refer to the disaster. "We watched you take comfort in food. We knew that you'd put on several pounds, and we waited for you to come around, to stop that. But starving yourself isn't any better. It's no more a solution."

I spoke to my mother's framed photo. "I haven't been starving myself."

My father said, "Then work with us." His tone was so reasonable that I had to turn to face him. To face all three of them. "Prove to us that you're eating."

"What? You want me to videotape every meal?" I felt like a rebellious teenager.

This was all about Drew, a voice whispered in my head. They didn't like him. They'd never liked him. They were trying to drive him away, trying to make my life so difficult, so unappealing that no man in his right mind would stay with me.

Before anyone could say anything to make me even more furious, Maddy stood up. "We want you to keep a food diary."

"A what?" I sounded incredulous.

Maddy crossed toward me, sweeping a piece of paper from my father's desk. Sure enough, it read "Food Diary" across the top. The page was broken into sections, carved up for morning, midday, evening. There were three extra blocks for snacks.

"I don't have time for this!" As I protested, my father set his jaw. I knew then that he would ignore every one of my arguments, no matter how logical they were. I turned to Maddy and Jules instead. "I have a show opening in a month! You guys know what that means! I won't have time to do my laundry, much less write down every bite I eat."

Maddy merely shook her head. "It doesn't take that much time. You don't need to calculate calories or fat grams. For now."

"For now?" I was incredulous. "Is that a threat?"

Dad answered. "Kira, I know you're angry right now. I know you think that we're against you. But nothing could be further from the truth. All three of us just want you to be happy. If your life is out of control, if you have too much pressure to function in a healthy manner, we owe it to you to intervene."

He was absolutely, utterly serious. Maddy took advantage of my speechlessness to add, "You can do this. You're a stage manager. You keep perfect notes for your productions. Just keep track of your food for a month."

I wanted to refuse. I wanted to tell them that they were

collectively nuts. I wanted to tell them that I was hurt, insulted, furious.

But I knew that they *were* only speaking because they loved me.

Okay. How hard could it be to keep a food diary? I ate enough, every single day, that I would easily disprove their concerns. And, even though she'd been trying to flatter me, Maddy was right. List-making did come easily to me.

"Fine," I said. "I'll keep your stupid diary." I looked at the three pairs of eyes, at the three people who loved me most in the entire world. (Except for Drew. He loved me more. But he wasn't exactly a fair test, under the Teel-ish circumstances.) "But it's only going to prove that you're all wrong."

"We can live with that," my father said. "We can live with that, and we know you can, too." He offered me his hand, just as he had when I was a child, when we were agreeing to stupid things.

I could have refused to take it. I could have refused to shake. But that would only make me look more defensive, more like a woman out of control.

I closed my fingers around his and pumped once, earnestly. He took a deep breath and exhaled, as if he were profoundly relieved to have our conversation behind him. "Now," he said to all of us, "how about if I take you ladies out to dinner? Anywhere you'd like—my treat."

Back in my bedroom, a rib-eye steak and loaded baked potato later, I was feeling a little more charitable toward my father and my housemates. If I'd only been able to share a glass of the shiraz my father had poured so generously, I likely would have overlooked the entire intervention, considered it just another one of those quirky signs of love and friendship that we'd all laugh about, years from now.

As it was, I continued to feel that I'd been treated unfairly, talked down to as if I were a child. But since we were all on the brink of food coma, I wasn't going to pursue the matter any further with my housemates that night.

I leaned back against my pillows and caught a whiff of Drew's shampoo. We'd already been together for three weeks. Time flew. Three weeks of his absolutely undivided attention. If I was completely honest with myself, I was grateful to have this evening off, even if my separation from Drew had meant the showdown with Dad, Maddy, and Jules. That didn't make me strange, did it? I mean, everyone needed a little breathing room from the love of their life.

Didn't they? Even if the person they wanted space from was so stunningly gorgeous they were still a heart-thudding surprise each and every morning?

No, I remonstrated with myself. My desire for an evening away from Drew didn't mean that I would ever dream of taking back the wish that had brought him to me.

I wouldn't forfeit my new body, either. Sure, I should have handled things a little differently. I could have adjusted my wardrobe gradually, instead of startling everyone with apparent overnight changes. I could have made my actual food likes and dislikes more clear, instead of letting Maddy and Jules think that I was going all anorexic on them.

And I wouldn't have given back my first wish, either. I definitely wouldn't have forsaken my job at the Landmark. Sure, the gender-switched production was strange. Yeah, Bill Pomeroy was making the show more and more bizarre with his daily design changes. Absolutely, we were pushing the envelope for a Twin Cities theatrical production. But I was learning new things every day, proving myself every single time

I set foot in the theater. No Fox Hill director would ever have shown the imagination for an entire production that Bill cast off in a single day.

No Fox Hill director would ever have chosen to wrap his set in plastic, three weeks before opening night.

Damn. I still had to let John know about the latest Pomeroy inspiration. I glanced at my watch. It was only nine-thirty, even though it seemed much later. I dug my cell phone out of my backpack, along with my well-used phone list.

Chewing on my bottom lip as I tried to figure out a way to break the news, I punched in John's number. One ring. Two. He answered halfway through the third. "Hey, Franklin." Ah, the joys of caller ID. "*This* isn't going to be good news."

Music played in the background, loud enough that I raised my voice a little. "I bet you say that to all the girls."

"Only to the stage managers who call me after nine. Just a sec," John said. With a slight grunt, the music was cut off midphrase.

"What was that?"

"Duke Ellington. 'Take the "A" Train.'"

"You thinking about getting out of town?"

"That all depends on what you're about to tell me. What's Bill got in mind now?"

I took a deep breath to fortify myself. "'I just want to say one word to you,' Bill told us today. 'Plastic.'"

There was silence for a long time, and I could picture John measuring out the new command. I was certain he was running a hand over his mustache. "Shouldn't that be plastic*s*?" he said at last. "With an *s*?"

Great. We both knew *The Graduate*. I gritted my teeth and told him about Bill's innovation.

"Jesus, Franklin! The actors are going to break their necks!"

"We tried it today, with plastic bags over their socks, and we only had one injury."

"What happened?" He sounded truly concerned.

"Nothing serious. Stephanie slipped. Cut herself on the edge of Drew's notebook." John muttered something that I didn't catch. "What?"

"Nothing. How many stitches?"

"None! It wasn't that bad. I mean, I could handle it with my first aid kit."

I heard him swallow something, and I realized he'd probably been kicking back in his living room, relaxing with some jazz and a beer. Maybe reading a script for some future show. Or a novel, something totally unrelated to work. The last thing he'd needed was my interrupting his night with more design bad news. "I'm really sorry," I said. "About this latest change."

"Don't be," he sighed. "This is just Bill being Bill."

"Genius that he is." I thought it would come out sounding light, funny. Instead, I just sounded tired.

"How you holding up, Franklin?"

There was honest concern in his voice, a frank tone that made me swallow hard. He understood. He knew what I was going through, what this production meant, what it was taking to hold it all together. He'd traveled all the way from *Texas* to join the show; he had to be questioning whether he'd made the right decision.

John would understand if I admitted that I was tired. That I was worried. That I might have bitten off more than I could chew.

Blinking back sudden tears, I reminded myself that I would not give back any of my wishes. I loved where I was in my life. I loved what I was doing. And even a transgendered, underground, slime-filled *Romeo and Juliet* beat the LSAT. Any day.

"Franklin?" John's voice was soft, as cautious as if he were whispering to a newborn. I could see him sitting up in his chair now, bottle of beer abandoned on whatever passed for a coffee table in his cheap, temporary apartment. I could picture him leaning forward just a little, flexing the hand that wasn't holding the phone, trying to funnel the tension of concern down his corded fingers.

"I'm fine," I said, but I couldn't raise my voice above a whisper. I cleared my throat. "Just a little tired, is all." There. That was better. "I'm fine," I repeated, but I couldn't think of anything else to say.

As if he knew I needed a little longer to recover, he said, "Well, don't worry about the plastic. I should be able to get something at Lyndale Garden, that heavy-duty black stuff for putting under flower beds. We can double it up and store it on spools, use a heat gun to add grommets, so the crew can attach it to the set."

I listened for another minute as John talked to himself, working out the problem. I could imagine him taking notes, sketching out his requirements as he talked. I could picture his steady, firm hand, dashing out letters and numbers on a sheet of paper. As he took hold of Bill's mandate, as he crafted a solution, I felt the tension ease in my shoulders. My momentary tears retreated, leaving a path of soggy exhaustion in their wake.

"You still there?" he said as he finished his calculations for how many square feet of plastic we'd need.

"Yep," I said, sniffing and stifling a sudden yawn. "Do you need me to get any of that? What can I do to help?"

"Don't worry about it. I can load it all into the truck."

"You make it sound easy."

"It'll all work out. Bill might be insane, but we'll stay one step ahead of him."

I smiled at his grim determination. "You don't fool me, John

McRae. I know you love this stuff, no matter what you say about Bill."

"I'm not trying to fool you, Franklin. Not trying to fool you at all." The reply could have been innocent enough. They were casual words, directly responsive to what I'd said. And yet, there was a layer of meaning sifted over them, a careful seasoning that warmed my cheeks. I could picture his earnest chestnut eyes, warm beneath his shaggy hair.

I cleared my throat. "Then I'll see you tomorrow."

"I'll be there." He started to say something else but settled for repeating, "I'll be there."

"Thanks," I said, surprised to find that I was whispering.

"You sleep well now, Franklin." He made his voice as soft as mine. "Good night."

My phone was warm in my palm as I cut off the call. I sat up and realized that the remnants of my flame tattoos were tingling. I rubbed my fingertips together idly and wondered what John had been about to say, what words he'd swallowed during our conversation. I fell asleep, though, before I could figure out anything he might have meant.

CHAPTER 14

A WEEK LATER, MY TEARY LITTLE BREAKDOWN SEEMED like ancient history as I made a face at myself in the Landmark's bathroom mirror. I knew I was making more out of the night's dinner date with Drew than I should be. We were just going out for burgers. It was no big deal.

Nevertheless, I'd dashed out to Macy's during our lunch break, finally splurging on the cashmere sweater I'd wanted for years. It was a deep hunter-green, a color so rich that I expected it to smell like pine every time I brushed my fingers against its softness. The sweetheart neckline was delicate without being dainty. I'd coveted it forever; I'd hinted heavily to TEWSBU that it would be a perfect birthday gift, and then I'd been too heartsick to buy it for myself after he left me.

But I had bought it that very afternoon. To wear with Drew. *For* Drew. For myself.

Truth be told, I'd bought it as a sort of magic talisman. Now that Teel was gone, I needed to grant my own wishes. And ever since that night a week ago, the night that Drew and I had spent apart, my boyfriend had been grating on me just a little.

I told myself that was normal. I told myself that every couple went through a few weeks of absolute bliss before settling into the ordinary annoyances of daily life in the real world. I told myself that I was personally responsible for some of the things that bothered me the most—Drew was clingy because I had wished him to be that way. He touched me constantly because I had made Teel magically bind him to do so.

I glanced at my fingertips. If I held them at just the right angle, the flame tattoos were still visible, a reminder of everything I'd asked from my genie. I wondered if I'd be stuck with them for life, secret marks that would always remind me of the crazy time when I'd had magic at my beck and call.

Or maybe they would fade after I put Teel's lamp back in circulation. With the crush of the play, I still hadn't found time—*made* time—to leave it somewhere. I knew it wasn't fair for me to keep putting off the transition. Teel needed to find two more people, grant six more wishes so that he could enter the Garden.

I closed my eyes, trying to re-create the feeling of nothingness that had surrounded me when Teel had taken me to that timeless, spaceless place. What *did* the iron gate really look like? How *had* the flowers perfumed the air?

I sighed. I'd never know. For just a heartbeat, though, I wished that I wanted something—anything—as much as Teel had obviously wanted to enter the Garden.

I ran my fingers through my unruly hair one last time, then stooped to pick up my backpack. My stage-manager clothes were shoved in with utter disregard for the possibility of wrinkles. I dug beneath them to extract a little clutch purse, and then I was ready to go.

Drew and John were the only people left by the time I walked into the lobby; the rest of the cast and crew had scattered as soon as rehearsal ended. John was explaining, "There'll be posts every six feet. The fencing will be sturdy enough, even if you walk right into it." He paused and ran a hand over his mustache. "*When* you walk into it. There probably won't be enough light to see it once we paint the fencing black. But don't worry. It won't fall down."

Just that morning, Bill had delivered his latest bombshell: we'd perform the play in the dark. No theatrical lighting at all; nothing that David Barstow had created was dim enough, *grim* enough to capture Bill's somber vision of Verona. Instead, each audience member would be given a flashlight, a high-power beam to illuminate whatever he or she wanted to see on stage. Some would naturally focus on the actors, others on the set. A few would probably be jackasses and aim their lights at each other, but that was the price we had to pay for full audience immersion in our theatrical world.

At least the supertitles would cast a little bit of light onto the set.

I would have to order dozens of flashlights and scores of rechargeable batteries. We'd need a crew member to swap out old batteries for new after every performance. It would take a couple of hours to unscrew each flashlight, drop in fresh cells, screw the things back together, test, and plug the dead batteries in for recharge. Overtime at union wages, countless batteries, the flashlights themselves… More fodder for the "it's only money" campaign.

Of course, all afternoon the actors had been worried about little things (Read: Their safety, life, and limb). They were afraid of slipping on the slimy plastic set and braining themselves on wrought-iron frames while their wet suit costumes split open to reveal their sweat-slicked bodies and the supertitles raced on overhead, getting ahead of whatever lines other characters were actually emoting on stage.

I had to admit, they had a point.

Drew looked up as I approached. "Dude, this isn't going to work. Tell him, Kira." He settled his arm around my waist as I stepped up to the table, and I squelched a tiny flame of annoyance. John's glance flickered toward Drew's hand, and he nodded slowly, as if I'd confirmed some close-held suspicion. I stepped away, pretending that I needed to move so that I could make out the latest version of John's plans.

The drawings were as masterful as ever, every line clear and dramatic. Bill had recently decided to go without any of the painted backdrops John had already created. Despite their grays and blacks, their subdued metallic malevolence, they were now deemed too soft for our hard-edged Verona. Too conventional. Besides, the flashlights weren't going to have enough power to reach that far upstage.

Instead, Bill had mandated hand-forged wrought-iron fencing, huge panels of it, making a jagged barrier across the back of the set. John had shouted him down, citing the weight and the time it would take to complete the welding. They'd finally compromised on lengths of standard hurricane fencing, painted black. John had reluctantly conceded the need for iron support posts instead of aluminum—only iron would have the right tone as the actors clanged against it with their pipe swords.

Drew pointed to a particularly narrow passage that now existed upstage. "We'll never find *that* in the dark. Right, Kira?"

Despite my initial annoyance at his physicality, I smiled at Drew, touched that he thought I could solve all of his problems. "What do you think, John? Can we add more glow-tape?"

"We might as well paint the whole damn thing fluorescent orange," John snarled. Drew leaped back like a kicked puppy.

I hurried to smooth ruffled feathers. "Come on now, it

could be worse. We could have the producers breathing down our necks."

In a stroke of genius, Bill had convinced all of the show's producers, all of the dreaded moneymen, to stay away from our rehearsals. He'd argued that they'd hired him to blow their minds with a radical new production. If they watched it change incrementally, from day to day, they'd never experience the full body blow of everything that Bill envisioned. Okay, I'd been a little surprised that they'd actually bought the argument, but I was relieved to have one less pressure as we raced toward our opening.

I continued to placate both men beside me. "Shows always feel like this a few weeks out. It's totally normal to worry about pulling everything together." John tapped his drawings into a neat cylinder, and I smiled at him. "Bill being Bill, remember?"

John darted a glance at me. "Franklin, you and I both know it's way too late to make changes this drastic. Bill's never been like this before. Not with his wildest concepts."

It felt odd to have him talking to me this way, so directly, so personally. It was like we were continuing the phone conversation that had started a week before, even though Drew was now standing right there. Of course, Drew was more interested in twisting a lock of my hair around his finger than he was in the latest tangle of aluminum and iron Maginot Lines that Bill was demanding upstage.

"It's going to be fine, John," I said with as much confidence as I could muster. Drew nodded his passionate agreement.

John barely spared our leading man a frown as he said, "My name is going on that design, Franklin. My name is associated with this production."

"So is mine," I said, and I sighed. "It's the Landmark, John. We're supposed to—"

"Supposed to take the lead in contemporary American

theater." He rubbed his face, as if he were waking up from a bad dream.

"Kira's right," Drew said. "She's totally…" He trailed off, as if he were trying to string together words in a foreign language.

His loyalty was touching, but I came close to wincing as he struggled to shore up his statement with facts. He was supportive, always, almost to a fault. That was one of the things I loved about him, one of the things that made me most grateful to Teel. I just wished that sometimes Drew would think things through before he spoke, that just once, he would demonstrate that there were brains inside that gorgeous head.

John waited politely for Drew to finish making his point, but accepted that no other argument was forthcoming when Drew bent to nuzzle my neck. I edged away, thoroughly embarrassed. I was grateful when John changed the topic of conversation. "Where are y'all going?"

Surprisingly, I had trouble meeting his eyes when I said, "Mephisto's. Just to grab a burger."

"Did Mike change the dress code?"

I forced myself to shrug, to act like our destination was no place special. "I've been living in my theater clothes. I wanted a change."

"Oh, you have a change, all right." Once again, I had that eerie feeling that he and I were back to the previous week's phone conversation, that we were having a private dialogue, with half our lines unspoken. My fingers prickled as I brushed my hair back from my suddenly flushed cheeks.

"Come on, Kira," Drew said. "I'm hungry." He offset his whine with a goofy grin, reminding me once again that I actually *was* enjoying his attention. I loved my dating life as belle of the ball. I had never been happier.

Drew picked up my coat and shook it out, holding it behind me. I swallowed a flash of annoyance and caught my sweater sleeves with my fingertips, sparing them from riding up to my elbows as I fumbled to find the coat sleeves. What would I have to do to break the New and Improved Drew of that little etiquette tradition?

Fishing my hair out from the coat's collar, I asked John, "Coming with?" It would have been rude to just walk out on him.

"I'm going to wrap up a couple of things here," he said. "I'll see you later. If you're still there."

I wasn't sure why he thought that I'd be gone—if he was alluding to my fleeing from TEWSBU, or if he thought that Drew and I would be…otherwise engaged. Neither possibility left me with an easy answer, so I just shrugged and said, "Don't worry about the show. It's all coming together. The play will be fine."

"Isn't it pretty to think so?"

Drew cocked his head to one side, his eyes creasing into an adorable—if maddening—squint. "What's that from? *Peanuts*?"

Peanuts? He thought the line was from a comic strip? "Hemingway," John and I said at the same time. I hurried toward the door before Drew could ask which play.

It was bitterly cold outside, but no snow was falling. We'd driven to rehearsal together; Drew's Mazda was parked three blocks away, halfway to Mephisto's. As we started walking, he reached for my hand, lacing his fingers between my own.

"Hey, Drew," I said.

"Hmm?" Again with the goofy grin.

"I thought we had an agreement."

"I'll agree to anything you want, Kira. You know that."

Yeah. I did. He'd agree to anything, say any words I wanted, just to keep me happy. And he honestly meant it, too. At least until he forgot, five minutes later.

A sudden realization smacked me between the eyes, and I stumbled to a stop.

I was dating a golden retriever puppy. A really beautiful, totally loyal, wonderfully intentioned, incredibly dumb golden retriever puppy.

Drew turned to look at me, concern creasing his forehead. He leaned in and planted a quick kiss on my lips, the sort of casual affection that was guaranteed to make my belly swoop, even in the face of other, less positive, realizations. "What, Kira? What's wrong?"

He wanted to please me. He wanted so badly to please me.

"Nothing," I said, forcing a smile. "It's just that you promised. You promised that you wouldn't touch me in front of the cast or crew, and back there, in front of John…"

Drew pulled his hand away from mine, as if my fingers had burned him. "I'm sorry! I thought that you liked me to touch you!"

"No!" I said, feeling like an idiot. "I mean, I do! I love it! It's just that when we're in the theater, when we're surrounded by all of our coworkers, I don't think it's appropriate."

"We weren't surrounded by coworkers. That was just John."

I pictured the set designer's slow appraisal, his gaze flicking over Drew's hands, his laconic nod as he accepted the public display of affection. My cheeks burned. "John counts," I said to Drew.

"It's not like he's the director, or anything. He's not in the cast. He's just the *set designer*."

My throat worked; I wasn't even sure how to respond to that. Too many actors looked at their technical crew as "just" those people. Some actors truly believed that they could do the show on their own, that they could perform without the bother of a lighting designer, a costume designer, a set designer. A stage manager.

When my silence became uncomfortable, even for happy-go-lucky Drew, he said, "Okay, Kira. I get it." But he really didn't. He said, "I don't want to make anything more difficult for you."

I shivered and took the easy route. "I know you don't," I said. I pulled my coat closer around me. "Come on. It's freezing out here."

It was plenty warm at Mephisto's. Mike was standing behind the bar, setting a Jack and Coke onto an already-laden tray. The tables in the front room were filled with customers; the restaurant was steeped in a healthy weekend buzz. Nevertheless, Mike looked up automatically as we walked in. He nodded, then did a classic double take as he recognized me. I could only flash a smile as Drew reached for my collar, eager to take my coat. I picked a path through the tables, navigating so that Drew and I ended up beside the bar just as a harried waitress swooped in for the tray of drinks.

Mike took advantage of the temporary lull in hostilities to give me an appraising look. "Kira," he said. And then he seemed to notice the man standing beside me. "Drew! I haven't seen you here in a while."

Drew smiled, his best, happy grin. "I've been too busy, dude. This Kira, she's a slave driver."

Mike looked at me, with an expression that was at least halfway down the road to disbelief. He recovered quickly, though. "Well, you know you two are always welcome. The Landmark group is back in the Shakespeare Room."

"Fitting," I said. And then I concentrated on making a question sound offhand. "Is, um, Stephanie there?"

"No," Mike said, shaking his head as he finished shoving limes onto the rim of my glass of tonic water. "They're not back there."

Drew didn't catch the plural pronoun as he accepted his Sam Adams. I, though, flashed a grateful smile at Mike. "Thanks," I said.

"Just part of the service at Mike's Bar and Grill." He gave me a mock leer, looking exactly like the debauched devil that had earned the place its nickname. Before I could express my appreciation, Mike got pulled away to mix a half-dozen cocktails.

Drew and I made our way back to the Shakespeare Room. I nodded to the assembled cast members, slipping into a seat on the far side of the table. Drew immediately joined me, resting a casual hand across the back of my chair. As his fingers traveled to the back of my neck, I was irritated by the physical attention, particularly since we'd just discussed it five minutes before. I offered him one pointed look, but I decided not to build mountains out of molehills. When the waitress came in, we both ordered burgers and fries. I was really hungry—I went with the black and blue, and I asked her to add bacon.

I resisted the urge to whip out my food diary then and there. Even if I left half the food on my plate, the fat and cholesterol should go a long way toward satisfying my overconcerned housemates and father.

I still hadn't reconciled myself to their stupid food diary. I found myself thinking about it at odd times, obsessing over whether I had recorded something, whether I had accurately estimated the weight of a chicken breast cut up on a salad, whether I had been fair when I said that I ate half a cup of mashed potatoes. The diary was almost having the opposite of my loved ones' desired effect—it was so damn hard to write down everything that I ate, that I was tempted to just eat nothing.

But that would only bring about more problems. It was easier to give in now. Easier to prove that they were all wrong, with their overprotective stance. Easier to manage the situation than to let it continue deteriorating.

"Kira?" I looked up to see Jennifer Galland at the far end of the table. She had her fingers wrapped around a stein of some light beer, and even at this distance, I could make out a couple of nasty bruises on her forearm. Rehearsals had not been kind to our gentle Romeo. Her iron pipe sword had tripped her up just yesterday. She likely would have kept herself from falling, if her wet suit–clad feet hadn't slipped on the slimy plastic sheeting.

Bill had been impressed with the string of profanity that Jennifer had let loose. He'd decided that Romeo would be thinking in just those terms as he contemplated fighting the hated Capulet crowd. It had only taken me three phone calls to determine that we could, in fact, change the supertitles, to make the language more foul, even though they'd all supposedly been finalized the week before. There would be a charge, of course, a substantial one, but Bill insisted it was all worthwhile.

I'd needed to deliver the new supertitles over the phone to jump-start the modification. I wondered what my father would have thought if he'd seen me standing in the Landmark lobby, seeking out the best pocket of cell phone reception so that I could enunciate words that would have guaranteed my mouth being washed out with soap when I was a kid. I had to spell some of them, too. All those years of playing Scrabble with Maddy and Jules came in handy. Sort of.

"Kira," Jennifer said again, when she had my attention. "Can't you talk to Bill? Ask him if we could carry flashlights, too?"

I shook my head. "I already tried that. He wouldn't go for the idea. I think he's afraid it'll look silly, like kids around a campfire." I mimed holding a flashlight under my chin. "You know, 'There was a hook, caught in the car door.'"

They all laughed, and Drew leaned over to kiss my cheek, as if he were rewarding me for a great witticism. I would have pushed him away, but our waitress chose that moment to come in with our food. The aroma of the burger made my mouth water; I was hungrier than I thought. I closed my eyes and took a bite, actually moaning a little as the bacon crunched between my teeth, as the Cajun spice danced at the tip of my tongue, and the creamy melted blue cheese flooded my mouth with flavor.

Heaven. Sheer culinary heaven.

Even if I did need to grab for my napkin to wipe juices from my chin.

"You'll need this for your fries, Franklin." I looked up to see John laughing at me from the doorway, holding out the bottle of ketchup that the waitress had just passed into our crowded room.

"Hi!" I said, surprised. "I didn't think you'd make it."

"Wouldn't miss it for the world." I wasn't sure what his tone meant. It was steady and calm, merely stating a fact. He'd clearly made a conscious decision to set aside his frustration over Bill, over the ever-changing set design. I felt guilty, though, that I hadn't insisted that he join us, back at the theater. "If I'd known y'all would be telling campfire stories, I'd've brought along some s'mores."

I laughed. Before I could think of something else to say, though, two more people ducked through the curtain.

Stephanie Michaelson. And TEWSBU.

The bite of burger in my belly turned cold. Stephanie and my ex were laughing too loudly, holding each other up as they stumbled into the room. "Sorry we're late," Stephanie brayed. "We stopped off at Orlando's for a drink after rehearsal."

More like for a bottle, I thought. They were both drunk. Not a pleasantly giddy, Friday-night flush after a week of hard-won rehearsals. No, Stephanie actually swayed as she stepped into the room. TEWSBU didn't help her; he was peering around the room, his head held a little too far forward on his neck, his gaze a little too uneven to be sober.

I realized that neither of them had drinks in their hands. I couldn't be certain, but I suspected that Mike had taken one look at their condition and declined to serve them further. I gritted my teeth. I had a problem with TEWSBU under the best of circumstances, but I remembered all too well that he could be a heartless drunk.

It was just my luck that the only empty chairs were on my side of the table. Drew was already scrambling to his feet, pushing in his own seat and edging toward the wall to make it easier for the newcomers to get by. I thought about scooting up as close as I could to the table, but it was easier to follow Drew's lead, to stand against the wall and let them go by.

Stephanie edged past first. The smell of alcohol was so strong that I wondered if she'd spilled at least one drink down her front. She giggled as she walked by, clutching the back of my chair to keep her balance.

And that's when I saw it—an engagement ring with a diamond as large as an egg. All of the oxygen was sucked out of my lungs, making it impossible for me to swear, to shout out a string of epithets that could have inspired yet another remake of the supertitle slides. Instead, my gasp was loud enough to draw Stephanie's attention.

"My ring?" she said, following my gaze. "Don't you like it?"

I knew that I was supposed to say something civil. I knew that I was supposed to give her my best wishes. I was supposed to turn to TEWSBU, to congratulate him, to follow through on all the social niceties that had been drummed into me since I was a child.

But the cold glints from that gigantic diamond froze the words at the back of my throat.

TEWSBU had never given me an engagement ring. He didn't believe in them, he'd pontificated. They were a primitive gesture of ownership. I'd gone along with whatever he'd said, of course. I hadn't needed a ring. I'd known that he loved me, and no silly block of compressed carbon was going to prove anything more.

At least my lack of an engagement ring had made things simple in the end. I hadn't needed to consult with Miss Manners about broken-engagement etiquette rules. I hadn't needed to return anything to my lost love.

It had all worked out for the best.

Stephanie apparently forgot that she was waiting for my response. She staggered past me and collapsed into a chair. And then I was face-to-face with TEWSBU.

He might be drunk, but he was still handsome. Not in the conventional way, not like Drew. TEWSBU was too tall to be traditionally good-looking; I had to crane my neck a little just to look him in the face. He was too skinny. His face was carved into planes, and his nose was a little too long. His cheekbones jutted out a little too hard, leaving behind hollows that whispered about the emptiness in his heart. When he became an old man, he'd look like Ichabod Crane.

But he was brilliant, in the theater. He read plays and truly *understood* them, carried those meanings to the public with an ease and a confidence that was the envy of every director I'd ever known (Bill Pomeroy likely excepted). He elicited emotions from his actors, pulling truth from them and displaying it onstage. He was excellent at his job—that was what had first attracted me to him, and that was what I'd most often mooned about during those long nights spent mourning what might have been.

He stumbled as he stepped past me, falling against me with his full weight. My arms automatically reached out to steady him, and he clutched the back of my chair, keeping himself from going down to the floor. He ended up, though, with his nose planted at the center of my sweetheart neckline, as if he were trying to breathe in the cool pine scent that I had idiotically imagined emanating from my treasured cashmere sweater.

Then he pulled himself up to his full height. He twisted his neck from side to side, like a pianist trying to work out the kinks before mastering a concerto. He took a deep breath, a sobering breath, and he exhaled fumes strong enough that I worried I might have an allergic reaction then and there.

Everyone in the room was staring at us. They all knew our history. Every single person was waiting to see what he would say, what I would say, how we would spin out our own sorry drama for their personal pleasure and enjoyment.

And TEWSBU gave them what they wanted. "Those," he enunciated carefully, "are extraordinary tits. Where did you get them?"

A flood of adrenaline actually kept me from hearing the crowd's reaction, but I could see the discomfort on every face in the room. I heard Stephanie screech something wordless. I felt Drew step up behind me, lay a protective hand on my arm.

And even as I cringed at TEWSBU's crude words, I was grateful for Drew's presence. I was grateful that somebody was going to defend me, that someone, that a *man* was going to tell TEWSBU that he had stepped out of line, that he had been utterly inappropriate, that he was wrong, wrong, wrong.

Drew said, "Hey, dude. They *are* pretty great! Come on, now. Sit down."

I whirled on my supposed boyfriend. "I can't believe you just said that!" I was so astonished that my voice broke.

"What?" he said. "He's drunk. Never argue with a drunk, dude." My dim-witted puppy leaned in close, whispering in a *voce* that wasn't *sotto* enough, "Besides, he's right. You've totally got a great rack! And they're real, so what's the problem?"

I needed to escape. I needed to get away from all of them. I needed to get away from my burger and fries, which had turned into a cold, plastic representation of food, nauseating in frozen grease.

I shoved an elbow into TEWSBU's side when he didn't move quickly enough, pushed Drew away so that I could reach the curtained doorway. I marched across the dining room, absurdly grateful that Mike was too busy to look up. I grabbed my coat from its hanger by the door, blindly shoving my arms into the sleeves.

On the sidewalk, I realized that I was in trouble. I didn't have my car; Drew had driven us to rehearsal. I would have to phone Maddy, see if I could reach her, see if I could beg her to leave Herr Wunderbar, to come rescue me. I started to dig for my cell phone, fighting back tears that I had been so stupid, that I had let myself believe in Drew, that for one blinding moment I had actually thought he would make things *better* in front of TEWSBU. TEWSBU, who had proved once again that he was a coldhearted bastard, theatrical genius be forever damned. I caught a sob in the back of my throat.

"Need a ride?"

I recognized the voice before I turned around. The Texas twang was easy, comfortable. The sentence was truly an offer, an option, a choice that was open to me, something I could take or leave with no consequences, no penalties. I turned to find John framed against the light of Mephisto's plate glass window.

"Yeah," I said.

We walked to his truck in absolute silence. He opened my door in absolute silence. He walked around to the driver's side, put the key into the ignition, fired up the engine, pulled out of the parking space, all in absolute silence.

"You okay?" He finally asked, keeping his eyes on the road. Leaving me room to answer.

I shook my head, then said, "I will be."

"They're all jackasses. Everyone back there."

"Some more than others."

"You can say that again." We drove another couple of blocks. "Want to tell me where we're going?"

We were going to be the gossip of the entire cast and crew of *Romeo and Juliet*. We were going to be the laughingstock of every theater professional in the Twin Cities, once our play opened. We were going to be changing careers—at least I was—as soon as my public ridicule was complete.

I shrugged.

He pulled up to a red light and said, "You didn't get a chance to eat much of your dinner."

"I'm not hungry now."

"Well, I am," he said. "Keep me company while I get something."

I shrugged again. He nodded as the light changed, as he worked the truck through its gears in the comforting predictability of first to second to third.

In the end, he took me to a restaurant I'd never seen before. It was some sort of dive-y diner, the perfect place to order a large bowl of chicken noodle soup. The waitress brought us hot bread and butter that was creamy and soft. John told me they served a chocolate silk pie to die for. He remembered that I didn't like to share. He ordered his own apple pie à la mode, and we matched each other, bite for bite.

We talked about everything other than the disaster of my personal life. I told him about growing up in the Twin Cities, about the Winter Carnival, about walking out on the ice of Lake Calhoun in the middle of the winter.

He told me about summer dust storms where half of East Texas blew into his Dallas backyard. He talked about growing up one of seven kids.

When the waitress brought the check, I glanced at my watch, realized with astonishment that it was past eleven o'clock. "Can I drive you home?" John asked, as he slipped a couple of bills out of his wallet, waving off my offer to pay for my food.

"Thanks."

I gave him directions in a hushed voice. It was late enough that there wasn't a lot of traffic. He drew up in front of my house, hovering beside the parked cars and putting the truck into Neutral, pulling the parking brake. The porch light was on, but none of the others. The Swensons were asleep. My housemates were in their rooms, or gone for the night.

I stared at my hands in my lap. I didn't know what I wanted to say, wasn't sure what I wanted to do. It seemed rude to just say good-night, presumptuous to say anything else.

Before I could figure out some way to express my confusion, John's tanned fingers closed over mine. He left his hand there for just a moment, just long enough for me to register the warmth, the weight. And then he leaned over and set his lips against mine. One chaste kiss—a little salty, a little sweet, like the echo of our night at the diner.

He squeezed my hands again. "Go on, Franklin. Head on in. I'll wait till you're safe inside."

For once, my key slipped easily into the front door, and I turned to wave. He acknowledged me with one brief toss of his own hand, and then he put his truck in gear, drove off into the night.

I was still awake as the sun came up, wondering what I was going to do to fix the tangled mess of my life. I needed to give Drew his walking papers—genie's spell or not, absolute faith in me or not, there was no way that I could condone his gleeful objectification of my body. Especially not when he'd been speaking to *TEWSBU*. He had to know what TEWSBU had done to me, how he'd left me stranded. Everyone in the theater world did. Drew knew, but he didn't care, and that's what made his offhand crudity the worst insult of all.

Somehow, I feared that even my double-strength coffee wasn't going to make my day any easier.

CHAPTER 15

THE MORE I THOUGHT ABOUT IT, THE MORE I CONSIDERED calling in sick.

That was the thing about stage management, though—about all of our jobs in the theater. There wasn't any way to cop a sick day. I didn't have an understudy, a trained professional who could hold the baton while I said, "You guys go ahead and do today without me. I'm just going to crawl back into bed, pull the covers up to my chin, and alternate being furious with my ex-fiancé, enraged with my current boyfriend, and mystified by my even-tempered, knight-in-shining-pickup-truck coworker."

The show must go on, and all that crap.

So, I stood beneath the shower for ages, long enough that the water began to turn cool. I made a point of choosing my skinny jeans, a fitted black tee, and a crimson lamb's wool sweater that made my cheeks look healthy and flushed. I took the time to apply makeup, even opening my eyes wide for two coats of mascara. I brushed my hair until it shone, and I remembered to add a pair of dangling earrings. I was going to look my best, gossiping cast members be damned.

I dug in the refrigerator for breakfast, excavating a container of yogurt. I was still hungry when I finished that, so I found an apple. And a banana. I thought about topping off my feast with a handful of Cap'n Crunch, but that made me think of Drew, of all the breakfasts he'd eaten sitting at the same table.

I broke off my kitchen rampage and completed my food diary entry. I scowled as I wrote up my morning consumption, and then I added dinner with John from the night before. I wasn't worried about the amount of food, and I had no idea of the actual caloric content, but I was getting damned tired of writing everything down. Still, a deal was a deal. If my maintaining records would keep my father and my housemates off my not-actually-anorexic back, then it was worthwhile.

Still frowning, I spent the entire drive to the theater writing conversations in my head.

I told Stephanie that I was happy about her engagement, and I reminded her that there were several excellent therapists in town who would be happy to help her out when she found herself betrayed by the man who had sworn his undying love and affection.

I told Drew that he wasn't in college anymore, that his frat-boy indulgences were boring and immature.

I told John…

I wasn't sure what I wanted to tell John. Every time I thought of him, I caught myself smiling. I kept remembering the feel of his fingers on mine, the gentle pressure as his hands closed over my own. I kept reliving the touch of his lips, the absolute…honesty of his kiss. I kept recalling the quiet confidence on his face as he watched me leave, as he waited for me to get safely inside my front door.

I wanted to thank him. I wanted to tell him how much it meant that he had taken me away from Mephisto's. I wanted to say how much I appreciated his standing beside me through the entire crazy production, through the incredible insanity that was Bill Pomeroy, that was our show's bizarre take on *Romeo and Juliet*.

I couldn't figure out the words.

Don't get me wrong—I was an expert at conversation. I had spent my entire professional life crouched over a script, listening to actors deliver their lines. I knew how dialogue really sounded, how it worked, what a pause meant when it was measured out just...so, what the perfect word signified, how it balanced out the ideal scene.

Of course, it helped when the author—the playwright, the stage manager organizing her life, whatever—knew what she wanted to accomplish with that single, ideal scene.

I was still trying to write perfection as I parked my car. I wrote it as I collected my backpack. I wrote it as I climbed over a snowbank. I wrote it as I pushed open the door to Club Joe. I wrote it as I got in line to order my coffee.

I gave up on the lines, though, when I saw John unfold himself from a table, gesturing to an empty chair beside him. I crossed the room without being fully aware that I was moving, and then I tried to sound casual. "Hey. Let me just get my coffee—"

He pushed a thermal mug toward me. "Large latte. Four shots of espresso."

"Thanks." I sat down and hugged my coat close. If he regretted anything that had happened the night before, he sure wasn't showing it. Instead, he looked as calm and steady as ever, as ready to listen as he was to talk. "How long have you been waiting for me?"

He gestured toward his own cup, a small drip coffee, black. Steam still curled off the surface. I was willing to bet that he hadn't stirred in sugar. "Not long."

I nodded, but I wasn't sure what to say next. I wanted to tell him how much I had enjoyed our evening, but the words sounded lame in my own head. Besides, he'd obviously enjoyed himself too, or he wouldn't be here, wouldn't have waited for me. Wouldn't have remembered the type of coffee I drink.

"About last night," I finally said, and I squelched a nervous laugh. *About Last Night* had been a mediocre movie, a film version of David Mamet's *Sexual Perversity in Chicago*. As soon as I thought of the play title, I blushed.

John spoke as if I'd actually finished a complete sentence. "I designed a set for that once. Not an iron fence in sight. Not a single manhole cover. One of the best damn sets I've ever built, too. Mamet beats the hell out of Shakespeare. At least this production."

I was grateful for the tiny joke at Bill Pomeroy's expense, but I forbade myself from dwelling on our looming stage disaster. "Seriously," I said instead. "Thank you."

He didn't pretend to misunderstand me, pretend that his rescue had meant nothing. Instead, he inclined his head and said, "You're welcome." If he'd worn the Stetson that seemed to be his birthright, he would have tipped it at me. As it was, I half expected him to say "ma'am."

I was glad that he didn't.

"Why did you come here?" I asked.

"I figured you wouldn't want to walk into rehearsal alone." He said it like a man might comment on the weather. "Not that you have anything to be ashamed of. Except for the fact that a lot of your friends are idiots."

My mind flashed back to the rock on Stephanie's finger, to TEWSBU's drunken leer as he stumbled into me. TEWSBU. My former fiancé. Norman Kapowicz. "Norman isn't my friend." It was the first time I'd said his name in more than a year. It sounded funny as it left my lips. Norman had always hated his name, but I'd told him I loved it. I'd said that it had character. That it was special. That I looked forward to teaching everyone how to spell my new surname.

I'd lied a lot during that relationship.

John frowned. "I wasn't talking about Norman."

"I know." I gulped down more coffee, trying to swallow my apprehension about seeing Drew. After all, I was the one who had gotten him into our relationship, against his will. Or more specifically, against his knowledge. Teel and me; we'd stolen Drew's right to make up his own mind about who he was, who he wanted to date. Damn that genie and his wishes.

But I knew it wasn't Teel's fault.

I had chosen poorly. I had chosen Drew because I'd been stunned by his physical attractiveness. I'd somehow put on blinders, ignored how incredibly *stupid* the man could be. I sighed. "We might as well get over there."

John nodded and climbed to his feet. "Might as well," he said.

Drew was waiting for us, of course, just inside the lobby door. "Kira," he said as soon as my foot touched the carpet. He ducked his head and looked up at me through his thick fringe of eyelashes.

He hadn't shaved that morning, and despite my still being furious with him, my fingertips twitched, drawn to the golden glint of his new beard. His T-shirt was wrinkled, as if he'd pulled it from the bottom of a pile of clothes. His hair was rumpled, and I knew that he'd been running his fingers through it—I could close my eyes and see the familiar action.

I forced myself to meet his gaze. His eyes were the now-familiar mix of mahogany and emerald, sparkling, even as he looked subdued. His face was still as perfect as it had been on the day of our first rehearsal, a breath-stealing balance of rugged masculinity and perfect bone structure. His lips were still moist, conveying a message of seduction even when they were silent. That one front tooth was still skewed the tiniest bit, making him human.

I knew this was the guy I had crushed on for weeks. This was the man I had dreamed about, the man who had made me a spiteful, jealous harpy when Teel had minced her way through rehearsals. This was the guy my genie had warned me about, when he had warned me about making my last wish out of jealousy.

I should have listened when I had the chance.

I felt nothing for Drew anymore.

That wasn't true. I felt annoyed by him. Angry with him. Frustrated, disgusted, repulsed.

And yet, I felt guilty, too. I had bound him to me, using Teel's magic. One glance was enough to assure me that his attraction to me remained strong. The spell wasn't broken, just because I'd realized he was an immature baby. He wasn't free, just because I'd come to my senses.

"I tried to call you," he said, glancing nervously at John. John just stared back at him, tall, silent, inscrutable.

"I turned off my phone." I heard my voice, but I wasn't entirely certain that it was mine. That voice was speaking steadily. With confidence. It didn't sound like a woman regretting her genie-empowered choices.

Drew pleaded. "I drove by your house, but the lights were off. I didn't want to get you in trouble with the Swensons. I didn't want to make too much noise."

I hardened my heart against his thoughtfulness, against the restraint that he had shown. "I went to bed early," I lied.

Drew reached toward me, curving his fingers as if he were going to cup my jaw. I shied away like a wild horse, but I almost regretted the move when I saw the baffled pain in his eyes. He said, "Kira, I'm sorry. Sometimes I just say stupid things. It's not like I mean them, it's not like I even give them any thought.

The words are just *there*, like lines in a play." He paused in his desperate explanation long enough to look over his shoulder at John. "Hey, dude, can you give us a minute?"

John didn't even spare him a glance. Instead, he took a half step toward me and said, "Franklin?"

I wanted him to stay, to stand beside me with his cowboy lankiness and his solid, supportive silence.

But there were some things that should be said in privacy. I owed Drew that much. I'd taken the guy's independence with Teel's spell; I'd stolen his free will. A little time alone was the least that I could give back as I broke his bewitched heart. I nodded at John. "It's okay. I'll see you inside."

He looked at me for a long moment before striding into the theater. As the door opened and closed, I could hear the cast chatting loudly inside. Bill was probably waiting for us, growing impatient at the delay. I looked down, as if I could magically discover a script in my hands, a concrete reminder of the conversation that I'd written in the car, on my way to work. I found that I was still holding the travel mug of coffee, my gift from John. I resisted the urge to fortify myself with more caffeine, to put off even further what I had to say.

"Drew," I started. "I'm sure that when you were in college, you had a bunch of friends. I know that you could joke with them, that you could say whatever you were thinking. You could call them 'dude,' and slap their backs, and talk about all the hot babes, and you knew that they'd always be there, laughing with you, hanging out with you. I get that. I totally understand it."

He nodded, a pitiful smile of gratitude flooding his face. For just a second, my heart stopped beating as I took in the beauty of his features.

But then I continued with the rest of my message. "But

you're not in college anymore. You can't just go around saying whatever you're thinking. This isn't some frat house. We're not hanging out at an endless beer-pong tournament."

His lips trembled. Those lips, which I'd spent the past six weeks kissing. Those lips that softened the rugged handsomeness of his planed face. "I'm sorry, Kira. But I can't help what I think."

"You weren't just thinking! You were talking!" My anger was closer to the surface than I'd thought.

"I didn't mean it!" he yelped, and I suddenly pictured him as a little boy, as a freckled Tom Sawyer explaining his way out of some childish prank. His mother probably let him get away with murder. But he stumbled on now, trying to fix what he had broken with me. "I mean, I *did* mean it. When I said it. You *do* have a great rack—"

I shook my head, suddenly completely exhausted despite the coffee from John. "Drew, it wasn't just what you said. It was who you said it to. You knew about Norman and me. *Everyone* knew about Norman and me. And yet you had to say it. You had to talk about me, like that, to him. To Norman."

Gee. I went without saying the guy's name for more than a year, and now I couldn't stop myself.

Drew shrugged. "I wasn't thinking. I'm sorry."

"I'm sure you are," I said. "But you have to understand, I can't be with you right now."

He nodded, taking my decision better than I'd expected. "But we can get dinner tonight? After rehearsal?"

I gritted my teeth. I should have written a less ambiguous exit line. "No, Drew. We aren't going to dinner."

"Oh. Is it already time to deliver the rent check to your father?" I shook my head, but he went on. "Are Maddy and Jules going to be home? I was thinking that maybe we could order from Indian Palace, instead of getting Chinese. We could all get appetizers. Share them." He was getting more desperate. "Maybe play a game of Parcheesi!"

I shook my head. "No. No dinner, no rent check, no ordering in, no games. No more, Drew. We're done."

I'd read in books that people went pale with shock. I'd seen dozens of plays where characters remarked on each other's pallor, where they noted surprise and astonishment. But I'd never really seen it before, in real life, never seen the color drain from a grown man's face. He stammered a little as he said, "Wh-what do you mean?"

Hating myself for what I'd done, for how I'd used Teel's powers, I pressed on. "We need to stop seeing each other."

"Kira, I love you!"

I winced.

Drew didn't love me. Drew didn't even know that I existed. Not when he was himself. Not when he was free. Not when he was spared the tendrils of Teel's spell. "No," I said. "You don't."

He clutched at me, closing his fingers around my upper arms. "You can't do this to me. To us. I made a mistake, I know it, but you can't just walk away like this. It was just one stupid thing that I said!"

One stupid thing. That was true. Under ordinary circumstances, I wouldn't doom an entire relationship because of one idiotic comment.

But these weren't ordinary circumstances. "Drew, stop and think. You don't even know me. This has all happened so fast, you just *think* you're in love with me." The immediate panic was fading from his grasping fingers. I continued my patter, as if I were gentling a frightened animal. I kept my voice low, singsong, making my words as private as possible. "You know how it is when you're working on a play. We both do. You think that you've got something going with the cast. The crew. Everything seems to mean more, to be more important."

He shook his head, getting ready to deny my appeal to his logic. Before he could say anything, though, the door to the theater exploded open. Bill Pomeroy stared at us, raising his eyebrows in mock surprise. He extended his arm with exaggerated exasperation, stared down at his missing watch. "Kira?" he asked, conveying an entire lecture in the two syllables of my name.

"Yeah, Bill," I said. "Drew and I were just going over his last scene. He had a question about his motivation."

Bill's lips curled in a sardonic smile. "I think the rest of the cast can speak more to Juliet's motivation than you can. Let's go. I have a special announcement to make."

I wanted to take exception to Bill's imperious tone, but it was more important for me to get away from Drew, to get him back to rehearsal, back to the life he had led before Teel got in the way. Before *I* got in the way. "We were just coming in," I said.

Drew followed me into the theater, and I purposely made my way up to the front row of seats. I collapsed next to John, grateful that someone's casually discarded coat filled the seat on my other side, making it impossible for Drew to sit there. I heard him throw himself into the row behind me, but I didn't allow myself to turn around, didn't permit myself to gauge his frustration.

I could feel everyone's eyes on the back of my head. The entire cast and crew were assembled; everyone had watched my late entrance with Drew. Even the people who had not been at Mephisto's the night before must known what had happened there. Gossip burned through theater people faster than boiling water melted snow.

I fished my notebook out of my backpack, craving the distraction as I burrowed for my favorite pen. "What?" I thought about screaming. "What the hell do you think you're looking at?"

I scrunched lower in my seat, pretending that I needed to balance my notebook across my knees. John leaned down beside me and whispered, "You're a lot braver than you look, Franklin."

His smile was lazy, slow, and I felt an answering grin blossom across my lips. "Thanks a lot, McRae."

Bill began speaking before John could say anything else. "Now that we finally have everyone together…" he began, with a pointed look at me. His gaze skirted off behind me, and I couldn't help but turn around, couldn't help but see Drew staring at me, wounded, like a puppy tied to the back porch while his owner went off on some exciting journey.

Bill rubbed a hand over his skull. "I've made a decision," he announced.

I glanced at John, but he shrugged just enough to let me know that he didn't have any idea what Bill's latest announcement would be. My belly tightened a little in dread, and I wondered what technical feat Bill was planning for us now, what disaster he was going to unleash with less than three weeks to go before the first preview audiences crossed the threshold. I settled my arm a little more firmly on my armrest, knowing that the action would take me closer to John. He didn't pull away.

"There comes a time in every production…" Bill began, and I immediately thought of the conversation I'd just had with Drew. Bill was breaking up with us. He was telling us that the relationship we thought we'd built was over. Broken. Gone.

But no, he was saying something worse. "We've reached that time," Bill was saying. "We've reached the moment when our show has to stand on its own two feet, when we have to let our child venture out into the world on its own. We've reached the time when we're ready for previews."

John was on his feet before I was. He didn't bother to keep

his voice down, didn't bother to hide his Texas twang. "We still have three weeks."

Bill gazed at him with the peaceful satisfaction of a Buddhist monk. A monk dressed in black leather, but a monk all the same. "We *had* three weeks," Bill said. "I made some changes to our schedule. The critics will join us on Tuesday, along with our producers and the first paying audience members."

John didn't back down. "We're not ready to go."

Bill looked over the entire cast before he answered, and when he finally did reply, he used the patronizing tone of a parent instructing a very young child. "We're doing something special here, John. We need to find our proper audience. We need to invite everyone in early, so that the people who *need* to know about us will find us, will be with us, will celebrate what we're doing. I hardly have to tell you that we're building a very unique show. A very unique show deserves a very unique launch. Three weeks of preview performances is perfect for what we're doing."

I wanted to point out that our *Romeo and Juliet* couldn't be "very unique." Unique meant one of a kind. Our show couldn't be "more unique" than any other.

I realized that I was obsessing about English language usage so that I could avoid the import of what Bill had really said. He was throwing us to the theatrical wolves. He was ready to unveil our monstrosity of a play. He was launching the last show I would ever work on, the last production in my professional life, the *Romeo and Juliet* that would go down in history as the worst play ever performed in the Twin Cities.

No one would ever hire me again.

I might as well walk out of rehearsal. I might as well head over to the library and start studying for the LSAT. It was time to turn my life over to reading comprehension essays and analytical problems, logical grids and whatever else they were going to quiz me on before my lifetime practicing law.

"We're not ready," I said, before I realized the words were out of my mouth.

Bill stared at me incredulously. "Of *course* we're not ready, Kira! We're *evolving!* With a show like this, with a show that speaks to the essential break between the genders, with a show that embraces the entire human condition, we'll never be *ready!* We won't be ready the night we close!"

If Bill had his way, we might be closing the same night that we opened.

But he continued to wax eloquent about our development process, pouring himself into his rallying speech with all of the charisma that had made his name, that had built his reputation for years. "All of you actors have been so brave. All of you have been so brilliant. And now we're going to share your accomplishments with our audience. We're going to bring the audience into our process. We're going to let them see, let them share, let them know the very complicated ways that art—that *life*—comes into being."

A quick glance at the cast showed that they were eating out of Bill's hand. All of them stared at him with the intensity of war-torn citizens of Verona. Most were nodding. Several were actually taking notes, recording every last word of Bill's dramatic manifesto.

I had a choice.

I could stand up. I could disagree with Bill. I could say that our production was intolerable, untenable, unwatchable crap. I could argue that our only hope was to exploit the next three weeks, to take the twenty-one days that remained before our scheduled previews began, to smooth down the roughest of the rough spots, to create the barest bones of a viable production.

I could step to the front of the room and say that the emperor had no clothes.

I looked at John, to see if he would stand beside me. His face was pulled into a mask. At first, I couldn't tell what he was thinking, what was going on inside his head.

But then, I recognized his expression. I identified the thoughts that deepened the lines beside his mouth, that creased his forehead.

John had moved on. He was taking the "A" train. He was stepping back, letting *Romeo and Juliet* devolve to its logical, disastrous end. He was freeing himself from Bill.

And as I realized what he was doing, I recognized the same emotions in myself. There wasn't anything left for me to change. There wasn't anything left for me to do to make this show a success.

We were going to stage a gender-shifted, iron-bound, water-stained, flashlight-lit, hip-hop-supertitled, heartbreaking production of Shakespeare's classic love story. And when it bombed, my life as a stage manager would be over. I'd be nothing but a punch line to a Twin Cities theater joke.

I'd hardly care, when I was ensconced in law school somewhere. Law school. My own personal "A" train.

Utterly unaware of my thoughts, Bill clapped his hands together three times. "Let's go, people! Kira? Get the set wet down. Actors, in your costumes. We'll start in five. Remember, everyone! Three more days, and then the public sees our masterpiece!"

Bill glared at me, and I cleared my throat. "Okay, everyone," I said, faking my best stage-manager-in-control-of-everything voice. "Places in five minutes!"

As the stagehands rolled the giant manhole-cover frames into the wings, I knew that things were going to go very, very badly on Tuesday night. Not even a grim smile from John was enough to melt the chunk of ice in my belly.

CHAPTER 16

TWO DAYS AND SEVEN HOURS OF SLEEP LATER. Opening night. Brain dead. Words. Lost.

Despite my best efforts to keep the cast and crew on track, we were running nearly an hour late. The lobby was filled with a restless horde, the critics and avid theatergoers who had responded eagerly to Bill's attempts to drum up early business.

Everything was insane backstage. Just that afternoon, John had discovered that the iron manhole-cover frames were rusting, leaving dried-blood streaks across the set every time they were dragged to a new position. Bill loved the effect; he'd ordered the crew to drag the frames around in random patterns.

The theater smelled vaguely like a swamp—Bill's brilliant plastic sheeting was retaining puddles of stagnant water. Costumes were splitting at the seams, and I'd already made two emergency runs for additional hot-glue guns. The printer had not been able to complete our programs on our expedited schedule; we'd been reduced to photocopied black-and-white pages. The projector for the supertitles jammed. One of the running crew dropped a crate of flashlights, breaking more than a dozen bulbs. The sound system developed a hum that sounded like the birthing pangs of feedback.

Ordinarily, I thrived on the rush of adrenaline that came with a show's opening night. Tonight, though, I knew that we were pitifully unprepared. Tonight, we were displaying our unformed show to hordes of fascinated critics, to eagle-eyed professionals who were going to destroy my theater career forever.

When a show was in crisis, however, I moved onto another plane. My stride lengthened as I walked up and down the aisles, draping programs over seats because we hadn't lined up ushers for our early opening. My fingers tingled as I applied my hot-glue gun to costume after costume, encouraging the actors to use more baby powder to ease on the balky things, to reduce the pressure on the seams. My lungs burned as I climbed up to the catwalks, as I disassembled and reassembled the balky projector. (We lost one slide, which melted into a hopeless pool of goo, but I figured the audience wasn't going to understand a word of the foul-mouthed hip-hop gibberish anyway.)

This was why I lived in the theater—this feeling of being alive, of being poised on the edge of disaster, of having the power to save everyone, to save everything. This was the energy—the charge—that I would miss when I settled down to take the LSAT. To apply to law school. To commit my life to maximizing profits per partner.

At least my father wouldn't be in the audience. Our theatrical change in schedule had caught him by surprise; he couldn't get out of a charity benefit that he was hosting. Likewise, my high school debate coach was unaware of tonight's chaos; he still had tickets for our originally scheduled debut. This would be my first opening night that either of them had missed, but I was actually relieved.

I took a deep breath and completed my preshow responsibilities with the brisk efficiency that had always served me well at the dinner theater. I reminded the actors when they had half an hour left, then fifteen minutes. I peeked out from the theater's wings to see some of the most prominent critics in the Twin Cities, some of the most vocal voters for our local Ivey Awards. I could see Bill pacing at the back of the theater, arms crossed over his chest, head freshly shaved. His black turtleneck made him look pale, cadaverous.

"Do you think it's too late to get out of Dodge?" John's question was a whisper in my ear, and I realized that I'd subconsciously heard him come up behind me, felt his broad chest against my back.

The last few days of chaos had solidified the trust between us. We'd worked side by side to salvage the show, to make it presentable to the public. We'd seen each other at our worst—tempers flaring; and at our best—cajoling our crew into delivering more than anyone had thought humanly possible. We'd stolen meals together whenever we could, trying to convince ourselves that fast-food grease was actual nourishment.

Along the way, we'd shared more than a handful of kisses. The night before, we'd collapsed on a couch in the prop closet, sneaking a few hours of exhausted sleep before we attempted to work more of the impossible to meet Bill's insane deadline. I'd let myself relax against John's hard body, felt his arms fold around me with an ease, a simplicity, that I'd never known before, not with any other man.

When I had awakened, he'd been propped up on his elbow, his expression inscrutable in the light that filtered in from the dressing room. I'd raised my hands to his face, traced the line of his mustache. He caught my fingertip lightly between his teeth, making me gasp in surprise. His palms ranged down my body, awakening more energy than I had dreamed possible in my exhausted, preshow frantic state. Only the arrival of the carpentry crew interrupted our idyllic interlude. John kissed me hard, to silence my giggles, and I nearly followed through on our original plan, carpenters be damned.

Now I let myself lean against him, and I answered softly, "Maybe we're just too close to the production. Maybe it's better than we think it is."

He turned me around to face him. "Franklin, you *are* an optimist."

"Yeah," I said. "Or else I'm just ready to be committed."

He brushed a kiss across my lips. "*That* sounds like the stage manager I know and love."

I started at the last word, immediately told myself it was just part of a familiar phrase, a cliché. It didn't mean anything. Couldn't mean anything. I didn't have time to think, didn't have time to feel. I glanced at my watch. "I have to call five minutes."

John stepped aside, his face unreadable behind his mustache. "Break a leg," he said.

I started to answer but ran out of words. I settled for finding his hand, squeezing his fingers. Then I escaped to the dressing room for my final call before the show began. After notifying the actors, I darted up the ladder to the production booth. I could hear the expectant hum of the crowd below.

Taking my seat, I looked around, making sure that I had my script ready, my headset at my fingertips. Even as I scanned the booth, I realized that something was strange, something was out of place. My nose twitched, and I squinted into the shadows in the corner.

A large vase of roses loomed on the edge of my desk. In the shadows, their crimson petals were black. I fished the card out of the arrangement reflexively. I already knew what it would say. "I love you. I'm sorry. Can't we try again?"

That was the message Drew had left on the dozen roses he'd had delivered to my apartment on Sunday night, after I broke up with him. And the dozen that had waited for me in the lobby yesterday morning, on Monday. And now here.

He was an actor. He had to be as broke as the rest of us. Now I was going to make him bankrupt, in addition to making him miserable. I gritted my teeth and wished that I had some way of reaching out to Teel, some way of forcing the genie to make all of this right, to correct the absolute and utter disaster I had made out of poor Drew's life.

Besides, if I still had that third wish, I could have used it to salvage our production. I could have harnessed Teel's magic to redeem *Romeo and Juliet*, to transform the show into something boring and ordinary and successful. I could have saved my reputation and the reputation of every single person working on the show.

But no. I'd squandered my last chance at magic. I deserved the disaster that was about to unfold.

I cursed and settled my headset over my hair. It was time to sink or swim.

"House lights to one half," I said. My blood sang as the lights dimmed. The audience's chatter faded away. "House lights out," I said. "Projector cue one, ready. Projector cue one, go."

The first slide was projected on John's velvet curtain. Our Prologue, one of our few male actors, pummeled the set with an iron pipe, and then he bellowed,

"Two households, both alike in dignity,
In fair Verona, where we lay our scene,
From ancient grudge break to new mutiny,
Where civil blood makes civil hands unclean."

As the echoes of metal clanging on metal died down, the actor waved toward the supertitles that flashed above him, translating the Bard's poetry into a poor excuse for a joke:

"God-damn Verona-town, I say,
Two fam'lies raise their old AK-
Forty-sevens…"

I couldn't make myself read any more; I didn't have time to watch the ridiculous words slipping from slide to slide. Instead, I listened to the murmur of the audience, their growing uncertainty as the stage remained pitch-black. I could hear the confusion, the polite mystification, as every single person wondered whether the stage manager—whether *I*—had forgotten to call a lighting cue.

We'd handed out the flashlights, but no one seemed to understand what to do with them.

Swearing, I contemplated using the public address system, the emergency microphones that were intended to let the audience know about fires, earthquakes, floods, and other disasters at least half as serious as an entire production proceeding in absolute darkness. But then, a single feeble light flickered across the stage. Another followed it a moment later, picking up the Prologue's face. A few more chimed in, exploring the tangle of metal, the reflective sheen of puddled water.

The audience had figured out what was going on. With the lighting, at least.

I forced myself to settle back into my chair, to call the next dozen cues. I could sense the crowd's confusion, though, as more and more women came on stage, posturing and beating the set with iron bars, swaggering like caricatures of warriors in extreme fighting contests. Which, of course, they were. Caricatures. Not warriors.

It wasn't until Jennifer entered and the other actors started calling her "Romeo" that I heard a collective sigh of relief. People were catching on. They were beginning to understand. Not that comprehension helped much when it came to building audience rapport. By then, the supertitle slides had flashed some of their most offensive contemporary language, n-words, and c-words, and m-compound-nouns leading to several surprised gasps.

The actors seemed thrown by the audience's reactions. Either that, or they were terrified they were going to slip off of John's set. The plastic seemed much more slick than it had in rehearsal (although that was probably an optical illusion, created by the near darkness that enveloped the stage). I winced over at least three tumbles, grateful that I'd left extra Ace bandages in the dressing rooms.

Somehow, we limped through the first act. We got through the masquerade where the star-crossed lovers met, through the balcony scene, through a dozen more chances for every single actor to work out his or her frustrations against the iron set. Romeo and Juliet fled to the meddlesome Friar Laurence, and the priest agreed to perform his secret wedding.

"House lights to half," I called into my headset, and I was rewarded with seeing the audience for the first time since the show had begun.

Or, rather, I was punished by the sight.

I'd stage managed a few shows where the audience didn't realize it was time for intermission. I'd witnessed that uneasy silence, when they didn't know if they were supposed to clap, when they didn't know whether they were supposed to react.

But every other time that I'd worked on a…challenging show, I'd solved the problem by bringing up the house lights. Audiences *wanted* to work with actors. They wanted to like productions. They wanted to applaud for shows. Even when they weren't certain that it was time to clap, they always obliged when the lights actually came on.

But not for us. Not for *Romeo and Juliet*. Not for the titanic disaster that was capsizing in front of us.

Not a single person applauded. Instead, they started talking to one another, murmuring, turning the pages of their programs as if they were certain that they had missed something, overlooked some note that explained how they had stumbled onto this bizarre postmodern comedy performed in an incomprehensible foreign language.

I thought I was going to be sick.

But I didn't have that option. I took off my headset and made a quick round through the dressing rooms. The actors were silent. They knew the show was flopping.

Drew sat in front of his mirror, a bandage in his hand as he assisted Stephanie Michaelson with wrapping her knee. She was leaning close to him, pursing her lips. Unkindly, I wondered if she was actually in any pain, or if she was just reveling in Drew's attention.

I couldn't keep from glancing at her hands. No engagement ring. She must have removed it for the show; it didn't exactly match Bill's vision of Verona. Or maybe she'd given it back to Norman, after his little performance at Mephisto's. Maybe she had moved on from my former fiancé to my former boyfriend.

I tried to care, but I just wasn't able to summon the emotion.

In any case, as soon as Drew saw me, he forgot that Stephanie was alive. He sat up straighter, tracking my every movement with his eyes. I saw the eagerness that stretched his muscles, as if he were a hound scenting a rabbit in the underbrush.

He wanted me to say something about the roses. I had the power to make everything all right for him. I could redeem even the disaster of our production. All I had to do was tell him that I loved him.

Instead, I looked away and said, "Fifteen minutes, please." Out of the corner of my eye, I saw his shoulders slump. His absolute despair made my eyes water, even as Stephanie leaned closer to him. She whispered something that I suspected was supposed to be encouragement.

Steeling my heart, I climbed back into the production booth. I dug into my backpack to fortify myself with some snack, but I found that I'd depleted my supply during the past crazy couple of days. Without an edible morsel in sight, my food diary mocked me from the bottom of the bag.

With my stomach grumbling, the second act didn't get any better than the first. So many people had left at intermission that we had completely insufficient lighting for the second half of the show. I realized that I'd never set up a box for people to drop off their flashlights, so we probably lost a third of our stock. The supertitle projector jammed again. The plastic sheeting caught on a corner of the iron framework, sending a shower of noisome water into the first three rows of the audience. Stephanie's costume split during curtain calls, baring her chest for the entire audience to see.

Even with Stephanie's overexposure, the curtain call was accompanied by only the most perfunctory of applause. I had to believe that most of that came from Bill Pomeroy himself. And maybe his aged mother, who was sitting in the center of the front row, shivering in her now-damp blazer.

The cast was silent as they sponged off their makeup, as they peeled out of their costumes, as they returned to their anonymous street clothes. I heard one halfhearted suggestion that everyone go to Mephisto's, but no one joined the chorus. The company trickled out in groups of two or three, their heads hung low.

No one was greeted at the stage door. Even friends and family texted messages that they'd see people at home, that they had to run, that vague, undefined emergencies had come up.

Bill Pomeroy was nowhere to be seen.

Drew lingered as the rest of the cast trickled away. I tried to ignore him, making myself extraordinarily busy as I supervised the crew mopping up the set, as we rolled up the plastic sheeting, as we applied hair dryers to the bottom of the iron frames in an attempt to retard their further rusting.

He finally gave up and slunk off, but not before I saw him slip a gold-wrapped package inside my backpack. Chocolate, my mind registered immediately, recognizing the classic lines of the box. Expensive chocolate. Expensive chocolate that no former boyfriend should be splurging on for me. My belly reminded me that it was empty, but I told it to hold on just a little longer.

I was switching off the lights in the dressing room when John materialized out of the gloom. "Hey," I said, swinging my backpack over my shoulder. "Where have you been?"

"Talking to Bill." He ran his hand across his face, smoothing down his mustache, leaving behind canyons of exhaustion.

"Where is he? The cast expected him to come in and say something."

"He caught up with me after getting his mother into a cab."

I heard something beneath John's words, a confusing mix of anger, and frustration, all the negative emotions that had been swirling backstage since the audience's ominous silence. But now there was another emotion as well.

Relief.

"What?" I asked. "What did Bill tell you?"

"He's closing down the show."

"What?" I asked again. I couldn't believe that I'd heard right.

John sighed. "He's going to announce that some flu bug got into the cast, that we don't have enough understudies. He's going to put the show 'on hiatus' until everyone has recovered."

The blossom of hope that had started to unfurl shriveled. "And after the 'hiatus'?"

John shook his head. "There won't be any 'after.' The Landmark'll stay dark for two months. If they're lucky, they'll manage to launch the next show a few weeks early. Try to recoup some costs there."

I imagined the media flurry, the cyclone of theater gossip as news of our colossal failure spread. I thought about the pots of money that the Landmark would have to burn, the tickets they'd have to refund—at least to season subscribers who hadn't had a choice about what horrific productions they'd be forced to see. I imagined the stacks of unpaid bills sitting on the producers' desks, the invoices from the ironworkers, and the supertitle company, and everyone else who had been dragged into our little corner of artistic hell.

"I can't believe he's pulling the plug," I said. "I can't believe it's over." And then, the full import of John's news hit me.

I was done.

No one else was ever going to see *Romeo and Juliet*. No one else was ever going to offer me the chance to stage manage another play. I really was going to have to take the LSAT.

I started to cry.

"Aw, Franklin," John said. His arms were strong around me. He pulled me close to his chest, made all of the appropriate shushing noises as my silent tears grew to sobs, expanded into great, gasping torrents of loss. I choked on my own hysterics, ashamed of myself, unable to stop. He smoothed my hair, ran his hands down my back, told me it was all going to be all right.

But he was wrong. It was never going to be right again. My life in the theater—the only life I'd ever wanted—was over.

At last, I managed to catch my breath. He pulled away enough to fish a handkerchief out of his pocket, and I ducked my head, imagining the mess of my swollen eyes and smeared makeup and slimy nose. He let me avoid his gaze, but he settled a steady hand on my arm, led me toward a handful of chairs that were scattered against the wall.

"I might as well tell you the rest of it," he said.

I could tell from his tone that whatever he had to say, it was going to be worse than the failure of our show. It was going to be worse than my wasting my wishes on a career that I was never going to have.

He was going to tell me that he was gay. (Read: That he was a greater actor than everyone in our entire professional cast, combined.) He was going to say that he was married, that he had a perfect wife and two point four kids and a dog, all waiting for him back in Texas. He was going to announce a religious epiphany, a decision to move to an ashram half the world away.

He chewed on his lower lip for a minute, and then he said, "I'm heading to New York."

"New York?" I croaked. My voice didn't belong to me; it sounded like a cross between a frog and a dying goat. I sniffed and cleared my throat. "What's in New York?" Of course, I knew what was in New York. Broadway. More theaters per block than anywhere else in the world. The "A" train. I swallowed hard and said, "What show?"

"A revival of *Long Day's Journey Into Night*. Big-name cast. Traditional staging."

Even as my heart was breaking, I said, "No manhole covers?"

He grimaced. "Not one in sight."

"Why didn't you tell me?"

"I thought we'd have more time here. Another couple of weeks at least. Working until the scheduled opening."

I couldn't blame him. A lot could happen in a couple of weeks. A lot had happened in a couple of *days*. "Break a leg," I said bravely, when the silence grew too loud.

"Come with me."

I was knocked over by the crush of relief those three words sent through my body. I was lucky I was already sitting; my knees started shaking so badly that I could barely breathe. "I—"

He interrupted me before I could stammer out an answer. "I know this is fast. I know we barely know each other. But surviving nearly three months of Bill Pomeroy is like spending three years on any other play. I think—"

I finally dared to look at him, and the expression on my face must have dried the last words in his mouth. "I can't," I said. I shook my head, hardly believing what I was about to say. "I promised my father. I have obligations to my housemates. I can't just pick up and leave. I can't just... I can't."

If I hadn't already shed enough tears to fill Lake Minnetonka, I might have started again. John waited for several heartbeats, as if he expected me to come to my senses, expected me to change my mind. When I just shook my head, though, he said, "I could only hope." He shuddered, like a dog shaking off rainwater, and then he clambered to his feet. He looked over his shoulder at the chaos of the set. "We won't start striking this thing until tomorrow. Can I give you a ride home?"

"I've got my car here."

"I'll follow you, then. Make sure you get there okay."

I was too tired to protest. Instead, I collected my coat from the dressing room. I picked up my backpack. I looked around the theater, realizing that it would take us less than forty-eight hours to eradicate every last sign of the worst *Romeo and Juliet* known to man.

John held the door for me as we left the theater, and he blocked the wind as I locked up. But he kept his distance as we walked to our cars, merely nodding at the unlikely coincidence that we were parked next to each other, right in front of Club Joe.

I let myself into my own vehicle. I started my engine, giving it a minute or so to warm up. When I pulled into traffic, he followed me, silently, protectively. It was after midnight, and the city streets were quiet. We wove around Lake of the Isles in tandem, and I thought about changing my mind. I thought about asking him to come up to the apartment.

But what was the use? I'd lost my last chance at happiness in the theater. I wasn't going to listen to the siren song of New York. I wasn't going to imagine what life would be like on the Great White Way, how my career might prosper and grow beside John's.

I was going to be a lawyer. I'd promised my father. We'd shaken on it.

John waited while I pulled into a parking space just a couple of car lengths from my driveway. I sank back into my seat, wanting to listen to the engine tick as it cooled, wanting to close my eyes and fall asleep and wish all of the crazy night away.

I knew, though, that he'd stay there until I got inside, safe and sound. That was the gentlemanly thing to do. That was John, all over.

I sighed and picked up my backpack from where I'd tossed it on the passenger seat. As I pulled it over the gearshift, a golden box tumbled to my feet. Drew's expensive chocolate.

My stomach constricted, reminding me that it hadn't been fed in ages. My fingers scrambled for the fabric ribbon that held the box closed. I fumbled for a chocolate, tossed it into my mouth like a starving woman. Which I was.

I bit down, already relishing the bittersweet melt across my tongue. I swallowed reflexively, and then I started to gag.

Alcohol. Liquor. Bourbon or rum or something that my taste buds had forgotten how to classify precisely.

My cheeks flushed even as I spat the last of the chocolate into John's handkerchief, which I'd kept after my sobfest. My lips tingled, as if I'd swallowed a particularly unpleasant hot pepper. My throat started to itch.

Drew had given me liquor-filled chocolates. And I, completely distracted, had not even thought about testing the treat.

My reaction wasn't life-threatening. I wasn't collapsing in anaphylactic shock. I could head inside and pop a Benadryl and be fine in the morning.

But the searing of my reddened cheeks was the final nail in Juliet's coffin.

I stumbled up the walk to the front door, swiping away fresh tears. I didn't even bother to wave goodbye to John, although I heard him put his truck in gear, heard him drive away. I locked the door behind me quietly, praying that the Swensons wouldn't think I was some sort of crafty burglar with a key.

I could hear voices upstairs, even before I turned the key in the apartment's lock. Maddy and Jules fell silent, though, as I opened the door. They'd been laughing, but now they stared at me, pity stark across both of their faces. They hadn't even been at the show, but they'd already heard about the disaster.

"Kira," Jules said, but I only shook my head, heading directly into the bathroom.

I raided the medicine chest, found the antihistamines, then swallowed a couple of pink pills with water cupped in my hand. I took a minute to splash my face, shaking my head when I realized there was no way to hide that I'd been crying.

By the time I got back to the living room, I had pasted on a fake smile.

"Kira," Jules said again, as perky as if she were greeting me for the first time that night. "Have you eaten?"

I glanced over at the dining room table and saw the collection of take-out containers from Hunan Delight. My stomach growled, but my tingling lips spoke of their own accord. All of my anger and frustration, all of my sorrow about the production, about John, about Drew, all of that negative emotion flowed over in a torrent of rage. My helpless fury was a flood directed at the two people who best understood me, best knew what I was going through. I screamed, "I don't need you guys to tell me when to eat!"

"We just—" Maddy said, sitting up on the couch.

I shoved my hand into my backpack, ripped out my food diary with enough force that several pages tore away. "I've been writing down my food, okay? I've been recording every single bite! You can go ahead and read it! Go ahead and call my father! Want my phone? Want to call him right now? I made a promise to you guys, and I keep my promises! I always keep my promises!"

"Kira!" Maddy said, her voice severe enough that it shocked me into silence. "We just wanted to know if you were hungry. We were celebrating, and we saved some for you."

I was shaking, but I managed to ask, "What could you possibly be celebrating?"

"We both got news tonight. Good news."

I felt a little stupid, standing there with my torn food diary, and my stomach grumbling loudly enough that I was certain they both could hear. Without a word, Maddy pushed herself off the couch and started piling food onto a plate. As I stared like a sleepwalker, she carried my dinner over to the microwave.

Jules filled the awkward silence by saying, "We heard about your show."

"Who told you?" I asked, consciously deciding to let exhaustion replace my outrage.

Jules cast a quick look at her coconspirator. "We got a few phone calls." Great. The rumor mill must have tied up every cell tower in the Twin Cities. The triple beep of the microwave spared me the need to reply. I crossed to the table and accepted the plate that Maddy put in front of me. The Hunan chicken was heaven in my mouth, and I barely resisted the urge to swallow an entire carton of rice without chewing.

"Yeah," I said after I'd downed another three bites. "So much for my brilliant Landmark debut."

Before I could say anything else, Jules passed me a glass of water. The diamond twinkling on her finger rivaled the one that Stephanie Michaelson had shown off at Mephisto's.

"Oh my God!" I said, nearly knocking the water to the floor as I grabbed her hand. "Justin finally proposed?"

Jules's teeth flashed white in a perfect smile. "They voted him in as partner, tonight. He came by as soon as he had the news."

Maddy rolled her eyes. "You missed it, Kira. He was down on one knee, holding out the ring, asking for her hand, the whole traditional thing. The four of us cheered so loudly that Mr. Swenson came upstairs."

I made a face, even as I continued chewing. Mr. Swenson could live with one night of noise. Jules had been waiting for this night for years. "Wait," I said, swallowing. "The four of you?"

Jules raised her eyebrows, clearly instructing Maddy to continue. For the first time since I'd met her, though, my bluff friend was silent. Instead, Maddy was suddenly fascinated by the edge of a cloth napkin. She rolled it between her blunt fingers, then smoothed it flat, repeating the process as if it could capture the mysteries of the universe.

"Who?" I said at last, snatching the napkin away. "Who else was here?"

"Gunther," Maddy said softly.

"Herr Wunderbar," Jules reminded me helpfully.

"Oh!" I couldn't help but look at the whiteboard calendar in the kitchen. A disbelieving tally, and I heard myself say, "What is it? Almost three months?"

Maddy's eyes were shining, even as her face crinkled in annoyance. "It's not like that's so unbelievable."

Jules answered before I could clear my mouth of chicken and vegetables. "Yes, it is. Three months in Maddy time is like three years in an ordinary relationship."

The food turned to sawdust in my mouth.

That was practically the same thing that John had said to me. Three months. Three years.

I pushed my plate away.

Maddy glared at Jules, but then she laughed and said, "I'm going to New York with him. With Gunther. People are already talking about the work he's doing for Shakespeare in the Park. He's got lots of offers, all sorts of possibilities. And I'll find work, too."

I knew what I was supposed to say. I knew what I was supposed to do. Years of living in the theater came to my rescue. I responded perfectly. "Maddy!" I said. "I'm so happy for you!"

New York. With the man of her dreams. Perfect.

And Jules and Justin were getting married. Perfect, too.

And I'd be left alone, living above the Swensons in an apartment I couldn't afford. Looking for strangers to be my housemates. Studying for the LSAT. Preparing for law school. Getting ready for my life as a lawyer.

"I'm so happy," I said again. "For both of you!"

"And to celebrate," Maddy said, "we have our fortune cookies!" She presented the cellophane-wrapped treats on a plate. "I waited until you were here, Kira."

"What a sacrifice," I said, trying to keep my voice light.

Jules opened hers first. "'Everything will now come your way,'" she read. The light glinted off her engagement ring as she set the curl of paper on the table. "Hopefully only good things!" She laughed.

Maddy looked toward me, but I nodded for her to open her own cookie. "'You are filled with life's most precious treasure—hope!'" She made a face. "I'm filled with Eight Treasures Chicken, but that's close enough, I guess."

Jules laughed. "I hope Gunther wasn't attracted to your ability to think in abstract terms."

Maddy grunted. "I'm a lighting designer. Not a philosopher." She turned to me. "Come on, Kira. Open yours."

I was tired of the game, weary of the lighthearted banter. But I wasn't going to argue; there was no reason to fight. Better to get all of this best-friend camaraderie over. Finished. So that I could retreat to my bedroom and collapse into sleep.

I tore open the wrapper, broke the cookie into two neat halves. I cleared my throat as I unfolded the slip of paper. "'You are going on a journey,'" I read. Unanticipated tears blurred my vision. More tears. How could I have any tears left? "Whoops, Maddy. I must have gotten yours by mistake." I shoved the fortune toward her, along with the broken crescent of my cookie.

I heard the shakiness in my voice. I knew that they could hear it, too. That's what best friends were for, after all. But I didn't have time for social niceties. I didn't have time to be polite. I had to get away from them, away from their happiness, away from their sickening, perfect lives.

I said, "I'm even more tired than I thought. I have got to get to sleep. I'll see you both in the morning."

And because they were my best friends, they pretended to believe me. They let me escape down the hall toward my bedroom.

Before I could sequester myself away, I saw the flurry of sticky notes attached to my door. Jules's neat handwriting. Maddy's forceful notes. "Drew called." "Drew called again." "Drew."

I tore them off the door and crumpled them into a ball as I threw myself onto my bed.

I wanted to scream at the top of my lungs. I wanted to tell Bill Pomeroy that he had ruined my life. I wanted to swaddle myself in my baggy black sweatshirts, my shapeless black sweatpants, the disguises that had protected me during my year of mourning Norman. I wanted to scream at Drew, to tell him that he didn't love me, that he'd never loved me, that it was all a horrible lie.

I rubbed at my face, trying to scrub away the last of the alcohol-induced itch. The rubbing only irritated me more, though, and I forced myself to fold my hands in front of my eyes, almost as if I were praying.

A golden glint caught my attention.

I opened up my hands, turned my wrists in the overhead light. Unbelievably, I could *still* make out the shape of golden flames, the glitter of the tattoos that should have faded weeks before.

I scrambled onto the floor, swiping my hand beneath my bed until I found the abandoned brass lantern. It was warm to my touch. Warmer than any metal had a right to be in Minnesota, in March.

I caught my breath and squeezed my thumb to my forefinger, pressing as hard as I could. "Teel," I said, working hard to keep the single syllable even, firm. As if I believed my genie would appear.

Fog flowed out of the lantern—emerald and cobalt and ruby and topaz. I caught a shriek against the back of my teeth, dropped the lamp onto my bed. I staggered back a couple of steps, unable to believe my eyes as a body solidified out of the mist.

Teel looked like the lawyer I dreaded becoming. Her sleek blond hair was cut in a neat bob that curled perfectly at her jawline. She wore a white blouse and a navy suit, the skirt cut an inch or two below her knee. Her legs were encased in silky stockings, and her ankles were steady in sensible pumps. She gripped a briefcase in her right hand, as if I'd summoned her just as she was about to walk into court.

Only the ring of flames tattooed around her wrist broke the stolid, boring image.

"Teel?" I whispered.

"At last!" she said. "I thought you were *never* going to call me back here. Are you ready to make your last wish?"

CHAPTER 17

"WH-WHAT ARE YOU DOING HERE?" I STAMMERED.

Teel stared at me as if I'd lost my mind. She thrust her head forward and raised her perfectly plucked eyebrows. "Hello? I'm a genie? I'm bound to stick around until you make your four wishes?"

"Four?"

She clicked her tongue like a frustrated nanny. "Parlez-vous anglais? Sprechen Sie Englisch? Habla ingles? Quatre. Vier. Cuatro."

I waved her off, trying to make sense of the situation. "Yeah, yeah. I speak English. But what do you mean by four wishes? Don't I just get three?"

Teel sighed in exasperation. "Didn't you read the paperwork?"

"*What* paperwork?" Astonished as I was, I was becoming more than a little exasperated myself.

Teel set her briefcase on my bed, triggering the locks with two expertly manicured nails. She lifted the lid of the container and shuffled through a stack of manila folders. "Joan Frankel… Carl Franken… Jeanette Frankovich…."

"Franklin," I said. "You went past me."

"Frankel," Teel repeated through gritted teeth, brandishing a folder. "Franken." Another folder. "Frankovich." She frowned, and rifled through the rest of the briefcase's contents. When she looked up at me, a deep line was incised in the center of her forehead. "You don't have a folder."

"Maybe that's because you never gave me the paperwork." Despite my exhaustion, despite the absurdity of our conversation, I sweetened my voice. (Read: I loaded my tone with saccharine, betting that Teel would let my insubordination slide.)

She harrumphed and passed me a sheaf of pages covered with tiny print. "Well, it's not too late. You can read and sign them now."

I took the pages by reflex. "The party of the first part… The party of the second part… Hereinabove mentioned forthwith…" I looked up. "You *do* realize that lawyers gave up a lot of this jargon ages ago, don't you?"

"Read," she said imperiously, producing a fountain pen from somewhere in her briefcase.

I can't promise that I understood everything that was in the document. I can't swear that I grasped the intricacies of the indemnities and the indemnifications. I wouldn't testify in a court of law that I had mastered the language about severance and inheritability and third-party beneficiaries. I was virtually certain that I was missing something about the subordination clause, and it seemed to me like "novation" should have something to do with weddings.

But there was one clause that was crystal clear. One clause that even an idiot could understand. One clause that even an exhausted, emotionally rattled stage manager could glom onto: "Term and termination: This agreement shall terminate upon the granting by Genie of all elements and subelements of the Fourth Wish ('the Final Wish') made explicit by Wisher."

I grabbed the pen before the words could change. Slamming the contract down on my desk, I scribbled my signature across the bottom of the last page. Teel took a step closer on her sturdy, practical heels. "And initial there," she said, pointing to a space on the first page. "And there. And circle your state of residence there. And add your mailing address there. And if you decline to purchase insurance from us—"

"Enough!"

Teel pursed her lips before tapping a perfect fingernail under the final clause. "Read this and initial beside it."

I picked up the paper and turned it to better catch the light. "Confidentiality: Wisher shall not disclose to others (including but not limited to Wisher's family, legal counsel, and targets of all Wishes) the existence of this Agreement or any of the terms herein. Wisher explicitly agrees not to disclose the actual number of Wishes granted herein. Wisher further explicitly agrees that disclosing the actual number of Wishes granted herein will result in irreparable harm to Genie, which harm may be enjoined to the full extent of law and equity."

I recognized the hodgepodge of words, identified each individual strand of legalese. I knew that my father would forbid me from signing such a document, at least until he'd had a chance to pick it apart, clause by dependent clause.

But I also knew that my father was never going to review my genie's documentation. I knew that Teel had the magical strength to keep me from revealing what I knew, even if I were inclined to do so. She'd already shown me that power numerous times, when she'd kept me from talking about what was going on, even before I'd known there was a fourth wish at stake.

Initialing the confidentiality clause was a formality. A formality that would get me my fourth and final wish. I scribbled KF in the margin, crossing the F with a final flourish.

Teel nodded precisely and stacked the pages, tapping them against my desk until they were perfectly aligned. Then she reached up to the pink shell of her earlobe, tugging firmly once. She passed me a newly materialized duplicate of the contract, countersigned with her own sprawling one-name signature on the last page.

"So," she said. "Your last wish."

"Wait a second," I said, finally able to think clearly. "Where have you been? Why haven't you been nagging me, the way you were for the first three wishes?"

"Nagging?" She sounded offended.

"Dragging me to your invisible Garden. Staring off into space all wistful."

"The Garden," Teel sighed, her longing cutting through the ridiculous business of the contract. She blinked, though, and shrugged. "I made a promise."

"You what?"

"The last time we went to the Garden. You made me promise I wouldn't bring you there again. A genie always keeps her promises."

She made it sound so simple. So straightforward. "Oh" was all that I could say.

"If you *want* to go back to the Garden—" She raised her perfect nails to her ears.

"No!" I had no desire to be back in that nothingness, no desire to float in the neither here nor now.

But what would I wish?

I could tell Teel that I wanted to undo the previous three wishes altogether. That would erase everything that had happened at the Landmark. That would save me and the theater-loving world from Bill Pomeroy's abomination of *Romeo and Juliet.*

Well, that wasn't entirely true. Bill would still have done his play, even if I'd been nowhere in the vicinity. Some other stage manager would have taken the hit, though. Maybe someone with more on the line than I had. Someone with a spouse to support. With kids.

Besides, I didn't want to miss everything that had happened. I certainly didn't want to miss my time with John.

I raised my fingers to my lips, remembering how gentle his first kiss had been. Remembering that he had just asked me to move to New York with him. I'd told him no, I'd said that I couldn't abandon my life here. But that was before I'd come home to find out that my housemates were abandoning me. (Okay, a tiny, logical part of my mind said. They weren't *abandoning* me. They were living their lives.) That was before a fortune cookie had told me I was going on a journey.

John and I were still at the very beginning of our relationship. If I hadn't ruined things tonight—and I had to hope I hadn't, had to believe that I could still go back, still make things right—there was so much potential. Potential that would be rubbed out if I erased all of my wishes, made it so that I'd never set foot in the Landmark.

If I turned back to John, though, if I even started to pay serious attention to the possibility of going to New York, I would be forswearing my obligation to Dad. I could use my final wish to end my promise to my father. I could wish to be free from my obligation to take the LSAT, to pursue law school and a staid job at a firm and the highest profits per partner that I could generate.

But I didn't need to waste a wish on that. I could make that happen on my own, without Teel's powers. All it would take was courage—the strength to tell my father that despite his grandest dreams for me, despite his love and care and support for so many years, I wasn't going to follow in his footsteps. I wasn't going to be the lawyer my mother had always dreamed of being.

It would be rough for him, sure. But he was my *father*. He wanted what was best for me. He'd always wanted what was best for me. No need for magical intervention there.

"Anytime today," Teel said.

"I'm thinking," I snapped. She hadn't believed it was important enough to tell me the full terms of our deal at the beginning. I certainly wasn't going to let her bully me into wasting my last wish now.

"Six out of ten people—"

"I don't care," I said automatically. Who knew what crazy statistic she was going to spout? Where did she get those numbers, anyway?

But that wasn't fair. Teel had consistently used her statistics to warn me. To guide me. She had tried to tell me that I wouldn't be happy with some of my choices. She had tried to say that most women chose to change their bodies, chose to reshape their physical selves, but she'd hinted that those changes weren't always successful. Satisfying.

I looked down at my reshaped physical self.

Sure, things had gotten complicated. I'd needed to convince my father and my housemates that I wasn't starving myself to death. I'd been subjected to Norman's disgusting comments, to Drew's stupid follow-up.

But I had to admit, I didn't mind the new body itself. I'd come to enjoy dressing it; I liked the changes Teel had built in. I had enjoyed the time that Drew and I had invested in discovering each other's bodies; I had liked the way this new physical me responded, the way I felt when I'd been with him. Nope. I wasn't going to give this body back, not without a fight.

But Drew… I'd taken Drew by the unfair advantage of a wish. I'd only snared him with Teel's assistance, ignoring my genie's most vigorous protests. I'd made him miserable. I was rapidly making him broke.

He didn't know me. He didn't care about me. He didn't even remember the first thing about me—tonight's alcohol-filled chocolates had proved that.

I had thought that I'd be happy with him. I had thought that the secret to my success was being wanted, being needed, being loved. I'd fallen victim to every romantic daydream, every cheap fantasy sold to every schoolgirl who had ever scribbled her name on a piece of wide-ruled notebook paper, adding the last name of her so-called One True Love in a giddy dream of wedded bliss.

I closed my eyes and summoned up Drew's face. Oddly, though, I wasn't able to picture him. Not all of him. I could see the line of his jaw, glinting in a ray of sunlight, bristling with a beard that he hadn't bothered to shave in the morning. I could see the sparkle of emerald swirled into the chestnut of his eyes. I could see the line of his teeth, the tiny imperfection that made him human, made him real. I could see the firm edge of his lips; I could even remember the feel of those lips as he woke me for the third time in the night, stirring me to passion I'd never dreamed I could enjoy.

But I couldn't see *Drew*. I couldn't see all of him. I couldn't see the man that I had bewitched, the man whom I'd bound to me through my genie's spell.

My eyes still closed, I bit my lip, trying to increase my concentration. Drew. This shouldn't be difficult. I'd slept with the man for weeks. I'd mooned over him at rehearsal for ages before that. Drew.

Try as I might, though, I couldn't summon a full and complete portrait.

I opened my eyes. Teel had settled a hand on her hip; she was a full-color illustration for a textbook on annoyance. "Ready?" she asked.

"I wish that Drew Myers would fall out of love with me."

Teel narrowed her eyes. I felt like I was on the witness stand as she said, "Drew Myers? You're wasting another wish on him?"

"It's not a waste," I said.

"You don't need to unwork the magic, just because you're bored."

"I'm not bored!"

"Bored. Guilty. Whatever." With a tight wave of her hand, Teel managed to connote professional disapproval, as if my wish violated some secret lawyer pact, broke the genie rules.

"Look," I argued. "You told me to make my fourth wish, and I'm making it. Weren't you the one who told me that nine out of ten women who make wishes out of jealousy regret their wishes?"

"I'm flattered," she said haughtily. "I didn't think you listened to anything I said." She stopped her rebuke long enough to peer into my face. "Wait. You really want to do this? You really want to spend your last wish forever, unmaking your third one?"

There were lots of other things I could wish for. Fame. Fortune. Finding a job in New York with John.

But fame brought its own disasters; Exhibit One was Bill Pomeroy's topple from the heights of local theater celebrity. And I didn't really need much money to be happy. And things were either going to work out with John or they weren't. After watching me break down like a sand castle at the beach, he might decide he didn't want anything else to do with me, ever again.

I thought of Drew's happy-go-lucky charm. His "dudes" and

his "totallys." His stunning good looks. I thought of how deflated he'd looked at the end of the play—not dragged down by the audience, not devastated by the critics. Broken by me. By his unrequited love for me.

I met Teel's eyes, remembering the rules of the genie game. This time, my wish was simple. I didn't feel the need to explain, the compulsion to clarify, to make sure that Teel understood every possible mistake I might have made. Teel knew the parameters of what I wanted. Teel would make it all right.

"I really want to do this."

She nodded. "Very well, then." She collected her papers and put them in her briefcase. She flipped the combination locks closed, spinning the dials to eradicate any trace of her secrets. She extended one slim hand, her tattoo glinting incongruously against the cuff of her blouse. "It's been a pleasure working with you. I regret that we won't be able to do business again in the future."

"This is it, then? You don't have any other hidden papers? No secret messages that you'll be coming back again and again and again to deliver?"

Her smile was so small I almost missed it. "This is it. Good luck, Kira."

"Thanks." And because that didn't sound like enough, I said, "Seriously. Thanks for everything. It hasn't all been good, but the past three months have taught me a lot."

"Three months." My genie lawyer shook her head. "Eight out of ten people complete their wishes in less than a week." She raised her fingers to her earlobe. "Goodbye."

"Goodbye. And thank you! And good luck getting into the Garden!" The last words caught in my throat. Teel's lips crooked into a graceful smile, and she inclined her head, accepting all of my good wishes. I stared at her for a long moment, thinking about everything I didn't know about genies, everything I didn't understand. I sighed and said, "I wish that Drew Myers was no longer in love with me."

"As you wish," Teel said succinctly, and then she tugged twice with all her might.

The flame tattoo around her wrist blazed out, golden light that shimmered up her arm, around her head, consuming her body and breaking it into tiny particles of fog. The minute jewels sparkled for a full minute before flowing into the lantern on my bed. I picked up the brass lamp and tried to peer inside it. The metal had lost its luster, lost the brilliant gleam that I had shocked into existence back in the costume shop at the dinner theater. It was cold, almost icy against my palms.

I rubbed my hand against it, then tried to polish it with my comforter, but the lamp remained dull. Lifeless. Ordinary.

I held my own hand in front of my face, turning my fingers this way and that, attempting to catch the glimmer of my personal flame tattoo. Try as I might, though, I could not pick up a hint of the mark that had bound me to Teel, that had given me the power to summon a genie.

For good measure, I pressed my thumb and forefinger together, firmly clenching them. Nothing. No electric tingle. No juddering metallic shock.

Teel was actually gone.

I leaned back on my pillow. For one fleeting instant, I caught a whiff of Drew's shampoo. I wondered if he would call me to announce his sudden freedom. If he was going to come find me, the way he had when Teel first made him fall in love with me. If I would know that my final wish had worked.

I realized, though, that there wasn't going to be any call; there would be no passionate proclamation to wake the Swensons. After all, what would Drew say? "I suddenly realized that I don't know you at all, and I have no idea what I've been thinking for the past month?"

And that was just as well. Because I couldn't imagine what I would say back to him. "You're gorgeous, but you're dumb as a rock, dude." That didn't speak very highly of him. Or of me.

I cradled the lantern against my chest. I was tired, spent from the days of theater hell, from the pressure to mount our show, from the living terror as I saw our creation unfold into something I never wanted my name associated with. I was exhausted from my sobbing, from my hysterical realization that my life wasn't going to be the one I'd always dreamed of, the one I'd always wanted.

I closed my eyes and fell into a swirl of dreams, all colored with glints of fading jewels.

Standing outside my father's office door, I hesitated. "Go ahead," Angie said from behind me, her voice sympathetic around her wad of gum. "He's only got fifteen minutes before his two o'clock."

I steeled myself and knocked, barely waiting for my father's muffled "Come in" before turning the handle. Dad was sitting behind his desk, the business pages of the *StarTribune* spread out in front of him. He hurriedly finished chewing the last bite of his sandwich as he stood to greet me. "Kira! To what do I owe this pleasure?"

"Sorry to interrupt you, Dad." I eased into one of the chairs across the desk from him.

I had slept late that morning, sacked out from physical and mental exhaustion. A shower and a bowl of Cap'n Crunch later, though, I felt like a new woman. Even though I'd dug the "Variety" section of the newspaper out of the trash can, where one of my housemates had hidden it. Even though I'd brushed off orange peels to read the review of our play. Even though I'd cringed at the snarky tone, the high-and-mighty critique of every last aspect of Bill Pomeroy's masterpiece.

Even though I'd read the black-edged box beneath the review, noting that the show had been placed on hiatus. Black-edged. Like an obituary.

At least I was lucky; Dad hadn't reached the "Variety" section yet. He always started with the stock reports, with the minuscule print that told the story of his clients' rises and falls.

Tiny print, like Teel's contract that I had read and signed. I could still feel my internal debate as I chose my final wish, remember it like a fever in my bones.

And I could recall my sudden clarity regarding my father, emerging from the middle of that debate. I could recall that instant of *knowing*, of *understanding* that I needed to talk to Dad. I needed to explain the truth to him. I needed to tell him who I was, what I wanted, how I was going to live my life.

I had dressed for the occasion—neat wool trousers, a creamy silk blouse. Anyone passing me in the hall would have mistaken me for one of the firm's eager associates, one of those lawyers who thrived on research and writing, on investing every waking moment in pursuit of the brass ring of partnership, in communion with The Law.

My father knew better, though. He sat back in his chair and steepled his fingers in front of his chest. "You're never an interruption, Kira."

I glanced over my shoulder at my mother's portrait. Dad had never bargained for the single parent game. He'd never asked to raise me on his own, to deal with the trials and tribulations of a sometimes headstrong daughter. But we'd made it through my teen years remarkably unscathed. We'd figured out our path through college, even when I'd wanted a major that Dad considered utterly irresponsible. We'd made it through an endless procession of plays.

We'd make it through this, as well. But only if I took the proverbial bull by the horns. "I'm not taking the LSAT, Dad."

He remained absolutely impassive. "You've lined up your next theater job, then?"

"No," I said. "Not yet."

He gestured toward the newspaper in front of him. "With *Romeo and Juliet* on hiatus, it'll be difficult to pin down something else, won't it? Something stable by your May deadline?"

Damn. I'd always *thought* he read the business section first. I raised my chin. "It might be difficult to find another theater job, if I were going to stay in the Twin Cities."

Again, with the poker face. "Where are you going?"

"New York." It sounded more dangerous when I said the words out loud. In the privacy of my own mind, New York sounded exciting. Bohemian. Romantic. But when I named the city here, my decision to move halfway across the country sounded shockingly irresponsible. Especially since I hadn't even spoken with John about it. Better to stick to the facts. Stick to the plan, however new it might be. I met my father's gaze.

"I thought we had an agreement, Kira. I thought you'd promised to take the LSAT."

"We did, Dad. *I* did. But I had to change my mind."

For one instant, he looked trapped. My beloved father, the brilliant lawyer, the man who had stood by me through every harebrained scheme of my adult life, looked trapped. I saw him consider one reply, another, yet a third. And then, he took a deep breath and said, "Why?"

That was better than I'd expected. That was better than his getting angry. That was better than his ordering me out of the house, me and Jules and Maddy, before all of us were ready to go our separate ways. Not that I'd truly believed he would turn me out. Not that I'd ever doubted he loved me.

Nevertheless, I had to stand up to answer him; I had to pace. My nervous steps carried me away from his desk, toward the bookcase, but I turned back to face him before I spoke. "I know you want me to be a lawyer, Dad. I know that's what Mom wanted to be. I know that you want me to be safe and successful." I glanced at my mother's photo, at her perfect smile. "But I know that, even more, you want me to be happy."

"Kira—"

"Being a lawyer would have made *Mom* happy!" I said, interrupting him. "But not me." I flexed my fingers, wishing that I could paint with words, that I could show him what I thought, how I felt. "There's an energy in the theater, Dad. Even when the show is terrible, even when the director is insane, there's a power in what we do. I love that energy, Dad. It fills me. It *fulfills* me."

"You'll learn to feel that way about the law, Kira. You'll argue in a courtroom, in front of a judge and jury. You'll find the same energy there."

I shook my head, a little sad that I couldn't make him understand. "No. I won't. Dad, you've taught me that I can do anything. You've given me all the training I need, taught me to stick with what I've chosen. I've chosen the theater. And down the road, in five years or ten or twenty, if I change my mind, if I realize I actually want to be a lawyer, I can choose that, too. And I promise that you'll be the first person I'll share the news with."

I was astonished to see tears glinting in his eyes. "Kira, you've chosen something so difficult. You've made your life so hard."

I glanced again at my mother. "I've chosen what's right for me. That's what you always wanted, isn't it? Both of you?"

He stood up. He walked around the desk. He looked at the framed photograph, for long enough that I imagined he and Mom were having some sort of silent conversation. And then he held out his hand.

Our handshake. Just like we'd always sealed our agreements. Just like we'd always reconciled, ever since I was a little girl.

My fingers closed around his, and I pumped once, firmly. Then, I let my father hug me. He kissed my forehead, and he said, "I suppose you already have everything worked out about the house? With Maddy and Jules?"

"Of course," I said, smiling in relief. "But I'll tell you about it later. You have a two o'clock meeting."

"I'll tell Angie to hold it. I want to hear your plans."

I fortified myself with a final Club Joe coffee before returning to the scene of my theatrical crime. The crew was set to arrive at five. Instead of setting up the show for a full run-through, though, we were going to take apart the set. We'd likely get the lion's share done in one night; it was always easier to tear things down than it was to build them up in the first place.

The theater was full of life lessons like that, I mused as I sipped my coffee, browsing through my food diary. It had taken me days of recording every single bite of food that I consumed, every sip of milk-fortified caffeine. And yet, I could destroy the entire compilation with one well-placed spill of coffee.

Or not. That would be a waste of perfectly good java. I tore out every page of the diary as I reviewed what it said. My father and my friends had meant well when they'd demanded that I keep the records. They had only wanted to help me gain control over my life.

But I knew the truth. I knew that scribbling a few words in a notebook was never going to do that. Continuing to track my behavior so closely was only going to drive me insane. I wasn't anorexic. I'd never *been* anorexic. My keeping the diary had been a lie, as much as my saying I would study for the LSAT.

It was time to toss the pretense.

As I walked out of Club Joe, I dumped the ravaged food diary into the trash can.

I was still marveling about how much lighter my backpack felt when I arrived at the Landmark. I started to fumble for my keys, but the door swung open before I could find them. I jumped back just in time to let Drew and Stephanie step into the light of the setting sun. She had her arm slipped through his, and their heads were close together, as if they were sharing a secret.

"Oh!" I said. "What are you doing here?"

Whoops. That sounded more accusing than I'd intended.

Stephanie only smiled, though, pulling Drew closer. Her ostentatious gesture highlighted her bare hands—no megadiamond in sight. A tiny part of me hoped that she hadn't returned Norman's ring.

Drew nuzzled her neck before answering me by holding up an envelope. "Picking up our paychecks," he said.

It felt strange to talk to him. Strange to stand beside him and Stephanie. Strange to realize that Drew and I had spent night after night rolling around between my sheets, at the same time that Stephanie was bedding my former fiancé.

Now Drew and Stephanie were quite obviously together, and I felt…nothing.

Okay. I felt a little surprised that Drew was such a fast worker. I'd only freed him from Teel's spell at, what, midnight? And he was already attached to Stephanie like a limpet? Of course, she *had* been throwing herself at him the night before, and her costume malfunction could only have furthered her cause. But they both got high marks for speedy recovery on the romance front.

I shrugged. I didn't feel a hint of the anger that had bolstered me through Norman's abandonment. I didn't feel a ghost of the thrill when I'd first crushed on Drew, that burning longing for him to look at me, to talk to me, to do anything at all to acknowledge my existence.

Nothing.

"What are you guys going to do?" I asked, when I realized that the silence was stretching on too long.

Drew answered; Stephanie was busy weaving her fingers into his belt loop. "Bill is casting the Scottish Play. He's asked us both to read for him."

A thousand questions crowded my mind. *Macbeth*? I wanted to scream, even though I knew that any actor within earshot would cringe, frightened off by the old stories about the show's title bringing bad luck. What theater was idiotic enough to ask Bill to direct another show? When had he managed to land the job, in between ill-fated *Romeo and Juliet* rehearsals? How was he planning on corrupting that bloodiest of Shakespeare's plays? But most important: who would be stupid enough to sign up for another round of Bill-Pomeroy-destroys-the-classics?

Drew grinned, and I pictured him waltzing into the next round of rehearsals, riding the wave of Bill's destructive creativity with nondiscriminating good nature. He'd make a gorgeous Scottish laird. And if the costumer put the men in kilts, every woman in the audience would be so taken with Drew's muscular legs that she wouldn't realize just how bad the show was on stage.

As for Stephanie? She could play a manipulative madwoman, I was certain.

"Well," I said. "Good luck."

"Thanks," Drew said. "I'll see you around, right?"

I thought about telling him that he wouldn't. I thought about telling him I was leaving the Twin Cities. I thought about telling him how much my life had changed in the past twenty-four hours, how I'd finally decided to stand up for myself, for what I believed in, for what I wanted to be.

But we'd never talked like that. Our relationship had never been about what we thought, how we felt.

"Yeah," I said. "I'll see you around. Take care, both of you."

Stephanie smiled vaguely. I was actually grateful she was there. Her presence eliminated some awkward leave-taking with Drew that I didn't really want. I darted inside the Land-mark before anyone needed to say—or do—anything else.

The stage already looked like a war zone. A cold breeze told me that the loading dock was open in the back; I could hear a truck engine revving, and I assumed that the manhole-cover screens were being carted off to their final rusty reward. I hoped that someone could melt them down, redeem the scrap for something worthwhile.

Two members of the crew were pulling up the plastic sheeting, exclaiming about the stench of trapped water, even as they mopped up the stage. Another person was sitting in the audience seats, fiddling with the projector for the supertitles. Two different lighting technicians were up on the catwalks, collecting the gels from the lighting instruments that hung over the audience. The colored pieces of plastic would be saved for the next production that required the re-creation of a cold, gray dungeon.

I exchanged greetings with everyone in sight and announced that I'd be back in the dressing room. Ordinarily, the Landmark stored its costumes, in case they could be used in future productions. I had my doubts, though, about whether anything could be redeemed from our slick, glued bodysuits.

The dressing room was chaos. Dispirited by the audience's reaction the night before, the actors had left their stations in utter disarray. They'd be coming in, one by one, to collect their personal belongings as they picked up their paychecks, but for now, it looked as if a bomb had gone off in a fetishist's closet.

I shook my head and tried to figure out where to start. One corner was as good as another. I picked up a wet suit equivalent of a Verona ball gown and shook it out, releasing a cloud of baby powder into the air. I sneezed three times in quick succession.

I love the theater. The theater is my life.

As I thought my mantra, I had the strangest attack of déjà vu. I'd been here before, cleaning up a costume shop. I'd sneezed before, standing under bare fluorescent lights. I'd shrugged before, knowing that I had chosen this career; I had chosen to be a stage manager, no matter what disasters might occur on stage.

And then it all flooded back to me. The costume shop at Fox Hill, the day I'd found Teel's lantern. As if I were allergic to the memory, I sneezed again.

"Bless you."

I knew his voice before I looked; the Texas twang just barely seeped into his vowels. When I turned around, John was leaning against the door frame, watching me. He seemed taller than he had in days. Stretched out. Relaxed.

"Thanks," I said. "It looks like you got a good night's sleep."

"For the first night in a long time," he said. "Without all this to worry about."

"I know what you mean."

It should be strange talking to him. It should be uncomfortable. He had invited me to move halfway across the country with him, and I had refused. He had watched over me, riding herd, following me home when I was at my most distraught, but I had told him I didn't have room in my life for him.

But it wasn't strange to see him. It wasn't uncomfortable. It just felt right.

"About last night," I said, and then I laughed as the ghost of Mamet's play raised its head again. "Is your offer still open?"

"New York?"

I nodded.

"Absolutely."

He crossed the room and took the costume out of my hand. Without hesitation, he crammed it into the nearest trash can, dusting his palms off when he was done. "I can't promise anything, Franklin. I know I've got a job, and a place to live. And I have a dozen friends who know who's who and what's what. And they have friends. It'll be rough for a while, though. Sink or swim."

The image called to mind our underground Verona. We both smiled at the same time. "I think we can handle that," I said.

"You said you have things to take care of here. Family. Friends."

I shrugged. "Sometimes things get taken care of faster than we expect. Sometimes things change."

He closed the distance between us with the easy confidence I'd come to trust. His fingers twined in my hair as he kissed me—a long kiss that hinted at the passion banked behind his honesty and left me clutching his arms for support. "Some changes are long overdue," he said. I laughed as his lips moved down my throat.

He pulled back enough to look me in the eye. I recognized the desire on his face. But I could read much more. I could read the thoughts of the man who had rescued me from myself, saved me from a life I'd outgrown. I saw the man who had talked to me about hopes and dreams and a lifetime of plans, all while sharing slices of pie in a diner that had no name. I saw the man who set me on my feet, who gave me the strength to walk away from my old demons. The man who gave me a choice. "You're sure?" he asked.

"I couldn't wish for anything more," I said, and then I paused. "Except…"

He took a step back, eyeing me with curiosity. Amusement. Confidence. "Except what?"

"Do you think that we could grab dinner at Mephisto's when we finish up here? Burgers and fries? And we can sit there long enough to finish every last bite without any disaster making me run out of the place?"

His laugh was contagious. "I think we can manage that," he said. "Dinner's on me."

We started planning our move to New York as we cleaned up the chaos in the costume shop.

★ ★ ★ ★ ★

But the Garden is still just outside Teel's grasp.
Come back to see the next set of wishes!
When Good Wishes Go Bad
Available next April!

ACKNOWLEDGMENTS

NO BOOK FINDS ITS WAY INTO READERS' HANDS without the help of dozens of "behind the scenes" people. My agent, Richard Curtis, continues to find paths through the thorny thickets of publishing, providing me with endless career advice and moral support. The folks at Harlequin/Mira always make me feel at home. Mary-Theresa Hussey and Elizabeth Mazer lead the way, but I know that they represent dozens of hardworking souls, including but by no means limited to Alana Burke, Valerie Gray, Mary Helms, Amy Jones, Margaret Marbury, Linda McFall, Diane Mosher, Emily Ohanjanians, Marianna Ricciuto, Lola Speranza, Malle Vallik, Stacy Widdrington, Amy Wilkins, Donna Williams, and Adam Wilson. I offer special thanks to Margie Miller, for her great work on the cover design for this new series.

My relatives have always supported my writing, from the original Klasky Clan to the expanded Timmins, Maddrey, and Fallon family. I cannot tell you how much I appreciate the phone calls, e-mails, and other support when I'm at my writing wit's end.

A special thank-you goes to my husband, Mark. He was the one who insisted that we could make my full-time writing career work. Every single day, I am touched by his support and his unwavering certainty in me.

Of course, no writing career is complete without readers. I look forward to corresponding with you through my Web site at www.mindyklasky.com.